Nosferatu Unbound

edited by

Steven Paulsen &

Christopher Sequeira

This is a work of fiction. The events and characters portrayed herein are imaginary and are not intended to refer to specific places, events or living persons. The opinions expressed in this manuscript are solely the opinions of the authors and do not necessarily represent the opinions of the publisher.

IFWG Publishing International
Gold Coast

www.ifwgpublishing.com

Table of Contents

To my dear pal, Jack Dann, who is always there for me come hell or high water (SP).

To Bryce Stevens, dear brother-in-fiction, fellow traveller on that mysterious road where stories are told (CS).

WHAT WE OWE TO F. W. MURNAU'S NOSFERATU

Leslie S. Klinger

The legal issues surrounding the filming of *Nosferatu* in 1922 are ably recounted by Dacre Stoker elsewhere in this volume. I do not intend to discuss here the legal position of F. W. Murnau in making the film or the justification for Florence Stoker's desire to destroy all of the copies. Instead, this foreword considers briefly how different our view of *Dracula* would be today if Murnau had not produced his film.

First, we must credit Albin Grau's script (and Murnau's embrace of the script) for the idea that vampires are injured or destroyed by sunlight. Though this now seems to be a well-settled tenet of vampire lore (espoused by creator after creator, including, for example, the Christopher Lee/Hammer films, the Frank Langella 1979 *Dracula* film, and the highly influential television series *Buffy the Vampire Slayer* (1997-2003), created by Joss Whedon), it is clearly not a part of Bram Stoker's *Dracula*. Scene after scene of the novel includes Count Dracula walking around during the day, wearing his unfashionable straw hat, without any ill effects. Though many tropes of the vampire—the need to rest in a box filled with one's native soil, the fear of running water, the ability to shape-shift— were codified by Stoker's novel, this one was not.

Where did the idea come from? It had its origins in the folklore of vampires. Revenants—the walking dead or the "undead"—were the original vampires. As creatures without souls (as explained by Augustin Calmet, in his treatise *On the Apparitions of Spirits and on Vampires* (1746), they were naturally associated with the dark and the night, when supernatural creatures achieved their

1

greatest strength. We see in *Dracula* suggestions that the Count is less than fully powered during daylight hours, and folklore associated vampires with the dead risen from their graves—at night—to prey on the living. Hence, vampires were not creatures of the day. But diminution of powers is not the same as a killing effect. It must be said that Grau invented this idea, and forever after, it has been a matter of canon that vampires are destroyed by sunlight. Murnau's brilliant film was the first to reassure us that while our human abilities to conquer the vampires among us may be less than needed, our sun can protect us from becoming just fodder for vampires.

Second, *Nosferatu* made much of the voyage of the *Demeter*. Probably the most lasting image of the film is the depiction of the creature on the foremast of the *Demeter*, enroute to England. The image is so striking and horrific that it has been widely shown and copied, most recently in the 2023 film *Voyage of the Demeter*. The voyage receives short shrift in the novel and is rarely depicted in filmic versions—yet it is one of the most powerful images in the entire book, as the lone occupant of the *Demeter* brings it to the shores of Whitby. In the 1931 film, for example, it is Renfield who is featured on deck. While his madness is in itself terrifying, the scene lacks the power of seeing the vampire-king himself arriving on the ship.

Nosferatu is an example of how adaptations can take on a life of their own, achieving a power and resonance far beyond the original. For everyone who has read the book, dozens saw the 1931 film or later adaptations. Unnumbered multiples of the original readership have by now undoubtedly seen Murnau's masterpiece. While the film draws heavily on the novel (and rightfully credits the novel as the basis for the film), Grau brought new ideas to vampire lore and saw the importantly terrifying aspects of the tale. While it was not the first adaptation of *Dracula*, it is for many reasons the most important.

This volume is further testament to the power of the vampire legends. Our fascination with blood, our desire to overcome death, and our conviction that some among us have supernatural (that is, more than natural) powers have engendered centuries of literature and myth. Specifically, Murnau's *Nosferatu* has nurtured the brilliant tales that follow, in which we may consider (in the words of the scholar Nina Auerbach) "our vampires, ourselves"—the vampires we need and the vampires we deserve.

One more thing that *Nosferatu* indirectly contributed to the world—my favorite dialogue from any vampire film: The following scene is from Mel Brooks's 1995 *Dracula: Dead and Loving It*, when Harker finds Lucy, who has just propositioned him, is lying still in her coffin:

Harker:	Now she's dead!
Van Helsing:	No, she's not!
Harker:	She's alive?
Van Helsing:	She's Nosferatu!
Harker:	She's Italian?

A STOKER FAMILY PERSPECTIVE

DACRE STOKER

F. W. Murnau had been an actor, an artist, and had an interest in the occult prior to directing *Nosferatu*, which may have led to his working relationship with producer Albin Grau, who was also keenly interested in the occult. What is of great interest to me is what led these very creative filmmakers to make their film *Nosferatu* (1922) without seeking a licensing agreement with Mrs Florence Stoker, the rightful heir of the Bram Stoker Estate, the holder of the dramatic and film rights for *Dracula*, published in 1897.

Adapting unauthorized source material was nothing new for director F. W. Murnau: his earlier horror film, *Der Janus-Kopf* (*The Head of Janus*, 1920), was also an unauthorized adaptation of Robert Louis Stevenson's novel *The Strange Case of Dr. Jekyll and Mr. Hyde*. It appears that this infringement did not make it to the courts. Although the *Nosferatu* case was quite possibly the earliest novel-to-film copyright infringement case in history, this was not only new territory for the courts, it certainly was for Florence Stoker.

Having spent the past 12 years on a quest to learn what I can about my great-granduncle Bram Stoker's life and his research and writing of *Dracula*, it is only fitting, given the 2022 centenary anniversary of *Nosferatu*, which was also the 125th anniversary of the publication of *Dracula*, that a member of the Stoker family has the opportunity to provide Florence Stoker's perspective.

Today the *Nosferatu* case is generally studied in law schools, and discussed by legal scholars, to introduce concepts related to legal remedies available for copyright infringement. In this case, after the ruling against them, Prana declared bankruptcy, and since there was no money to pay restitution to Mrs Stoker, the German court ruled to have copies of the film destroyed. Although the court case and its ruling seem to be the focus and garner the most interest, there were other extenuating circumstances regarding Florence's attempts to protect and capitalize on her late husband's intellectual property, namely the legal licensing of the stage rights to *Dracula* in Great Britain and the film rights later in the USA. Bram was no stranger to the law; in 1871, while still at Trinity College, he worked as a clerk in the Petty Sessions legal department of Dublin Castle, and later, in 1877, he was promoted to Inspector of Clerks throughout Ireland. During this time, he compiled a legal manual appropriately named *The Duties of Clerks of Petty Sessions* (1878), and this manual was in use until the early 1960s. Furthermore, Bram wrote many of his own publishing contracts, and contracts in his position as manager of the Lyceum Theatre. Therefore, legal rights surrounding his novels were something about which Bram was acutely aware. As an aside, in 2013 Ms Margaret Wood of the US Library of Congress discovered that Bram, contrary to popular opinion, had in fact followed the proper procedure for filing the copyright for his US edition of *Dracula (1899)*. Confusion apparently stemming from the fact that Bram was also referred to as Abraham created a filing error, which led to this long-standing misunderstanding.

Florence was widowed in 1912; she was 64 years old when *Nosferatu* first premiered in Berlin in 1922. Since then, records have been lost, first-hand accounts are difficult to source and verify, and as a result, I have found a lot of hearsay and rumor which has been difficult to separate from fact. I am deeply indebted to Mr Holger Mandel, a German film historian, for his assistance in my research. David J. Skal has provided a lot of important information on the subject in his excellent book *Hollywood Gothic*, published in 1990. In fact, David devotes three chapters of his book to the complicated issues of the nine-year period involving Florence Stoker and the representatives of the Incorporated Society of Authors, New York and Hollywood stage and film industry. Over this period multiple studios, agents, and apparently even Bela Lugosi got involved in the negotiations of the film rights.

Florence, outgunned in numbers and experience, certainly held up her end with perseverance and resolve to do what was right on behalf of her deceased husband. Her health was waning but luckily her son Noel, a chartered accountant, was able to assist his mother during this difficult time. What is unsettling to me is how many articles I have read that make broad-based assumptions and provide misinformation on the subject. One issue that needs clearing up from the start is one of the most frequently repeated claims that the Stoker Estate would not grant the rights to Prana to make a film adaptation of *Dracula*. My sources within the Stoker family are Florence's great grandsons, who were raised by Bram and Florence's son Noel. There are in possession of various Stoker family papers, and they are well aware of any other papers that have been donated or sold to various archives over the years. With their assistance, I have been unable to find any records that Florence was ever approached to sell the film rights to Prana.

Bram died April 20, 1912 at his home on St Georges Square in the Pimlico district of London. His health had been in decline over the past two years, having suffered two strokes. This caused him to lose his eyesight. In addition, he suffered from Bright's disease, a severe condition of the kidneys. He had been employed by Sir Henry Irving for 27 years, ending with Irving's death in 1905. Bram struggled financially for the last seven years of his life. Royalties from *Dracula* and his other novels barely made ends meet, and Irving did not make any arrangement for a pension for his loyal Lyceum Theater Manager for his 27 years of unwavering and dedicated employment. Nor did Bram receive any form of inheritance from Henry Irving. Florence's son Noel was working as a chartered accountant and did provide support for his mother. Bram's brother Thornley, who died only 4 months after Bram, did leave Florence £2,000 in his will. Bram did have the foresight to protect the dramatic rights to *Dracula*, by conducting a staged reading on May 18 1897 per the established laws of the day. It would be a while before these rights were exercised, but when they were, they provided Bram's widow

Florence the financial security she needed. The film rights were closely related to the dramatic rights but they were not the same. Since Bram's death in 1912 his novel *Dracula,* assisted in 1924 by publicity from stage adaptations, generated a lot of publishing success around the world, before it went into public domain in 1962.

In early 1922, to monetize what Bram left her, Florence was in the process of pursuing a stage adaptation of *Dracula* with Hamilton Deane when she first become aware of the release of the film *Nosferatu* by Prana Films. It is not clear how she found this out, but more than a few sources have stated that she received an anonymous note telling of the World Premier on March 4 1922 at Der Marmorsaal (Marble Hall) in the Berlin Zoo. At that point the film had already been screened in Holland as well as in various other countries in Europe.

Florence approached the Incorporated Society of Authors to support her efforts to protect the integrity of Bram's novel. Although Bram had been a member, it was pointed out that Florence was not a member of the society and that she was obviously joining because she needed their financial assistance. Florence wrote numerous convincing letters to Mr Thring, the Secretary of the Society who in May of 1922 was finally given permission by the committee to inform Florence that they would take up her cause.

Letters in the British Museum Library indicate the correspondence between Florence, the Incorporated Society of Authors, and their German lawyer, but unfortunately no records or correspondence have been discovered which reveal Prana's position in the matter. These letters show that in 1924 the German court ruled in favor of the Incorporated Society of Authors on behalf of Mrs Stoker and again in 1925 after an unsuccessful appeal. However, additional correspondence indicates that in 1931, well after the initial court case had ruled in their favor, their German lawyer pointed out that the film *Nosferatu* had resurfaced and had been shown in Berlin. It was obvious that not all copies of the film were destroyed, per the court order. What a disappointment to Florence and the Incorporated Society of Authors this must have been.

This would have been most troubling to Florence as she was in the process of working with Hamilton Dean and John Balderston on the stage adaptation of *Dracula* in both London and New York. Within a few years Universal Studios had shown interest in purchasing the screen rights of the stage version. Finally, a legitimate path forward to turn Bram's *Dracula* novel into a film, and a substantial payout for Florence. However, with the resurgence of *Nosferatu*, correspondence indicated that Florence was very concerned that even though her efforts, and those of the Incorporated Society of Authors, had prevailed in the German courts, this pirated version floating around might scare off any legitimate studio from a proper and legal licensing agreement for the film rights.

Later in 1931 Florence was in contact with studio executives, agents and intermediaries; they all gave advice and sent offers back and forth, indicating that they were close to a deal. It turns out that for some reason, possibly practical, or it might have been a legal one, Universal ended up buying the rights to the stage play *Dracula* which was owned by F. Stoker, H. Deane and J. Balderston, and not the film's rights-to-novel itself.

Not lost on today's fans, *Nosferatu* has become a sort of cult classic. It certainly was an example of German expressionism and advanced filmmaking, although probably not something appreciated by my great grandaunt. It was also a horrifically good movie retelling of Bram's story in a manner very close to the original book, something audiences are still demanding today. Notwithstanding that it was an unauthorized film adaptation, legal scholars argue that *Nosferatu* has significant, independent artistic merit as one of the great, early horror films, and that the court erred in permitting Mrs. Stoker the right to have copies of the film destroyed. Such scholars point out that but for the fact that Mrs. Stoker was unsuccessful in having all copies destroyed, the world would have lost the film because of the remedy determination by a judge (implying that judges are not in the best position to make determination that affect artistic expressions). I am sure there are many horror fans who would agree.

THESE PALE SHADOWS

Kirstyn McDermott

Breath frosting in the chill night air, Ghost leans from the car window and speaks her name into the intercom. After a few moments, there comes a quiet, metallic click and the iron gates swing open, smooth and close to silent on their hinges. She makes her way along a broad bitumen driveway that doesn't have any right to be as long as it is, not less than twenty minutes from the centre of Melbourne. That's Toorak, though. Money older than sin and twice as wicked. Massive mansions squatting like poison toads in the middle of sprawling, manicured gardens, protected by eight-feet-high stone walls and the kind of security you absolutely do not fuck with.

She parks her Toyota opposite this particular mansion's front doors, keeping within the yellowish glow from the twin coach lights perched either side of the entryway, then taps out a message to Cassidy on her phone. *Arrived 10.14pm.* After a minute or two, when no one comes to meet her, Ghost grabs the package from the passenger seat and gets out of the car.

Melbourne in the middle of winter isn't a patch on London, but it's still not beach weather. Even though Ghost grew up in this city, and has been dragged back here more times than she cares to consider, she's forgotten it can happily freeze the nipple off a witch's tit if it has a mind. Her light trenchcoat might be made from chiffon for how easily the wind slices through it, but she assumes the place will be heated comfortably inside, carbon footprint be damned.

She assumes wrong.

The front doors swing inwards before she even has a chance

to press the ringer, the camera above presumably alerting the controller to her presence, and a wall of frigid air greets her.

"Fuuuuck," she mutters beneath her still-frosted breath. At least the wind will stay behind. No butler or housekeeper or executive assistant emerges as she steps into the spacious foyer, but the doors close again as soon as she passes beyond their arc. She waits, taking in the lavish floor-to-ceiling jacquard drapes that shield the windows, their colour a perfect match for the burgundy rugs and runners protecting the highly polished floorboards. A staircase curves up to the first floor, the runner ascending with it like a giant tongue unfurled.

On the opposite wall hangs a portrait of a middle-aged man wearing a once-white ruffled collar, an elaborately feathered hat and a severe, snobbish grimace that says he has just this minute returned from viewing Shakespeare's latest effort and, gentlemen, he remains unimpressed. Ghost drifts over for a closer look. Notes the discolouration and cracked varnish, the antique wooden frame. No signature, but the skill of the artist is undeniable. The man looks like he could step off the canvas and start pontificating at any moment.

If he did, Ghost suspects she'd want to punch him right in his supercilious face.

"I see you've met my father," a voice calls from behind her, from above her.

Ghost turns around. Her current client waits at the top of the stairs, dressed in an understated black suit that likely cost more than her car. His short blond hair is late-stage Bowie, sweeping up and away from his thin and angular face.

"I didn't care for the man any more than you appear to," he says, descending with the type of deliberate grace commonly associated with cats, or fictional sociopaths.

She can't place the accent beyond vaguely European. From this distance, he doesn't look that much older than her, mid-thirties, maybe forty at the outside—certainly nowhere near old enough for the arsehole in the portrait to be his father, which tracks with what Cassidy has dug up. So to speak. "Mr...Orlok?" The name feels stupid in her mouth, but it's all she has.

He nods, points at the package under her arm. "That cannot be what I asked you to fetch."

"It's part of it."

At the bottom of the stairs, he pauses. Tilts his head to one side. Closer, his porcelain-pale face has a weird, ageless quality that reminds Ghost of septuagenarian celebrities on a Botox bender. She remains motionless, allows him to appraise her without comment. Driving out here, she'd fretted about this moment more than she wanted to admit, especially to Cassidy. Now she's surprised to find herself infinitely more curious than scared.

"Well then," the creature who calls himself Orlok says at last. "If there are further negotiations, I propose we remove this discussion to my study." He smiles, or attempts to, his lips quirking oddly at the corners. "I have set aside a delightfully aged brandy, of which I'm sure you shall be quite enamoured."

He's not wrong about the brandy. Ghost indulges in a second modest sip, then sits back in her chair while Orlok slides the film canister from the padded bag in which it's travelled from her Airbnb north of the city. He opens the metal lid and sets it down on his desk, then removes the reel carefully with both hands. His nails are on the longish side, but neatly rounded at the tips. Harmless. She hasn't yet gotten a good glimpse of his teeth.

With a delicate touch, he locates the end of the film and unspools a foot or so, holds it up before the hooded desk lamp — an incongruently modern design, all matte black powder coating with a bright LED globe and a neck that swivels. Almost imperceptibly, his eyes widen; if Ghost hadn't been paying particular attention to his face, she would have missed it.

"Tinted?" he whispers, the question perhaps directed only to himself.

Ghost answers anyway. "Faded, as you'd expect with a century-old print, but yes."

After examining several dozen frames, Orlok packs the reel away once again, pausing to study the flaking label on the outside of the can before seating himself behind the desk. He reaches for his own brandy glass, swirls the honey-coloured liquid around the sides before taking a mouthful. Swallowing.

"You can drink?" Ghosts asks. "I mean, other than…"

"When occasion demands." That odd smile again, a mannerism too long out of practice. "It passes through without effect, alas, and the flavour is dulled."

"Well, I can vouch for this." She lifts her glass. "It's magnificent."

"Take the bottle with you when you go." He taps the canister. "This is the first reel."

"Yes. And I have the other six."

"Six? Then, altogether…there are seven reels?"

"One more than the usual number for this film. But you knew that."

"I'd *hoped* for it. That was the whisper on the wind." There's a sharpness to him now, his formerly languid demeanour shed like a cloak. Those oil-dark eyes glimmer and fix upon her; worms prod and writhe in her brain, thickening her thoughts.

Ghost leans forward to place her glass on the desk. "Please don't."

"My apologies." He breaks his gaze; her head clears. "Old habits."

"This isn't about payment," she tells him. "A contract's a contract, and you know my reputation is solid. You wouldn't have sought me out otherwise."

"I might have. There are vanishing few who possess such a remarkable talent as yours."

"Still, I honour my word, and I don't make promises that I don't intend to keep."

"Yet, here we sit with only a single film reel between us."

"You withheld pertinent information. Once my colleague found out—"

"Ah, *Cassidy*, the driver of hard bargains." He all but hisses her name.

"Yeah, *Cassidy*, who has saved my arse more times than I can count. Workplace health and safety is kind of her jam, so what we're negotiating here tonight is a secure handover. You'll get your film—all *seven* reels—and I'll walk away with nothing altered beyond my bank balance."

"Because I also have a reputation, or at least my kind does."

She nods.

"The reputation of humans is far from benign, you realise. Rampaging, wrathful, avaricious wretches. Territorial too, even when they've no honest right to what they claim. And murderous, let us not even begin to debate murderous. *See here: this one is different; this one is ugly; this one has something I would much prefer to be mine—let me kill it and be done.*"

"Fair," Ghost says, trying not to let her fingers dig too hard into the padded arms of her chair. *Don't antagonise him*, Cassidy advised earlier. *He's much stronger than you, and that's only the start of it*. She can feel her heart beating faster.

Orlok smiles, with a hint of genuine warmth this time. "Shall we then set aside reputation and deal with one another as people? Tell me, how did you locate it?"

"I can't… It's not something I can explain, even if I wanted to." Except, all at once, she really does. "It's a sense I have, like an internal radar for lost things. The closer I get, the louder it pings—or twangs, really. You know when you stretch an elastic band and flick it? Like that, *twang*. That's the feel of it, stupid as it might sound and—shit!" She gets to her feet, anger riding bitter on the back of her tongue. "Stop doing that! Or I'll burn your precious fucking film to ash, I swear."

His laughter is almost—*almost*—human. Those elongated and sharply pointed incisors not so much. "I am sorry, dear Ghost. Truly. We have stepped on each other's toes this entire dance, the two of us so clumsy. Please, sit down, drink your brandy."

She does sit, once she's pretty sure it's her own decision, but leaves the brandy where it is.

"You are right," Orlok is saying, "this needs to be equitable."

"Meaning?"

"A question for a question—with my sincere promise that your answers may be given freely, and we may both exercise a right of veto. Come, your curiosity glows so bright we scarce have need of this lamp. There must be things you would know of me? Things not even your dear Cassidy has been able to discover with all her clever tricks? Let us trade, on equal footing."

Ghost considers the offer. "All right," she says at last. "But I get to go first."

It's well after 3am by the time Ghost drives back to her accommodation, the promised bottle of brandy belted safely upright in the passenger seat, and the streets of Melbourne are far more sparsely trafficked now. She's still wearing the fine grey cashmere jumper Orlok fetched, with apologies, once he noticed her discomfort. *I am no longer bothered by the cold; it is a waste to heat this mausoleum on days when my staff are absent.* He waved a dismissive hand when, at the front door, she went to remove it. *Please, the colour suits you.* It doesn't really, and the size is too voluminous, the sleeves too long, but at least it doesn't feel lost.

They've arranged a time and a very public place to meet again, although Ghost now feels quite certain she could safely bring the remaining reels to the Toorak mansion for handover. It's not that Orlok isn't dangerous—she has no doubt he's exsanguinated an unfathomable number of victims over many long and lonely centuries, some perhaps more willing than others—but above that, he prides himself on what he refers to as his honour. *My reputation, as you might call it, a suitably insipid word for these thin and rational times.* Ghost isn't prey; the two of them are bound by an honest bargain, and it would stain him indelibly to harm her.

Never mind his honour, Cassidy said when Ghost called to check in as the steel gates closed behind her. *Just be sure to carry a damn stake.*

Ghost doesn't think stakes will have the desired effect.

We are very, very difficult to destroy, those few of us who yet remain. He shook his head even as she opened her mouth. *It would be rude to ask such a thing, and my refusal may offend. Myth and rumour, we excel at. Fold a lie until it feels like truth and send it fluttering into the world. Set aside your garlic and your crosses, your running water and your earth-filled coffins.*

Sunlight?

Shall we meet for afternoon tea? You can see for yourself.

For his part, Orlok was keenly interested in the film. How she found it, and precisely where. Despite her *remarkable talent*, the bulk of what Ghost does—or what Cassidy does, when it comes down to brass tacks—is good old-fashioned detective work. Ghost can't find anything unless she's physically close enough to catch a lost thing's plaintive bleats. Which, depending on how lost it is, and for how long, how much it has been missed, or the strength of the desire that seeks it out, can mean the measure of half a city, or merely a single heartbeat.

An original print of *Nosferatu*, Orlok's whispers had assured him, was still in Berlin.

Beyond that, nothing.

It wasn't the most obscure lead Ghost has ever had to start a job, but it came close. And so, to work. The German director, F. W. Murnau, was enticed to Hollywood in the mid-1920s, making only two films by 1931 when a rogue truck ran his car off the highway outside of Los Angeles, dealing a fatal head injury to which he succumbed the following day.

Likely, he wouldn't have regained consciousness, she pointed out. *No time for last words. Perfect conditions for a lost thing. A precious one.*

Murnau died in California, not Germany.

Ah, but he went back to Berlin, just for a few months, in 1927.

Where Cassidy was pretty sure he met with Albin Grau, one of the founders of Prana Film, the studio that made *Nosferatu*. Bankrupt by then, of course, the infamous plagiarism suit decided in favour of Bram Stoker's widow, with all copies of the film ordered destroyed.

Barn doors and horses, as we all know by now. Ghost allowed herself another sip of brandy. *Several prints had been dispatched to other countries in the meantime, and none were about to give them back. Do you really think the producers wouldn't have hidden away at least one copy for themselves, though? Especially Grau—it was his baby from the start, and he was obsessed with all that occult shit.*

As I understand it, you cannot find "hidden" things.

She grinned. *I cannot. Not hidden and forgotten, not stolen, not regretfully given away. Only the genuinely, truly lost.*

Which this precious, wholly complete print of *Nosferatu* might well have been. If Murnau, pockets bulging with fresh Hollywood paycheques, did indeed meet with Grau and make him an offer. If Grau agreed to sell him his remaining print. If Murnau, not willing to risk travelling with the reels while the court orders still stood, stashed them in his residence in Berlin.

Oh, say, in a cavity behind a false wall. Safe and secret and naturally climate controlled.

All seven reels?

I'm sure it was only meant to be temporary. Until he could figure out how to get them out of the country securely. Or possibly return with enough clout to screen Nosferatu *in Germany again. We'll never know.*

The last hurdle had been convincing the nice, middle-class German family who now owned the place to let her take a sledgehammer to the wall of their guest bedroom. But the reels had twanged so hard from their cell behind the brickwork, their call at once eager and forlorn, spilling shadows of ships and rats and craggy, cobwebbed castles into her brain, that she knew she was in the right place and, honestly? If you offer people enough Euros, they'll let you sledgehammer your way through just about anything.

Ghost pulls up beneath the carport of her rented place and turns off the engine. She's exhausted, probably too exhausted to have driven back alone in the first place, but she wasn't about to ask Orlok if she could crash in one of his spare rooms. There's honour, and then there's the matter of a warm-blooded guest sleeping but a few swift steps down the hall, throat bare and pulsing a siren call.

Why do you care so much? she asked near the end of their conversation. *I mean, it's a good film for what it was, back in the day, but you're...what you are. Don't you find it offensive, what we think of you? It must be like blackface or something, right?*

Orlok leaned back in his chair. *I find it instructive, and often amusing. It's not a mirror—which would reflect us, by the way; we haven't managed to circumvent the properties of light. It's more a pane of glass, warped by fire, by trauma. We can learn from the way others see us, use it to our advantage. Make…adjustments. Evolve.*

The mansion housed quite the collection of artefacts, he informed her with unmistakable pride, without question the most comprehensive of its kind in existence. Not only films, although there are many, many of those, but also literary works—Stoker, Rice, King, Harrison; all the canonical names to have progressed the lore—and worthy entries from the visual arts. Heavily weighted across the 1900s, with the twenty-first century showing no signs of slowing down. *Even though there are concerns far more pressing to you now, or there should be.* Naturally, he already possessed a print of Murnau's masterpiece—the very first cinematic representation of his kind—but the one Ghost has found is different. Infinitely more valuable.

Because of the hand-tinting? Until now, there was only one other print with trace colour left, right? The one they have in France?

Correct. Orlok averted his gaze, ran a fingernail along the rim of the canister. The scratching sound, more akin to metal on metal, made her flinch. *The tinting is very rare.*

There's more to it than that. Ghost retrieves her phone from the hands-free, taps out a quick message. There are a couple of days before she hands over the reels, to allow for the payment to come through and be confirmed. Plenty of time for what she has in mind, so long as Cassidy can work out the logistics. Less than two minutes later, she has a reply. *Leave it with me. Get some sleep.* Ghost wonders if Cassidy ever takes her own advice.

Orlok isn't your real name, Ghost remarked at one point. Not a question, but also, yes.

He raised an eyebrow. *As Ghost is not yours.*

Too sensitive a trade, they both exercised their right of veto.

She half-expected the address to belong to a dilapidated movie palace, one with old-fashioned projectors and flip-down seats, their velvet upholstery worn to bare threads by decades of use. Instead, Cassidy's contact lives in an ordinary brick veneer house, albeit newly renovated to include a lavish home theatre and temperature-controlled archives. Having received a brief tour, Ghost now waits in the kitchen, drinking the best coffee she's had in months and nibbling on wafer-thin almond bread, while Bastian Payne makes the necessary preparations.

He will not be rushed, that was made clear from the start. And he will absolutely not not *not* be rolling a one-hundred-year-old print through any machine, not even his own immaculate, top-shelf setup, without a thorough examination first. Depending on the condition, he may elect not to roll it at all. No, she cannot pay him extra to take such a risk.

Money solves many problems, young lady, but not this one. He ran a deferential hand over the film canisters, regarding them as a priest might a holy relic. Although, to a man who's devoted most of his sixty-odd years to cinematic history and film restoration, the reels are likely even more precious to him than that.

So: coffee and almond bread and enough downtime for Ghost's nerves to start jangling. She messages Cassidy. *You trust this film guy, right?*

With your life, the response bounces back immediately.

Not yours?

Only one person I trust with that, G. At the end, an emoji winks up at her.

Ghost finishes her coffee. Traces a fingertip along the grey veins that weave through the pale stone countertop. It looks like a genuine marble slab, not the engineered stuff. Film restoration can't pay that well, surely. Lowering her head on her arms, she closes her eyes for a minute.

Someone taps her on the shoulder, says her name.

Startled, she jerks upright. The light in the kitchen has changed. Her back hurts.

"Apologies." Payne stands a little to her left. "Didn't mean to scare you."

"No," Ghost says, stifling a yawn. "Just resting my eyes."

The man ushers her into the theatre, gesturing towards the half-dozen plush red armchairs arrayed before the screen. Ghost chooses one at the back, near to where twin projectors are set up, the reels laid out neatly on a bench beside them.

"The condition is remarkable, considering their age. How have they been stored?"

"Well, I presume. Beyond that, I'd rather not say."

"Trade secrets, of course, of course. The first reel is missing—you knew that?"

"My client's already taken delivery."

"Shame not to be able to view it through. Still." He rubs his hands together, then pulls a small black remote from his pocket and dims the lights. "It won't be the classic experience, I'm afraid. The print's far too valuable to mess about with changing reels in the dark, so we'll bring those up in between. Won't take a minute."

Ghost smiles. "You sound excited, Mr Payne."

"Please. Anyone who brings a new version of *Nosferatu* may call me Bastian."

The second reel opens with the frightened villagers and, Ghost is ridiculously pleased to see, the hyena-cum-werewolf stalking briefly through the supposed wilds of Transylvania. She watched the movie at the very start of this job, and it's odd now to see the same footage overlaid with colour, however faded it may be. Otherwise, the story is very much as she remembers, although of course the intertitles are in the original German. With no soundtrack, she's able to catch Bastion murmuring translations to himself over the whirr of the projector.

They work their way through five reels. The room is warm and dark, the chair exceedingly comfortable, and Ghost tries her best not to nod off. She holds focus well enough, the film concluding no differently than she remembers. A cockerel on the rooftop sounding in the dawn. Max Schrek, bald and bat-eared, hunched over his supine prey. Sunlight shining through an open window. The famous fade-out, reducing the monster to a paltry puff of smoke. Sinless Ellen, dead in her beloved's arms. And a ruined castle, brooding still.

"The final reel is unnumbered," Bastian informs her, bringing up the lights again. "But there are the initials *H.G.* Which is interesting, being that Henrik Galeen wrote the screenplay for *Nosferatu*. Most of it, at least."

"Most?"

"Murnau himself rewrote the ending. Allegedly, Galeen's last dozen pages were missing from the director's working copy and he whipped this up on the fly. Perhaps the original was similar to what we've just seen, perhaps Murnau had better ideas and the lost pages story was nothing more than diplomacy, or perhaps there's another explanation."

Ghost nods. "Let's see what's on that last reel."

The lights dim. She leans forward in her seat, elbows resting on her knees. There's no tint to the frames this time, the images slipping across the screen in stark black and white.

"Is that?" Bastian swallows a low gasp. "Did you see?"
Ghost doesn't move. "I think so."

She's fully awake now, eyes wide and fixed to the screen.

Abruptly, the footage ends, the film left flapping in the projector for a second or two before Bastian comes to his senses and stills it. "An alternative ending," he marvels, switching the overhead lights back on. There's a soft tremor in his voice; whether it's purely excitement or something else altogether, Ghost doesn't know him well enough to tell. "The *original* ending."

"It's more than that." Ghosts stands to face him. "You know the sort of stuff I deal in, right? Cassidy wouldn't have sent me to you otherwise."

He clears his throat, collects himself. "Of course." With careful hands, he removes the reel and examines the last couple of feet of print, satisfying himself that no damage was done before returning it to the canister. "It is a privilege to have viewed it, nevertheless."

Pacing in a tight circle, Ghost runs scenarios in her head, weighing up pros and cons, winnowing and discarding. Time, as ever, is the enemy. "You got everything set up here, right? For your restoration work?" She taps the cans. "These don't have to leave the house?"

"To do what?"

She tells him, gives the deadline.

He shakes his head. "Not enough time. The print may be in excellent condition but it's still very old, very fragile. I would want to do it manually, frame by frame."

"Not the whole film, just this last reel. What was that, five minutes? Less?"

Bastian rubs his lower lip. "Yes," he says at last. "This one reel, I can do."

Orlok is late. Only by a few minutes, but Ghost had him pegged as the punctual type. Perhaps, after many centuries, a few minutes amount to less than nothing. A couple of seconds, her time. The span of an anticipatory breath, held. Overhead, winter sun filters through the atrium roof, filling the bar with soft afternoon light. It's the primary reason she chose this place, a close second being the stellar selection of gins on offer. She takes a sip of hers, on ice with a sliver of blood orange, and when she looks up again, Orlok stands two paces away.

"My apologies for the tardiness." He's wearing a blue suit. *Blue* blue, the colour of summer skies and the plumage of tropical birds, and she must have been staring too long. "I'm trying something new." Gracefully, he undoes a coat button, sits down in the chair opposite.

"What, colour?"

"It's been a while. We can become stuck, if we allow ourselves." He nods at the roller-case beside her. "The remaining six reels?"

"I've watched them." Ghost looks into his eyes, unblinking. "All of them."

He laughs, exposing a glint of incisor. "I expected nothing less."

"Can I ask?"

She half-expects him to cry veto, but instead he leans across the table and snags her gin. Swallows half in one mouthful. "You may ask."

"It's just, I've never seen, or even heard of…*that* before."

"We have taken great care to keep our most vital secrets from the light. There was a source on set. Once one of our number learned what had been filmed…well, as you know, *Nosferatu* now ends somewhat differently." He waves his ungloved hand through the air. "The sun, as you can see, harms us no more than it would a possum or a bat or any other nocturnal creature. Still, the trope serves as a useful diversion."

"And the court case? Was that—"

"No, that was all the widow's idea, and who could blame her? Such blatant plagiarism of dear old Bram's work." He slides the remainder of her gin back across. "We may have had an influence on a certain judge's orders to destroy the film, however."

"Why? If that…*scene* was removed?"

"We are ancient, my dear. Unfortunately, great age does not preclude great pettiness."

Ghost finishes the gin. "Which is why I've had a digital copy made, uploaded to a highly secure server." His eyes sharpen; for a moment, she can feel him skimming the edges of her mind, sniffing for the truth of it. Her stomach churns. "It's safe, as long as I am—as well as the person who made it. He'd better live to a ripe old age, okay? No rogue trucks."

He shrugs, a smirk lifting the corner of his mouth. "Pettiness, as I said."

"But we're good? You and me?"

It happens too quickly for her eyes to track. How he rises from his seat, moves to stand beside her, one hand gripping the handle of the roller-case—and are his nails longer now? Sharper? "You may speak of it to no one, nor show it nor write a word describing it, however obliquely. Not even in the guise of a fiction. Understand?"

She swallows hard, wishing there was more gin. "Of course."

"Then why would I allow harm to come to you, dear Ghost, when I may very well have need of your talents again someday?" Another movement too swift to catch—but she would swear he planted a *fucking kiss* on the top of her head—before the creature whose name definitely isn't Orlok is at the sliding doors. As the glass opens, naked sunlight streams through, backlighting a silhouette that for a fraction of a second seems to flicker and fade.

And then, like all precious things lost to time and to memory and to breath, he is gone.

THE LAST DEAD GIRL

Leverett Butts

I.

It was past midnight. I sat at my desk, feet kicked up, staring at the skull on my bookshelf. Slow raindrops crawled down the office window, dyed scarlet by the taillights outside. They set me dreaming about the cleaning lady. Miss Rosa Flores. A nice piece. Ruddy. Lovely neck. The vein on the left side throbs when she reaches up to dust the ceiling fans. I can watch that thing for hours. Not that I'd ever harm her. One thing I've learned in all my years is not to shit where you sleep.

Anyway, as I dreamed of Rosa's throbbing jugular, a voice pulled me from my reverie.

"Are you Mr. Orlok?"

"Depends on who's asking?" I looked over. If I had any breath to lose, it'd be on a milk carton. Ellen Hutter stood in my doorway.

She hadn't aged a day since I last saw her in 1920, just before I met Fred Murnau and got mixed up in that damned film.

I looked again, though, and realized it was not my Ellen, just a brunette girl, maybe thirty years old. She walked into my office like a nun entering a speakeasy. She smoothed her skirt as she sat in one of my client chairs (ever the optimist, I have three). Her wrists were silky and supple. She bent her head down examining her work, and I got an unobstructed view of her nape. Heaven. "My name's Greta Wegener," she said. "Someone has stolen my identity."

II.

She had awoken the previous day in strange clothes on a bus near Forsyth Park. Her purse contained no forms of identification. When she went to her apartment building, her name was not listed on the call buttons.

"Where'd you sleep last night?" I asked.

"I don't know." She shrugged. "I woke up this morning on a bus heading downtown."

Her heart rate remained regular. Probably she was telling the truth. I looked at her face and thought of Ellen.

"I charge $500 a day plus expenses," I said.

She rummaged in her handbag, pretending to look for her wallet.

"I generally ask for a day's retainer, but we can make other arrangements if necessary."

"Thank you." Her carotid pulsed as she smiled. A man has bills to pay, but he also has to eat.

It had stopped raining. I followed Greta from half a block away, scaling the walls like a spider. Nobody looks up in this town. Even if they did, the streetlights date back to the nineteenth century and don't illuminate enough for a nearsighted beggar to read his own sign.

She walked south on Ann Street, then turned left on Oglethorpe and south on MLK. Hopped a bus at MLK and Turner. I can move faster than most humans can see, but I can't move that fast. I leapt to the roof of the bus and held on as it traveled south.

Riding on top of a bus, trailing a skirt through the streets of a coastal town was not how I 'd imagined my afterlife. I'm not sure what I expected.

I don't remember how I came to be a vampyre. One day I was alive, and the next, not so much. This memory lapse has irritated all of my biographers. Jim Rymer, the first person to hear my story, claims I was turned after betraying Cromwell, but that doesn't make any sense. Unless Cromwell was undead, and I assure you he was not. Of course, he also can't decide if my true name is Bannerworth (it isn't), so everything he says is suspect. Except throwing myself in a volcano. I did that. And turning young Miss Crofton, but not for vengeance. Okay, I did a lot of what he says, but he can't decide if I'm the hero or the villain of his story, and the book suffers terribly for it. Truth is, like anyone, I'm neither one nor the other. I exist. I do things. Sometimes they're bad things, sometimes good, often neither.

Murnau claims I was turned by Belial, lieutenant of Satan himself. It's a better story than the Cromwell thing, sure, but still ludicrous. I doubt Satan even exists, much less his upper management.

However I was made, once I learned I couldn't die (not by the sun; not even by volcano), I mostly continued to live as I always had. Bought a house in Bremen, fell in love with a married woman, convinced her to leave her boor of a husband and spend eternity with me.

Eternity lasted just north of eighty years. Then Ellen grew bored, with me or with immortality I never knew. I rose one evening to find she had left and had taken her coffin with her.

Then I met Fred Murnau, may he rot in hell. I knew he was a filmmaker, had even seen a few of his flickers, and I knew how well Vlad had done with Stoker's novel. I thought flickers were the coming thing (they were) and that my story would do for film what Vlad's had done for penny dreadfuls (it didn't). Turns out my story was merely a flimsy stake upon which Fred tried to drape a thinly plagiarized *Dracula*.

The rest is history: Mrs. Stoker sued Fred, and Vlad hasn't spoken to me since he threatened to destroy me a century ago.

After the *Nosferatu* debacle, I hopped a ship for the new world. I tried a few more times to get my story told, all to varying degrees of failure. Since even the undead need money and I had read Chandler and Hammett, I settled on sleuthing as a profession. What else was I going to do? The only other jobs available to me, given my aversion to sunlight and near total lack, at the time, of documentation, were third shift fast food worker or late-night janitor. I'd been a knight and a count. I was nobility. The least I could be was my own boss.

And private investigation works perfectly: It's mostly done at night, and the job's relatively easy: I mainly follow cheating husbands or wives and photograph them for their betrayed spouses. Sometimes I investigate prospective employees for local businesses. Once I even found a lost puppy.

Greta left the bus after nine stops, then walked north. We were in Carver Heights, which once had known better days, maybe back when Georgia was a prison colony. It'll see them again, once the wealthy realize its potential for gentrification and jump the claims of the riffraff. I followed her on foot. The streetlights here were completely out. After about a block, she entered what looked like an abandoned school converted into low-income apartments. It had all the public housing charm: no expense had been spared on cinder blocks. The entry door led to a hallway running right and left, punctuated with scarred veneer doors. I've seen nicer graves.

At the end of the hallway, Greta inserted a key into a deadbolt, opened the door, and disappeared inside. Before I could follow, a claw grabbed my left shoulder.

"Where you going, cueball?" The voice had the mellifluous tone of a backed-up garbage disposal.

"Cueball?" I asked. "That's hardly nice." I turned around. The light was dim here, so I couldn't be sure, but I was restrained by either a yeti or a wolfman. Maybe the ghost of Robin Williams. Anyway, somebody hairy. "I've been led to believe"—I ran my free hand over my scalp—"that bald was beautiful."

"Listen, mosquito." He leaned in. I could see him better now. He looked like a middle manager masquerading as a bum. His jacket was ratty and his jeans faded, but his aftershave smelled expensive, and despite his hairiness, every strand was in place and not likely to move far. Fella used a lot of product is what I'm saying. He shook me and growled, "Scram."

"That's the best you can do?" I chuckled. "Scram? Read a lot of *Dick Tracy*, do you? Gonna ask if I'm some kind of wise guy next?" I winked at him. "I am, by the way."

"I'm asking nicely," the well-groomed hairy hobo growled. "Next time maybe I don't ask so nicely."

"I'll be out of your ample hair as soon as I talk to the girl down there."

He cast his eyes down the hall, shrugged. "I don't see no girl, and in about three seconds, I better not be seeing you."

"Can you say, 'Get out before I gets you out?'" I asked. "I think I'll have a Hard-Boiled Bingo."

"Walk away, shamus." He turned me toward the door. "You don't, you're not going to like what you find."

I smiled. "I rarely do." I twisted my shoulder under his hand and shifted my weight. He loosened his grip for a better hold. I dropped and jabbed my right hand into his left kidney. When he buckled, I jumped up, leapt to the wall, and crawled along it toward Greta's room.

Before I could get there, someone dropped an airplane on me.

When I opened my eyes again, I was leaning against a glass door. I looked up:

Night Vesper Investigations

F. V. Orlok, P.I.

Savannah, Georgia

Clearly Robin Williams knew who I was. He called me "mosquito," so he probably knew what I was, too.

The world seemed a bit too bright. I blinked twice, rubbed my eyes, and realized it was dawn. I rose to my feet, bracing myself on the door frame, and entered my office.

I needed a nice nap.

III.

There are many things I hate about being a vampyre in the twenty-first century. Popular media paint immortality as a fairly sweet deal. No responsibilities, no roots. The ability to go anywhere, do anything you desire. Hell, even the most morose of immortals can at least be sad on mountaintops overlooking sweeping vistas or from the height of a penthouse in Times Square.

The reality is different.

Try getting a business license when the sunlight sears your flesh. Or a driver's license. Christ, try buying a house after the sun has set in most towns, even large towns. Sure New York may be the city that never sleeps, but even there, the banks close at dusk. And I don't live in New York.

But what about computers, you ask? Sure, a lot of business can be taken care of on-the-line nowadays, but I can't do it. I've known octogenarians who can't figure out television remotes. For a man who knew Oliver Cromwell personally, I'm going to understand this webnet thing?

It's enough to drive a man to alcoholics.

That's where Knox comes in.

"No record of a Greta Wegener in any of the databases." Knox was a computer technology student when I bit him. "I looked at property records, birth certificates, driving records." He typed at the computer in the corner.

"Did you check German records?" I was kicked back at my desk sipping a lowball of blood. Every evening Knox meets me in the office with a bandage about his left wrist, offering me a glass of freshly decanted claret. Knox smokes, which gives him a pleasant, woody flavor.

"I'm not an amateur, Frank." He seemed irritated that I'd even ask. Vampyre familiars are rarely the fawning lunatics popular culture describes. Just because Vlad chose Renfield, whose belfry, let's be honest, was already overfull of bats, doesn't mean we all have moon-dazed assistants. No, Knox knows his stuff. All my familiars have been masters of their fields, all the way back to the original, the real estate lawyer who set me up in Bremen. His crazed portrayal in that damned film was just another in my long list of grievances against that fucking Murnau.

"Hold on." Knox snapped his fingers to get my attention. "This is weird."

I leaned over and inhaled the aroma of his neck. Looked longingly at the two healing puncture holes. Maybe later. He pointed at the screen. Fifteen entries for a Greta Wegener appeared: an address, a car registration, employment histories, her school and university records. Even an application for a library card.

"This wasn't here a minute ago." Knox shrugged.

"Any pictures of her?"

Knox clicked a button and the screen showed the face of a

young brunette woman. "That her?"

"Apparently." I tapped the screen beside her picture. "This isn't where I followed her last night, though."

"I reckon you'll be going there tonight then." Knox reached into a desk drawer, removed a black thermos, and began to unwrap his bandage. "I'll pack your lunch."

IV.

Something I've learned through years of traveling, especially in the American South, is that the reality of a place rarely fits its portrayal. If a film wants to imply an old Southern aristocratic family fallen on hard times due to their own depredations, for example, they'll live in a crumbling plantation house, columns overrun with kudzu and Spanish moss (even where Spanish moss doesn't thrive) and built conveniently on swampland. There will often be a crack or two running from the foundation to the roof. Very metaphoric.

As anyone actually from the South knows, these houses, by and large, don't exist. Decadent Southerners from old families generally live in ritzy subdivisions near golf courses.

Greta Wegener's address, though, brought me to just such a house in the swampy backlands of Ebenezer Creek, about an hour north of town, on an island near where Ebenezer empties into the Savannah River. I parked off of a private road and walked the rest of the way. Even from the shore, I could see the house's widow's walk above the tree line across the water. Folklore gets many things wrong about vampyres. We cannot transform into mist or hordes of rats, for instance. Nor can our shadows move independently of our bodies (though admittedly in the film, that scene was the tits). We're also perfectly able to cross running water, so long as we can swim or there's a boat.

Sadly, I found no boat. I stashed my coat and wallet under a tree root, and waded in.

One myth that is true is that we cannot enter uninvited a home occupied by the living. I found it curious, then, that I crossed the threshold of Greta's house unhindered (except for the lock I'd picked). On one hand, this implied that the place was abandoned. However, the furniture and dust-free floors suggested otherwise.

The door had been locked from the inside, too.

The lack of clutter, though, argued for at least recent abandonment. Most people maintain a modicum of untidiness in their homes. Books scattered on tables, magazines draped across chair arms, toys on the floor. Generally, the only time houses are this clean is when the owners are selling them.

Or are expecting company…

I moved carefully through the house. Upstairs the beds were made. I bounced a quarter on one of them. The bathrooms were spotless: no toothpaste tubes dripping onto the sink. No toothbrushes, for that matter. The toilets were pristine.

Back downstairs to the kitchen. Empty sink. Dishes stacked in cabinets. Bare refrigerator.

A door under the stairwell led to the basement. Here were the first signs of neglect: the air was damp, smelling faintly of must. The walls had a patina of mildew. The floor was only slightly spongy.

And in the corner, against the wall, leaned a coffin.

"You're a tough nut to break, Mr. Franklin Varnae Orlok."

Jojo the Dog-Faced Boy loomed behind me. The must on the air hid the scent of his mousse and aftershave.

"A tough nut to crack." I grinned. "If you're going to speak in clichés, at least get them right."

Jojo seemed not to hear. "You got a chance to walk away." His right arm moved to his left shoulder. Almost certainly a gun. "Don't, and the sun back in Wisburg won't do half the job I'm gonna do."

"Wisburg isn't real." I replied. "It was Bremen. And the sun thing never happened. Murnau was low on money and needed to end his picture."

He didn't seem the least bit amused. "I'm asking you nicely. Go back to your office. Look the other way." He nodded upstairs. The light there had brightened. "The sun may not kill you. But it'll hurt a great deal, I believe. And it's rising directly."

"I'll leave in just a minute." I said, nodding to the corner. "Who's in the box?"

Jojo said nothing.

I shrugged and turned to the coffin. As I reached it, the air around me exploded, and I saw Knox's blood spatter on the coffin. Son-of-a-bitch had gut-shot me.

"You dumb fuck." I turned around, trying to hold my guts in while the wound healed itself. Jojo stared at me, his mouth attempting to catch flies. "You don't know shit about vampyres." I nodded to the casket. "Have a word with your boss. They clearly didn't prepare you." I nodded at his iron. "Place your gun on the ground with two fingers only. If not, you should know I haven't fed well," I nodded toward the spatter behind me, "and you just blew most of that away, so I'm peckish. You use more than two fingers, I'm going to quench my thirst."

He dropped the gun.

"Now kick it over." He did. As I reached down to pick it up, a raspy voice behind me spoke with a faint German or Eastern European accent.

"It's good to see you again, Frank."

And for the second time in as many nights, I woke up elsewhere. This time in my car. My wallet lay in my lap, my coat folded under my head. The inside pocket vibrated.

I sat up and pulled my phone from the coat. I saw two texts from Knox. The first read: "Do you know who Greta Wegener was? You probably knew her."

The second, sent about thirty minutes before I came to, was a grainy picture of a woman in her thirties sprawled in an alley off what appeared to be River Street. She wore a black leather bustier over a pink miniskirt and knee-high black leather boots. Clearly a working girl. Knox's note read simply "Exsanguinated." I looked again at the girl's face.

She had been my client.

V.

"Greta Wegener," Knox explained the next evening, "was the married name of Greta Schröder." Knox slid a stack of papers across the desk. "She married Paul Wegener a couple of years after you knew her."

"Who was Greta Schröder?" I asked.

Knox looked at me as if I had just asked who Frank Orlok

was. "You don't remember?"

"I've been around a long time and forgotten a good bit." I tapped the papers. "Including apparently, who the hell Greta Schröder was."

Knox shook his head and smiled. "She was in that film about you. Played Ellen Hutter." He shrugged. "Our Greta is her great-granddaughter."

Fucking *Nosferatu*. Film's done nothing but make my existence a living hell for a century. Since Murnau used my story to tell his own version of *Dracula*, I'm constantly confused with Vlad. When people meet me, they express surprise at how little I resemble my portrayals. When I explain who I am, they lose interest. Or accuse me of plagiarizing Vlad's story, though I predate him by a good hundred years.

I've got to hand it to Vlad: he has a great public relations team. Look at who plays him on screen: Bela Lugosi, Christopher Lee, Gary Oldman. Who wouldn't want to be bitten by that? Here's the thing, though: he's not nearly as attractive as the flickers make him. Short and dumpy. And that stupid mustache. Like Josef Stalin after a five-day drunk. But no one cares. On screen he looks dreamy, so he never hunts for food. Dames line up around the block to get his teeth in them.

Who plays me on the silver screen? Fucking Max Schreck, Klaus Kinski, and Willem Dafoe. Talented actors all, for sure, but not exactly heartthrobs. Other than the baldness, not one of them carries my disarming charm. So I glut on vagabonds, hospice patients, and the occasional asshole. Well, and Knox, bless him.

I came to America to escape the film. To start fresh. I thought that was what America was for. But every time I turn around, Murnau's monstrosity finds yet another way to screw me over.

And now this.

Knox had been busy while I slept. Once he made the connection to Schröder, he set about researching her family on something called the CODIS. It's a webnet thing, he explained, a way of tracing ancestors.

"We're interested in her descendants," I said. "What do her ancestors have to do with it?"

"It's got data on both, Frank." Knox told me. "The largest DNA record collection in the country. Let me finish my story. We're burning moonlight here."

He was able to trace Schröder's descendants all the way to a granddaughter-in-law in Atlanta, Georgia, whom he called.

"I told her I worked for a personnel vetting firm, and that her daughter Greta had applied for a job," Knox said. "I tried to get as much information as possible before she realized I was lying and clammed up." Knox pulled a notebook from his pocket and read from it. "Our Greta attended Georgia Southern as an English major. Received her Master's there as well. Couple years ago, she applied for and was accepted to a doctoral program in Atlanta."

"And?"

"Dropped off the face of the earth." Knox shrugged. "Mrs. Wegener hasn't heard from her since. Had no idea if she even started graduate school. Didn't know her daughter was living here. I'm fairly certain she was unaware her daughter was turning tricks. Mrs. Wegener reported her missing after three weeks of not hearing from her, but the police never found her. She was pretty broken up about it."

"Uh-huh."

"I did find out something interesting about her family, though." Knox turned the page of his notebook and smiled at me.

"You gonna tell," I asked, "or is it a guessing game?"

"Sure." Knox said. "When I asked about the last time she heard from her daughter, Mrs. Wegener starts crying. Says she should have known something would happen. I asked why.

"'Because of the curse,' she says. What curse? Well, turns out every single one of Schröder's descendants have either died young or disappeared."

I leaned in. "Elaborate."

Knox shrugged. "Just that. Mrs. Wegener was widowed shortly after Greta was born. Her father-in-law left on a business trip in the 1970s and never came home. Her sister-in-law, Greta's aunt, was found overdosed on heroin behind a Piggly Wiggly in 1994." Knox shrugged again. "All the way back to Schröder's divorces, the first of which happened right around the time *Nosferatu* was filming, and her descent to almost total obscurity and bit parts." He looked at me. "You know, nobody even knows when Schröder died? Some say April 13, 1967, others June 8, 1980."

A family curse, a girl with amnesia recently dead, and a hirsute heavy. And everything circling back to that damned film. A film supposedly about one vampyre but actually about a completely different and more popular vampyre. The coffin in the basement.

I rubbed my chin and looked at Knox.

"Gonna need your help tonight," I said. Knox sighed, and began unwrapping his wrist. "No," I shook my head. "Something else."

VI.

I approached the plantation house with all the subtlety of a flatulent rhinoceros in St. John's Cathedral. Knox had rented a motorboat without a carburetor to get me across the water. I was wearing my blue suit, light enough to wake the dead, which I hoped to do.

"Vlad!" I yelled as I scoped the yard. There was an unlocked tool shed in the back. Other than a few yard tools, though, it appeared empty. I stepped onto the porch. "Wake up."

Nothing. I tried the door. Unlocked.

"Vlad?" I entered the house, leaving the door open behind me. A fire burned in the fireplace. Lamps cast a warm glow over the furniture. The air smelled of sandalwood. I stepped into the room and looked around. No one.

I made my way to the stairs. The air shifted slightly as I reached the basement door. Someone had silently entered the hall behind me. I felt the faintest wisp of breath on my neck and caught just a whiff of cologne, and before you could blink, I had turned around, grabbed Benji by the scruff of his neck and buried my fangs into his carotid.

I intended to drain him only enough to make him groggy, more prone to answering questions, but it had been years since I'd let loose and drained a victim more than a couple of pints (other than the occasional hospice patient), and I went too far. When I finished, Benji sank to the floor with a thud.

"Well, that was anticlimactic." The voice behind me was accented, not as raspy as the night before. It was also decidedly feminine. I turned from the hairy corpse on the floor.

Greta Wegener leaned against the basement door frame, smiling as she pared her nails with what appeared to be a silver dagger.

"Hello, lover," she said, "been a while."

"You're not Greta," I said. Something about the voice…

"Well, not since 1980," she chuckled. "And not before 1967." She clicked her tongue three times. "Come on, Frank. It's been over a century, yes, but surely you remember me."

Then I did.

Ellen Hutter sank her dagger into my heart with one hand and delivered a left hook to my jaw with the other. Since I'd recently had so much practice, I passed out without any trouble.

VII.

One thing people don't realize about detective work is how little intelligence it takes. You don't have to be Sherlock Holmes (hell, I knew him. Even Sherlock Holmes wasn't Sherlock Holmes). All it takes is reasonable observational skills, a decent grasp of common sense, and an ability to take a beating until somebody tells you what's going on. Detective work is mostly just pretending to be a punching bag.

When I came to, I was sitting in a Queen Anne armchair in the living room. I tried to rise and found my arms and legs bound tight. In front of me, Ellen poked at the fire with an iron rod.

"I have been waiting a century for this," she said over her shoulder. "Ever since you and that Murnau ruined my life."

"What are you talking about?" I asked. "You left me. I never ruined your life."

"I wanted more than spending eternity in Bremen feeding on farmers and shopkeepers. But you said Bremen felt like home and wouldn't leave." A log fell into the coals of the fire with a crackle and a hiss. "Then you told our story to Murnau and the two of you conspired to make me look weak and foolish."

"What are you talking about?" I asked again. I've never been great at holding up my end of a conversation.

"That damned film!" Ellen yelled as she turned around and leapt toward me. She held the red-hot iron poker under my chin. "You made me a fool! You painted me as a mealy-mouthed housefrau without the gumption or wits of a half-rotten radish." She touched my right cheek with the poker. I heard the sizzle. Smelled my flesh singe. Felt the burn. I didn't scream. I've survived the sun and Vesuvius, after all.

Ellen rose from me and stomped her foot on the floor. "You made me out to be the doting little wife to that braying jackass, and made him the hero. As if he ever did anything more interesting than watch other people act. I left him for you, and you weren't any better. Though honestly, you're more interesting now."

"I'm a late bloomer." I said, but she didn't hear.

"I spent years taking my anger out on the actress because I couldn't find you, and Murnau was too well-known." She smiled before turning back to the fire and reheating the poker. "I interfered with every relationship she had. Sometimes I lured her men away, even turned one or two. Sometimes I let men think I was her." She turned back to me, waving the poker. "You know I killed her in '67? Should have done it sooner, really. Old blood tastes so thin, don't you agree? Like seltzer water gone flat."

Something moved outside the window behind her.

"You killed her," I said, "then took her identity."

Ellen smiled. "She stole my life. I stole hers."

Outside, I heard a faint shuffling sound from the shed. "Why'd you stop in 1980?"

"Bored." Ellen shrugged. "I couldn't do it forever. After all, humans must die eventually. And her grandson's family had moved here."

"You killed him too, I'm guessing." The shadow moved across the window again, "and mesmerized the great-granddaughter. Took her identity, too. Turned her out on the street at night for what? Kicks?"

"I want Schröder to know, wherever she is, that I am not the frail violet she made me out to be, and that my vengeance spans generations. Sins of the Mother and all that." She leaned down again and waved the iron poker. "I will not be trifled with by anyone living or dead." She gave me a matching brand on my left cheek. Again, I didn't scream, but I thought long and hard about it.

"I was going to go after Murnau and his family, but he was

long dead by the time I got to America, and he had no children."
She looked at me. "Did you know he was an Arschficker?"

"We say gay now, but yes." The air in the hallway behind us shifted.

"Someone took his skull a few years ago, right from his grave." Ellen shook her head and stared into the ceiling, lost in thought.

"Shocking."

She returned her attention to me. "That left *you*. Imagine my surprise when I followed young Greta here, and found one of your advertisements on a park bench."

"So you planted the idea for her to hire me." It wasn't a question.

"And you took the case." She shrugged. "She was no longer needed, and I was hungry."

"I don't suppose," I said, "it would help my case if I told you I'm not exactly a fan of the film either?"

"Perhaps," Ellen chuckled. "If I believed you."

"But you don't believe me?"

"No." Ellen reached out with her left hand and pulled my lower jaw down, opening my mouth, forcing my eyes to the ceiling. I heard the faint sound of socked feet on hardwood. "This won't kill you," —she raised the poker to my mouth, and I could feel it searing the roof— "but it'll hurt like all the flames of hell."

"This actually will kill you." Knox appeared behind her and swung a rusty axe. With a sound like a cleaver cutting steak, Ellen's head flew across the room, landing in front of the fireplace. She looked startled. Her body fell to the hearth. The clothes began to smolder.

"Took you long enough." I said.

Knox began freeing my legs. "It's rude to interrupt someone monologuing."

Epilogue

Maybe the news of the burning, abandoned old house would make the papers. Maybe not. It was pretty isolated, and I'm fairly sure the whole place went up. Looked that way from the car, anyway.

Knox left me at the office. I leaned back in my chair and stared out the window. It was almost dawn. I thought about that damned film. I thought about Ellen's century of hatred. I thought about my own.

Truth is Murnau wasn't alone. No one's ever told my story well. Rymer wrote an uneven, confused tale that no one other than English majors read. That broad in New Orleans gave me blonde hair and made me a damned rock star. The mook out West kept me as a gumshoe but made me a preening fratboy with a conscience.

Yes, Murnau's film had problems. He so wanted to film *Dracula* that he used me and twisted my story to do it. Now if anyone even remembers my name, they assume I'm just a cheap knockoff of Vlad. Hell, mostly they think I'm called Nosferatu. I don't even bother with aliases anymore. I can't ever escape the stupid film anyway. I hear they're even working on a new one.

"Well, Fred"—I winked at the skull on my bookcase—"if nobody else can tell my story right, I'll have to do it myself."

IN THE LANDS OF THIEVES AND PHANTOMS

Nancy Holder & Alan Philipson

Palermo, Sicily, 1902

Moonlight streamed through the ruined palazzo's atrium, illuminating the crumbling gallery railings and enclosed courtyard below. Two men sat on the cobblestones beside an empty fountain, legs extended, arms raised overhead, wrists chained to the rim.

From the edge of the darkness that surrounded them, a tall fragment of shadow broke free—a shadow on two legs. Neither prisoner reacted as Mezzanotte swept forward in his long, black coat. Their trousers and vests were dusted with the fine ash that ringed the fountain's base, their faces snow white, shirt collars spattered with bright drops of blood. Dozens of purple puncture wounds decorated their throats and wrists, as if they had been set upon by ravening beasts.

Mezzanotte leaned closer.

One of the mafia clansmen was dead. His chin rested on his chest, eyes open, staring vacantly at the unmoving dome of his stomach. The other criminal still inhaled and exhaled, but barely. Looking up at Mezzanotte, eyes brimming with tears, he wheezed, "Have mercy!"

For a murderer, thief and extortionist, a predator of the defenceless, mercy was never an option. From the moment of his capture there was only one way forward, and it was neither easy nor quick.

The sound of a violin filtered through a shadowed doorway behind the fountain. Individual notes of perfect pitch stretched on and on, swelling in volume until they became an unbroken moan.

The chained corpse twitched, then a violent shudder shook it from head to foot—and lifeless flesh began to stir. Still not breathing, eyes open but not seeing, the chin slowly began to rise from its resting place.

"Minchia!" the surviving mafioso shrieked, hurling himself as far from the wakening horror as his shackles would permit. Words spilled in a torrent from his bloodless lips: "Dear Lord, no, this cannot be! I watched him die, I watched Carlo die. Only witchcraft could have brought him back like this—a rotting puppet without a soul. Is that my fate as well? I beg you, destroy me now with fire, crush my bones to powder, before…"

Carlo stared at his fellow captive, eyes swimming with darkness.

"A line has been crossed," Mezzanotte said, "and a point must be made."

"Desecration and black magic have never been the way of the clans. We are men of true faith. Your capocosca, Don Falde, has sworn the oath, signed it in his own blood."

"I do as I am bid, with the means at my command."

"Then you are a monster!"

"We are *all* monsters," Mezzanotte said.

The mafioso started to protest, then fell into convulsions, frothing at the mouth as Death took a firmer grip.

Mezzanotte tested the shackles a final time. Satisfied that they were secure, he followed the strains of the violin, around the fountain, through the doorway, into the palazzo, and down the pitch-black corridor leading to the dining hall.

He walked past heavy doors ripped off their hinges, into a narrow, high-ceilinged room with stone block walls and wooden crossbeams. Moonlight streamed through a row of curtainless windows.

On the scarred oak table, amid the scattered plates, overturned goblets, dust and cobwebs stood the violinist. Eyes closed in rapture, with exquisite tenderness Hannah Krugerhof played a melody of passion spent, of desire fulfilled. Turned by Dracula in a Salzburg graveyard in 1895, Hannah would be forever seventeen, blonde, slender, waif-like, with huge blue eyes. In life she had been a meek music student; in death, she was a lioness, always first to the blood.

Slumped in chairs beside the long table were Peter Moresby and Johannes Vilnes, both sated to the point of immobility. Peter was the son of a British admiral, a family disappointment, and would-be poet. He'd met the vampire in 1893 in Amsterdam's De Wallen red light district. Johannes, a young Swiss outdoorsman, had been murdered and resurrected by Dracula on a moonlit path beneath the Jungfrau.

The Italian noblewoman Zenobia di Schiani sat at the head of the table. Cascades of wavy black hair framed startling green eyes that matched the glittering emeralds encircling her slender throat. She had been plucked from life in Florence's Boboli Gardens in 1891, at the pinnacle of her youth and radiance.

Mezzanotte smiled at their torpor. It was always so peaceful after they had fed. They could be reasoned with. They could all enjoy a carriage ride or a leisurely passagiata down Via Roma, even take in an opera or concert with no danger to innocent bystanders or fear of public exposure. It was nearly five in the morning, too late for anything but a short stroll.

He said, "Shall we get some air while the moon is still high?"

Peter groaned and waved off the suggestion. A smear of dried blood decorated the right lens of his spectacles.

"Give us a story instead, Master," Hannah said, lowering her instrument and taking a seat on the edge of the tabletop.

"Yes, please give us a story," Johannes agreed.

"You know which one," Zenobia said.

He took in their expectant, happy faces, ashen cheeks flushed with the living blood they had gorged upon. He had loved them all before he ever met them. Their tragedies and his were inextricably, eternally interwoven.

Mezzanotte pulled out a chair, sat down, and began the tale his charges never tired of hearing.

I came into being in a land of phantoms.

Not as a seed nourished and nurtured in a loving womb, as you were. Not as a baby thrust forth into the world, as you were.

I awoke a fully formed adult, naked in the murky depths of a storm-tossed lake, my mind blazing with images of horror and carnage, and an insatiable thirst for blood. Not just to spill, but to drink. Hundreds, perhaps thousands, of victims—legions of men, women, and children—flickered though my consciousness. I saw them chased to exhaustion, cornered, their pulsing throats torn open and drained. I saw their terror, their vain struggles, their inevitable surrender. Through a veil of blood I saw shimmering ghosts of steam rise from their heaped bodies.

Alone in the dark at the bottom of the lake, I covered my ears with my hands and screamed.

The revolting memories and urges were not my own.

I knew I had done none of those things. I knew I was only just born. I had never set foot on dry land, had never set eyes on another living creature. I had never tasted blood. But if the memories were not mine, to what unspeakable monster did they belong? How did they get into my head? Why, why wouldn't they stop?

I struggled to free my feet from the thick ooze of the lake bottom and battled upward towards a faint glow. As I broke the surface, lightning flashed across a stormy night sky. Foam-crested waves, formed by howling wind, slammed into my back and face. In towering waterspouts, spinning columns of mist, I saw the same tableaux of subjugation and slaughter that infested my brain. And above the images of struggle, glittering in the slanting sheets of rain like an enormous unfolded banner, a row of letters spelled a name I recognized—but could not place.

DRACULA

The raging gale pushed me towards the shore. As I bobbed helpless under the light of a moon half-hidden by black clouds, I could make out the lake's surround of shadowy, densely forested mountains. Perched on a promontory that jutted out over the lake, I saw the jagged parapets of an abandoned castle.

I crawled out of the water and collapsed onto the muddy beach. I should have been gasping for air, but I wasn't. How I knew this, how I knew anything, I could not say.

I wasn't breathing at all.

When I forced myself to my feet, I realized the path leading to the ruin lay directly in front of me. Carved from bare rock, crooked stairs marked the face of the massive outcrop. I staggered upward towards shelter, lashed by the wind and driving rain.

Above me was the castle; a weathered crag of gray stone blocks—cloaked in lichen and moss, it looked like a headless giant seated on a decaying throne. Irregular rows of empty windows stared down at me as I climbed over the tumbled-down arch of the entry gate.

Beyond it stood a luminous form.

Human-shaped, like me. Not entirely human, like me. The being had a rat-like face and pointed ears, bald head, needle-like protruding front teeth and dark circles around even darker eyes. It was dressed in a black velvet cloak, its colorless spindly arms folded across a narrow chest.

As I approached, it recoiled from me in shock. Fluttering its long, spidery fingers, it nervously clicked their curved, seven-inch nails. Lightning flashed overhead, illuminating the littered courtyard, and I could see through its body as if it were made of smoke.

More memories surfaced unbidden, more memories that were not mine. Of crossing a raging sea in a sailing ship and rising from a coffin in its hold. Of devouring the ship's captain and crew. Perhaps all the horrid memories belonged to this wretched thing?

"Are you Dracula?" I asked.

The creature's bushy eyebrows arched in surprise; then a strangled laugh erupted from its throat. Its eyes twinkled as it spoke. "The answer to your question is yes and no—but mostly no. That's something you and I have in common."

"I don't understand."

"We are kin, of a sort. The explanation is complex and lengthy, and here you stand cruelly exposed to the storm."

I was naked and dripping wet, but not cold.

"Please, come out of the rain and let me show you my temple of delights." The creature half-turned and gestured at the sprawling ruin, revealing a hunch on its back. "I am called Count Orlok. Or was. Not to put too fine a point on it, I am all that remains. What is your name?"

The question took me aback. I had no answer.

Orlok seemed amused by my paralysis. "Follow me inside, No Name," he said. "To a more comfortable place where we can talk. You can remind me of life as our Master lived it. You can tell me what you have seen through his eyes. What you have tasted."

When I did not move, Orlok threw a spindly arm around my back and urged me forward. "Come along, brother," he said, "and I will show you my secret treasure."

Hoping for answers, I let him lead me into a dim passageway. The instant we stepped across the threshold, howls and shrieks erupted on all sides, throbbing like heartbeats against the rough stone walls.

"What is that?!" I asked.

"A symphony of mourning," Orlok replied. "Of agony that never ends."

"Whose agony?"

Ignoring the question, he ushered me into a cavernous chamber lit by scattered torches embedded in rusting sconces. The wailing continued, rising and falling like the wind outside. Rain from a breach in the roof spattered the marble floor. In a huge stone fireplace, flames suddenly leapt to life, dancing and crackling. But they gave off no heat. Shadows drifted across the walls, obscuring, dissolving, reappearing. Like a cloud of hungry flies they swarmed around my host.

Orlok squinted at me, rat teeth protruding over his lower lip. "You resemble him," he said. "Certainly more than I."

"Whom do I resemble?" I asked.

Bending over a worm-eaten, lidless wooden chest, Orlok said, "Should you wish to cover yourself, here are furs of the finest quality." The chamber's shadows darted around him, swooping and diving as if in attack. "Take what you want. They are no longer of any use to us."

I puzzled over his last word.

"Are you hungry?" Orlok said. "Do you want blood?"

The images that popped into my head sickened me.

"There are rats in the castle of course, and rabbits in the forest outside, quite juicy," Orlok went on. "And for something more filling, peasants in the tiny village to the south. It's not far."

"Is that what *you* eat?"

"We don't eat. I myself have not taken sustenance for fifty years."

Again, the mysterious plural. "We?" I said.

My host spread wide his skeletal arms. As if at his command, the shadows whirling around him slowly morphed into pale, translucent shapes. Distorted, vague, but human-looking. "These are my trophies," Orlok said. "The mementoes I gathered and brought with me from the other side of death. Their suffering mine to enjoy forever."

The chorus of misery rose in volume until it drowned out Orlok's laughter. His form flickered before me, the edges of its perimeter dimmed, and then he disappeared, but the spirits remained.

I was surrounded by them, their faces elongating, melting, reforming. The only constants in the chaos were their black eyes—or the holes where their eyes had once been.

The shape of a young woman materialized before me, gradually becoming more distinct. Rows of ringlets framed a gaunt, hollow-cheeked face and dark eyes full of pain. She wore a ruffled, gauzy nightgown.

"Where am I?" I asked.

"In a place that does not exist and never has," she said. "Nothing here is real, not even our unending torture."

Feeling a sudden chill—not from the air or the damp, but from her words—I lifted a robe of soft fur from the lidless chest, slid my arms into the sleeves, and belted it. It was clean and fit well. There was considerable weight in both side pockets. I dipped my fingers inside.

On upturned palms I showed her fistfuls of bright coins. "What use do spirits have for gold? Or luxurious furs, for that matter?"

"They do not belong to us, they never belonged to us," she said. "That robe and the gold were the property of your progenitor, the ancient and powerful vampire known as Dracula."

"Orlok said I looked like someone else. Is that who I resemble?"

"You have Dracula's height and build, his black hair and chiseled face. You were created from an infinitesimal speck of his essence. Using forbidden magic in this unholy place, the vampire transformed himself into other beings, other forms."

"How do you know this?"

"I watched him leap from the promontory into the waters of Lake Hermannstadt and burst into millions of glittering fragments."

"What was his purpose? To escape his enemies?"

"I don't know. Perhaps to populate the world with his like-nesses."

As improbable as it sounded, it explained the images in my mind and my strange "birth" in the lake. It also explained my knowledge of things I could never have seen.

"I was called Ellen Hutter," she said. "I sacrificed myself to Orlok to destroy him, to protect my husband and others I knew and loved. I was his last living victim. He drank me all night, and when he was caught in the rising sun, he fell to dust before my eyes. When I died moments later I was certain I would go to heaven. But instead I was drawn here, a prisoner of Orlok's ghost, condemned as are the spirits of all his innocent victims."

She stepped into the pelting rain that fell through the roof, and tossed back her head. As she looked upward, arms outstretched, the drops passed through her and splashed in the puddle on the floor. "Why can't I, why can't *we* be washed clean of this filth?" she cried.

Ellen Hutter was a wraith. Made of vapour. Breathing or not, I appeared to have substance. As I dropped the coins back in my pockets, I felt an urge purely my own: to right a terrible wrong.

"Did Dracula create Orlok?" I asked her. "Is that why he calls me kin?"

"Orlok was the product of Dracula's first attempt at dispersing his essence, a test of the magic spell's power and effect. He was created from a shard of fingernail that Dracula cast into the lake. The experiment failed. Its result was hideous to look upon, a single-minded predator, spreader of plague, able to make legions of corpses, but unable to create more vampires."

She gazed deep into my eyes. "But in you, Dracula has made a perfect copy. You may possess the power to do everything he could do—or to undo it as you see fit." Standing in the downpour, undampened, she clasped her hands together. "Have pity on our poor souls. Release us from this nightmare!"

A chorus of assenting wails rose from all around.

Save us save us save us. For the love of God, save us.

"You are our only hope," Ellen Hutter pleaded as her luminesce and that of the others winked out, smothered by a taloned hand.

"You still have his memories, your Maker's," Orlok said to my back. "I had them too, until I made my own."

I faced the failed experiment, the spawn of a fingernail clipping. The spirits had vanished but I could hear their keening, braided with the shrill wind. "Do you keep your victims with you to drown out the memory of him?"

"No, I keep them because their misery was my only act of creation. The gift of spreading seed, of making progeny was denied me, but perhaps you have it."

"I am not a vampire. I cannot create vampires."

Orlok chuckled, his hands opened at his sides, long fingers and even longer nails fanned out in white spikes. "There is only one way to find out. But elsewhere. We are all dead here. You must go among the living."

He gestured at the chamber door. "You must go now."

Leaning into the wind and rain, I paused at the tumbled-down arch and glanced back at the courtyard. Ellen stood at the head of a writhing mass of lost souls.

"Don't abandon us!" she cried.

I felt her pain and desperation, but I knew Orlok was right. This was not the place to find my power. "Ellen, you'll all be released," I called back. "I'll find a way, somehow."

With that, I departed the land of phantoms. Scrambling up the mountainside, I looked back from its peak. In the light of the moon I saw below me a shallow valley carpeted with black forest. The mystic lake was gone, the castle gone, Ellen and the others gone.

Forever beyond my help.

My promise forever a lie.

Mezzanotte lifted a drowsy Hannah into her coffin and gently lowered her head to the pillow. She weighed next to nothing, an angel of darkness he was sworn to protect, and who in turn protected him. Folding her hands across her chest, he slid shut the lid.

The others had already crawled into their coffins in the windowless chamber. One by one he closed the lids. That they hadn't been able to stay awake to hear the end of the story didn't matter, they all knew it by heart.

I descended barefoot to the path on the other side of the mountain, pockets full of gold, my brain, after a few moments of respite, seething anew with Dracula's urge to feed and destroy. I knew eventually it would overwhelm and prevail, turning me into the monster he had intended.

I had to find a way to defend myself, and in so doing, protect the innocent, and atone in some way for the crimes of my progenitor. I knew I could not do that alone. I had to reach outside myself.

Of all the horrors that filled my mind, the most vivid and most repeated were the most recent. Hannah, Peter, Johannes, and Zenobia had been Dracula's final victims, their tragedies replayed over and over. I loved them for their perfect innocence before evil touched them, for what they might have been, for what they had become. Like me, they were blameless. I sought them out. I found them. I became their caregiver, and they mine. To that end I created a symbiosis. A way for us all to survive and move forward.

A life made from death.

Mezzanotte returned to the palazzo's courtyard wearing dark spectacles. Dawn was breaking over Palermo, the atrium filling from top to bottom with lavender light. The mafiosos chained to the fountain had long since turned. No longer alive, no longer human, they bared their fangs at him, snarling like wolves as they jerked taut their restraints. Pulled back from the dead, reborn starving for blood. Beyond the reach of reason.

But not justice.

A ray of bright sunlight cut across the atrium's cobblestones at Mezzanotte's feet in a thin line, widening, spreading out towards the fountain. Sensing destruction, the new vampires shrank back as far as they could, and began to scream. No longer cries for mercy. They sounded like gulls fighting over scraps at the edge of the bay.

Mezzanotte did not step back into the shadows. Though it was unpleasant, he could endure daylight. He watched as it devoured them, turning their dead flesh and bone to ash, instantly silencing them. The manacles fell empty, clanking against the fountain. Twinkling dust climbed slowly into the spire of light.

Sicilian clans like Don Falde's usually left victims' bodies in public places to instill fear among their prey. Murders for offenses between *cosche* required a more delicate touch because if evidence were ever discovered, such killings would start a war. That situation called for a different sort of message. And a *specialista* to deliver it.

The message just sent to Don Falde's competitor was this: Cross me again and you, too, will vanish like you were never even born.

The *specialista* was called Mezzanotte.

He had no other name.

THE VAMPYRE'S SHADOW

Sal Ciano & Peter Rawlik

The Twenty Sixth of March, Eighteen Hundred and Thirty-Nine

For so many months, you have been my only true companion. Too many months, far too many if I am honest. I do want to thank you though, dear diary, without you I would have been lost—fully and completely. When my dear and darling husband left me here on his search for the origin of that mysterious plague that brought so much death and whispered rumors to Wisborg, striking without rhyme or reason and leaving families decimated in its path, I confess that I felt terror for him and horror at the idea that he would willingly head to that town to study this disaster, but I was not surprised. My darling Edmund is a scientist, a man of medicine, and a great man and, as my mother always said, a great man would never shy from his duty, and so—while the plague had not come near to England, he still felt it his duty to investigate—he set out as quickly as he could arrange with one goal that he related to me: find out why it stopped as it had, such a terrible plague should not have just ceased. He and his fellows who studied such outbreaks of disease were all in agreement: that such a terrible, unfathomable disease should not have simply halted when, if anything, it seemed to be gathering strength. Such an occurrence needed to be investigated.

That was weeks ago… No, that's wrong. It was months ago. Weeks ago was when I last heard from him, but you knew that already. I've complained and lamented many times to you over those days and weeks, how those minutes and hours without a word from him were hellish, that his lack of communication was worrying at best and selfish at worst. You, my confidant, have heard it all. I wrote of my loneliness, of how each day away from my love was agony. I wrote of my misery when Edmund had been reported missing after they could not locate him in his rooms a few weeks after he arrived in Wisborg, and I wrote of my cautious joy and optimism when they found him in that abandoned home a few days later. I have spoken to you about everything, everything but the words I am about to write, the words I have longed to write for several weeks now: Edmund is returning home! I received word just this morning that he is now fully risen from the state of catatonia that the doctors in Wisborg were treating him for and he even managed to ask to come home, though he was unclear as to where he was exactly and how he had arrived there. The doctors wrote that they feel that this fugue state will pass, and he will recall exactly what led him to that house but—to be perfectly honest—I don't care what he was doing in that empty home, I'm simply impatient for him to arrive. In the meantime, they begged me to be patient with Edmund, and they cautioned me that he is still very ill and would need plenty of bed rest in the coming weeks. I care not though; he is coming home! I would care for him for a thousand years as long as he greeted me each morning with a kiss and a whisper and said goodnight to me in the same fashion, I missed him so and I cannot wait to see him again. I shall write more here after he returns to me. In the meantime, I need to attend to some errands I have put off for far too long, and I need to visit Mr. Sandu later to drop off some of the dessert I made earlier. That's right, I baked to celebrate the good news. It is a shame, dearest diary, that you have no mouth to eat with or a tongue to taste with or I could share a world of confectionery delight with you! Then again, who knows what kind of terrible gossip you'd be if you had a mouth to move and a tongue to form words with! I will write more soon!

The Seventh of April, Eighteen Hundred and Thirty-Nine

I cannot stand it any longer. I did not want to write about any of this, but I can no longer stay my hand. If I do not speak or write about this, even if it is just to you, I feel as though I will explode. Everything is awful, my world is falling apart one piece at a time. It started when the doctors arrived here with Edmund in tow. When I saw him, I was, and still am, at a loss: The stranger in my house is not the man who once held me in his arms and danced with me for hours on end. He is a scarecrow version of my Edmund, a terrifying effigy which has done nothing but rot since they brought it back from Wisborg. It's true, the man I am caring for is little more than a living and breathing corpse and I am left wanting for the return of my real husband as this forgery withers up and turns to dust. Reading over that last sentence, I seem hysterical like a poor, lost housewife. I am not, though. I am not some helpless or hapless member of my gender; I am a strong and independent manager of my home and ruler of my life. I was raised by several powerful women to be a powerful woman myself, one capable of springing into action in the face of disaster, and so I went ahead and tried to manage this situation on my own. I followed the instructions left behind by the doctors. They told me to keep him confined to bed, that rest was key to his recovery as were the various powders and poultices they left behind. They explained that they did not know what, exactly, was wrong with him; they could only say that he was not contagious and so they felt it best that he recover at home. They could also offer no explanation as to how Edmund arrived at the location where he was eventually found or what he was doing there. Edmund, they said, was able to eat and move but they cautioned me that he no longer spoke and was prone to staring without blinking for long periods of time. He would, they promised as they left, be no trouble at all, save for his chronic somnambulism. They lied of course; the trouble started almost as soon as they left.

I went to the room where the doctors had carried him when they arrived. It would have served as our nursery, but we have so far been unsuccessful in producing an heir to our vast and glorious holdings. So instead, it has served as a sometime-guest room and sometime-storage room and now it is Edmund's sick room, where I shall nurse him. I remember taking a deep breath and steadying myself before I opened the door. I tried to put on a happy expression as I stepped into the room. I did not want Edmund to see the concern on my face or hear worry in my voice as I find that healing happens best in a healthy environment. The room was almost pitch black; the window was closed, and the curtain drawn, and a single candle cast a guttering and flickering light which hardly moved the darkness that crowded the room. Shadow clung to Edmund, the thin light did little to illuminate the handsome face I missed so much. I walked to the dresser where the candle sat and picked it up, guiding it carefully as I went to Edmund's side. The flame did not dispel the thick darkness which permeated the room and I found myself increasingly frustrated as the shadows danced and writhed in the candlelight, obscuring Edmund's face. The darkness was odd in that way, it did not respect the light. I frowned and put the candle down, reaching with my free hand to wipe the darkness away from him but I paused and chided myself for my foolish reaction to some shadows. Instead, I left the candle where it was and walked to the other side of the bed to the window. *Let the darkness be gone,* I thought to myself as I whipped the window coverings aside and threw open the shutters to let the sun in. I heard a whimper and a hiss behind me as the daylight streamed into the room and then a thump as I whirled around to see what was wrong. The bed was empty, and I rushed around the side in time to see Edmund lying in the pooling darkness that the far side of the bed provided from the sun. He was face down, his feet reaching under the bed and his hands limply lying palms down next to his head. I rushed to him, I knelt and grabbed his hand to lift him up and…well that's the problem, isn't it? I don't want to even write down what happened because I don't believe it myself but…no, I have to write this down. I suppose, for accuracy's sake, I will need to set aside the skepticism of my own mind and trust that what happened, however it happened, did in fact happen.

Kneeling there next to Edmund I took his hands gently in mine, but he did not stir, and I sat there for a few moments, gently stroking the back of his hand and wishing with all my heart that I could have him back as he was; begging God to let me hear him laugh or to see his smile again. I seem dramatic—I know I must—but if you think so then you do not understand the sort of love I felt for my husband and just how drastically he had changed in the months since he left. He was wasted and gaunt, with skin pale and tautly stretched over his skeletal frame, and his head and face were covered in sores and dry skin. His hair was falling out in patches and his eyes were so deeply sunken that I could not see anything but darkness welling up in the pits left behind. His eyes! When I lifted his head to see if he was injured in the fall from the bed, I felt overcome in the moment with a need to see his eyes; it was a need to establish any kind of normalcy in a dire situation, I suppose, and his eyes were what caught my attention when we first met all those years ago. I can, even now, remember how they sparkled with life and were filled with joy on the day we met at the town fair. I remember how tender and full of love they were on our wedding day. I remember now and I remembered then, and I needed to see that they were still there, but they were dull, lifeless things, a sad reflection of what they once had been. Staring into his dead and dark eyes, I thought some of the fresh air and sunlight I had allowed into the room might do him good, so I picked him up to put him back onto the bed and into the sunlight that shone on the bed there. He was lighter than I thought he would be, but even so his weight was a burden and I struggled to lift him up to the bed, managing to only lift his torso off the ground. I grunted and swore softly as I tried to drag him up and I started to entreat him to help me, although I knew it would do no good. His limp form offered no resistance and no help as I struggled with it. I heaved with all my might and finally cleared his torso from the ground and guided him back up towards the bed. His head cleared the edge of the bed as I lifted, and sun streamed onto it, and I dropped him in shock as he was wrenched violently from my hands. We fell back to the floor, and I tangled up with him; I flailed about in a panic. I scrambled free and then crawled back to him, desperate to ease his suffering as mewling sounds of pain escaped his throat, but as I got there, he was pulled backwards, backwards by something under the bed! The first pull dragged him halfway into the darkness beneath the wooden frame, and the second tore him from my grasp and he disappeared fully into the darkness there. I fled the room and the house in a panic and raced to the home of my neighbor, Mr. Sandu. I pounded on his door but there was no answer. I sat there in the relative safety of his doorstep, terrified and shaken, trying to make sense of it all. In the waning hours of the afternoon, I think I managed to convince myself of the truth: my dear Edmund had rejected me, had pulled himself violently away from me and was even now choosing to waste away rather than allow me to care for him. Well, I decided through the sobbing and the tears, I would not allow that to happen. I marched resolutely back to our home, and into the nursery I saw immediately that he had not moved from under the bed, though I fancied I could see two cold predatory eyes—not the eyes of my husband—staring at me from the darkness. I shuddered but decided that I would play whatever game my husband's feverish mind was involving itself in, and so I closed the window and drew the coverings, again leaving the room in darkness save for the single flickering candle. When I turned around Edmund was back in bed, covered in shadows and sheets as if he'd never fallen out of it in the first place. This happened in mere seconds, and I never heard so much as a rustle of the sheets. I felt an overwhelming rush of terror at his sudden reappearance, and I must confess I—blinded by fear—left him there without so much as checking to see if he was alright. Afterwards I despaired. That all happened a few days ago. There has been no change since, I am still full of despair, and he is still a shadow of a person. He accepts what liquids I give him; he takes the medicines without complaint, he even eats the food I place in his mouth and—eventually—fills the bedpan, but he did not and does not do any of those things of his own volition, his body only going through these motions when I require it to; otherwise, Edmund lays there unspeaking and unmoving. The poultices are not working, and he is not getting any better. Every day he gets a little gaunter, a little thinner, the dry and broken skin spreads a little more, and his breath smells a little fouler and there is nothing I can do…I just want my husband back.

The Fourteenth of April, Eighteen Hundred and Thirty-Nine

Vermin. As if my husband's illness was not enough, I noticed the first rat a few days after the incident with the open window as it scampered across the kitchen floor. Where there is one, there will be more, is what my mother always said about rats, and I know now she was right. I am not sure why they have arrived now, just another test from God, I suppose. I am starting to sympathize with Job's plight more and more each day, though I recognize that my suffering is not nearly as great as Job's and even less so than what my husband is going through. I will use some of the Paris green that Edmund purchased the last time we had an infestation, and my rat problem will go away, just like that. In recognizing such a simple solution as that, I can see how overdramatic I am being. I think I am just overwhelmed and looking for any reason to not write what I really need to talk about, what I really need to share here: what happened with Edmund not even a few hours ago. I am still shaking…

It started with a cracking sound, a brittle sound that made me think of dry twigs snapping in winter, that roused me from a fitful nap. I have not been sleeping well and when I do sleep my dreams are feverish and fretful—my mind always on the verge of waking. When I woke, I found myself at the kitchen table unable to fully recall what I was doing before I fell asleep or why I was awake. The night arrived while I was sleeping and filled the room with its obscuring presence and so I lit the lamps in the room, searching for what half-remembered sound woke me. As light filled the room, the snapping sound came again and this time it was accompanied by mewling, pain-filled whimpers; the same sound a newborn kitten might make if stepped on. At first the sound was everywhere, the cracking surrounding me and the mewling filling my ears but as my ears adjusted to being awake again, I realized that the sound came from the nursery, from my Edmund, and I rushed to the door. I reached out timidly; I know that I should have thrown it open and raced to his side, but fear stayed my hand. I paused, my hand hovered just over the doorknob as if there were flames on the other side heating the metal handle; I took a deep and steadying breath, and then I froze as I heard a voice from the other side of the thick wooden slab that separated my husband and I.

"Plllleeeeaaassseeee," a voice filled with fear and agony whined weakly. What followed was another sharp snap and a screech, and that is when I did find my fortitude and threw open the door. The light from the lamps spilled into the room from behind me, my shadow stretching before me, and illuminated Edmund, kneeling with one arm extended towards heaven with an open hand and the other trying to pull his arm down. The light from the doorway mixed with that from the single candle that I now kept permanently lit in the room. It flickered and flared in the sudden rush of air and the shadowed corners of the room swelled and shrank as if the lungs of a giant creature were inhaling and exhaling. My husband whimpered again, a pleading and awful sound that contained no words I could understand. I looked again at his strange stance and his wide eyes staring away from the doorway, gazing up as if he were being held aloft and that was when I noticed the figure standing there in the breathing shade—in the dancing darkness—holding Edmund aloft by one arm, and I raised my hand to my mouth to stifle a gasp as I took the scene in.

My mind reeled as it tried to process the moment—even now it is a fragmented phantasmagoria—but what I saw was a figure, as much made of darkness as cloaked in it, holding Edmund with one hand in an iron grip. No matter how much Edmund struggled he could not get free, even though it looked as if the stranger were just casually holding his hand. The figure gently reached down and caressed Edmund's head with its other hand, its overly long fingers casually twining themselves through some of the last strands on his almost bald scalp. As it did so, my husband's expression turned from one of fear to one of ecstasy wrought at the hand of a lover. Then suddenly it ripped the tuft of hair from his scalp. Edmund screamed and I did too, and the figure glanced up at me.

Edmund's free hand went to his scalp as his shadowed tormentor waved at me and pointed down to Edmund's other hand. It reached down and closed its hand languidly around Edmund's little finger and with a vicious wrenching motion, violently pulled it up, causing it to make the same brittle snapping sound that had roused me. Edmund and I both screamed again, Edmund in anguish and I in rage. Incensed, I raced into the room, and snatching the candle off the bedside table, I rushed the bed and shoved the tiny flame in the face of my husband's torturer.

The figure reacted to my assault by releasing my husband and diving to the floor before I could get a good look at it, though now that I was close enough to make out some detail, I saw that my husband's assailant was tall and thin, though hunched a bit in his shoulders (I am assuming gender here, but the presence in the room felt malignantly masculine). His head appeared to be somewhat malformed, though, again, I only had the briefest of glimpses before he dropped into the space between the wall and the bed. I did not hesitate, I placed the candle, its flame quivering wildly, back on the table that I had snatched it from and grabbed Edmund—whose fluttering, racing heartbeat, whose lightness as if full of hollow bones and whose fragility made me think of a wounded bird—and dragged him from the bed. His limp body was slick and damp with sweat, but I was able to keep him propped up as I pulled him towards the beacon of light that was the doorway. I looked down at him as we entered the rectangle of light pouring in from the kitchen and I was horrified by what I saw: his skin was gray and pallid and coated with an oily, glistening sheen and his countenance was a ruin. That very morning when I had gone in to see him, he had half of his hair remaining; it had been falling out steadily since he'd arrived, but I'd been warned that one of the side effects of his powders would be hair loss and I had not been alarmed. Now, though, his pate shone bare in the light and covered in angry red sores where the hair had been ripped free from the scalp, and I pictured that foul intruder covering my weak husband's mouth with one hand to stifle his screams while the other wrapped those spidery fingers lovingly over each lock before yanking it free. The vision broke a sob loose from somewhere deep inside me, but almost immediately that sob turned into an anguished scream as darkness snaked out from under the bed and wrapped itself around my Edmund's ankles. I frantically dragged Edmund toward the doorway, but to no avail: no matter how hard I pulled, Edmund was held in place by a terrible strength. A moment passed this way and then with a monumental pull, and, yes, this time I KNOW it was a pull and not him pulling away from me, he was torn from my arms and dragged under the bed. I dove to the floor and scrambled after him. Reaching under the bed with both hands, I grabbed hold of one thin wrist, and I pulled him toward me as hard as I could. Almost instantly, I felt what must have been a horde of hairy bodies writhing against my arms, like thousands of flies or spiders traversing my flesh. My skin crawled in revulsion, but I did my best to hang on to my husband's wrist. Once, when I was a child, I fell into a bramble, and my arms and legs became covered with dozens of prickles, which were agony to remove. What was happening to my hands in the darkness under the bed was a similar sensation but magnified tremendously. I tried to use the floor and the bottom of the bed to scrape off whatever it was that was assaulting me, but to no avail. Whatever was attacking me simply flowed away to another part of my flesh, and continued to inflict me with what seemed an endless barrage of stings. Inevitably, I found the growing agony unendurable, and I had no choice but to momentarily loosen my grasp. This was all the opening my opponent, whatever it was, needed, and my husband's wrist was torn from my grasp. I caught his fingers for a second, as they slipped through mine, but it was only for a second. I pushed further in to try and recover the grasp I had lost, but instead of my husband's hand my fingers brushed up against something large, with coarse fur that stabbed into my fingertips. My hands recoiled from under the bed, and I stared at them in horror, for they were now covered in tiny, bite-like wounds, many of which oozed blood. I scrambled back away from the bed and to the doorway and then into the hall as the light reflected back from dozens of tiny eyes. I crawled forward as quickly as I could and pulled the door shut and struggled to find my footing. I sat at the table for the rest of the night, an array of weaponry—kitchen knives, a hatchet, a mallet, and a fire poker—in easy reach of my seat should that monstrous intruder make another appearance. I know you, if you were real, would ask me why I did not run to the authorities with this incident and I would tell you, "Because I do not believe it myself." If I cannot believe what I just recounted as fact, then how would anyone? I would most certainly be confined to Bedlam within minutes of concluding my story. As for Edmund…well, I am not sure, but I feel like whatever is happening to him is absolutely a fate worse than death. Speaking of, I checked on Edmund not long before I started this passage and from my vantage point in the doorway I could see that he was resting comfortably again. I could also see a tall, dark shape holding very still in the corner, the still area in the room noticeable because it did not dance in time to the candlelight's rhythm as the rest of the shadows did. I did not react, simply told Edmund that I would be in shortly to give him his medications soon and to feed him some broth, the only thing he's been able to keep down the past week or so. (As an aside, the doctor who visited after Edmund first stopped eating said that he was not exhibiting any real signs of starvation despite his constant vomiting of normal food, oatmeal and the like, that I could spoon into his mouth.) I stepped back and closed the door and started this passage a few minutes later. I had to write it all down before I convinced myself it was a dream or a hallucination or that I have contracted whatever brain-fever ails Edmund. No, what I saw was a demon. An incubus or a succubus perhaps, I have heard that these beings haunt good men until they drive them to ruin and eventually death. I'll need help to deal with this.

The Sixteenth of April, Eighteen Hundred and Thirty-Nine

He arrived at the table as dark fell last night. I was not expecting him but there he was, cloaked in shadow and changed so much that I barely recognized the scarred, bald and malformed beast that sat there before me as my husband. You, my faithful friend, are wanting to hear that I met him with a doctor in tow, or the police, or a priest perhaps, that we were able to capture his shadowy tormentor and bring him back to health, but that would not be the truth and I promised you that—if only here—I would not lie. So, the truth: I fell into a fugue and sat despondent after the events of the last entry, for a day and a night, at the kitchen table. From time to time, I heard the scurry of rats in the walls around me, and more strange noises and whimpers of pain from the nursery, but I was not paying them too much mind; I was fixated on what I had seen in that room. What had the strange "person" in my Edmund's room been doing?

That question was on my mind as Edmund announced himself with a spidery flicker of fingers dancing lightly on the back of my hand, and I gasped and jumped with fright. I had not heard his approach or when he seated himself at the table across from me, in his usual spot. I pulled my hand away instinctively and he left his hand on the table as I turned to regard him. He was cloaked in shadow—and I mean this quite literally, a cloak of darkness deeper than the gloom of the room hung upon him— his eyes were hidden completely in deep pits of darkness and his skin had become like gauze or paper over his cheek bones. His head seemed misshapen as well, though I imagine that was his newly bald pate throwing me off. I looked at his hands and saw his fingers were all longer, the skin pale and bruised at the knuckles and joints. He lifted one hand languidly, and it seemed to me in that deep gloom as if the shadows covering him moved first and his fingers danced like a marionette in reaction instead of their own volition.

"Please listen to me very carefully, my dear," said Edmund, his voice a raspy whisper. "I am still somewhat in control, at least my mind is my own for now, even if my body is not. My darling, do not touch me for it will kill you if you do. I am in control now, but only barely, and this…disease…I think it did not realize I could still control myself; I allowed it to be overconfident and now I can finally tell you what happened…and what needs to happen."

I reached for him, heedless of his warning, and the shadow around his lips pulled back as I leaned in and peeled open his mouth in a parody of a comforting and kind smile, full of feral-looking, jagged and broken teeth. Without thought, my body recoiled from the sight, and I pulled my hand back as Edmund resumed speaking, his voice low and hurried.

"In Wisborg, I was attacked. I…went to a house there in the city in search of the last people known to have succumbed to the terrible wasting disease, that plague. The house was largely undisturbed when I arrived, the bodies had been removed but the house was largely the same as the day the bodies were discovered. I tried to learn more about what happened, but the locals and the authorities were not forthcoming, other than to tell me the couple was beloved in the community and that the husband traveled often for work. I was excited to learn about this man, this Hutter, and I hoped that he would be the source of the plague, or at the very least that he could provide the vital clue we were missing. That perhaps something he brought back in his travels…" He trailed off for a moment. "In the house, in the bedroom there, something happened, and it took hold of me. It's not a person. I know you must think it is. But it's not. It's the plague, it's a malady of corruption: of the soul, of the body, and of the mind, and I am terrified of what happens if I do not cure myself. There is only one way that I can think of to do this, so I need you to…" He grunted as he lifted his hand and I saw a piece of paper below his palm. "Take this note to Sardu…"

"Sandu, dear." I corrected him automatically; he was always calling Mr. Sandu by the wrong name and so my reminders of the correct pronunciation were just as constant and, for a moment, the air grew thick with a bittersweet nostalgia as I was reminded of the well-oiled routine and banter we'd once shared. I reached for the note, hesitating as I did so. The hand stayed where it was, hovering just above my hand, but the shadow that clung to him reached for me frantically as I snatched the note from under his hand. "When did you write this?" As soon as my hand moved back to my lap, from darkness back into the dying light cast into the room from the window, his hand relaxed—as did the writhing, shadowy parasite that I knew was killing him. I am not so much a woman of reason that I will discount the supernatural as some of my husband's peers and co-workers do, men of Reason who decry the existence of the Supernatural while trying to tell me that God (a supernatural being if ever there was such a thing, I would think) would not allow such claptrap to exist. I think they just say that so they can be justified in believing that there might be bogeymen in the world, creatures outside their limited capacity to understand and in doing so they cling to the idea of all-consuming light that defeats the darkness but—in my limited experience—it's what exists in the absence of light that can do the most damage, a way of thinking that has allowed me to approach this situation with the outwardly calm demeanor I try to present each day to Edmund as he lies there being tortured.

"It is weak during the day, but so am I. I am unable to move much when the sun is up, my body… It feels incredibly heavy and I find it hard to will myself—or want to will myself—to move but, more importantly, *it* sleeps then as well. The daylight creates an adverse reaction, you see, and I was content to rest when the torment paused for those few hours at a time. But today the whispers changed, and so I felt I had to move…had to do anything. Its hunger is growing, you see, and now it is whispering that it—no, *we*—need more sustenance. It cries to me even now that the rats will not do any longer, for there are no more rats, are there? Not under the bed, at least, and the rats were fine but now they are gone, and it wanted you, and that is why…I had to move." Edmund trailed off as something scurried along the right side of the room. I could see that it was a rat, a large rat, and it was running along the wall toward a hole near to the nursery door. Edmund never looked at it, but I know that he saw it nonetheless; for even as he looked at me, the shadowy presence lunged predatorily at the rat and fell atop it in a blur of darkness. Edmund sat there for a second as the darkness stretched away from him, frantically trying to tear the rat to pieces, and said, "Help me." In the moment before he followed the darkness— before he bolted from the table then in a herky-jerky motion, a marionette of flesh being pulled viciously at the behest of his shadowy puppeteer—and fell onto the terrified rodent with a savage glee, I saw him clearly and I saw a ruin of a man, filled with pain and wanting his suffering to end and then he was gone. He moved so quickly that I barely registered it, one moment he was in the chair imploring me and the next he'd scurried across the floor and was hunched over the rat, having scooped it up off the floor where the darkness had accosted it seconds before. I thought that he was going to tear it to pieces, or perhaps bite into it, but instead he seized it and stood up— he was taller now—and raised the rat with two hands above his head, holding it firmly upside down with its head just even with his mouth. For a moment I expected him to bite down on the rodent's head, when instead he twisted and squeezed with a violent wrenching motion, opening his mouth as he did so. The rodent's frenzied and frantic squeaks and squeals were cut off abruptly as the contents of its body poured from its mouth and eyes and into my husband's mouth. He brought the rat's head down to his mouth, wrapped his lips around it and sucked hard as if drinking from a bottle. His mouth made thick, syrupy slurping sounds as the rat's body deflated under Edmund's ministrations, euphoria radiating from him as he ate. Unheeding of the danger, I turned away and rushed from my seat to the window, where I vomited up the meager meal of broth and bread I'd eaten today. When I straightened up and fearfully cast a glance to where they'd been moments before, I found that Edmund and the shadowy presence had vanished and that the door to the nursery was once again closed.

The Seventeenth of April, Eighteen Hundred and Thirty-Nine

I delivered the note to Mr. Sandu last night after Edmund left, making my panicked way there just as the sun vanished and the darkness of the kitchen filled me with fear. After Edmund disappeared, I hurriedly packed a bag with some clothes and you, dear diary, took the note Edmund had given me, and then I fled across the street as the sun set and darkness unfurled into the street. After I knocked, I handed him the note and he looked at it and then, with a sharp look full of barely concealed fear, looked me over, scrutinizing me in a way that I was unaccustomed to and then—saying nothing—closed the door. Despairing, I turned away and started heading back to my home, and I am ashamed to write that I wondered if Edmund was going to kill me when I returned. The thought made my feet move a little slower and my head hung a little lower.

"Veere urrr uuu goen?" The jumble of words caused me to turn around and find Mr. Sandu standing there. His wispy gray hair flew about in the night breeze and the eyes in his heavily wrinkled countenance looked at me with sympathy and sorrow and understanding. Nail heads protruded from between pursed lips, which accounted for the jumbled speech, and as I glanced down, I saw that he held a sheaf of papers in one hand and a hammer in the other. He strode past me and down the lane towards my house.

"What are you going to do?" I asked, but he did not offer a response. He simply walked to the house and began methodically nailing pieces of paper to the front door in a maneuver I felt he must have borrowed from Martin Luther, though I do not know how the 99 Theses (or were there only 94 or 95? I can never remember) could help in this particular circumstance. He hammered the last nail into the door and then hung a cross on the door that he produced from one of his pockets. He went around to the windows next, closing the shutters that were open and hanging crosses and nailing pages to them as well, and he worked on Edmund's room last. A few minutes later he stood back and nodded.

"That should hold for a while at least," he said. "Come with me now, back to the house. We have not a minute to spare. There is only one way to solve this, I am afraid, and you will not like it. But Edmund knows what needs doing, that is why he sent you to me. We spoke of this very topic once and I will tell you now what I told him then. This disease is fatal, for the victim, certainly, but also for everyone around the victim though the victim will be responsible for those deaths. I can see you understand what I mean."

I nodded, frantically, eager to share my experience, "Edmund is different now, I thought…just now, in the kitchen…he wanted to…his face…the rat." I tried to articulate what had transpired but the words refused to come. Horror overwhelmed me and the world swam with too-bright light and too-dark shadows, all warring for my attention. Hands, firm and steady, caught me, and then strong arms were holding me up as the world shut down to a narrow tunnel which steadily closed until darkness overcame me. When I woke it was morning, or rather it is morning as I write this. I found myself in Mr. Sandu's spare room, a spartan affair if ever there was one, on a too hard mattress, and here I remain as I write down the events of yesterday. I cannot believe that so much has transpired in such a short time. Everything is wrong and it may never be right again but…I must confess that I feel much better now that I am getting the proper assistance. Edmund always spoke highly of Mr. Sandu, whom he referred to as a scholar and a theologian and a priest and a doctor. An enigma, he once confided in me, that he could not get a full accounting of Mr. Sandu (to which I gently reminded him it was Sandu…) and that made the man a total mystery. Edmund was never satisfied with a mystery, and I imagine he took the time to try to get to know our neighbor, for they seemed to get along well enough to share the occasional meal. I will write more later after I speak to Mr. Sandu.

The Eighteenth of April, Eighteen Hundred and Thirty-Nine

There is blood on my hands. It is dried under my fingernails, it has stained the lines of my knuckles and palms, and left freckles where there were none previously. There is blood on my face. I can feel the spattered drops drying there even now, even though I have long since washed my face, and I am not entirely sure that I can convince myself that I will ever be clean again. Not that it matters. Edmund is dead. Nothing matters anymore.

After I finished the last entry, I left the room and found Mr. Sandu sitting at the kitchen table. Two plates of food waited there as well as a valise case, much like the doctor's case that Edmund took from place to place each day when he was working. Mr. Sandu said nothing as I walked up to the table and sat down, he simply picked up his fork and started eating and I did the same. The food was delicious, and I felt terrible and guilty for enjoying it, but the eggs were seasoned in a way I was not used to, as were the potatoes he'd cut into wedges and fried with the fat from the bacon he'd cooked. Richer still was the thick dark drink which I do not know the name of as I never did ask him, but I assume that it came with him here from lands much farther away than our small English hamlet. As soon as I finished eating, he picked up our plates, put them in the sink, and then he walked purposefully back to the table and looked down at me.

"There is only one thing to be done. There is only one cure for what ails him," he said as he laid down the note that Edmund gave to me to deliver. It read: NOSFERATU. RELEASE ME. PLEASE. I know I gasped at this; even though I did not recognize the first word, deep down I had already come to the same conclusion. Mr. Sandu did not speak again; eyes brimming with loss and sorrow, he picked up the bag and left. I followed him, though I knew he was giving me a choice. In the end, I knew there was no choice at all.

We crossed the lane and went to my home; the sun was out, and it was a beautiful day. The papers nailed to the threshold fluttered in a light breeze and made the house look condemned and dangerous. I opened the door and Mr. Sandu pushed past me and I found myself wondering how he planned to do it exactly, how was he going to release my Edmund. I assumed that Edmund was asking for death, and that he and Mr. Sandu had discussed something along these lines in the past, but I did not know how to ask. It never occurred to me that I might need a friend one day to perform as great a service as Mr. Sandu was about to grant Edmund, and I found myself profoundly glad that he was here. I was not equipped to do any of what might be necessary to defeat whatever fell spirit had a hold of my husband, and I knew I definitely could not have done what Edmund had asked of Mr. Sandu. I could not kill Edmund; I could not release him as he asked. I would only have been able to guide him along as he wasted away, unable to hasten the process to conclude before its time. But with Mr. Sandu, I saw a way to end Edmund's suffering in the here and now.

"Wait, what must I do?" I asked as I gripped Mr. Sandu's arm to give him pause as he stood in the hall. He turned back to me and snapped open the case.

"We will find him and then we will provide him the only cure for this that I know, this…" He trailed off as he pulled an elaborately carved spike from the bag. It was tipped and capped in silver, and the shaft of the spike was stained a deep crimson, almost black, carved with shimmering letters that danced in the light. I didn't need to ask what it was for; it was evident that it would be the instrument of Edmund's release. I nodded, fighting back tears as I came to terms with what was about to happen, and opened the door for him. He strode through the dark house and set the spike and his bag down on the table and, in the meager light trickling in from behind the shutters and the doorway, I watched as he reached into the bag and withdrew a large hammer, a lamp, a candle match, a nail and a cross. While he did that, I crossed the kitchen to open the window there, but he stopped me with a raised hand. "We do not want any attention to come to what we are about to do," he said, and lit the lamp with the match.

Warm light filled the room and Mr. Sandu walked to the door of the sickroom, carrying the nail and the hammer. He gently tapped the nail into the door and then picked up the cross and hung it from the nail. He nodded at his handy work and then returned to the table once more to pick up the spike. At his indication, I picked up the lamp and followed him to the door of the sickroom, where he paused.

"Why are you stopping?" I whispered.

"To give you one last moment to reconsider. He will not survive this and there is no time to say goodbye," he replied.

"You said it was the only way, and his note…it begged you for…well—" I couldn't finish the thought. I could hardly think straight.

Mr. Sandu did not ask again. He opened the door and strode

into the darkness, leaving me to follow with the light. I hesitated, a pause that saved me as Mr. Sandu vanished into darkness. He became a shadow among shadows, a cruel puppet about to end an awful play as he raised the hammer above his head and positioned the spike above Edmund's heart. I heard the sound before Mr. Sandu, I think, that dry rubbing and rattling of fur and bone mingled with the clicking of hundreds of nails, and by the time he did hear the sound he was hearing it from the bottom of a horde of tearing, clawing, biting bodies that rushed from under the bed. He dropped the hammer and the spike on Edmund's chest as he fell back into a surge of tiny, furred things and they covered him completely as I rushed forward to aid him, thrusting the lantern before me. The light from the lantern revealed a writhing pile of creatures that appeared only barely rat-like—horrible, shriveled creatures that seemed to be bags of loose flesh covered with fur, with bones piercing the skin and dripping with darkness. I caught a glimpse of one that had a long tear in its side, and I could see that it was empty inside but for the skeleton, the undead thing twitched horribly as it joined the horde and scurried away from the light and back towards the safety the underside of the bed provided. As the horde retreated somewhat in the face of the light, I was able to see the ruin that once was Mr. Sandu. In the seconds that he'd been submerged, the rodents had chewed apart his face, leaving the flesh torn and ruined and streaming with blood. One eye was missing and the other had no eyelid over it and was wildly and spastically glancing about while seeing nothing. His nose was gone, and his mouth was stretched open, with the rotten, desiccated body of one of the creatures struggling to crawl down his mouth, and I thought to reach for its tail and pull it out when I looked further down and saw that Mr. Sandu's throat was distended and multiple tiny heads were protruding from his neck as the beasts sought egress from the confines of Mr. Sandu's body.

In the moments following the revelation of utter carnage I panicked and—with a scream that I did not recognize—leapt onto the bed to avoid the rats, even as the throng streamed back under the bed and away from the light. My swinging lantern revealed a nightmarish version of Edmund; his skull was completely bald and scabrous, and his jawline was more pronounced, as were his cheek bones. Sharp and jagged teeth rested atop his bottom lip, and I felt a moment of terror as I considered that he had wanted to use these horrible and jagged things to do to me what he'd done to that rat in the kitchen—what he'd done to the rats that I had just seen decimate Mr. Sandu. That fear turned to rage as I met Edmund's gaze. His eyes were still wells of darkness, but floating there in the middle of each pool was a cold and merciless iris that made me think of the pitiless stars on the coldest winter nights, and they were the eyes of a stranger. That was where my rage stemmed from, that this curse could take my husband away before I could tell him goodbye, and it was this rage that helped me to act. Without thought, I set down the lantern and snatched up the hammer and spike.

Of its own volition, the hammer seemed to raise itself and a ringing sounded out as it came down on the silver-encased end of the spike. Then a second ringing sounded out, then a third, a fourth, and then merciful silence as the hammer finally ceased its work. The rustling of the rats stopped as well. I reached out and caressed Edmund's broken and twisted face. I tried to wipe away all the blood that spewed forth from his mouth as the hammer fell but I only succeeded in spreading it around and staining my hands. Then I sobbed, with sorrow and with relief, as I saw that those two hateful orbs were no longer floating where my husband's kind eyes should have been. There was only darkness. I climbed off the bed, and I had to push aside the semi-decayed furry bodies that covered the floor. I shudder now as I think on it—those rats must have been puppets like my husband, vicious little marionettes tasked with protecting Edmund and whatever dark forces that possessed him. I looked again at Mr. Sandu as I stumbled from the room and saw that the rats that had been working so hard to escape the confines of his throat had mostly failed, with many of them still halfway out as their animating force left them.

And now—with the blood of my husband covering me—I am finally confident enough to write that I have taken care of almost everything else, all that's left is to throw you out the window before I close it again for good. Not to worry though, I will wrap you in the weather-proof satchel that Edmund used to travel with. I will wait here with Edmund and Mr. Sandu as the flames from the fire I started in the root cellar eat the house away. The floor is already getting hot, so I must hurry here. I coated all three of us in lamp oil, just in case. And—again, just in case—I mixed a generous amount of the Paris green with several glasses of the good brandy that Edmund kept for visitors and special occasions, and drank them down, one after another, until I felt a bit numb. I think our deaths would qualify as a special occasion. The Paris green is working, as it is getting increasingly hard to focus and my stomach is starting to ache fiercely. So, this is goodbye, thank you for being my confessor and my confidant. I hope that this account is found, and that it answers any lingering questions anyone might have about what happened here.

My God preserve and save our souls,

Mary Stuard

LAST OF THE SACRIFICIAL WOMEN

Deborah Sheldon

In the weeks before, Tilda Mueller senses his approach in the shifting tide of her blood. It is a strange pulling sensation, the iron of her haemoglobin straining towards a magnet that keeps dragging her gaze to the sea, to the sea. Tilda lives alone in a rented cottage on the promontory. In the weeks before, she often sits outside at night and stares across the restless waves, which moonlight and phosphorescence limn in shades of silvery green. She feels him staring back at her across the nautical miles. He is on a boat, his cargo of many coffins filled with Romanian dirt to sustain him. In the weeks before, he whispers through her haemoglobin, *I'm coming to you*. Tilda can only put a hand to her throat. *I know.*

She has always known. The curse was first told her by Granny and Mother in childhood. Then reinforced throughout puberty and early womanhood—apparently the most dangerous times—yet he hadn't appeared. For 59-year-old Tilda, the taut, breathless suspense of expecting him every single day of her life has been harrowing, exhausting, crushing. Her parents emigrated to Australia to escape him or, at least, to slow him down. Perhaps the vast distance from Europe was the reason behind his tardiness. On occasion, Tilda has also thought that he hasn't shown because he finds her distasteful.

Now that he is coming, she has no one for support. Both Granny and Mother are long dead. But the curse, told to her so many times, is branded inside her heart. It is a curse that has passed through seven generations of women descended from

Ellen Hutter of Wisborg, Germany, the one who met him first. Ever after, the eldest-born daughter was fated to play a similar game of cat-and-mouse with him. Taught by maternal elders from the nursery how to lure his bite near dawn, find the inner strength to willingly let his sucking mouth drain her almost dry so that the sun's rays can turn him into mist, and stay his plague-riddled hand if only for a while.

And in return, endure a half-shadow life of malaise, fatigue and melancholy. The sacrificial women survive, yes, but never recover. Tilda still nurses bitter memories of Mother's insomnia, sleepwalking and bad dreams, the countless hours of her lounging at the bay window only to gaze blankly at nothing, eyes empty, skin sallow and jaundiced, her vitality snuffed out by his bite.

So, after years of desperate terror spent waiting, waiting, it is finally Tilda's turn. Lucky number seven. Instead of making plans for wile and treachery, however, she begins keeping a hammer and wooden stake close to her person, always close, because she decided long ago that she won't blindly do what all her maternal ancestors have done.

This curse will stop with Tilda Mueller.

She chose to never bear children. And to that end, never married. Never even dated; what would have been the point? She stayed aloof, withdrawn, the virginal spinster. This lonely life, foisted upon her, seems especially cruel because the curse doesn't make sense. That fateful meeting between him and Ellen Hutter in 1838 had been random, surely? Yet the curse has endured, unbroken, via the family's maternal line. Via the mitochondrial DNA. Long ago in medical school, Tilda learned that DNA exists outside the cell's nucleus; just 37 protein-coding genes from the human body's vast collection of 25,000, a meagre clutch gifted to the child by the biological mother. Why? Science has no answer. Neither does Tilda. But those outlier maternal genes must mean something to him, or else he wouldn't keep coming back.

The weeks pass and he reaches land.

She knows this because her tortured haemoglobin finally quivers in place, aligned, trillions of compass needles pointed at Tilda's one and only north. She also knows this because of the hired landscape gardeners at her work.

Her work is at a building set high on a cliff as if it were a light-house. This building is a hospital. Originally it was a convent dating from 1851 where female postulants and novices lived. After religion was abandoned, it became a charitable institution; next, a university campus; now, a palliative care hospital where the terminally ill come to take their last breaths amongst paid strangers. Inexplicably for a 19th-century Australian building, it features medieval architecture with stone walls, flying buttresses, ribbed vaults and columns, pointed archways, tall and vast windows. The building's layout has a horseshoe shape with gabled wings so that every coastal-facing window might overlook the sea. It is a sober, dispassionate, imposing edifice.

This evening, motoring from her nearby cottage along the hospital's steep and winding driveway, Tilda is struck as always by the skeletal fingers of the building's various pinnacles and spires against the sky at dusk. Then she sees the hired landscape gardeners, still fussing at a soil bed, and coldness grips her branded heart in a fist.

The three men pause as she pulls her hatchback into a parking space and kills the engine. The engine ticks as it cools. She touches her voluminous handbag, squeezes it, feeling the reassuring shapes of the hammer, the stake.

She watches the men as they watch her. Shouldering her handbag, she gets out of the car, locks it, approaches the men on her way to one of the hospital's rear doors, her crisply starched uniform crinkling and whispering with each step. The men are hunched, dirty, their eyes shining brightly out of gaunt faces. She tries to feel brave. They watch her still. She lifts her chin as if to ignore them. Her foot on the first stair, she changes her mind and turns.

"Gosh, you're working late," she says. "Don't tradies usually knock off at three-thirty?"

"We're running behind," one of them says. "The boss wants us to make up time."

Deferential, they can't meet her gaze with their hangdog eyes. They cringe as if she might draw up imperiously to her full height and strike them. But she is short for a woman, barely five foot one, and thin. Bony, in fact. Short, bony, pale, anaemic with thin mousy hair, a nobody without beauty, charisma or gravitas, one of the perpetually overlooked and invisible. All the women in her maternal line were brunette, gorgeous, willowy and tall, yet Tilda inherited her father's characteristics. Perhaps his contrary stubbornness too.

The rapt attention of the gardeners is glaring, out of place. Her haemoglobin quivers.

Tilda looks at the garden bed. It is long and narrow. The turned earth, dark and ripe, reeks of loam and rotted compost. The men recoil at her scrutiny. One of them gasps, leaning back on his spade. Their fear gives her strength.

She points. "What is in here?" she commands. "What have you planted?"

The tallest one, panting a little, murmurs, "Herbs, milady."

"Such as?"

They regard each other. The tallest one stutters, "Rosemary. Thyme. Parsley. Sage."

"No garlic?"

Speechless, the men gape. With a sly smile, Tilda clomps her sensible shoes up the stairs and enters the rear door.

The door closes behind her. The familiar smells of stone, old wood, antiseptic and death fill her nostrils. She pauses, alert and afraid, waiting to feel his presence. There is no distinctive sign except the beating of her heart and the singing of her blood.

Tilda has worked here as a palliative care nurse for some 28 years, believing that it would be an unobtrusive location for his plague to take place. Since each patient is expected to die, no autopsy would be required, nor requested. She doesn't enjoy medical work. An avid and talented painter in her youth, Tilda yearned for a career in the arts, but his long shadow cast a pall over that part of her life just as it ruined her chances at love and children.

The interior of the hospital is dim despite the lamps, fetid despite the open windows, full of pained moans and sobbing whispers of the dying despite the stern and stoic uprightness of the architecture. Tilda puts her handbag, laden with hammer and stake, beneath the desk of the nurses' station. It is almost time for night shift to start. Tilda has always opted for night shift because she has always wanted to be ready for him. Since graduating as a nurse, she has rarely spent time in sunshine. Her skin is so pale that the blue veins show in her face and throat.

"Hey, Tilda," Franny says, walking out of a room holding a roll of dirty sheets. "How was your weekend?"

Tilda spent the weekend alone, the nights awake, fretting. "Good, thanks. Yours?"

Franny rolls her eyes. "I took Matt to a day spa and paid for our mud bath. Guess what?"

Tilda grins patiently. "He hated it?"

"Bingo! Ugh, he's such a heathen." Franny laughs and heads towards the laundry.

Now Tilda is alone and her smile drops. She stares down the long hallway. At its far end through a stone arch, the hallway intersects with a corridor to another wing. She expects to see him scuttle past the stone arch, long-limbed and insect-like, tall in his black frock coat, a cockroach on hind legs. She watches, waits, watches, waits…

Yet he doesn't appear.

Have the hired landscape gardeners left? No, she won't look out the windows to check. She mustn't give any sign that *she knows*. Instead, she should attend to her rounds.

In this wing, a half-dozen wards are on either side. Faint mutterings sound through the arched doorways. In each four- or six-bed room lie those who are nearest to death, which is why they are nearest to the nurses' station. None of these patients will live another week. A few have had their rally, which doctors call "terminal lucidity", where full cognitive function miraculously returns and the dying appear eerily like their old selves before their sickness and decline. Day-shift nurses must explain to relieved and joyful relatives that this rally is not a sign of recovery, but of impending death. Most patients have already seen deceased family members. Last Thursday, an elderly man's childhood dog talked to him with proper words like a person, and that night, comforted, the man passed over. Most patients ask about people in their rooms that the nurses can't see. Tilda is used to these hallucinations, these spiritual insights, these truths, these whatever-they-are phenomena—

A patient's buzzer sounds.

It pains Tilda to leave her handbag unattended, as if the hammer and stake are her babies. Determinedly, she walks the corridor to the blinking light over the arched doorway and enters the room. There are just two people in here, a man and a woman. It's the woman, Nelly, who has pressed the buzzer. Tilda cancels it to stop the buzzer's light and sound.

"How can I help you?" Tilda says.

Nelly turns her grey, flabby face. "There was some creepy bloke in here."

A prickling of prescience crawls through Tilda's blood. She looks about the room. The other patient is facing the window, still and quiet beneath his blankets, unmoving, the oxygen tube hissing in his nostrils like a snake.

"What kind of creepy bloke?" Tilda says.

Nelly fusses with her sheet. "Very tall. White. Bald with big ears. He wore a black coat and seemed to be whispering at George over there. You know, like cheek to cheek."

Tilda steels herself. "Can you still see him?"

Nelly roams her gaze. Tilda's heart leaps and flops in terrible expectation.

At last, Nelly says, "No. He must have left the room. But I didn't see him go." With anxiety in her eyes, the woman clutches at Tilda's hand. "He moves as quick as a wink."

"Okay—"

"Don't let him get me! Please don't let him."

Not knowing what to say, Tilda replies, "Of course I won't."

Nelly drops her voice to a thready whisper. "I think he's the devil."

She gently breaks Nelly's grip. Tilda heads over to the other patient, George, lying still and quiet, and discovers that he's dead. Two small marks are on his throat, side by side, inflamed and slightly raised, as inconsequential as mosquito bites. Doctors will sign off his death certificate without question because the man was suffering from advanced and incurable pancreatic cancer.

Tilda returns to the station, calls the doctor, starts the paperwork.

As her pen scritches across paper, her haemoglobin jitters and jumps. She keeps looking up from the document. The long hallway is saturated in patches of shadow. The lamps are many, but the stone and high ceilings seem to suck away the luminescence. She keeps expecting to see the intensity of his eyes, the whiteness of his face, his long-taloned hands, but he is not there. Where is he? He's somewhere about this old building, floating through its rooms, spreading his plague of death, watching her through the walls.

Where is he?

In the following hours, other patients die, exsanguinated. He is hungry, insatiable.

When Nelly is found dead with twin mosquito bites on her neck, Tilda feels a painful sense of sadness and horror, a heavy guilt. It's all Tilda's fault, isn't it? The only reason why he is here? Nelly may have lived longer if not for Tilda leading him to this hospital.

Did Ellen Hutter feel the same responsibility for Wisborg's procession of coffins?

Franny theatrically wipes a hand over her forehead. "Phew, this must be a record!"

Then she disappears into the bowels of the building, following the distant buzzers of patients in distress. Tilda is left with more paperwork. The shadows along the hallway seem to darken and clench with muscular tension.

A buzzer goes off nearby. Tilda must attend. She walks the echoing hallway.

Trembling, the dying man regards her with terror, with tears in his bloodshot eyes. "There's a monster running around in here. Call the police! He's got teeth like a rat."

Tilda, without a doctor's permission, increases the dying man's morphine to put him to sleep. It's all she can do. Petrified, she thinks, *Help me, Mother. Help me, Granny.* There is no answer from either of them.

Instead, her haemoglobin sings, *I'm coming to you.* Tilda puts a hand to her throat. *I know.*

Later, after midnight when all patients are drugged into a fugue state of deep and dreamless sleep, Tilda goes outside. The hired landscape gardeners and their truck are gone. Overhead, the moon looms. The hospital grounds look grey and drained. From the edge of the cliff, the tossing, griping, moaning ocean pounds ceaselessly against the promontory's rocky face as if demanding to be let in. The air smells briny. Salt crystals settle on Tilda's cheeks from the onshore breeze. Nervous, she edges towards the new garden bed, the bed that is supposed to hold a range of herbs except for garlic. She stops.

The bed is exploded open, dirt everywhere, as if a grenade has gone off inside it. The ground appears to be moving, crawling, wriggling. Holding her breath, Tilda approaches.

Rats.

Three or four dozen, maybe more, clambering among and around and over each other as if frantic. Tilda steps back into a shadowed window recess, claps her hands over her mouth.

The vermin are grey, black, brown, with long pink tails and pink feet, rounded ears. They scuffle frantically at the dirt, clawing, whining and squeaking. All at once, as if responding to the same invisible trigger, they notice Tilda and freeze. Gaze at her with shiny, black button eyes. Sniff with twitching, whiskered snouts.

Strangely, they appear to be scared.

She is reminded of the landscape gardeners, who also seemed to recognise and fear her.

Now that the boiling mass of rats is still, she can better see inside the exploded garden bed. It contains a giant wooden coffin. His powerful flinging open of its lid is what erupted the dirt in all directions, the Romanian dirt he'd carried with him on the ship's voyage. The rats must somehow sleep in that coffin with him. But how? How can they fit inside?

As one, the rats begin to advance.

Quailing, Tilda retreats towards the hospital, stumbles up the stairs. The door closes behind her. Another buzzer goes off. More death. She can hardly bear it. More and more death. Oh God, is he planning to suckle the entirety of the hospital's patients, all in one night?

Tilda remembers tales about the 1838 plague of Wisborg, how the procession of coffins kept marching on and on through the town's central street, portending that the whole population would soon be wiped out. Until Ellen Hutter's sacrifice.

What should Tilda do? It seems that every patient in the hospital has seen him, yet he's hiding from Tilda. How does she force a confrontation if he won't appear of his own accord? Since deciding to vary from the curse's script, she's lost and confused, bewildered, making it up as she goes along. She should have made a backup plan using wile and treachery to trick him into drinking her blood at sunrise. How crazy that she didn't do this! Why did she believe herself to be smarter than all the cursed women who came before her? Smarter than him? But it's too late to change course.

Too late…

Clearly, Tilda Mueller is not up to the task. She is weak. Her maternal ancestors were made of sterner stuff. She will fail and he will prevail.

The last of her courage flees.

She locks herself into a toilet cubicle and weeps bitter tears, even as her haemoglobin shivers and jumps like magnetised iron filings. He is close. So very close. She has existed solely to face this moment, yet now she can't face it. Outside the hospital is the cliff. She contemplates running and launching herself out into space, to dash herself on the rocks below and end this curse through an unexpected route that just might work…

Or would it? Again, she has no way of knowing.

Ellen Hutter had a sister. If Tilda Mueller removes herself from his preferred gene pool, might he swap his attention to the matriarchal line of Tilda's distant great-aunt? To women who would have no idea of the demonic hell that would be unleashed upon them?

Tilda wipes her eyes. Starts to unlock the toilet door. Stops. Her blood pounds and pulses. Is he here inside this bathroom? Is she cornered? The hammer and stake are in her handbag at the nurses' station. Dawn is hours away. Regardless, this bathroom doesn't have any windows to let in sunlight. Right here, right now, if she tries to conquer him, Tilda Mueller will lose. He will bite her and suck her blood until she dies of exsanguination. And then, unchecked, would his deadly plague spread beyond this hospital? Across Australia? Across the planet? Would humankind suffer because of Tilda Mueller's selfish desire to end the curse and be free? She doesn't have any answers.

Help me, Mother. Help me, Granny.

Sniffling, Tilda holds her breath. Leans her cheek against the toilet door. Listens to her haemoglobin. Breathes out. Relaxes. Closes her eyes. Allows her consciousness to float and billow like a sail in a bracing sea breeze.

And at last, she senses him.

In her mind's eye, she views him at the neck of a patient, his teeth sunk into the carotid, the Adam's apple in his stringy throat bouncing up and down, up and down as he swallows the life-giving nectar. For the moment, he's distracted. Hasn't noticed her.

Tilda flings open the door, flees from the toilets. The high walls lean over as if the ceilings might fall. The sounds of her rapid, running footsteps echo against the harsh stone of the corridors, bounce back, concuss her eardrums. The echoes prick his ears, too. He has stopped drinking, has lifted his head and cocked it, listening, like a feral animal. Like a sniffing rat.

Short-winded, Tilda reaches the nurses' station. Throws herself into a chair, reaches under the desk. Grips the security of her handbag and lets out an involuntary sob of relief at the shapes within. *The hammer. The stake.* She's been waiting all her life. Throughout the long, lonely, empty, unlived years.

A buzzer sounds. Tilda ignores it. Where is Franny? Perhaps he is keeping Franny away.

Tilda walks towards one of the giant, arched windows and gazes outside. The grounds are silvered with moonlight. The night seems quiet and still. Even the sea is hushed. Across the grounds in the neighbouring wing, she glances at a window and sees him with her own eyes for the first time.

After decades of waiting and imagining, he is a jolting, alarming, shocking sight.

A bright white and triangular head, bald. Wide and piercing eyes, unblinking. The pallor of freakishly long fingers and nails standing out against his black frock coat. Despite the distance, his penetrating gaze is intimate and rubs against her face as if made of sweeping lashes, murmuring lips, searching and probing tongue, nibbling teeth.

I'm coming to you. Tilda puts a hand to her throat. *I know*.

The blood in her veins feels animated, ready to leave her body, the haemoglobin lunging at him with abandon. Her heart pounds, faint with inexplicable ferocity.

She turns from the window, ready to run at him.

Yet Franny appears, scared, with tears on her cheeks and a trembling chin.

Tilda feels a duty of care. Franny has been her colleague for 11 years. That counts for something, doesn't it? Even if Franny hasn't expressed the slightest interest in Tilda's life; has done nothing but talk about herself, herself, herself, and ignored Tilda's timid attempts at conversation with vainglorious, silly and conceited counterpoints. Franny the narcissist. Franny the self-absorbed egotist. Momentarily, Tilda wants him to attack Franny because Franny is nothing but a hoggish bitch.

Tilda thinks in a moment of doubt: *Am I nothing but a hoggish bitch?*

Maybe. Probably. Well, according to Christianity, everyone is a sinner.

She glances back through the giant, arched window, across the grounds to the doppelganger window that framed his blackened, hellish image, and now it's empty. Tilda feels eviscerated.

"I think there's an intruder," Franny says. "A murderer."

"Huh?" Tilda says, collecting herself, gathering her thoughts. "Wait, calm down."

"This shit going on is *wild*." Franny laughs, grimaces, whimpers. "Are you keeping track of how many patients have carked it tonight?"

"Stay here. I'll go check the building."

Franny's eyes widen. "Are you nuts? Let's just call the cops."

"Have you actually seen an intruder?"

"No, but our patients—"

"Are hallucinating," Tilda interrupts. "They're end-of-life patients. Come on, Franny. Sometimes coincidences happen. We've got a higher number of deaths tonight than on other nights. So what? Sometimes the stars align."

Franny considers. "They're seeing a man in black."

"Visions are normal."

"But the same man in black?"

"They're hearing each other's stories," Tilda says, rubbing the other's upper arm in what she hopes is a comforting manner, "and suffering from social contagion. That's all. We're the nurses. The trained staff. We ought to keep our heads."

Tearfully, Franny giggles. "Yeah, while others are losing theirs."

The truth in that rejoinder makes them share a sober, frightened moment. Then Tilda taps Franny on the shoulder in a jaunty way and smiles.

"You stay here," Tilda says. "I'll check the building, okay?"

Franny considers. "Okay."

Coward. *I still hope he bites you*, Tilda thinks viciously, and turns to go down the hallway.

"What are you taking your bag for?" Franny says.

"It's got my phone." Tilda hesitates. "And my can of mace."

Franny gives her a thumbs up. "If you're not back in ten minutes, I'm calling the cops."

Tilda mulls this over, then nods. "Fair enough."

The interior of this medieval building is drenched in pools of deep shadow. He could be hiding anywhere, ready to pounce. Tilda walks in a direction without thinking; to the furthest wing from the nurses' station, as it happens. She sighs in and out, spurred like a sail by the breeze, her mind's eye feeling for him, following the shimmer of her haemoglobin.

A turn through an archway into another long, empty corridor.

Tilda utters a little shriek.

There he is. Standing at the corridor's end, blanch-faced, charcoal-eyed. Tall, narrow and spindly, shoulders hunched, clothes dark as a raven. Frozen as if lifeless, yet real. Flesh and blood. Tilda's cursed and branded heart feels squeezed into a cramped little ball, which takes her breath momentarily.

Now or never.

She chooses *now* and walks towards him, shivering.

He watches her, unblinking. His front teeth are long and yellowed, hanging over his thin and white lower lip. The irises of his eyes are too black to distinguish the pupils, if he has any. Tilda advances within a few feet of him. Stops. Waits. She is terrified, shaking, yet ready to take an empty-handed leap for better or worse.

He smiles, lifting the right side of his pinched mouth, and points to her bag by slowly extending one taloned finger. "Mal sehen." *Let's have a look.* His voice is deep, creaky, old, dusty, disused.

He speaks German instead of Romanian. Tilda isn't surprised. That's how he has communicated with all of Tilda's ancestors since 1838, when first arranging to buy a property in Wisborg from real estate agent Thomas Hutter.

Tilda says, "Es ist eine überraschung." *It is a surprise.*

"Für dich oder für mich?" *For you or for me?*

It's about three o'clock in the morning, sunrise many hours away. Tilda should have arranged this fated meeting closer to dawn in case Plan A failed. Too late now. Too late.

Hands trembling, Tilda unzips her handbag. She expects him to spring and bite her neck. He doesn't. At least, not yet. Patiently, he waits while she rummages inside her bag. Upon his bloodless lips is a faint, eager smile, like a child anticipating a gift. She wonders if he has read the intention inside her heart.

Tilda grips the hammer and stake. Puts her handbag down and shows him the tools. He regards them solemnly. Time passes without words. Tilda bends over, places the hammer and stake at his feet, and stands up again. She feels awkward. Short, bony, pale, anaemic with thin mousy hair, a nobody without beauty, charisma or gravitas, one of the perpetually overlooked and invisible. At 59 years of age, her gift might not be enough.

He says, "Was ist das?" *What is that?*

She blushes. "Mein Treueschwur." *My pledge of allegiance.*

He regards the hammer and stake, harmless on the bluestone floor. He lifts his eyes to glare at her. His penetrating gaze fingers and probes through the chambers of her branded heart and sees her lonely, fruitless, spurned existence. And in return, he allows her to peer inside the depths of his black eyes to reveal a similar emptiness, but one that has stretched across many centuries. As Tilda has always suspected, they are two lost and unloved souls.

His bushy eyebrows lower. The ferocity of his gaze softens. He opens his arms to her. She approaches. He reeks of sepulchres and rot, vermin and disease, yet to Tilda it feels strangely like a homecoming, a throwing off of her life's constraints and countless disappointments. She presses against his body. It is like pressing against the fragile ribs of a chicken carcass. Tears flow. Tilda will no longer be alone. Will never be alone again. Will always have the love of someone, of *this one*, to lean into and against, for as long as eternity might last.

The restless sea pounds and smashes against the cliff face, yet above the tumult, she fancies she can hear the frenetic squeaking of rats. In her mind's eye, the wooden coffin invites her to take a long-deserved and comfortable rest. She accepts.

He puts his lips to her throat. The sweet penetration of his teeth gives Tilda a wave of heady pleasure. He drinks, and the sucking makes her weak. She feels it between her thighs and cries out. So, this is why Mother, afterwards, could only sigh at windows, staring at nothing; it was sorrow for that single taste of ecstasy that would never be felt again.

He offers Tilda his own throat.

His skin feels cold and dense like clay, but it opens a moist slit to accept Tilda's small, blunt, human teeth. The molasses of his bloodstream floods over her tongue. Now they will be wedded forever. His fierce grip on her heart tightens. Tilda licks her stained lips.

"Ich liebe dich," she whispers to her lord and master. *I love you.*

And with that heartfelt proclamation, the curse is done.

NOSFERATU

Jim Shepard

EXTERIORS

Six weeks of exteriors: the Carpathians, the Baltic towns of Wismar, Rostock and Lübeck, as well as ocean vistas of Heligoland and the Frisian Islands in the North Sea. All shooting, exterior and interior, must be finished by November 1921. We begin here, in Czechoslovakia. Half the company has yet to arrive; those who have are filled with questions. Nothing of course has gone as planned. To add to the confusion there are my daily visits to foreign doctors, to say nothing of the visits of nurses to me. What time I have is often expended in elegiac dreams about H—. But already the film takes me from the soft anguish of idleness and drives me from any room where I cannot work.

7/12/21. This is intended to be for the patient readers of *Der Querschnitt*, the journal of a filmmaker's progress: an ongoing chronicle, from rough notes composed day to day, of the trials and tribulations of this new project. I hereby pledge to do my utmost to prevent this diary from becoming a "melancholy school of posturing and dreary self-deception." Frankness and clarity will be the goals. If I will not, cannot be truthful with myself here, where can I be?

With this film, I will not aim at poetry. I will try to build a table. It will be for you to eat at it, criticize it, chop it up for firewood.

It seems appropriate in this confessional form to chronicle the beginnings of my slide from the status of a young man of promise into the regrettable position of filmmaker. Late in 1913, with my career in the theatre—specifically, with Max Reinhardt's prestigious troupe—all but assured, I drifted into a moving-picture show to see the American D.W. Griffith's *Judith of Bethulia*. I was mesmerized by the giant figure of the wine-guzzling Holofernes, who towered over everyone. Where had they found him? In some circus, I supposed. I mentioned this to Reinhardt, who laughed and told me that the same actor had visited Germany a year earlier, and was shorter than he was. He had been made to *seem* huge by Griffith's camera. Reinhardt had had no idea how. He suggested I write to Billy Bitzer, Griffith's cameraman. I was possessed by the trick, and would have, had the war not intervened. I was twenty-five and as curious as a field dog about everything having to do with filmmaking.

In the 1914 war I served in the air corps, and came to understand aviation as a new way of seeing. (The air arm itself grew out of the reconnaissance service.) Airborne vision now escaped that Euclidian tyranny so acutely felt by the ground troops in the trenches; in this new, astounding topological field, air pilots already had their own special effects, with their own names: loops, figure-eights, falling leaf rolls. My understanding was transformed by the way the airborne observer's hand seemed to detach itself from the body and stretch out in freedom… The aerial body, looking down from a great height… Good training for the fledgling film director.

After the war I bought a battered old view camera and tripod in a Charlottenburg junk shop and began shooting pictures of everything within range. I even attempted to develop and print the footage myself in a converted coat closet. The experiment was not a success.

Eventually I progressed in the only way possible for me, which was to make every mistake until there were no mistakes left to make, and the right way of proceeding was the only way remaining. Like many of the early filmmakers, I thought myself an urbane bohemian and outsider, eager to experiment, one of the sensitive, nervous spirits of the age, a tinkerer and a visionary with what I hoped was a keen business sense.

Even then, the film world, to my dismay, did not fall prostrate at my feet. The truth was that I would have to become a bit less gangly and awkward, at least enough to overcome the distressing habit of falling over my feet, before I could impress that world with the idea that I was a gifted artist drawing on vast resources of experience and sophistication.

Dolny Kubin, Slovakia. Grau wants the names of Stoker's characters changed, but echoed. Harker has thus become Hutter. On the long trip here I wrote the first title from his diary, which will introduce the story: *Nosferatu. Doesn't the name sound like the midnight call of a death bird? Beware of uttering it, or the pictures of life will turn to pale shadows, nightmares will rise up from the heart and nourish themselves on your blood.* [Fade in a long shot of the town.] *For a long time I have been meditating on the rise and fall of the Great Death in my father's town of Wisborg. Here is the story of it: In Wisborg there lived a man named Hutter with his young wife Ellen.*

Wangenheim was a compromise choice as Hutter. I wanted Veidt, whom Grau proclaimed too old, too sinister-looking, and, he might have added, too intimately associated with me. Neither of us is happy with Wangenheim, but he was available. At the first production meeting, he looks over the room assignments and complains that the rooms have been apportioned hierarchically. The top floor, the one with the view, has been divided between art director Albin Grau, cameraman Fritz Arno Wagner, scenarist Henrik Galeen, and myself. Everyone looks to me to quash this kind of petty revolt. Wangenheim offers his chin and makes a face. He's a left-winger and an aristocrat and probably feels isolated in this crew.

There *is* a hierarchy, I inform him. I congratulate him for having noticed. The arrangement is so our collaboration can continue at any and all hours. Grau, handing out room keys, suggests he spend less time worrying about accommodations and more worrying about his performance. Wangenheim then wants to know why his room is below Spiess', and why in fact Spiess has been brought along. One of those film company spats, unpleasantness tinged with subtextual insinuation. Why was there scrimping and saving on one end and splurging on the other? Spiess, I remind everyone, has lived in the East and could prove invaluable. The usual grumbling before the rebel angels retreat, quiescent for now and more trouble later.

The company, like a class of children, never understands: it's not a matter of severity or love, but devotion to the work at hand. Behind my back, they poke fun at my unwillingness to show emotion even in disagreements. It is simple, simple, simple: by remaining master of myself, I remain master of the company. This is all I need to remember. Without that first mastery, all other authority is quickly at an end.

Persistent thoughts of H—. Lasker-Schüler claims to have no more information. Have I tried everyone else? Are there memory tricks that would release new answers?

(—Record everything; revise later with *Q* in mind.)

The week before we left, *Der Film* finally announced the founding of the Prana Film company, with a remaining capital of 20,000 Marks, the rest already having been spent. Two managers were named: Enrico Dieckmann, a merchant in Berlin-Lichterfelde, and Albin Grau, an artist/painter in Berlin. The name of the company was explained (the reference was to the Buddhist concept *prana*, "vital breath") and attributed to Grau, who, we were informed, "reflects a great deal on the occult aspects of life." Accompanying the announcement was a list of nine films (!) scheduled for production next year, each illustrated with a drawing of Grau's. At the very bottom in small print we learned that directing Prana's first production, *Nosferatu, A Symphony of Horrors*, would be one F. W. Murnau. "Artistic direction"—apparently a separate category— would be handled by Albin Grau. "Together," the announcement concluded with a wan and affecting flourish, "they propose to construct the film on new principles".

We're filming in Dolny Kubin for the scenes involving the inn in the Carpathians. A dismal, crooked little town perched like a tooth on a hill. Father would say, "What kind of work would take you to a place like this?" I imagine him, when people ask, answering only: "He's in Slovakia." H— would be pleased to hear me imagining Father's thoughts, after all this estrangement.

The castle, Oravsky Zamok, is not far from town. Wagner

discovered it months ago, and sent a postcard. It was built on the river Orava in the 13th century, high on a curiously hollowed-out rock. The most elevated part is a watchtower that overhangs the Orava more than one hundred meters. The watchtower, shot against the light, will form the final image of the shadow of the vampire passing from the earth.

Tomorrow we begin shooting on the dilapidated terrace, with Wangenheim, who so far has had only useless ideas as to his portrayal of Hutter.

Still awake. This preparation, most of my life since December: how much does it avail me now?

We start with Hutter discovering the marks on his neck, writing Ellen. It will be in bright sunlight, against a ruined stone wall. We must make certain the vines have been cleared from the battlement. We must counter excess shadow with lamps. We must be ready should the weather not cooperate. If the terrace scene comes off we'll go on to Hutter's search for the coffin. After the arch I'll pass in and do the stairway, to the right of where he sees the bolted door leading down…

Sleepless, I wander the corridors. Napoleon said he made his battle plans from the fighting spirit of his sleeping soldiers.

Before the shooting, one must put oneself into a state of intense ignorance and curiosity, and yet see things *in advance*. My working method is to sketch out everything and then be completely open to impulse and improvisation. Recognize the true by its efficiency and power. The film's beauty will not be in the images (postcardism), but in the ineffable that those images emanate. To use prodigious, heaven-sent machines merely for belaboring something fraudulent—how would that appear, in fifty years' time? And yet it's from those mechanisms that emotion will be borne (born?) Think of the great pianists. (Bach, answering an admiring pupil: "It's only a matter of striking the right notes at exactly the right moment.") We evoke the pre-industrial world of superstition by creating an illusion that allows the viewer to forget the film's technical base.

In the darkness and stillness there are murmurs and flickering light under Grau's door. I knock softly, and enter.

Grau and Galeen are sitting cross-legged around a guttering candle. When they lean to make a point, shadows bend around the recesses of the room. Still uninvited, I sit. They share a bottle of Hungarian wine. We can hear mice gnawing at the walls' interior. Grau repeats his story of the old peasant with whom he was billeted in the army. The peasant was convinced that his father, who died without receiving the sacraments, haunted the village in the form of a vampire. He showed Grau an official document about a man named Morowitch exhumed in Progatza in 1884. The body showed no signs of decomposition, and the teeth were strangely long and sharp, and protruded from the mouth. The man was proclaimed undead, known in Serbia as *the Nosferatu*. Grau is an ardent spiritualist. His next project, he's informed us, will be something called *Höllenträume: Dreams of Hell*.

Galeen, too, has a vampire story, from a cousin who served in Austria-Hungary. Galeen is slightly off-putting, watchful and disquieting. He has a bulbous face, with lank brown hair and beautiful skin and an odd and pointless smile. He is only twenty-nine, four years younger than Grau and myself, and was born in Berlin. He reacted well to my revision of his treatment. He's a Rosicrucian; perhaps even one of the adepts. I learned that from others.

He tells us the following, in his smooth voice: After it had been reported in a nearby village that a vampire had killed three men by sucking their blood, Galeen's cousin was, by high decree of the local Honorable Supreme Command, sent there to investigate, along with two subordinate medical officers. This is the story they were told: only days after the funeral of a girl by the name of Stana, eighteen years old, who had died in childbirth two weeks previous, and who had announced in a fever that she had painted herself with the blood of a vampire, the family caught sight of the deceased sitting on the front steps of her house. The dead girl repeatedly appeared afterwards at night in the street, and knocked on doors. Children sickened and died. She had relations with an addled widower. When at night, like a trail of fog, she would leave a farm, she left a dead man in her wake.

Galeen's cousin and the other officers were taken to the graveyard to open and examine the grave. When they exhumed her, she was whole and intact with blood flowing from her nose, mouth, and ears. When the girl's mother saw her, she spat and said, "You are to disappear; don't get up again and don't move!" At those words, tears flowed from the corpse's eyes. After seeing that, the villagers pulled her from the grave, cut her into pieces and tied them with cloth. The cloth they threw on a thornbush which they set on fire. Whereupon a strong wind rose and blew after them, howling, all the way back to the village.

The first day is overcast. It's always a question of the intensity of the light. Wagner's assistants test it with orange filter glasses. We wait. At eleven I announce we'll set up the close-ups. For those we don't need sunlight. No sooner are we ready than the sun is out. We go on, but now Wangenheim and Greta are squinting; Wagner and his assistants have to screen with canvas the very sun we've been waiting for all day, fake the half-light we've suffered through to this point. Flies circle everywhere. The wind shakes a background I want still. The camera develops a tremor. Wangenheim abominable.

That night, the cold sweats, trying to sort out the next day's tasks. Confronted by the characters, I feel like an official called in to oversee a crowd of immigrants. They stand about, passive, while I regard them with growing dismay.

Day 2: More camera troubles. Drove off at nine in the morning. Spectacular trip. Stopped at a wine tavern, and then continued off the main road to show Spiess the avenue of Caspar David Friedrich trees Grau showed me earlier. Pointed out to him as well the pitched waterfall Hutter will see from his room in the castle the night of the greatest danger. Every time I view the place it's a revelation. Spiess astounded. The grottoes and clefts and riot of overhanging branches enclosed us within the sound and force of the cataract. We could see movement flitting above in the narrow and overgrown cliff faces. We were in a world where all was wonder, delicate and secret, and beside which all our clutter looked like a farce in bad taste. On the way home by a different route, I was talking to Spiess about the second inn, where Hutter is warned against proceeding to the castle, and round a bend all at one glance I recognized, down to the smallest detail, the exact setting I had resigned myself to having to build. Here were the windows for Hutter's view of the frightened horses, the old shutters with the carved hex signs, the doors and boxed-in bed, the stone well, the apples piled in an oaken bucket, everything! The interiors as good as the exteriors, with this quality of the luminous strangeness of the ordinary shining through the walls…

Spiess too is fascinated with the lore of vampires. He reads a number of Slavic languages, and has helped with the forbidding and disintegrating texts Galeen has pulled from the local libraries. We never have enough background material, and what we have always feels too vague. At night, sitting on my bed in my room, Spiess reports, his voice transforming the softest consonants into sounds that make my neck ache with desire. Among the Slavs it's reported that one may strew ashes or salt around headstones in a cemetery to determine, by looking for footprints later, if any of the bodies are leaving their graves at night. If a grave is sunk in, or if a cross has taken a crooked position, the deceased has transformed himself. Often there is visible a hole in the grave from which the vampire emerges. And the gypsies believe that if dogs are barking, no vampires are in the village, but if dogs are silent, then the vampires have come.

With this sort of story, everything, Wegener wrote when he was working on his *Golem*, depends on a certain flow in which the fantastic world of the past rejoins the world of the present. And yet how does one make judgements about emotional truth in such situations? Authenticity is a problem that remains unresolved in this country. Transylvania, with its evocative meaning ("beyond the forest") seems appropriate as our setting: that place which can only be imagined. Europe's unconscious.

Remember to flag sections to be excised for *Querschnitt*.

One of Wagner's assistants is spending the week filming the light at dawn (real) on the castle gates (constructed). His task is to open on a fade every morning until "morning's dawn" becomes "morning horror": *Morgengrau* becomes *Morgengrauen.* I have a specific effect in mind, and this stock can capture it. Then he'll be sent home to film the dilapidated salt storehouses of Lübeck, for the long shots of the Bremen house of the vampire. All those empty window-sockets, with their uncanny, anthropomorphic quality.

Dinners with Spiess and Wagner help us clarify our ideas. The shot is not a painting, dependent only upon the expressive content of its static composition; it's also a space negotiable in every way, open to intrusion and transformation, inviting the most unpredictable courses. It's necessary to understand the process by which the mood and tone of such spaces can change. If only the camera could move! If the question becomes not only "what is the image?" but also "how does it change?" we exploit precisely that connection between film and dream; spaces shift with the logic and fluidity of the dream state. The geography of the film must be evocative yet elusive; the vampire's castle and the wilderness concrete in their tone and unmappable in their contours. Reality, but with fantasy; they must dovetail.

Spiess agreed. Wagner offered in support the reminder that in Rubens' engraving of the sheep, which Goethe showed to Eckermann, the shadow is on the same side as the sun.

If only the camera could move! Imagine if the camera could move! Wagner too is excited about the possibilities. "When and if," he says dryly, "we have the budget to experiment accordingly."

Second full production meeting tonight. All of us—Wagner, Grau, Spiess, Galeen, myself, Max Schreck, who will be playing the Nosferatu—crowded into my room. Some wine and sausage. Talking about the sources of horror. Grau claims our new art has an advantage over literature because the image can be clear and concrete even as it remains inconceivable. That is the paradox that causes the hair on the back of our necks to rise. Wagner adds that what people look for in film is a way to load their imagination with strong images. The fact that these images are silent is a supplementary attraction; they're silent like dreams. I think he's right, for as Hofmannsthal points out, we have only apparently forgotten our dreams; in fact there's not a single dream that, reawakened, does not begin to stir: the dark corner, the breath of air, the face of an animal, the glide of an unfamiliar gait, all of it makes the presence of dreams perceptible. The blackness below the stairs to the cellar, the barrel filled with rainwater in the courtyard, the door to the granary, the door to the loft, the neighbour's door through which the beautiful woman casts into the dark and palpitating depths of the child's heart an unexpected thrill of desire…

We fall silent, passing the wine. Spiess says it's like travelling through the air in the company of Asmodeus, the demon who raised roofs and laid bare all secrets.

Wagner says he imagines a future film which will be nothing on screen but beautiful creatures and transparent gestures, looks in which the entire soul is read.

Grau points out that in Mediterranean countries, children born with red hair or unusually pale complexions were watched carefully for other vampiric signs. Everyone looks at me.

Galeen has been listening to all of this, his elbow on the arm of his chair, his palm cupping his fat face. It's necessary, he says, to correct the dictionaries. The majority of terms today no longer correspond to the ideas whose image they were intended to provide. Are love, friendship, heart and soul still the same concepts they were when the ancient dictionaries were composed? What do the old "fantastic" worlds of Grimm, Hoffmann, or Poe represent for us today? Let us, he says, consider them with modern eyes: they remain a source of inspiration, nothing more; for what we have daily before us goes beyond even Jules Verne. Douglas Fairbanks' flying carpet already bores today's young; they sniff out special effects and look for the artifice that made it possible. We're no longer astonished by the technically unheard-of. We're surprised on those days the newspaper does not trumpet new breakthroughs. So we look for the fantastic within ourselves. We notice the child or the dog who walks to the mirror, caught by the miracle of this doubled face. We wonder: if this second self, the Other, were to come out of the mirror's frame… ?

Empty wine bottles are pyramided on their sides against the wall like artillery rounds. Grau, slightly drunk, eyes Spiess. There's been more tension as to his presence on the payroll. Prana, as a new production company, according to Grau can afford little extravagance. This despite the fact that Agnuzzo's delight with Lasker-Schüler caused him to pony up a check to cover "additional contingencies."

In Berlin, Grau quarrelled to the last minute about the additional spending represented by Spiess. He stalked around the station platform gesturing with the company's train tickets in his hands, and only gave in when I reminded him how much money I'd already saved by agreeing to cast Wangenheim instead of Veidt. Grau is ambitious, and given to wild statements intended to cow the listener. Prana is a creation of his will and rhetoric and is all he has. His painting career has not been a success. I told him Spiess was indispensable in helping me think, and dream, and important to the project in ways I could not yet articulate. Grau finally accepted my explanation. Spiess remains uncomfortable in his presence.

Wagner peers into an empty bottle. Grau is slumped to the floor, his head against the door of a low cupboard. Galeen still has his chin in his hands. Only Schreck seems unaffected by the wine, looking each of us over in turn.

The meeting has petered out. To finish, we toast the enterprise: Grau the good fortune of the company, Galeen the spirits around us who work with us, Schreck the undead, Wagner the new cameras ordered from Berlin, and myself my young collaborator Spiess and his contribution to my work. In the silence, Spiess' eyes shy from mine. Afterwards, he's the last to leave. He stands with his back to me, rummaging in the mess for his coat. He's still angry that I hadn't wanted him to come. I'm condemned not for having been unreasonable but for having come to my senses too slowly. I stand closer, still without touching him, and he eludes my hand nimbly, like a beautiful animal. I'm reminded of a title for which I can't find a place in the film: "She stands in front of him, still drawing back but trying to attract him to her".

This has become something unsuitable for public consumption. Where will I get the money to repay the advance?

Spiess refuses to talk about Lasker-Schüler's claim. We quarrel about this regularly. He notes only that the savagery of her claim indicates how badly I must have hurt her. He offers no further insight on this point, either. So my detective work is solitary and intermittent. Hans is the roundtable topic of my insomnia. I work through our time together the way a limited art student toils to copy a masterpiece. And what does all that effort represent? A man, frustrated, weeping for himself.

I have always been a fugitive and a vagabond. For a thousand years none of our family has remained anywhere without growing uneasy, without being seized by wanderlust. I am at home in no house and in no country.

The Murnaus have always been aloof, have always designed their own worlds. My father left a thriving business and went his own way, bought a magnificent estate at Wilhelmshöhe, with land, hunting, a carriage, and a horse. We children were delighted. The garden had everything we could wish for—a grotto, a ruin, a secret pond, a giant stone, a trapeze. It was a miniature paradise.

Bernhard was the first to visit me in Berlin after I'd cut off communication. The first night I joked with him about Father letting his youngest son out in Sodom, and he told me he'd been strictly forbidden to move in my "circles." When we met Spiess by accident, Bernhard took his leave, and did not meet me the next morning as planned.

I am both my father and Something Else, and remain mute before the ongoing miracle of the coexistence of the two.

Talked with Schreck about the Nosferatu. Schreck is a very strange man: narrow-shouldered, peculiarly stiff and clumsy, strikingly ugly without any makeup. At lunch he knocked over his water glass with a wooden sweep of his arm and then simply watched it, glared at me and then the water as it ran across the table. Intensely private, yet he's begun to follow me around, trying to absorb as much as he can. His performance is absolutely crucial. He has had very little experience but when I saw him bending without pleasure over a child on the Kurfürstendamm I knew he was the Nosferatu. I have begun talking with him about his role the only way I know how: trying to articulate the sources of my own obsessions. His silences seem equal parts hostility and understanding.

I talked of the vampire's parasitism—*you must die if I am to live.* I talked of the loathsomeness and the dread of his allure. I talked of the way the terrible inhumanness of him, the nightmarish repulsiveness, should move easily among the bourgeois naturalism of the costumes and acting styles of the rest of the cast—the way everyone must see him as in some ways *not out of the ordinary.*

More midnight work with Spiess on Galeen's script while the rest of the company sleeps. The hotel is silent. In the distance someone is drawing a wagon up the road.

Spiess reports quietly on his readings. He lays out on the bed charcoal drawings of amulets and charms, diabolic designs. The vampire he believes first appears in a Serbian manuscript of the 13th century in which a *vuklodlak* is described as a creature which devours the sun and moon while chasing clouds. Among the contemporary Slavs, *vampir* and *vuklodlak* (literally, wolf's hair) are synonymous. He reads aloud from a fragment of 15th century Turkish apocrypha: "The Force of Destruction is always near man and follows him like his shadow. For this reason man must always be restored. This restoration occurs in various forms: through the tears of the Force of Creation: water (bathing and washing); through the breath of the Force of Creation: air (ventilation of the house, and living outside); and through meeting every morning the first life-giving rays of the Force of Creation (which are sent from the sun)."

We trade ideas until the sky pales, building together an artifice superior to the work of either of our imaginations alone. We construct a new scene for Hutter's arrival: Distant mountains. Vratna Pass. In the background the fantastic castle of the Nosferatu in the evening light. A steep road leading straight up into the sky. Hutter abandoned by his coach. Something comes racing down—a carriage? A phantasm? It moves with unearthly speed and disappears behind a groundswell. Out of nowhere, reappears. Stops dead. Two black horses, their legs invisible, covered by black funeral cloth. Their eyes like pointed stars. Steam from their mouths. The coachman, whose face we cannot see. Hutter inside. Carriage drives at top speed through a *white* forest! (We'll use meters of negative, like "the land the sun travels through at night" so feared in ancient Egypt.)

If the camera could move *with* the coach— So that *we* could feel the terrifying capacities of evil—

Then the courtyard. The carriage at a halt. Almost in a faint, Hutter climbs down. As if in a whirlpool, the carriage circles round him and disappears. Then, very slowly the two wings of the gate open up…

Six days of shooting. The camera still trembles. The new one sent from Berlin is worse than the old one. I let them develop the bad takes in case the camera has performed some miracle of its own. Yet some scenes come off beautifully. The panicking horses Hutter sees from the window of the inn: on a grassy slope, the ground falling away toward the back. Night mists creep up the valley. The horses raise their heads as if frightened, and, scattering, gallop away. The white horse spun and shook perfectly, which he refused to do yesterday. The camera just got it. And one, after hours of work, *backed out* of the frame! The effect was marvelous. Even Wagner, for all his exhaustion, was excited by how it will look. The possibility of other people's fatigue never occurs to me.

Spiess proposes a trip to the South Seas to collaborate on an old photoplay of his entitled *The Island of the Demons*. I'm insufficiently excited about the idea. A horrible fight.

I must avoid a certain kind of coldness that results from the way I work. It would be fatal.

Spiess gone to Berlin for a few days for "personal matters." We fought again over Hans. Clumsy life going about its stupid work: even when we want to reveal ourselves we're so poor at it that we spend most of our time in self-concealment one way or the other. My experience of him is discontinuous, my attention uneven, my judgement and understanding uncertain.

He was gone all night and announced his trip the next morning. I said nothing. I was busy the entire day. That afternoon on his pillow in his room, I left for him one of the vampire's entreaties to Hutter:

Would you not like to wait a while with me, dearest worthy? It is not so long until the sunrise—

And during the day I sleep my best; I sleep most truly, the deepest sleep—

Long hours in the makeshift projection room last night. The coach arriving at the inn. Wangenheim crossing the little bridge to the "land of the phantoms." The forest he views on his journey. That last setup particularly difficult because of the terrain. Extreme long shots of landscape must be shot north or south so that the crosslight provides definition. Flat, dead-on light causes shadows to fall away behind objects so that there's no modeling, and backlighting is problematic in all but the clearest skies.

It's irritating to see so little, because the true rhythms will be produced only in the cutting. Can't find the take of the white horse turning with its balked jumpiness, and there's no trace of it on the labels. Awful if that shot lost.

With some of the vistas Wagner hasn't enough courage. He compromises and won't take a bold enough line. The result is a softness to his work that I must overcome. It's all too "beautiful." Whereas I want something more harsh to contrast with the beauty, a starkness and awed sweep…

Grau has done a marvelous job of turning what's innate in Schreck into the Nosferatu. Schreck's been bound into a three-quarter length jacket, buttoned up tightly. His makeup (I must show his hands today) will take three hours.

Endless discoveries. Water from a spring so pure the animals take the trough to be empty. The play of shadow off it in twilight like the marble ceilings of seaside hotels. Grau, in his other hat as producer, complains that we continue to fall behind our schedule. But what shots! Today an open cart-shed full of rakes and scythes, and that grey spider on the backlit orb-web. Broken sunlight through isinglass. Wagner's work, viewed each night, is breathtaking: in clarity, in richness of detail, in contour. One can find that same soft brilliance in certain kinds of silver polished with skins.

Greta came to me with an idea for Heligoland: her character, Ellen, waiting for Hutter's return at a seaside graveyard—stark crosses at oblique and neglected attitudes on the dune, with the sea beyond. A wonderful idea: the natural world enlisted and compromised by the Nosferatu. The natural world operating under the shadow of the supernatural. Enormous tranquillity in the context of unease and dread: for whom is she waiting?

A discussion grows out of our enthusiasm. Endless polarities—west and east, good and evil, civilization and wilderness, reason and passion, with the contested terrain in every case the body of the woman. The obsession is not with the oppositions as much as the areas between them—the possibility that they're not such oppositions. Hence the connections between Hutter and the Nosferatu, Ellen and the Nosferatu.

The differences between the Self and the Other start to collapse. In Stoker's novel, the woman from the village sees Harker at the window and identifies *him* as the vampire: "Monster, give me my child!"

Still no Spiess. Lunched with Galeen and Greta in Poczamok. Bathed in the river. Raspberries!

The publicity assistant back in Berlin sent Grau an article from the *Literarische Welt*, which he passed on to me: "Murnau has become a new kind of being who thinks directly in photographs. Murnau is a kind of modern centaur: he and the camera joined to form a single body." An image lifted from Lasker-Schüler's image of me as "made of leaf and bark / Of early morn and centaur blood." The article ends by announcing that "Murnau teaches us to *see* the modern film; others will teach us to *feel* it."

Still no Spiess. The headaches back. The doctors unhappy with my kidneys. Great pain while urinating. The crew sits about and waits. At times I'm ashamed of their confidence. What have I achieved so far?

A single day left to do scenes that should take three or four, which is always the way the schedules evolve. Wagner points out that for the negative footage the vampire's carriage must be painted *white* so it will remain black. In the same way Schreck must be clothed in white. Multiple disasters and new ideas make the last days on location always a nightmare of clumsiness. Everyone falls over everyone else while the light slowly disappears. Four of us splash paint over the carriage in a fever. Grau fashions a white cloak out of a bedsheet. Eight in the morning becomes five in the afternoon.

That night I dreamed of my father, the last time I saw him: on the platform of the Berlin railway station, standing amid the depressed and nondescript second-class passengers. I was leaning out the train window. For a moment we looked at each other; then the train moved off and he disappeared among the crowd. Then I was in a dead woman's apartment, gazing at the remains of an unappetizing meal, the head and bones of some smoked fish. A sort of ghost meal.

I lay awake afterwards, and scribbled down an idea for a general shot: Hutter looks around the room which seems to him utterly changed. The damp wallpaper, the stains on the floor, the rough furniture, the depressing well of the courtyard beyond. All these things exude a rank physicality, a bleak hostility, a hostility directed at him.

INTERIORS

Spiess is gone. Frau Reger handed me his note a few minutes after I dropped my valise in the front hall. It was typed. Civilization, as I well knew, had become unbearable, and he'd decided to flee from it and build a new life in the South Seas, perhaps the Dutch East Indies.

A day off work. Unreturned calls to Lasker-Schüler and Veidt. The company puzzled. Wagner attributes it to exhaustion.

Doubts about the whole project. There is an essentially trivial quality at the heart of film's fascination—a nervous, aggressive vulgarity.

I'm surprised, too, by the intensity of my despondency at Spiess' departure. As he once wrote me, "*Hans* is your obsession. I'm just the Catamite who helps you with all your ceremonies of regret."

Late for work the next day. Unheard of for Murnau. An inspection of the interiors built by Grau and his assistants at the Jofa studios at Berlin-Johannistal. More than a few ironies here: the largest film production studio in Europe has taken shape on the grounds of the old Albatros-Werke. I make movies now where engineers made planes for Allmenröder and me.

It's a hard place to get used to, a huge dirigible hangar of exposed steel girders and glass that makes all sound harsh and prone to echo. First check of the set of the castle dining hall. An arrangement like a child's playhouse in the middle of the vast space.

Grau was enraged by the way his sketches had been realized. He ranted, upbraided, drew new versions in the air, and tore down flats, while I stood by befuddled by his talent and passion. This is more often his production than mine, and he's the glue in the face of my weakness that holds everything together.

He disagreed about the layout of the great hall. He complained the scenic space gave the impression of being cut off by accident. I told him that the compositions were intended to seem part of a larger, organic effect; he said *No*, banging a table so that a plate jumped: the artistic decor ought to be the perfect composition at the center of which the action took place.

Wagner mediated, suggesting we weren't as far apart as we thought. I suggested a compromise: we do it my way. Grau left.

Wagner's steadiness is invaluable. I work beautifully with him, usually by anticipating him. I show him an inferior composition; he looks despondently at it; then gets excited, begins fiddling, and in minutes produces exactly what we need.

When Grau returns the three of us walk the set. I eliminate the chairs (too light and too modern), allow the fireplace (which doesn't work). Wagner shows us where he wants the second camera. We make fun of his precision. Grau gets onto his hands and knees with a slide rule, and I shout "Closer! Farther! Closer!" while he moves it incrementally this way and that. Spiess had watched us do that in Czechoslovakia and had said later that we'd seemed like a family he'd never be a part of.

Outside the studio we wait irritably for taxis. It's raining. Schreck leans against a wall in the darkness, his arms folded. He has no hat. Grau is staying at a nearby hotel. Wagner and I are going back to Grunewald. Out of the darkness Schreck asks what we think a vampire is. Wagner says: corpses who during their lifetime had been sorcerers, werewolves, people excommunicated by the church, excommunicated from their lives: suicides, drunkards, heretics, apostates, and those cursed by their parents. Grau, after a pause, looks at me and says: demons who dwell in the corpses of men, to instruct them in vice, and lead them to wickedness.

Some conversations with Leo, Spiess' brother, about his possible whereabouts. Leo is unsympathetic. The Spiesses were a great Baltic family. Leo is Kapomeister at the Staatsöper Berlin. There's no guarantee he'll even let me know if he hears anything.

I blame Spiess as often as I blame myself for Hans. Yet with who else can I share this obsession? He liked to call me the administrator of my own inhibitions. He amended Hans' nickname and called me Bayard, the Knight Soaked in Reproach. He was impatient with the subject of Hans. He said we were both to blame, always with that air of knowing the price of everything.

The shooting begins and the wolfhound that was Galeen's idea refuses to film. He takes his place all right but leaves as soon as the cameras begin to roll and returns when they're finished. We attempt the simple scene of Wangenheim in his room in the castle, a tiny whitewashed room with sharp angles and a huge, crib-like bed in the period style. He is to read from *The Book of Vampires* ("*THE NOSFERATU. From the bloody sins of mankind a creature will be born…*") and go to the window, throwing it open to look into the starless night, while beyond his door in the depths of the castle the horror gathers. He swaggers through the motions, ruining everything. Multiple takes, two or three quiet conversations with him. The film is nearly always finished before one's had the time to get the actors to forget the bad habit of "giving a performance".

Then, through the viewfinder, everything was too washed out. I begged Wagner to get more contrast into the shot, so we set about dramatizing the light, hanging screens to define the space and throw shadows on the far walls. Then Wangenheim began botching the simple actions, dropping the book, catching his foot in the bedclothes. I hid myself, thinking him more likely to manage with me not around. At last he made it without disaster to the window, but then it was Wagner's turn: the camera caught on its cable and didn't pan. Grau could stand it no longer, and left. We broke for five minutes and did it once more, with only an hour of time left, and miraculously, everything worked. Everyone relaxed. The scene fell together and even a cat wandered through as if it were at home.

At the end of each day, everything but the sets themselves is stowed away out of sight. The rights to *Dracula* have not been purchased and Grau has begun receiving inquisitive letters from solicitors representing Bram Stoker's wife.

Talked to Grau about Wangenheim's costume. Colours offer different sensibilities to light even in black and white photography. For the scenes in the castle, Wangenheim should have a blue waistcoat. This is not superstitious or fetishistic; it has to do with the value of grey that blue will provide.

Also: first day for Ruth Landshoff, who plays Ellen's sister. The daughter of the ship-owner, not even a professional actress, but someone I noticed months ago in the Grunewald on her way to school. Beautiful and refined, she reminded me of a picture by Kaulbach, and I went to great lengths to meet her mother and ask permission for her to take part in the filming during her holidays. I'm irresistibly drawn to the idea of *this* woman in my film, in this infernal vision of swarming rats, of pestilential boats, of men who suck blood, of dark vaults, of black carriages pulled by phantom horses…

During a half day's shooting she stands beside me, not sure where else to go. Wangenheim flirts with her. Wagner and I are filming Ellen's sleep-connection to the vampire. The only sounds are the turning of the camera and Wangenheim's whispering. It's customary to build additional sets while shooting's going on, a crowd of people standing nearby giving orders at the tops of their voices. But I work in silence, the silence of the film itself. A journalist from my parents' hometown compared work on my set to a memorial service, presided over by "a tall thin gentleman in his white work coat, standing a bit out of the way, issuing directions in a very low voice".

I don't understand how it is that this generation has not seen the rise of a true Poet of film. For all the arts, one is able to cite great masters born to understand them exceptionally. There should come geniuses of the screen who know instinctively what it alone among the arts has the power to do. At the moment we found our stories on novels, stage plays, etc. In the future, we'll think film and dream film.

More telephone calls to Leo Spiess. He's taken to hanging up on me.

Wagner took me aside with doubts about Wangenheim's performance. He said Wangenheim's aggressive terror inhibited his own. The hero, presented to us as bold/hardy/audacious/daring/venturesome and plucky, suddenly passes from all that to convulsive terror? I thanked him and reminded him it was too late to replace Wangenheim. It was not a comment timed to fill me with confidence.

For the vampire's arrival: lack of movement makes the eye impatient. *Use such impatience.*

Filmed Granach, as Knock, the house agent under the sway of the Nosferatu. A relief working with an old friend. During breaks he told the crew how as students of Reinhardt's we'd lie on the floor of the stage-box to hear and see him work with actors (he allowed no one to view his rehearsals). The scene came off perfectly. Granach reading the cabalistic letter sent by the vampire seems dropped in from another world, his spindly hunchback shifting and jerking, his ugly smile making sense of the strange symbols. A last touch was all his: raising his head upon finishing, as if greeting the evil. Wonderfully disturbing sense of the diabolism closer to home.

The happy accidents of art. As the Austrians say, "Es ist passiert"— It just happened like that.

Reminder to the labs: the lettering of the titles should be lanky and tortuous, like that of *Caligari*. The background, a poisonous green. A tooth is giving me great pain.

In Czechoslovakia, Spiess related to me a dream that he was Ellen in the film. He went up to the bedroom before his husband. At the side of the bed he heard the fluttering of a bird. The air was disturbed. He didn't light the lamp or draw the curtain. The streetlight provided the only light. He couldn't keep awake. In a park nearby, the wind moved the trees. It was as if he'd been chloroformed.

Even after his departure, he continues to provide information on the lore of the vampire. Alone in my room, unable to sleep, I go over, in his handwriting, the last three stages of the etymological history of the word: the Old Church Slavonic for *fugitive*, the early Common Slavic for *the one who drinks in*, and the later Slavic for *neighbour*.

First interior shooting of Schreck as the Nosferatu. Made up, he wanders the dining hall set in preparation, and the stone-work, windows, and doors come to life. It's we, in our modern clothes, who look like intruders, ridiculous ghosts. The scene of his dinner with Hutter: the hall through the camera appearing to have gigantic dimensions. In the center a massive Renaissance table. In the distance the huge fireplace. The Nosferatu reading Hutter's letter of introduction: sharp ratlike teeth over the lower lip. Over the top margin of the letter, his eyes, as he hears the clock strike midnight. A snake hypnotizing its victim. Wangenheim smart enough to stop acting as the drama reaches its height, understanding the audience will have already reached the required degree of tension. Afterwards some "executives" from Prana, friends of Grau's, in for lunch. A strange meal. Schreck, still made up as the Nosferatu, set his teeth on the table like part of the place setting while he ate his soup.

The pace picks up. It must. One set is struck and another built in its place while Grau and Galeen and I confer with the actors for the day's next scene. More kidney trouble has thrown us a week behind, and Grau called me at the Bühlershoh sanatorium to remind me that the rest of the shooting had to be finished in four weeks, by 1 November. He added that some sets I'd asked him to save had been struck, and that I had to work more sensibly and avoid unnecessary takes. Film stock already cost thirty marks a meter and there wouldn't be any more forthcoming. Even with the help of the big banks, inflation was making it impossible to raise money. Agnuzzo was apparently tapped out.

Twelve-hour shooting days. Many of us are fighting artificial sunstroke, caused by the arcs. Crew members rub raw grated potato on their faces to combat the burn. The Nosferatu greeting Hutter as it emerges from the darkness of the castle archway. Wagner suggests we use magnesium flares with the arcs to increase the effect of moonlight. Take after take. Schreck sweats and suffers under his makeup and his forehead looks as if it's been varnished.

Everyone thinking about future commitments: Granach going back on stage; Grau soon to begin scouting exteriors for Prana's next film. Wagner working with Lang. Galeen to direct his own *Stadt in Sicht*. We're all progressively losing the sense that we're held within the same dream; each of us is beginning to wake up.

My trouble is naiveté. What I should do is overnumber the shots so that as we progress the script girl could note increasing numbers accomplished each day, and Grau and Dieckmann would be steadily mollified.

Tensions continue with Grau over the schedule, our plans for the film, everything. As we get closer to the end more and more of his energy goes into promotion and distribution, which is necessary but seems premature. After he's interviewed by *Der Film* I have to read: "Each scene is given over to the director only when ready to be filmed; beforehand the artistic director has prepared it down to the smallest details, according to psychological and pictorial principles, and has sketched it out on paper. Each gesture, each costume (the era of 1840 approximately), each movement has been laid out with scientific rigor and calculated to produce a specific effect upon the spectator."

The publicity material prepared has achieved a tone that verges on provocation. One of the handouts:

Nosferatu was there. In the streets. Mongrels howled it. Babies cried it. Crooked branches traced its letters in the earth. The wind swept the word and carried it away, and dead leaves from the trees read "Nosferatu." It invaded everything. One could see it along walls, above streetlamps, in the eyes of those late to bed. It fastened to ganglia and sounded in bones. It clamored. It uttered cries like rats in a coffin. Maidens whispered it in their sleep. Above them in the darkness it formed, livid and ghastly pale, leaden and yellow, full of sulphur and fatal breath. And you? Do you still feel nothing? Nos-fer-a-tu — Nosferatu — beware.

Shot by shot I know my way through. I will not give in until I have what I want. But every morning there we are again on the set, with its dismal fraudulence, flapping wall, plaster gargoyles. Again I'll get worked up, pull my hair, go back to my room, start over again.

Determined to do ten shots today, despite Wagner's pace, Grau's complaints, and the arcs, which keep fusing. Horrible quarrel. Wagner's taken to calling me The Schoolmaster.

Fruitless check of steamship offices about Spiess. Found a gift he'd brought me at a dinner I'd arranged in my room in Czechoslovakia. An erotic drawing of two boys and a man. We'd been tense and awkward. Wangenheim had wandered by while I'd been examining the drawing. The whole thing had been a Feydeau farce. Spiess had become distracted and impatient. I'd become exhausted and short-tempered. He had left before dessert.

A telegram back from Meidner. No help about Hans. His response was full of questions.

The first stalking of Hutter. Discussions with Wangenheim beforehand. What matters is not what the actors show me but what they hide. Above all, *what they don't suspect is in them.* I cite for him the Baroness in *Schloss Vogelöd*, who after her husband fends off her kiss and announces his renunciation of everything worldly, whispers distractedly to herself, "I'm longing for evil — seeing evil — wanting evil."

We begin. The set deathly quiet. Hutter in his room in the castle, huddled behind the door. He opens it a crack. View deep into dining hall. By the fireplace the Nosferatu, motionless, arms down, confrontationally stark against the background. Horrible lack of movement. Hutter supports himself on the doorpost. Terrible realizations dawning. Shut the door, shut it quickly! No bolt. No lock. He rushes to the window. (View of the forest at night: undergrowth; wolves raising their heads, howling.) The contrast between Hutter's movements and the Nosferatu's: frenzied panic vs. the terrible evenness of the advance. Hutter on his knees by the side of the bed. Stares at the door, which opens to half its width; opens fully. Superimpositions of progressively closer shots of the vampire produce movement without movement, the figure swelling within the frame, the mechanism of nightmare. Wagner has the genius idea of having the figure penetrate a powerful light emanating from the side just as he enters the doorway. Four days of work.

Two weeks left. Hardly eating. The same woman journalist from *Der Film* who interviewed Grau told me today that my face was like two profiles stuck together. Ellen's room, her decision to sacrifice herself, the final approach of the vampire are all still left to do. Two days of work on Ellen reading *The Book of Vampires*, until my temples are throbbing, my cheeks burning, my whole frame shivering. A few hours in my room drinking hot soup. Realizing mistakes I made by plunging on at such a pace; but besides the lack of time, I feel myself fighting to prevent any kind of indecision at this point from demoralizing the unit.

My headaches worse. My kidneys breaking down. Berliners are tactless and cruel. On a bus yesterday a young lieutenant seated me with a flourish. The spectacle of this disintegrating thirty-three year-old seems to make people laugh.

Take after take of Ellen at the window, seeing the Nosferatu. She is pure (and therefore appalled by what she has to do) and she is not pure (since she makes her bed available to the vampire.) Greta not up to it. Wagner works with the inhumanity of all cameramen; he calibrates the lights at his own pace without noticing that Greta all that time is swaying on her feet. Grau looks on, his arms folded. The nerve storm finally breaks and she collapses. Wangenheim comforts her while we wait. The shooting goes far into the night.

This fear of coming to a standstill, of not being able to go on, of having to break off—it's connected to all of my other undertakings:

loving, observing, participating. Everything, in short, that has called for perseverance.

Little sleep; endless, crushing headaches. Granite pieces breaking behind my eyes. Cold sweat, palpitations, exhaustion. A full day without working at all. Grau in a frenzy of rage and despair over this preview, in a Marxist rag: "This occultism, which has victimized thousands of shaken minds since the war, is a strategy mounted by the industrial world to deflect the worker from his own political interests. Today the occult takes the place of religions that no longer attract clients. Workers! On your guard! Don't give your pennies to a spectacle designed to stupefy! Let the phantom "Nosferatu" be devoured by his own rats!"

Grau's response? Ever more publicity. Prana has now spent more on publicity than on the film itself. It seems clearer and clearer to me that the whole enterprise is an enormous bluff. Where is the publicity money to come from? Grau says "the Otto Riede Bank," but Wagner has told me that this bank does not exist, and that Otto Riede is a simple employee. Yet the madness goes on. Grau plans a party on the release date: Saturday, March 4, "Prana's Day." He's secured the marble entry hall of the zoo, and commissioned a prologue by Kurt Alexander inspired by the introduction from Goethe's *Faust*. He's hired Elisabeth Grube of the national opera to perform with the ballet troupe. For musical accompaniment there will be the great harmonium "Dominator," transported to the site at massive cost. And all of this, he announces, will be filmed!

Hobbled back to the set this morning accompanied by a nurse. Disoriented by the medication and exhaustion and worried all day by an oppressive sense that I'm out of touch with the world. Stagehands stood around in groups as if at union meetings, and eyed me. The whole film seemed moribund. Woke that night from dreams which seemed to move like dirty water forming monstrous waves. Neck hurt.

And then a late-afternoon wait in a pub across the street from the studio. Another problem with the arc lights. Wagner and I share wine, bread and butter, minced pork. I confess my fears, my inability to understand what I'm doing, or go on. Wagner tells me that I alone can do this. Seeing my face, he puts his hand to my cheek, there before the entire pub. That easily, his palm brings me a temporary peace. He tells me he's been viewing the footage, and that it's everything I've hoped for. He is such a mysterious figure, finally: cheerless and sober and intent on something outside my view.

A few hours' sleep. A breathing spell. The final sequence to be done, the Nosferatu's approach to Ellen.

The horror coming slowly, tensed like a predatory animal. A new idea, necessitating a new set at this late date by Grau: nothing but the shadow of Nosferatu on the wall of the stairs, mounting with dreadful slowness, then more quickly, an awful quick-footed walk, fingernails dripping, until it pauses beside the door. The hand and fingers extending elastically along the wall. In the room Ellen shrinks before the monster we still don't see, except for the black shadow of his hand spreading across her white body like ink. She jerks her head down in anticipation of his touch, as her husband had. The shadow fist seizes her heart. And then in the darkness, on the very side of the frame, obscenely unobtrusive, the Nosferatu feeding.

The shooting done. A week's rest. The unit comes back together one last time to view the rough projection before the final cutting begins. Grau, Wagner, Galeen, Wangenheim, Greta—all of this is now a memory to them, like a party they found puzzling and absorbing but not pleasant.

Galeen torments me with an article in the *Berliner Tageblatt*, reading for the group: "Of all the film directors, Murnau is the most German. A Westphalian, reserved, severe on himself, severe on others, severe for the cause. Outwardly grim, never envious, always alone, his successes and failures arising from the same source, each of his works complete, authentic, direct, logical, cold, harsh, and absolute, like Gothic art." Much hooting. Grau suggests it sounds like an obituary.

We view what we have. Some pleasures—the opportunity to make fluid human time, so painful in its rigidity, to arrange and rearrange it, our small triumph over the inexorable. Again struck by how often the camera could see what I couldn't feel.

Long stretches of footage so bad no one will comment. Enduring them I begin to tell myself I can still do what I set out to do; yet if there are faults in the work, they're mine alone.

In the darkness, the absence of Spiess is more comfortable and familiar. The more he pursued me, the more I restrained my passion for him. This sense of never being at home, with anyone, I feel more and more, the older I get.

More footage. My concentration dissipates. I remember living in a series of hotels, when I was very small, before father bought the estate. One small old hotel in particular, by the sea, a little room full of sun, where you could smell the apples and the waves.

Someone yawns. Someone shifts in his chair. In the silence of a changeover in reels, I can hear us all—Grau, Wagner, Greta— murmuring with pleasure and amusement. Behind the whirring of Wagner cueing up the final leader, we can hear the sound of many voices singing in the garden below: children outside our dark little room, shouting in the sunlight.

PAGES FROM A DIARY

Steve Kilbey

January 1, 1873. Prague

Awake in an intensely cold dark room
I remember who I am
Warm summery dream of the child gone
The damp is contagious and is attacking me
My guts in disagreement with themselves
As if I could vomit out my heart
And my bones and muscles contracted in a
    rictus of numb agony
My hands and feet of whitest ice
The nails like filthy hooks
My odour fills the room as a dismal stain
    might, creeping and corrupting
In the mirror the reflection so repugnant I
    never look
I stagger to the window and push out the
    wooden shutters
The city is still dark and smouldering
Here and there a candle flares against a pane
The sun does not want to rise today
In a century of wars and a week of murders
Europe killing itself and screaming in my ears
It amuses to remember myself as I was
I actually smile at the absurd memory of it all

A handsome young boy whose father was a
    lord
Mother so long now dead but her beauty stays
    with me
Such a pale face against such dark hair
Her crucifixes and Macedonian accent and her
    myrrh
It makes me laugh to think I had a mother
It's snowing
The loveliness of the flakes would make me
    cry
But now I have no tears for anything at all
I gaze down on this city and I feel nothing but
    hunger
Unending unendurable hunger and a thirst I
    can never slake
Some pale awful sun threatens to break
    through a cloud
I pull the curtains and retire back to shadow
I curl up in my deep anxiety and I dream
    horrible dreams

June 12, 1888. London

I feed and I hide and I hide and I feed
I have paid off the man who owns this hotel
He must obviously know who I am
He must obviously know what I am
A room in an attic I gaze out at dirty London
In Islington where I cruise camouflaged by the
    smoke
And Shoreditch where I stand under trees by
    an old mortuary
Almost unseen in the fogs and the wavering
    lights

In my cloak of burnt soot black
In my shirt of fetid silk
In my boots that fill my feet with nails
Yes there was a girl tonight like a girl from
    another night
A girl from the olden days who had lived in a
    different world
It angered me so that she wouldn't remember
    me
Yes she must have loved me once
But now in this form I am unrecognisable
Yes of course I must understand this
Still her gracefulness burns at my eyes
The sweet smell of her rushes into my nose
    and it's acrid
She fills me with hunger she fills me with
    thirst
I follow her patiently as she steps off the train
I must hunt I must eat I must drink
These things are the things that I am
She struggled as I drank and I drank
She whispered prayers and sobbing for mercy
I stagger away full of blood and throbbing
    shame
Yet not shame
But the diseased remnants of shame
Something about her made me have to have
    her
She tasted of iron and rusty like old armour
She tasted young and she tasted of some warm
    hope
Afterwards I hurry away
I scurry away down the crooked lanes and I
    climb over walls
I balance on roofs and I creep up the tiles
I lurk in the river's mists unnoticed by the
    rank and file

The more I drink the more I want to drink
The summer here is weak and rainy and the
    sun rarely shines
I come out in the long tepid grey afternoons
An unexplained magic means I attract little
    attention
In the warm drizzle beyond a doorway
And the moths in the lamplight and rain
The stupid police barking up a hundred
    wrong trees
The people go about their nights with caution
It makes my life harder if indeed this is a life
It makes the ice bite deeper in the street
And cruel black birds who follow me cawing
    hoarsely
The sights and sounds of London disgust me
The people seem ill and stunted and dirty
Then suddenly a flash of some profanely
    beautiful woman
The chimneys pumping out that awful smoke
Horses and ugly children and unmentionable
    things being cooked
Give me a forest any day
A dense tangle of dead trees around a disused
    wishing well
Where the white lilies float in the black lake as
    the snow falls silently
Sweet silence of no living thing

December 24, 1888. Dublin

Tonight a rabble has chased me and an urchin
    cast a stone
I stoop panting in the shadow of a castle
The mud up to my ankles

My skinny shins all chafed and in sores
Some terrible creature has emptied its stomach
    in the street
Nearby another has cast up its accounts of
    black beer
It's too cold to snow and some places reek of
    cold holiness
I hate Christ and I hate Mary and I hate God
I hate the devil who made me this way
I curse the day that I wandered down this
    gruesome street
I spend my time hidden in the earth on a ship
I want and I burn with the wanting
I sleep but my dreams are burning too
I wake up scorched in the freezing place I have
    found to sleep
In the gap between two floors in a boarding
    house by the river
I wait out the days that are short and are
    freezing
I feel the cold I feel the hunger
I remember the daughter of the poet
How I took her hand and led her down under
    the ground
And the winter was at its height and it
    towered all white
The houses that kept out no cold and no ghost
All huddled together in a shambles of
    crumbling wood and cracked plaster
The squelch of a shoe out there in the mud
In all my lamplit horror I will be discovered
I can see my eyes my animal eyes
Which can see I am an animal
Swift and shrewd and ruthless as I feed
I am delighted by the red of blood on the grey
    snow

March 3, 1892. Outside Zurich

A nasty policeman has found my bolt-hole
So I'm lingering in a cemetery in the hills
Misty and lit by a sick old moon
I am the cliche villain it occurs to me
I feast on the blood of poor peasants
Leaving them dreaming damned or dead I
    don't care
All the same anyway in the end I'm cold and
    I'm hungry again
Wandering up a cold road at dusk shivering in
    my miserable skin
There is no warm hearth or cup of warm wine
Waiting for me at the end of the street
No one dares speak or even knows my name
Wind whistles through broken glass and dogs
    howl far away
I am known to the thorn and the broken grave
Wrought iron angel with rust for hair
A path through the woods where lovers once
    had their trysts
A golden spider catching black fat flies
Spring is still sleeping in a darkened cave
An afternoon in a field as the yellow stars
    came out
Overland and on the run I traverse the
    continents and the years
A sad song begins the violins will start up
Wine is poured and commiserations made
No stranger to the coffin myself I am a study
    in grief
Time ticks into eternity and everything's
    reborn
Then everything returns again unto dust

September 19, 1900. Amsterdam

Abandoned windmill halfway into town
    hiding from the *Politie*
Secretly I hope they will catch me and end all
    of this
In a puddle a reflection more rodent than man
A sodden bed of earth where I try to sleep
Another reverie of youth quickly deforms
In a black and white world with monochrome
    villages
I followed a witch into a wood of hazel trees
She lifted her skirts and it was done standing
    up
She laughed and she spat and she drifted
    away
I drank her magical blood from her whitest
    neck
It was ambrosia and it was poison at the same
    time
That was long ago and faraway
when a woman would still
look upon me
In a city of merchants with their plump wives
    and daughters
I hunted at midnight in the alleys and lanes
In orchestra pits and cloakrooms and kitchens
In libraries of books unread and forgotten
In a courtyard at early morning's first light the
    broken path
Cracked sundial and weedy loam
The cathedral knells in the distance across the
    fields of poppies
Even I don't know of all the horrors to come
I sense it sometimes when I hear a train
Or come across a dead bird on my path

And the murmuring fountains that spout no
     more
A soldier with one leg begs for guilders
He belongs in this scene a piece of the puzzle
He stinks of hospitals and pity and scorn
I take in everything and put it all together
I'm always looking around for some quick exit
I need to know what I'm dealing with
I need to know the lay of the land

September 23, 1900. Amsterdam

And yet for all of everything I still fall in love
     easily
So easily like a child or a small dog I am
     stricken
I saw her today in the doorway of a church
She did not see me for I was covered in the
     shadow
With her auburn hair and her white skin
Haloed against the black maw of the church
Oh how I loved her then
And how I hated that church
I wondered how old she was in this new
     century?
Perhaps 20 or 21 I really am undecided
Her eyes seem green to me
That's how I would certainly prefer them
Her lips red
Her nostrils black
Her veins so feint blue in her swanlike neck
Elegant she seemed to me in her simple
     clothes
Holding a small navy bible in her bony hand
She gazed up into the sky like a prophetess

A sybil foreseeing all the terrible destruction
    still to come
I wondered about her name
I imagined her childhood
Her mother bathing her in a tub on summers
    evening
Eating wild raspberries and cream in a field
    with her friends and brothers
I longed for her and everything she was
I loved her like a cat may love a small bird
I loved her as a bear pawing at honey and yet
    the swarm of bees
I wanted to absorb her into me and bathe in
    her exalted ray
Bring her flowers I've stolen from a cemetery
    vase
Sing her words from an old drinking song I
    once heard
Perhaps my old voice could sing of other times
    too
If she couldn't see me yes oh then I would
    croon
Romania and winter in her mountains
How the snow would swirl around my high
    room in the castle
The bare trees in silhouette against the whitest
    sky
The long years of night
My morning-less life in margins and corridors
A crow in the air caws as it flies
The candlelight writhing throwing shapes on
    a wall
The cold crisp air in the room holding me
    awake and shivering
Of all this and more I would sing to her and
    perhaps she could understand

How the love for her just this once glimpsed
    roars through my blood
And the screaming need for her rips open my
    ears like bells ringing too loudly
I shrink back into my latest hole like the
    rodent that I am become
Still she fills my leathery spirit with a
    sickening hope that I despise
And as sleep claims me
It is her face I see on the borders of my dreams

October 2, 1900. Amsterdam

I follow her to a graveyard where she lays
    daisies on a cross
On a sullen autumn afternoon that has dried
    and cracked my hands
No birdsong disturbs the stillness here
World's end at the end of the world
Even time seems dead as she kneels and she
    prays
The clouds stopped in the sky
The sun forever hidden only the faintest palest
    stain on grey
The worms still in the earth
The earth still in the sky
The sky still above her softly falling auburn
    tresses
The sky matt on her shining white skin
Her slender fingers pressing together
Squeezing her Jesus out with sheer force
An entreaty to a god so faraway and distant in
    his heaven
A cruel and jealous god who has surely
    created me

I who am concealed in this afternoon
Licking my lips and wringing my hands
So cold and ugly even in here where I am
And with all my damaged heart and my
    broken love
And with caked blood cloak watching from
    the gloom
No beginner to necropolis or tomb
I hate life
I love death
Why should it be otherwise?
So she prays and I watch and everything stops
Cancelled out by each other these two actions
    produce a nothingness
Trapped in this second forever I could well
    imagine a terrible panic
The stretching out of time causes a vile nausea
    in my entrails and in my mind
In this eternity her god turns towards us at last
He smiles at her tender words
And his eyes penetrate me in my hidden
    miasma
And he is filled with disgust
And he turns away and is gone
I know now my endless days are coming to an
    end
The limitless has been bound by a broken
    slender thread
I will be discovered
Or some impending war will obliterate me
And I will be tortured and burnt and hung
    and shattered
And I will be hounded and hunted until then
I just grin to myself
The girl is still kneeling in prayer
Just to see her brings me some horrible joy
I will watch and wait forever then

Although forever is now foreshortened I'm
    sure

December 25, 1900. Romania

Shot it would seem by a silver bullet
My black life now ebbs away in a congealing
    trickle
Under my clothes I am drenched in it
They finally got me as it always had to be
Everything is laid out you know
All of this had to happen for some reason
Lured into a village where I saw a pretty girl
I followed her into the orchard beyond the
    candlelight
A premonition of the end was there waiting
    for me
The father stepped out from behind a tree with
    a rifle
and blasted
Lying in wait he must have been
Silver bullet worming its way into my old
    rotten heart
Still I will strangle him and throw him into the
    river
And somehow stagger back here
Feeling whatever this life is supposed to be
leave me
So long ago I came into this world
Might as well have been yesterday
All the horses and carts
All the summers and winters
All the Christs on their crosses
The beautiful women and the ugly old ladies

The handsome young men and the useless old
    fools
The castles and the forests and the long silent
    hibernation
Lamplight and crackling fires
And the lovely snow falling
Noel Noel goodwill to all men
The bells will ring at midnight
And by then I will be wherever I'm going
One day they'll find me turned to dust in these
    ruins
In a lovely time when I will not exist
And angels will wander this earth not
    monsters
And finally a peace has come to Europe
And a new morning born to this world
Now I feel oblivion upon me
Gnawing at the knots that keep me here
I will close my eyes
And finally I'll surrender

THE LATE STAGE

Jason Nahrung

Saturday's stagecoach from Geelong was unusually late, even accounting for the recent rain that flooded crossings and made the road muddy up to the fetlock or more in places. Sunday did not bring an appearance, however unlikely on the Sabbath, and Monday's, arriving after sunset in the glow of its lamps, reported no sight of the overdue coach between the southern coastal town and Ballarat. Which gave rise to that other great concern in the minds of many and, immediately, on the lips of one:

"Blasted bushrangers!" Roger Pendhurst's angry howl echoed in the polished halls of his hilltop manor. "Hang every bloody last one of them if they've brought ruin to that coach."

Though it was more common for the outlaws to strike on the rich northern road between Ballarat and Bendigo and further afield, where the hills afforded good lookouts and better hideouts.

Roger, whose wealth had begun with a pastoral lease before increasing exponentially with the Karpathen gold mine at nearby Creswick, screamed for his favoured henchmen. His stepson, who'd brought the confirmation that the Cobb and Co was not just late but apparently lost, rushed to gather them, thoughts of Tuesday luncheon abandoned.

Thompson and Heatherstone appeared presently, dressed little better than miners in cotton and waistcoats compared to their master's suit and cravat.

"I am expecting my nephew on that coach. He is bringing something from my brother that is essential to the expansion of the Karpathen. Worth a pretty penny, boys, not to be interrupted by ne'er-do-wells too lazy to take up the tools of an honest trade."

All hung their heads, awaiting the tirade that traditionally harkened to life on the lease and then on the diggings, wealth gained through toil and boldness. The litany was espoused to any within earshot, at the manor, the club, the races, especially if the brandy had been flowing. You took what you could with both fists and fought to keep hold of it. The gift horse was never to be looked at in the mouth, rather, whipped until it dropped, and be damned anyone who got trampled in the process.

"Get down to the camp and have that useless Sergeant Beckett put together a squad and go find my blasted nephew, with or without the coach. Hear me? I don't care if you have to drag him by his boot heels from the bar at Craig's, you bring him here."

The lackeys mumbled a "yes, boss" and made for the door, hats in hand.

Roger held them up with a shout. "And take this lad with you. 'Bout time my stepson earned his keep with something manly."

Both men grimaced, but not as much as the lad in question. It had rained all weekend, and he had been anticipating making the most of the break in the weather with some light accounting, a perusal of the newspaper his stepfather had finished with and an afternoon tea in the rotunda in the back yard.

"Sir?" the lad said, fighting the quiver in his voice.

"You heard me, Stewart. Pull on some britches and saddle up. No one steals from Roger Pendhurst."

Stewart's mother spoke up then, an overlooked shape in her black gown seated in the shadowed corner by the fireplace, her cross-stitch now suspended in her lap.

"Stewart's chest is hardly up for such an excursion, Roger."

"Tosh, Annabelle. It's just a horse ride, with Thompson and Heatherstone here to look after him. Plus a squad of our finest troopers led by our inimitable sergeant."

Stewart looked hopefully to his mother, her face a pale blur emanating concern. She had been especially mindful of his health since her husband's death in a cave-in. Roger, his partner in the mine, had barely escaped with his own life, a circumstance that Stewart often had cause to regret, for all that the man had taken in his mother and him. A frail woman to the eye, as though winnowed by sorrow if not the wind and cold of the country of her parents' birth, but strong enough to give Roger a memorable black eye and split lip in a post-nuptial tiff about a husband's rights. An accord had been struck that gave both widow and son some relief, even if the whispers of Roger's infidelities made socialising a tad fraught.

To her credit, Annabelle knew when to swing her punches and when to hold them.

"The leaves have barely begun to turn; the fresh air may reward him," Pendhurst said with a huff. "Rug up, Stewart, and stick close to Thompson and Heatherstone here. They will look after you. On their lives."

The men muttered their assurances, but their looks spoke of crossed fingers. Neither man was much of a friend to Stewart, and he did his utmost to avoid them. With his stepfather, they were the only witnesses to his father's demise, murmuring about cracking timbers and falling earth, and how there had been time to pull only Pendhurst from the collapse.

"Come along then, young Stewart," said Thompson. "Best be about it while we still have the most of the day. Meet us in the stables once you've got your riding clobber on."

"None of that fancy rubbish, mind," Heatherstone added. "We're for the road, not a Sunday promenade around the lake to giddy-ap the fillies."

Thompson chortled, spittle flecking his lips and beard. He whispered, well under the hearing of mother and stepfather, "I doubt too many fillies have been troubled by our young steed."

Stewart, blushing, exited by the side door with a mumbled farewell to his mother, a scant nod to Roger. Riding britches and boots it would be, along with scarf, coat, and a side trip to the drawing room to fill a flask of whisky. To ease the tightness in his chest and his jangled nerves. He suspected both would be tested on this blighted excursion.

As it turned out, the sergeant had no interest in sending a full squad of troopers on a fool's errand to dig out a coach stuck up to its axles in a creek crossing, and so Stewart found himself in the company of just two, the pair in dishevelled uniforms with stained shirts and a reek of rum and tobacco that may have influenced the sergeant's choice of personnel. The flinty looks they gave made Stewart stupidly grateful of the presence of the solidly built Thompson and Heatherstone, who, while not giving a toss for his wellbeing in general did have an appreciation of their boss's wrath. Still, he could not dispel the notion of winding up in a ditch with the troopers squabbling over possession of his riding coat, fob and boots, and so kept his mouth shut and eyes down as the five followed the rutted Geelong road in search of the overdue stagecoach.

"Can't imagine the widow's happy to have the precious heir sleeping rough," said Heatherstone, a foot hitched nonchalantly across the front of the saddle while he rolled yet another noxious cigarette.

Stewart braced for the whiff of coarse tobacco, his lungs already thick with the miasma of horse, mud and body odour brought to the simmer by afternoon sunshine undoctored by cloud or autumn breeze.

"Youngster has to learn the business someday," Thompson said, all four otherwise apparently oblivious to said youngster's presence on a tame piebald chosen for him by his mother. Little better than a carthorse, his stepfather had adjudged, but Stewart felt he and his steed were well suited, its quiet disposition welcome compared to the seething ribaldry of his present company, none of them able to tame a beard or keep a shirt stain-free and well stitched, it seemed. Guns and knives impressed on him a certain modesty in his observations; he found the trail most interesting and kept his eyes upon it, while his ears stayed pricked for any mayhem from his companions. But so far, just japes about his reserved mother and his spineless self.

"Maybe when we find the coach and Mr Pendhurst's treasure, we can reward the youngster with a roll at Nell's." Heatherstone leered at Stewart, the man's lips glistening from within their border of curly black hairs in a way that both horrified and fascinated, the effect diminished when the stained palings of his ragged teeth were exposed.

Stewart stared once more at the ground in front of his nag, cheeks flushed. Mother and the reverend at Christ Church were both very clear about the wages of sin; passing through the cesspit of Esmond Street on the way out of town had been enough to reinforce the lesson, men clearly at the bottom of desperation's pit dragging women and girls down with them, or vice versa.

He suspected he knew the nature of the treasure borne by the nephew, Thomas. He had heard his stepfather working out loud on a letter some months before, extolling the virtues of the mine and the need for capital to increase its stampers and pumps to pillage the river of gold locked in the quartz hundreds of feet below. Want of equipment was the only barrier to his team of well-drilled Cornishmen unlocking the vast bounty. The anticipated promissory note was a secret knowledge that Stewart kept to himself, a small leg up over his companions who were not so well versed in their master's business as they might think. A kernel of comfort on an otherwise bleak outing.

They rode on, afternoon heat stealing conversation but for occasional cussing at the flies that buzzed around them. The cloying smell of drying mud rose from the rutted road; sweat slicked Stewart's back and thighs and hat band; his legs protested the protracted time in the saddle. This was no mere doddle down to the lake for a Sunday picnic; the piebald plodded on with an air of resignation.

It was McRae, the portlier of the pair of troopers, who spotted the first sign of mishap. They had passed the most recent changing station a few miles back, a welcome opportunity to wash grime from faces, refill canteens and rest the horses. The grooms reported that Saturday's coach had not arrived for a fresh team, and enquiries of the Monday coach as to the absence of its predecessor had drawn a blank. Whether the coach had reached the next station down the road the searchers would need to ask on arrival, but as it was, they were spared that 15 miles or so.

"Thompson," McRae said, leaning low to point. "Would you

look at this, then."

A shattered coach lamp, sheared from its place aside the cab, lay at the base of a gum tree that stood at the fork of a scant trail, the impact marked by a clear scar in the smooth grey bark. The scent of kerosene still wafted, ghostlike, from the ruin.

"And here." Trooper Davis indicated a set of wheel marks still puddled with stale water, veering down the side track, the more recent coaches having left a clear trail across the earlier passage.

"Why on Earth…" Thompson said, surveying the scrub. The track was barely discernible, masked by shrubs and regrowth and lined tightly by trees as it wound its way out of sight up a thickly forested slope.

A creek gurgled nearby and a crow gave a rusty cry, but the air was still and nothing stirred, just the swish of tail and mane and clop of hoof as the horses shifted listlessly on the spot.

"A strange detour," Heatherstone said, spitting tobacco before he took another draw.

Davis unholstered his rifle, and Stewart would've sworn he saw the man's nose twitch, rodent-like, as though seeking to penetrate his own reek for the tell-tale scent of a nearby threat.

"Lost in the dark?" Stewart wondered out loud.

Thompson snorted. "The whips know this road better than the back of their hand, boy. No way to mistake this path for the main road. Anyone know where it leads?"

None did. Possibly to a miner's camp from the headier days of the rush, but more likely a sheep paddock or perhaps a homestead, but none could name a claim or holding nearby.

"Nothing for it then," said Thompson as he took hold of his rifle, the others following suit. "Look sharp. If the coach has been waylaid, the bandits may still be around."

Stewart, without rifle or pistol or even a blade other than his pocket knife, felt bereft.

"In the middle," Thompson ordered him, then led the way, with a trooper before and after Stewart and Heatherstone bringing up the rear. At least the man's noisome cigarette was behind, Stewart not having to breathe in the fumes, reminiscent of the smoke from a train billowing across the carriages.

It was a short time after that they found presumably the driver, whip near at hand, likely knocked from his perch by a low overhanging branch, and the passenger who would've sat beside him on the coveted box seat. Both quite dead.

"Hope he didn't pay extra for the privilege." Thompson dismounted and rolled the passenger onto his back in the bracken beside the track. Late afternoon sun filtering through the gums striped the corpse with shadow, but the bruising around the face and neck was unmissable. "Broken neck, most like. Quick, at least."

Davis nodded, tugged at the open neck of his coat as though against a sudden chill, then held his rifle at the ready across the saddle. He stank of rum, as though his day's intake was seeping out through his pores.

"Is it Pendhurst's nephew?"

Thompson shrugged. "Does he look like a Thomas?"

He rifled the man's jacket, retrieved a wallet and undid its strap to open it. He squinted hard at a piece of paper he took from inside. "Knock. Strange name. German, by the look." He withdrew another paper, squinted close, mumbled: "A deed? In Ballarat. Not in his name." Then said, louder: "Also not Thomas." He returned the papers and slipped the wallet into his saddlebag.

"The team kept going," Davis said. "Something must've got into them, to keep going on such a rough track without a driver."

"The coachers are bred for the part, it's true," Heatherstone said, making the most of his chance to roll another cigarette, "but a horse is still a horse." He licked the paper, the wet glisten of his tongue reminding Stewart of a lizard or snake. "Doesn't take much to spook 'em."

A kookaburra cackled and Stewart flinched, feeling the cold penetrate suddenly where he sat in the shade, the sun barely glinting through the glossy leaves as it sank low towards the crown of the hill.

Sweet wattle scent rose around them as they plodded on, the horses nose to tail as though seeking comfort, and Stewart was reminded of his father's funeral procession, the sprigs of gold and green on the coffin, the lilies, his mother's tears, the empty words of the priest and the flash of anger at the sight of Pendhurst's arm around his mother's black-clad shoulders.

Yet, here they were, at Pendhurst's bidding, the cold coming down with the night, his lungs already feeling the icy thickness settling within. He tightened his scarf, afraid to reach for his flask lest the four mouths around him demand a share. They had their own, were even now reaching for them, Davis in front tilting his at a great angle.

Stewart would have made for home but knew quite well he would not even reach the Cobb and Co station before the dark caught him, not to mention the wrath of Thompson and his stepfather once the fact of his cowardice had emerged. He would not put his mother through another harangue about the unfitness of the son that Pendhurst had inherited along with the widow's share of the mine. No, he would have to see it through and hope to avoid the threat of Esmond Street and whatever other bullyboy ideas his father's lackeys dreamed up between now and then. Return the nephew and the promissory note or whatever form the capital came in, and that would mollify Pendhurst for some time, at least until the next opportunity for disparagement arose.

"There she be," Thompson said, even as Davis pointed with his empty flask.

The coach was on its side, having crashed through wattle and saplings down a slope at a sharp turn. It may have rolled before coming to rest against trees, the shell cracked and misshapen, axles bare and wheels mangled. The coachers were dead in their traces, all four, a bloody tangle of limbs and harness and foliage, with mailbags and luggage strewn across the flattened area between road and wreck. Letters lay like breadcrumbs; a clothesline's worth of garments were draped on bushes and logs as though in the aftermath of a willy-willy. Like a battlefield, Stewart thought. He half expected to see spectral people slide into those awkwardly shaped shirts and petticoats and wander the field, looking for their missing pieces. He followed the carnage to the ruin of the stagecoach, thinking that was the place where the spectres would reside. The passengers, mashed together like ingredients in a stew pot.

He swigged whisky, welcoming the warmth in throat and gut, and none of the four with him noticed. None reached out a hand.

"My God," Davis said, raised his rifle, fired. "Put it down, you devil!"

Stewart, jolted by the sudden shot, had just enough time to see the tawny shape at the end of the barrel's direction. Crows, cockatoos erupted from the trees in protest, filling the air with screeches, banshees awoken from their slumber.

What might have been a shirt and trousers lying near the ruptured rear of the coach jerked as the wild dog released its grip and fled.

"Did you see?" Davis said, fumbling another round from his bandolier into the breech as he scanned the bushes. "It was eating him!"

"I'm sure it wasn't the first to take a morsel," Thompson said, easing back in his saddle, lowering his rifle. "Been here a couple days."

"Aye, bastard dog." McRae fired into the curtain of bushes. His horse jittered, and, as the shot rolled away, a howl arose, and then another.

"Mock away, you bastards," McRae said, standing in his stirrups as though the extra inches would reveal the pack.

Stewart swigged again, then put the flask away, his nape still prickling from the dingo chorus, the sensation travelling all the way to his balls. *Mockery?* Threat, more like, a promise to return to finish the meal. The piebald stamped but he held it. The horse seemed as keen to leave as he was but likely also lacked the courage to face the gathering night alone.

"We need to check." Thompson swung himself down. "Here, boy, hold the reins."

Stewart held them, then for Heatherstone and Davis, while McRae retained his vantage in the saddle, staring widely, the rifle, reloaded, held high.

"How many passengers were there?" Heatherstone asked, but no one had bothered to ask as to the manifest. A nephew and some prized object was all they knew.

"Check him," Thompson told Davis, who advanced cautiously

as though on a bushranger's camp and not a corpse. Perhaps he expected the dog to return, maybe with friends, and try for fresh meat.

He bent to one knee and patted down the body. "Nothing," he reported. "Must've crawled this far. He's fair beaten up. Tore up, too. I think the crows have had his eyes."

Thompson and Heatherstone peered through cracks in the coach. Heatherstone called a loud, "Hello."

"I think they'd know we were here," Thompson said, nasty like. He'd flinched at Heatherstone's sudden announcement so close to his ear and clearly didn't like it.

He stared at Stewart over his shoulder, as though daring him to grin. As though Stewart hadn't also startled, hadn't almost let go the reins of all three. And wouldn't that have been a pretty to-do? He clenched the leather harder.

Thompson scrambled up the belly of the coach to stand on the side, where the door stood closed. He pulled at it but it didn't budge, though the coach creaked.

"Jammed," he said. "Help me, Heatherstone."

The man clambered up, clumsy, but made the top and knelt and heaved in time with Thompson. The door came open with a crack of timber and Thompson fell back, two steps, caught himself, did not fall.

Another glance at Stewart, maybe reproach, maybe just checking he was still there with the horses.

"Oi, where's Davis?" the mounted McRae asked.

"What?" Thompson asked.

"He was there with the stiff. Now he ain't."

Heatherstone and Thompson made a show of looking around.

"Gone to water the horse, most probably," Heatherstone said.

"Here," McRae said, dismounting with a huff, then handing yet another set of reins to Stewart.

Rifle to shoulder, he strode methodically towards the corpse.

"Anyone in there?" Heatherstone asked of the carriage.

"For God's sake, Heatherstone, they're dead," Thompson said.

"I don't want to go in there," Heatherstone admitted. "Black as the pit, it is."

Thompson snorted, suspended himself by his arms, slowly lowered himself into the hole.

Stewart imagined him, boots touching down on arms, legs, chests, heads. Imagined them sprawled together in unnatural positions.

He hoped there wasn't a woman, before remembering there was women's clothing in the debris. He didn't like the idea of Thompson looking down at her. He imagined her to be young and pretty. He hoped her skirt was down, her modesty preserved from the likes of him. From the men around her, who had been thrown against her, who she had been made to suffer the touch of. Had been made to touch.

"I'll be buggered if one of these ain't a Chinaman," came Thompson's muffled exclamation. "I'll bet a bob to a pound that ain't the nephew."

"What in the—you gents need come see this." The fear in McRae's voice was unmistakeable.

"What's wrong?" Heatherstone asked, moving slowly, the coach creaking like an old porch.

"Still tied to the baggage rack, but it's broken loose, come apart. A crate."

"A crate? Yeah, scary."

"Nay, nay, it's what's in it. The shape of it. Basic, but a coffin."

"A box in a box? Are you sure it's a coffin?"

"Wider at the top than at the bottom. What would you call it?"

Thompson appeared, head and shoulders, like a digger from a shaft. "Just the one? Pity, because I count customers for a good six here."

"Why would someone ship a coffin?" McRae asked, his voice jittery.

"What's in it, man?" Heatherstone asked, his voice pitched high.

"I'm not opening the blasted thing!"

"Then how do you know it's a coffin and not just some fancy box?"

"Fine, then, but keep a good watch!" McRae approached the

crate as though it were a snake, struck a match and held it close. "Writing, here. Stamped on the wood. German, I think. A name: Knock. Your passenger, Thompson?"

"Just open the blasted thing and let's be about it," Thompson called back.

McRae jabbed at the timbers, finally told Heatherstone again to keep an eye out as he pulled a knife and sliced at the ropes to fully free the box so he could remove the shattered lid and work at the one within.

"I'll be," he said, standing back, hand to forehead under his cap.

"Well?" Heatherstone asked.

"Dirt. Just dirt."

"Well," Thompson said. "I'm glad that mystery's solved. Make a fire, will you? I'll get what I can, see if we can work out who's who." He vanished back into the coach, Heatherstone cussing softly as his perch rocked with the sudden motion.

"I'm gonna look for Davis some more," McRae said.

"Don't go too far," Heatherstone said. "This country will swallow you whole."

"Aye, like them boys at Daylesford."

"Just like 'em," he said, "but maybe no one will find your body."

"Light that fire. It'll guide me back."

The trooper vanished into the brush, calling Davis, and the dark seemed to wrap around Stewart. He tried to track the trooper, but his shape was lost, branches and trees taking on the appearance of figures crouching and creeping in the bushes. He imagined bushrangers there, taking aim, ready to slaughter and pillage.

It was a relief when Heatherstone clambered down, took the reins from Stewart and told him to dismount. Stewart flexed his fingers, his hand cramped from his tight hold on the leathers, the horses skittish.

"I'll tether this lot," Heatherstone said. "Grab up some wood for the fire."

"We're not staying here, are we?" Stewart asked, the words coming out in a wheeze, the fear all but choking him.

"Well, we're not gonna try to ride back to Ballarat in the dark."

"We can make the changing station, though. There's an inn there."

"Not in the dark. We need to find this nephew and whatever it is that has Pendhurst so steamed up. Sure as eggs it ain't a box o' dirt."

Far from the lights and fires of the town, the night came down like a blindfold, and without moonlight, even the well-blazed road to Geelong would be difficult to follow and treacherous under foot. He would have been prepared to try, but not alone. Too easy to lose one's bearings, as Heatherstone had said, and die of thirst or starvation or predation.

Just looking for firewood was no easy task in the gloom. Stewart winced with every crack and rustle of his step, feeling the eyes of the wild dogs and the maybe bushrangers following his every move. The recent rain meant everything was damp, bark peeling away in his fingers.

He had managed to gather an armload of reasonably dry kindling when a shot startled him and he dropped the lot. The report was followed by a screech, as though a galah had been set alight. The noise cut into him like a saw, right to the bone.

Heatherstone was on his arse, two horses bolting off down the track, the other three jerking at their tethers. He settled them, swore at Stewart. "Don't just stand there, you prissy prick—grab the rifle!"

Stewart stumbled across to the tree where Heatherstone's Martini Henry leaned against the trunk.

"There's one in the breech," Heatherstone warned him.

There was nothing to shoot at. Just tree trunks glowing in what was left of the day.

"Thompson!" Heatherstone shouted the man's name a second time, then added, "Get out here now!"

Thompson appeared, head and shoulders again. "What's all the noise?"

He slipped, fell, arms flailing. Screamed. The coach rocked. There came the knocking of things against timber. Then silence.

"Thompson!"

Heatherstone shouted his name three times, but there was no answer.

"Get that blasted fire lit, boy. Quick bloody smart. And give me that bloody rifle before you shoot your dick off."

A figure rose through the doorway of the coach, bald head mounted with elongated, pointed ears, wide eyes aglow with unmistakable malevolence, protruding front teeth sharper than a roasting fork. Brass buttons on its coat, the ghost of a gent or an officer, maybe. It floated free, arms by its side, nothing but air under it as it glided to the ground and moved towards them as though propelled by a zephyr Stewart could not feel. Could not feel anything but an icy dread locked around him. Heatherstone came up beside Stewart, muttering, the rifle clenched to his shoulder.

"Stop right there!"

The figure advanced, silent on the leaf litter and detritus, its arms slowly rising to reveal talons curved and sharp as bale hooks.

Heatherstone fired, the report rocking Stewart, filling his head like an avalanche. If the round found the mark, the figure gave no sign. Heatherstone grabbed for a new bullet, managed to get it into the breech. But then the creature was on him, dragging him to the ground, those misshapen fangs fixing to the man's throat despite the desperate, useless slapping and punching of its victim. The man's body arched as he emitted a final groan, one hand clenched in the wet earth at his side, then collapsed and lay still. The creature eased back on its haunches, its tongue lapping at the dark stains around its mouth, and fixed its black orbs on Stewart.

As dark as the starless night, those eyes, overshadowed by heavy brows, flanked by those pointed ears that made Stewart fear the head would take flight alone and attack his throat. The Martini Henry lay at his feet, but he lacked the ability to kneel, let alone shoot.

The creature's nose twitched above its almost lipless mouth, then it rose in a smooth, soundless motion like a pocket knife unfolding and circled him close enough to touch, a wild dog appraising its helpless prey.

"What is it you want?" Stewart managed to gasp. Clearly, the answer was all around him, yet he asked as though seeking to be told otherwise. For reprieve. God, he was so weak, he could barely hold the crouch he had slumped into, but feared to fall lest the creature be upon him. His hand was at his throat, as though to hide the temptation; through scarf and skin, he could feel the rush of his laboured breath, his blood, and wished them both to subside.

A moment of clarity, like a shaft of moonlight on a stygian night; a straw to grasp at.

"I…I can help you." He forced himself to his feet and lowered his hand, exposing his throat. The creature stood, head at an angle, as though awaiting his offer, or sizing him up. "I know a place. A house. There are people there. People everywhere." He imagined his stepfather, the unravelling of his cravat, a fist thumping uselessly on the floor in the drawing room as the monster mined its fill of the man's rich veins.

The creature advanced, close enough for its coat hem to brush Stewart's boots, for the musty reek of earth and blood to cloud around him. Its eyes bored into him, with intelligence if not understanding.

"I can get you what you need," Stewart said, straightening. He tapped his chest with his thumb. "I can be Knock."

His hand stopped shaking as he held it out, and he smiled as the creature growled its response—"Knock"—and placed its bloody claw in his palm.

The Doorman

Jim Krueger

Good evening to you as well.

Pardon me? You need to speak to me about something extremely important?

Well, my good man, it is a relief to know that I have nothing to fear or that you won't tell anyone my secret, but really, you have me at quite a disadvantage. I simply do not know what you are suggesting.

A what? You think I'm a what?

Are you mad?

You…you followed me on your nights off? You saw what? From a distance? You… Oh, I see. You have pictures.

I suppose that simply confessing I am some sort of serial killer and not a vampire at all is not really going to solve my problem, is it?

Let me begin by saying that you are in no position to negotiate anything.

Look at me.

Look closely.

Closer. In my eyes.

Now hand me your phone.

Thank you. Wait. Let me turn this around. Look at the screen. Unlock it.

There.

Now let me see these pictures of yours. Ah, well, the lighting is not what it could be and I'm afraid the composition is a bit off. Not a great loss.

There. All gone. Here is your phone.

Ah, you are a writer. I should have guessed as much. I remember the notebooks you once scratched your thoughts into. I remember how you looked, the disappointment, when you tore certain pages out. That was before you purchased your smart phone and it became the depository, I assume, of your thoughts and inspirations. When deleting became your preference to tearing and ripping. Though, you now see, if you did not before, how easy it is to have the invaluable lost in a moment because of this device.

I suppose I should also not be surprised that you came to the conclusions you did, even before you began to follow me. You have been a doorman here, at the Hotel Holloway, for a great many years. Almost as many as I have been a resident here. You see how guests come and go. I imagine, for someone whose sole focus is to open doors and guard the gates, so to speak, that certain cures for personal boredom would be sought out and would lead to the amplification of your observations. Maybe your paranoia as well. But, as this evening is the one it is, I suppose trying to talk you out of your summations would be ridiculous. And quite actually, when I am honest with myself, there is a freedom in being found out.

I am certain my goings and returnings, only in the nighttime hours, betrayed me, at the very least, to your imaginings and suspicions. Positioned as you are in this life of yours, I understand your hunger to allow your mind to wander through possibilities. Through the twilights and dawning of what might be. As well as the streets denied you most evenings. Streets you can only visit on those rare nights you are not working the so-called graveyard shift.

How do I choose my victims? At random most nights, though the healthier the individual, the less inebriated, is advantageous. But that has more to with taste and satisfaction than sport. More to do with the fat content of the blood. Or any viruses that might alter how quickly I will need to feed again.

Is it comforting to know that I do not choose my victims based on gender, ethnicity, orientation, or even age? For someone you say sleeps all day long, I am rather "woke."

Let me begin by saying you, too, have nothing to fear. You need to calm yourself. Even as it is right now, your heart rate is like a beacon. A siren call. But where I have not aged, not a day, you have. And not well. If you don't calm yourself, it will be you in fatal threat, and not because I will feed on you. But because your own body will. You are not well. I'm afraid you will be lost. And this is something I do not wish.

Actually, I think you are quite lost already. Again, I am not here to rip out your throat or to damn you to the likes of a lightless eternity.

Why am I telling you my story, now that there are no pictures? No evidence? Why did I say you were lost? Simply because you witnessed a number of murders. You took pictures. You could have gone to the authorities. Instead, you confronted me, and then tried to blackmail me in exchange for the story. Perhaps it is not fame that you desire, perhaps it is only significance. Regardless, you were prepared to let me continue in my way in exchange for a story. You would aid and abet me.

Simply put, you are not a good man. I am not saying you are a bad one, merely a weak one.

Please, I see that I have offended you. I am not a good man either. And I have no desire to be one.

Because of this, I will indeed give you your story.

It is not necessary that you swear to keep my secrets on your mother's grave or on anyone's graves for that matter. Graves are hardly a concern of mine as it is. It is the living, of course, which have been my source of focus for so many years.

So, yes, I am a vampire. Or, if you will, one of the Nosferatu. The people of endless night. A moonwalker. There have been many names for my kind. But again, there is no reason to fear.

Incidentally, the classic film, *Nosferatu*, was only titled that because rights to Bram Stoker's book could not be secured.

As for me, I have been *this* for a great many years, and I merely wish to tell you of the many doors I have walked through. Incidentally, there was *always* a doorman of sorts as I walked through these doors. Always a witness of the walking through, though some did not live long enough to even recognize the moment or what they were witnessing. And that is why you must be here this very night. Even as it evaporates into day.

I want to be known and there is much to confess.

So, my priest, let me begin. I do apologize for the strictness of my language, but I want to be cautious with how I speak in this moment, and want to make certain, as I talk of times past and times present, that I do not speak with the slang of the moment.

Let me begin by speaking about doors. To walk through one is to be changed. And I have been changed a great many times.

We are each of us born in blood. It needs to be wiped away and washed and, in all cases, cut from us from those first moments of life.

In fact, for the months leading up to our births, we all swim in blood and water on the other side of flesh.

The first door I ever walked through was, of course, birth. A violent wailing entrance into the day. From the dark I came, like we all do.

Is it any wonder then, for one such as I, that becoming a vampire felt like a returning to those first moments of consciousness? The hunger to be held in blood was still with me, like a returning to something forgotten? That is what it means to be a vampire. To drink blood is to once again know the joy of being cradled in the blood and flesh and darkness of another.

This is not as romantic as the words suggest. It is far more primal and removed from the words of authors who can only guess what it means to be once again so connected with the very source of life. And to know that it sees you. Recognizes you. Nurtures you. Perhaps if your kind knew what it was like to be my kind, the response would not have been to hunt us down and try to kill us. There should be *wonder. Appreciation.* Even if you are our prey.

When I was mortal, in those early days of your country's birth, I fought for your country's freedom. I walked with every other man and woman through the door that was the forging of your nation. I cheered like so many others at the doors being closed on England, when, with tail in hand, and a tailwind behind her, she mounted ships and returned to the little island from which she came.

But the soon-to-be foreigners of Europe left me with their gift. With this curse. Perhaps I spoke out about them too loudly. Or I drank too much and stumbled upon them, and not they on me. Or perhaps my victories on the battlefield of Lexington were a little too bloodthirsty, and they enjoyed the irony of showing me what "bloodthirsty" really was.

I will never know.

Incidentally, your George Washington knew of the vampires that came to your shores to oppose your revolution. He kept quiet and made certain word did not get out regarding their existence. Perhaps he knew how superstitious your people were. Or perhaps he thought that the sheer magnitude of what my kind would mean to yours would indeed be an obstacle to your countrymen's courage. I even sometimes wonder if those wooden teeth of his were a way to dispatch those, of my kind, who let their teeth show a little too brightly in those days long ago. I never knew for certain but suspected his very personal way to strike at the English was to bite back.

Before I was what I am now, I was not a good man either. And the many years since have not made me any better. I like to drink. This has always been the case. It is just the drink that changed.

It's very possible that the reason the Europeans bit me was to curse this new world. To allow a new red plague to spread through the Americas the way it once had through Europe. Perhaps I was to be a vehicle of destruction in the same way.

Before the revolutionary war, I and many of those I fought beside would pass poisoned blankets to the indigenous people of this nation. Perhaps becoming a poison myself is a well-deserved fate.

But I did not like the idea of making more like me. I knew power. Real power. So why would I share that with those that I wanted to feed upon? More of my kind merely meant less blood for me. And this was indeed America. Spreading the wealth has never been at the core of our nation's development and growth.

Let me also mention that blood is not all I thirsted for with this new "night life" that was bequeathed me. There was experience. Experiences. I had become a sort of immortal. And death, while once a fear, no longer was. Now it was only present around me. It was coming to meet everyone else. Not me. In fact, for those who sustained me, I merely provided an early introduction.

In the 1790s, during the rarely talked about Whiskey Rebellion, I realized that I was wrong to think that I was a bad man compared to my other countrymen. I was merely a vote. One that weighed little compared to the atrocities to come. During this rebellion, many refused to pay a tax for their whiskey to fund your new government, and though it would be years and years before your famed civil war, the tension between your federal government and the wants of its divergent regions, began to show its hand. Whether it was taxes, or state rights, or land, or wealth, or even the various races of people that found themselves often coerced to be here, there was a fight brewing. A contradiction of thirsts. A war between the hunger of individuals and a table set to feed all. It was a fight, in some cases, between the truly gifted and exceptional, and the swell of the mediocre. Am I being unfair? Or perhaps you think all should become like me? And what would we feed on then?

There is a lie at the heart of this country. It is the tension between the want for all to be equal and the truth that we are not. We never were. Some are beautiful, some are not. Some are strong, many are weak. Few are wise, but they fight to protect the rights of the foolish. Perhaps lies are more important to ensure a fragile peace than truth is. I have seen people ignore the truth over and over again. For the sake of a lie. A happy ending. A hope that is too good to be true.

I fought on both sides during your Civil War. When it appeared like I was dealt a fatal blow by the Northern Army, I waited until the smoke was too thick to gaze through, and I took the uniform of the so-called enemy and fought on their behalf, until again, that would lead to an apparent death. Blood was in ample supply. I fed well on both sides. And I found myself very much alive on that battlefield, walking through the revolving door of the North and South. I found myself singing and dancing in the mighty plantations, drinking mint juleps with a people that did not understand that the way they had always lived was now considered morally wrong. Days later,

I would condemn them for their selfishness and ignorance while lifting beer with my fellow Bostonians.

You see, viewpoints and opinions and convictions are doors as well. But for most, they are walked through slowly, over years, beginning in the circumstances of birth and family through the experiences they have and the tiny part of the world they are introduced to. But in those days when your country was divided—not that it is not today—I walked both ways. I eventually stopped caring for the better or more logical argument. Or who said what with greater passion or enunciation. And merely enjoyed being in both worlds and allowing myself to feed upon the melting pot of voices. It was a stew. Perhaps that is all it ever was.

Your first World War was interesting because now the war left your contradictory country and I found myself in Europe. Another door. I was there in the trenches, and when one of our men was killed, I made certain that their blood was not spilled in vain. I, of course, fed on the enemy as well.

I had never been to Europe before. One night, when the smoke was thick and the moans of the men on both sides of the trenches had reached a crescendo of sorts, I stole into the night. It had dawned on me—not that dawn is anything more than an obscure abstraction at this point in my life—that it might be good to check in on those who had given me this gift. I had over the years made certain that I collected information on those that had done this to me. Did I desire revenge? I do not believe so. As I said before, issues of justice and vengeance were not passions or character traits important to me anymore. Perhaps it was just conversation that I wanted. A chance to face them and let them see that I had not become the curse on my country that they intended. Or maybe, as the days behind me seemed nothing like the days before, I wanted a glimpse at my future. It was not to see them as much as it was to see me. What I would become.

Unlike the war for independence, the vampire that took my life and then gave me another, did not fight in World War One. He was still in England. Getting to London was not a problem for me. But I need to admit I was surprised that he did not go to where the blood was flowing. That he did not come to the killing fields for the amusement of not having to hide in the shadows when taking life after life.

Had he perished somehow? My death had not been a concept I had even considered for a long time. The fear of it was so distant, I could no longer recall its gravity on my life.

I remember being struck by another door that perhaps awaited me, one that would have been too terrible to walk through. What if he was somehow paralyzed in some way? What if some harm had crippled him? The idea of being a prisoner of my own body for all of eternity was a maddening and sobering irritation.

When I found him, he was sitting in a great chair in what I assume had been his home, a monster of a castle or manor of some sort. His dwellings were unkempt. Tapestries that looked as dusty as the giant area's rugs below them hung from the walls like shrouds covering the bones of the old architecture, and also covering the great windows, of course. Webs filled the arches of doorways that hadn't been walked through in years. And there was a smell. A rotted smell. I'm not certain if it was the summation of those that had died there, had been fed upon there, or if, instead, it was the stench of my host and benefactor, Lord Winsick himself. Lord Winsick did not pretend not to recognize me. But he also did not seem to show any surprise that I was there.

I wanted him to see me. I wanted him to realize that he had not loosed a plague upon my country. The truth is that there was nothing I did or said that seemed to provoke him in the slightest. He spoke little. My questions, all of them, went unanswered, save one.

I asked him why I should not kill him right there. Some say a vampire cannot kill another vampire, which is very untrue. Every animal, alive, dead, or undead, is capable of terrible violence toward its own kind. Our world, our countries, nature itself, is proof enough of this.

In answer to my question, he merely said it was because I was not a merciful man. That he had seen that in me those many years before. I asked him what he meant by that. He said nothing. I stood before him for maybe another hour, trying to get him to speak. But it was akin to speaking to the walls. Nothing.

I returned to the trenches. I returned to the fighting and the blood and drank my fill.

The America that greeted me upon my return was very different than the one I had left. One war had ended only to give rise to another one, a new kind of civil war. Between the elite and those that had even less than they had before. This was your Great Depression. Most lived in such terrible poverty and shame, little understanding what had happened. Others gambled and made their sad, bitter love in the jazz dens, dancing their way through their losses, still seeking ways to get from those who no longer even had anything left to be gotten.

Even the blood of the poor lacked the taste it once did. The blood did not flow like it had before. I am not speaking about the battlefield. I am speaking of the veins. Sadness can travel in veins in the same way a virus does. It actually damages the body quicker, perhaps because it opens a door for viruses as well.

Also, my intended meals did not run from me as they did before. Their heartbeats did not quicken those few moments when they recognized that their lives were coming to an end. Some knew the lore of my kind, and those that did, all of them, begged me not to change them because they did not want to have to think of more days like the ones they were living.

So, I fed upon the rich. I struck at them in their hardly-a-secret Gatsbian parties just out of reach of the hungry. Do not think for a moment that this was somehow an act of conscience. Simply put, the rich simply tasted better. Their blood satisfied me for longer periods of time.

This great depression led to the outlawing of alcohol and drinking, which hardly affected me since there was no actual law against drinking blood. Though I am certain that if your lawmakers knew of my existence, they certainly would have written such litigation.

Why does the inspiration for artistic endeavor and human invention increase in the midst of suffering? I have a theory. I have come to believe that art is the true prayer of your people. It is a form of worship, almost. An ordering and beautifying of chaos and sadness to support the imagined hope that things will become better. And this moment has a lesson for them that will justify their pain.

In the midst of all of the depression, your film industry made all things possible for me. Another door. This one to a flickering light that at least allowed me to see a sunrise again. I became quite the cinema fan. And not just of the genre called "horror". Though I did dabble in some acting and even starred in something of an autobiography.

Fortunately, your Second World War led to the reinvigoration of your people. There were jobs, and therefore wealth. And nothing tastes quite so good as the blood that is pumped through a body filled with patriotic and righteous conviction.

I found myself in Europe again. There was so much blood. So much nationalistic fervor on all sides of the equation. If it were possible for someone like me to gain weight, I certainly would have. But please do not think the so-called "death camps" were a lure of any kind. I had already drunk my fill of sadness. There were so many other places to feed.

Before returning to America, I did visit my old benefactor once again, now hoping that perhaps time had somehow reminded him how to speak. There was little left of the manor, largely due to neglect. There was also what I assumed to have been a struggle of some sort. The tapestry that had hung in the giant window had been torn down. And the chair that once housed the mute vampire that gave birth to me was no longer present. Perhaps he had been caught unawares by one of those so-called vampire slayers. I assumed at the time, though, that he had moved on, to another place, perhaps one with a better selection of blood. But I was quite wrong.

This was not a haunted house. But it did haunt me on my way back to America on the ocean liner, the Queen Mary. There were a number of soldiers, broken and still bleeding from the war, that made such a journey for me possible. There were many who knew they would never reach America. In many cases, I ended their suffering. But please do not consider this mercy. I am not merciful, remember this as you write. When I killed them it was more of a utilitarian choice. They were receiving blood transfusions as it was, and it all struck me as a terrible *waste.*

The America I once again returned to was now a place of such overwhelming hope and promise. People talked about the American dream of owning a home. Of having a family. They spoke of the great defeat of the monster, Hitler, and of their own virtue in a way that made me feed far more often than I needed to. Rock and roll replaced the elitist rhythms of the jazz and secret rendezvous of the Great Depression. One and all feasted on this era. The American Dream was never so delicious.

This, of course, was why it could not and would not last. Dreams change. Even the collective ones. The hope that made the blood of this era so exquisite began to tarnish upon its golden promises. New wars began without patriotic convictions. Those wounded in these wars, upon returning home, were not given the ticker-tape welcome that met those who fought in World War II. Mistrust began to spread, often the result of your elected officials. This led Americans to suspect the worst in each other where once they had hoped for the best. No one was aware of the diseases that were beginning to spread through a movement known as free love. "Free" had become the desire where "freedom" had held on for so long. Even the staunchest protectors and fighters for the concept of freedom were either imprisoned or murdered.

Perhaps the fear that spread across the country was not merely because of this, but was aided and amplified by the invention of the television.

The movies I loved I could now watch in the privacy of my room.

But so too could I view the assassinations, the diseases, the crimes, the mounting distrust. Television was a window, or a doorway, into all that was wrong with this world.

There were eras of greed late in the last century that made the taste of this country more pleasant. But those eras merely manifested into perhaps the worst of your social diseases.

Comparison.

Keeping up with the Joneses. Needing to have what someone else had. Perhaps even needing to have more. In this mentality, your people, as they are no longer mine, chose inequality over potential possibilities and equalities.

I know what you are thinking. I sound like an old man.

I wonder sometimes if Lord Winsick really did move on to redder pastures as I once surmised.

Perhaps this is not actually, as I said, immortality. Maybe it only pretends to be when it is actually the long death. A perpetual and slow bleed out from the wounds that made me what I am. There is no true healing, only a perpetual filling of a wound, like those on the Queen Mary that I fed upon, that will never fully heal.

What if, no matter how much blood I take, no matter how many times I try to fill this dripping bucket of mine, it still leaks? And has been leaking for so long?

I fear that I now understand the final fate of Lord Winsick. It wasn't greener or redder pastures. He did not move on. He was not attacked in his home by some slayer who knew how to expose him and pulled down the tapestry that kept the sun from him. He merely pulled it down himself. And he let the sun have its way with him.

He died of boredom. Well, he killed himself out of boredom.

I am an immortal. My body is young. I did not expect old age in any way, but I feel old. My thoughts are old. As are my words.

Time and history, I suppose, catches up to all of us.

Perhaps I have walked through too many doors.

But there is one last door.

One last door to walk through.

This one.

There will be a bit of a mess, I'm afraid. Mostly dust. But I know that sweeping the front entrance is part of your job.

I hope you have time to finish your book. Thank you for listening to an old man rant.

I have grown weary of saying "Good evening."

It is time once again to say… "Good Morning."

V IS FOR VERMIN

Steve Rasnic Tem

She vividly recalled what it was like as a young child before the accident: wandering through the woods behind their house, prying up rotting logs to see the teeming insects, the sad remains, the vermin feasting on both the living and the dead, a harsher version of the vivarium her class managed at school. Her parents worried over her apparent need to look under everything.

Then, after weeks lying in her hospital bed, feeling vulnerable and afraid of all those parasitic creatures waiting in the dark for her and everyone she loved.

Delia was on her belly wriggling through the crawlspace when she heard the commotion on the front porch. A chorus of vacuous laughter echoed through the dark cavity and the drubbings, vaguely suggestive of vandalism, sent drifts of dust raining across her head and back.

She saw no point in rushing upstairs to investigate because she had no means of rushing. She was too far into this debris-filled space, her bad leg throbbing from its awkward positioning, and the lack of traction against loose dirt, broken brick, and rat-gnawed fragments of wood made it difficult to turn around.

She could see little with her headlamp, but what she could view of the architecture exposed above the rubble—masonry arches and keystones, stone columns with antique candle sconces—looked well out of place beneath a thirties-era American bungalow. This hadn't always been a crawlspace.

The dust mask slipped off her nose and the headlamp kept blinking on and off. Every time she turned her head, some hard-to-fathom shape revealed itself, and then her surroundings turned pitch black again. Worse, she could hear the rats scratching about their fetid nests beyond the reach of the beam. Their acrid stench overpowering, a sour perfume of musky ammonia, not just down here, but throughout the house.

All this would be cleared, the upstairs stripped of damage, and she would experience the fullness of her impulsive purchase, but for now it appeared to be a half million dollars' worth of ruin.

By the time Delia got upstairs the vandals were gone. They'd graffitied a large white V across her beautiful antique door. She didn't understand the hate. Was it about her Jewishness, or the fact she was a lesbian? But how could anyone in her new neighborhood know these things? She shouted, "Vicious little freaks!" to any culprits near enough to hear. It was pitiful vengeance.

She hobbled down the steps, her leg almost making her fall, and limped to the street. She saw some teenagers with backpacks headed toward the library, talking and laughing. One glanced back and smiled. She was suspicious but couldn't prove anything.

"Did they tag you? They got my abuela's house yesterday. Kids like that, they have no respect." Delia turned. A short, dark-skinned woman with a dazzling smile shook her hand. "I'm Martina. You posted a flyer at the grocer's. Do you still need a worker?"

"It's dusty, hard labor."

"I'm fine with that. Show me."

Twenty minutes later they climbed out of that vile tomb she'd paid so much money for and peeled off their masks. Martina was strong and friendly, and she had some clever ideas to make the work go faster, including hiring a couple of her cousins who wouldn't charge much. Delia knew they would work well together. She made them some robust black tea.

"Did you know the Orloks?" Martina asked. "They were the family who lived here before. A woman and a really old man, her grandfather maybe. I sold them Girl Scout Cookies when I was a kid. My grandmother took me to every house in the neighborhood. She said it wasn't safe to go by myself."

"No. I bought the house through their agent. It was a bargain in this neighborhood, but you can see why. I figured I could restore it with some help. I've hired a company to exterminate the rats and the roaches and whatever else is living here. But they won't step inside until I've cleared the debris and made the structure safer. The agent said the house has been vacant a few years. Was it nice before?"

"I remember it being dark inside. The one time I was here, I remember this moldy odor when the woman opened the door. She invited us inside, but my abuela, she said no, we had to hurry. I was glad. The woman kept shouting things to someone in the back of the house. Grandmother said the language was Romanian. It sounded an awful lot like Italian to me.

"I could see the old man back there, moving in and out of the shadows. He had this bald, swollen head. He glanced at me once—I was an imaginative child, so you'll have to forgive me—but it looked like the face of a giant rat. Those deep-set eyes, and two long teeth in front."

"Your grandmother didn't talk about them?"

"Those weren't good times for people who are different. I guess no times are. My grandmother was sympathetic to immigrants. She knew what it was like. Other people in the neighborhood weren't so kind. They thought foreigners carried diseases from their native countries. People said that about Mexicans, too."

"And Jews. The Nazis said we were like lice and caused typhus."

"And gays. Parents won't let their kids play with you. They think it's catching." They exchanged shy smiles.

Delia put down her tea. "I have plenty of breathing masks. And gloves." She glanced down at the gloved hand holding the cup. She wore gloves so often in this house she forgot she had it on. "You're sure you want to do this? Maybe I should have hired a crew with hazmat suits. But I don't have much money left—"

"It's okay. My cousins and I will be careful. You can stay up here and clean and organize. Your leg—I don't mean to insult you—is that permanent? You shouldn't be messing around in that basement."

Delia bristled. There was an awkward silence. "A car ran over me when I was young. They fixed it the best they could. It was okay for a long time, but now, not so much. You're right, I shouldn't be down there. But now that I know you a little, I don't think I need to be. But be careful, I'd feel terrible—"

"Our Lady will protect me." Martina pulled an Our Lady of Guadalupe medal out of her neckline and showed it. "I'm not a good Catholic, but you know, just in case."

Delia moved into an apartment a couple of blocks away until the end of construction. Every night after dark she left her new house and walked back to the apartment. She remembered before her accident riding her bike around the old neighborhood at night. Neighbors would have their porch and yard lights on, their kids playing outside. They called out friendly greetings from the shadows—everyone knew her name and who her parents were.

Here people retreated indoors when the sun went down. No one knew her or appeared to want to. Many of the houses were so dark she could barely distinguish their outlines. Narrow bottom floors with low roofs, wide overhangs. From a distance they resembled upright coffins.

The cousins arrived the next morning in a rusty panel van, Martina squeezed between them in the front seat. They might have been twins, short and powerfully built. They nodded and smiled when Martina introduced them, then unloaded metal buckets, pickaxes, and shovels. They shook their heads when Delia offered them masks, pulling up their bright bandanas. The three went to work, forming a bucket brigade to transfer debris from the basement to a side yard. Delia sifted through the rubble looking for treasures, but at this stage found only a few coins and corroded metal, fragments of furniture, and unidentifiable adornments including a long brass handle engraved "ORLOK."

Martina brought out a trash bag sagging with lumpy contents. She held it far away from her body. It smelled awful.

"Your rats are eating each other. Every one of these bodies has been chewed on. I guess they don't have enough grub."

"I'm embarrassed you had to deal with that."

Martina shrugged. "*¡No hay problema!* Be careful sticking your hands into anything. The rabies vaccine is no vacation."

The work created clouds of dust throughout the house. Every evening Delia vacuumed. She wondered if it was even possible to eliminate all the dust, or if it would hide until the remodeling was complete, then creep out of the walls to ruin her things.

Three weeks into the cleanup Delia was working on the re-roofed second floor. She had no power in this part of the house and carried a small lantern bright enough to keep her from tripping. The windows had been screwed shut and painted over with multiple layers of black paint. Replacing them was going to be expensive.

She was removing water-damaged wall plaster and floorboards too far gone to salvage and checking for structural damage requiring professional intervention. Because of her leg she had to sit in a folding chair, but she had long pry bars and a block of wood to use as a fulcrum. The work was a struggle, but she would figure it out.

She'd encountered extensive rodent damage as well, chewed boards and posts, baseboards deeply clawed. She felt pity for the creatures, so hungry and desperate with only wood to snack on. Some of the damage could be painted over, but most would have to be replaced.

With all the gaps in the floor, the missing sections of wall, naked lathing and fallen plaster, wallpaper peeled in curls and landing in recumbent stiff folds, the lantern light created a confusion of expressionistic shadows across the room. The doors had been removed for refinishing, many of the closets partially deconstructed, so every time Delia moved the lantern some new mysterious realm of geometry was variously revealed.

The constant intrusion of unidentifiable sounds had been a distraction at first. Now she ignored them and focused on what needed to be done. She'd accepted that she'd be working around rats and spiders, cockroaches and other bugs, the occasional ferret or fox or squirrel which had found its way inside. So much disease, so much contagion. Martina gave her a can of animal repellent in case any of those creatures ventured too near, but she couldn't imagine having the sense to use it.

She was checking the floor joists inside a huge hole in the floor near one of the closets, moving the lantern around to find evidence of damp, when she heard a hiss. She scooted back, thinking there was a snake. A chalk-white face appeared beneath one edge of the floor, its deep-set coal-like eyes burning. It hissed again, moist flecks spraying her arm. Its breath was appalling. She dropped the lantern just as the creature appeared to bend around itself, long body clothed in fur so dry and patchy it resembled a rotting coat. Delia turned and tripped over the lantern, shattering it. She landed hard on her side.

"Sounds like a possum," Martina said later as Delia was trying to calm herself. "They're rare here, but they do exist."

"No. No. It was too *big*. It was gigantic! I don't know how it even fit inside the floor."

Martina was quiet for a few moments. "Maybe the exterminators—"

"I've tried. They won't come until the basics are done. I didn't like the way he talked to me, like I was some silly teenager who doesn't understand how things work."

"You haven't been down in the cellar in a while. There's much to talk about, decisions to be made. You and I will work down there. We'll let the cousins work up here. They can put in the new windows. That will help with…visibility."

Delia was stunned.

"I hope you like castle chic." Martina laughed.

"I was thinking more dungeon, or mausoleum." The excavation had exposed walls, floors and ceilings made from large stones fitted together, medieval-styled archways and columns. Martina and her cousins had placed floor lights to heighten the drama.

"I hope you're on good terms with your neighbors, specifically the ones left and right and behind you."

"I've never met any of them. Why?"

"Look at the size of this thing. It's been dug out part way under all their properties, and about halfway beneath the street out front. I'm surprised there's been no collapse."

Delia walked from one end to the other, looking up nervously. Roots had broken through from the ground above. "What am I going to do? They're going to sue me!"

"Maybe we can put some of it back. More immediately, something's been nesting down here. Maybe it's your possum, maybe something else." Martina showed her where shredded bits of cloth and wood and other scraps spilled from a large hole in the wall. She dragged out a tangle of polished wooden splinters and silky bits. Another of those metal handles with the engraving *ORLOK* appeared. "I don't want to alarm you, but do these look like pieces from a coffin to you?"

"It's an historic neighborhood. There are probably some abandoned grave plots. Not that I accept the notion I have pieces from a grave under my house."

Martina walked over to a patch of vines hanging down one corner of the cellar. She lifted the loose vegetation—it formed a flap covering another large hole. The stone and the rubble had been worn smooth here, suggesting frequent passage. "This is where it's been getting in and out."

"It was a big animal, but that seems a large hole for a possum."

"I wonder." Before Delia could stop her Martina was climbing through the hole. Not sure what she should do, Delia followed.

They were outside, halfway into her neighbor's back yard. She's seen him on his front porch, an older gentleman. The lot was badly neglected, a jungle of trees and thick vines, a sea of tall weeds containing islands of rusted machinery.

Martina pointed to a worn path. "There's a trail." She began to follow it. Delia glanced at the man's back porch, then hurried to join her.

The vague trail became vegetation worn down to bare earth, leading to a trash mound by the back fence. From there multiple paths ventured out in a spoke pattern, one leading back toward the man's house, several going under fences into other yards.

"Skeletons." Delia limped over to where Martina stood by the trash pile. Among the cans and rinds there were some definite remains, leg bones, animal skulls, fragments of rib cage. There were also small vertebrae protruding from the dirt.

"Tell me none of those are human, Martina."

Martina prodded the garbage with her foot. "Not unless they're babies."

"Martina!"

"They're animals, sweetheart. No reason to get the police involved."

Delia smiled. She didn't want to wiggle back through that hole into the cellar, but Martina suggested it was simpler than trying to explain to her neighbor why they were in his back yard.

Once inside, Martina took several large stones and cemented them into place, sealing the passage. Delia wondered if they should have made sure the creature was out of her house first.

The black hearse which pulled up in front was unlike any vehicle Delia had seen before. An apparent antique, it had large chrome tubes coming out of the engine compartment. Roaring Twenties-style grill and running boards. Shiny script identified the car as an *Excalibur*. The side windows were blacked out similarly to her windows upstairs. Two tall men stepped out of the front. One opened a passenger door and an even taller woman dressed in black lace emerged.

Delia and Martina watched from the front window. Delia could see the cousins preparing frames in the yard. They stopped what they were doing and stared.

"That's her, the Lady Orlok," Martina said breathlessly. "After all these years she's barely changed." Delia had never heard her friend sound less than calm before.

"She's...*elegant*." It was an understatement. The woman was so tall, so pale, moving like an exotic bird toward Delia's front porch. The two men remained by the hearse.

Delia opened the door before the knock. Lady Orlok stared, looking miffed. "Our door, pardon me, *your* door, has been *defiled*."

"I know. Vandals." The woman raised an eyebrow. "I'm having

it redone. It'll look better than new. Please come in."

Delia hastily prepared tea while Martina sat with the woman. She felt compelled to treat this strange woman like royalty. "Martina, here, she knows you," Delia blurted. "I mean she's met you."

"I was selling Girl Scout Cookies. I was just a child, of course."

Lady Orlok nodded, unsmiling. "Of course. How are you?" She did sound musical, like Italian, but different.

"I'm fine, thank you," Martina said. "Busy helping my friend here restore this wreck of a home. Can we help you with something?"

Delia gasped, but her admiration for Martina increased even more.

"I respect...directness," Lady Orlok replied. "When I left here, many years ago, I left something especially important behind. I was unhappy, and angry, and this made me do something irresponsible."

"Oh, I'm sorry." Delia sat down. "What was it?"

The woman closed her eyes. "You would know what I am talking about, if you were to have an encounter."

"Encounter?"

"Yes, encounter. Could you show me the house? Such a tour might precipitate...some activity."

Martina clearly wasn't happy, but Delia gave the lady a tour, starting with the basement. The woman had to duck to avoid hitting her head at the bottom of the stairs. Once inside, she stared at the walls in silence.

"Is it the way you remembered it?" Delia asked.

"Less clean. The furniture, many grand pieces, are missing. I left them behind. Were they less than suitable? Or did you sell them? Quite valuable as antiques, I would think."

"All we found were fragments. Splinters, really. A lot of rat-chewed, worthless wood."

The woman nodded. "There were many candles, then. The light from the candles did not bother him. He built all this himself. He dug out the common brick and he continued to dig. He brought in the stones. He was extraordinarily strong, even at such an age. He fit everything together from memory. He said it reminded him of the old country."

Martina interrupted. "This *he*? Was that your grandfather?"

Lady Orlok stared at her. "An approximation. An *honorific* if you will."

"He must have passed some time ago."

Again, the lady stared, as if considering her words. "We became estranged. I have not seen him in a long time. I regret this. I should not have left so quickly."

"It took forever to clean the wreckage out of here, you know. The way you left this house."

"Martina." Delia didn't know if she was embarrassed or afraid.

Lady Orlok looked from one to the other. "I do not understand. The house is vintage, but it was pristine when I departed, I assure you. I am sorry if there has been trouble. If there has been damage. I was not here to…control the environment."

The lady left a card, A. ORLOK, with a phone number written in elegant script. She instructed Delia to call "in case circumstances change." Delia had no idea what she meant.

The cousins left a week later. "Thank them for all their hard work."

Martina and the cousins exchanged a few words. "They say they do roofing all summer and fall. For them, this was a pleasant change." One grabbed Martina's arm and whispered. Martina smiled. "They say you should be careful in this house. They say even after all this work it hangs onto its secrets."

In Delia's dream she was a child again, lying in bed, her leg shattered, taped, and glued back together. She dared not move or it would fall apart. But instead of the hospital bed, she was in a bedroom in her new home, now all fixed and beautiful, the walls hung with flowery wallpapers and luxurious fabrics, paintings of peaceful country scenes, the rooms furnished in fine antiques Delia was surprised to have been able to afford.

But insects were creeping from between the paper seams and

flowing down the wall. Despite their terrible injuries, half-eaten rats were crawling out from under those beautiful antiques. But worse were the unintelligible whispers, and the sour breath of the thing lying beside her, now slipping out from beneath the sheets.

Delia slept late, and by the time she arrived at the house Martina wasn't there. Had she gotten impatient and left? Delia looked everywhere. She reached for her cell, but it wasn't in her pocket. She walked back to the apartment. It wasn't there, either. She realized she hadn't seen it since she fell upstairs at the new house. She walked back, her leg throbbing from the exertion, and searched. Nothing. She tried not to panic. Maybe Martina was tired of working for her. Maybe she'd been offended by the Orlok visit. Delia didn't have Martina's number memorized, nor did she know where Martina or her grandmother lived.

She knew there were ways to retrieve contact information, but she didn't know how to do that. She barely knew how to use the cell phone at all.

But she knew her phone was here somewhere. She sat and had a cup of tea, centering herself. She had developed a taste for tea. She had work to do. Eventually Martina or the phone, hopefully both, would turn up.

Something thumped in the area behind the kitchen. They'd barely made a start there. It was the old pantry, the back porch, a kind of mud room, the back staircase to upstairs.

She hadn't replaced the lantern yet, but she had a big old flashlight. She heard some scraping. She got up slowly, the flashlight in front of her like a gun. It was heavy. She could hit someone with it.

She heard a rhythmic creaking on the back stairs. Something going up, or something coming down. She swung herself around the corner, aiming the beam upwards.

A furry flood of rats scurried across the landing at the top of the stairs, their eyes gleaming red in the light. Something tall and stick-thin loomed over them. She raised the beam higher. Something moved into the shadows to the right of the landing, escaping the light.

Because of her leg, Delia had never much liked stairs, but these last few weeks had made her stronger. She braced herself, then ascended, one hand firmly on the railing, the other gripping the flashlight like a club, ready to use it that way if necessary.

She kept glancing at her feet, afraid of stepping onto a rat or into a hole. She reached the landing and turned, and still looking down, almost missed it, the shape moving through a broken closet space ahead of her. She jerked her head up.

The silhouette of his great, domed head came around the wall first, then she had full view of his chalk-white face, more rat than human, the pointed ears, bushy eyebrows, sunken eyes, beaky nose, a long V-shaped chin, and those gigantic rat's incisors. His coat was rotted and falling off. He was taller than the doorway and had to stoop. His talons clicked across the naked wood frame.

They both stopped and gazed at each other. He had his hands up—those incredibly long fingers curling and uncurling like eyelashes—to shield his reddening eyes against the light, then gradually lowered them. He stared at her a moment, then raised a finger to smooth down his gangly eyebrows, then to lightly dust off his shabby dark coat—fruitlessly, because that decaying garment demanded much more than a cursory tidying. As ancient as the thing was, as hideously ugly, he was still pathetically vain. Nothing seemed either wise or venerable about the creature.

His pale skin was stretched tight against his skull. It appeared heavily veined, but the veins were even lighter than his skin, as if these vessels were empty.

He shuddered, lifting his lips away from his velvety pink gums. A narrow, pale tongue peeked out as if to wet them, but she saw no saliva, and the tongue made a slight scraping noise as it crossed the lips.

Delia wasn't completely surprised to encounter this being. If anything, it was a validation of everything she'd felt since taking physical possession of the property.

"You need to leave," she said. "You don't belong here. This house is mine now." He made what appeared to be a vulgar gesture with those incredibly long fingers. "I'm serious. I paid good money—"

He lurched in her direction. She moved to the side, easily avoiding him. She wasn't sure how much he could see. The way he stumbled around seemed indicative of a serious vision impairment. She supposed his body remembered the location of things, but now with some of the walls removed he was confused.

His mouth gaped open like a snake's, and he hissed in her direction. His mouth was so dry, and smelled vile. She could see the terrible splits in his lips.

He'd lost his power of speech, it seemed. His mouth silently conveyed his rage. She supposed he was still a villain, but she couldn't help pity him.

He'd gone to all fours, and he found the stairs again. She could hear him hurtling down the steps, groaning and making hideous whistling noises. She no longer felt afraid, and followed.

She heard him crashing through the kitchen, then into the ruined space she hoped would one day be her lovely dining room. She heard him weeping, or at least his version of weeping, and it saddened her, thinking how trapped he must feel.

She followed him into the cellar, where bugs congregated into a moving carpet flowing across the floor. He crushed and smashed his way across them to the large debris-filled void in the wall, and clawing through the contents, tossing dirt and garbage and dry vegetation everywhere, he dug himself back into his nest.

Delia stopped, wondering if she should pursue. She didn't want to. She looked at the trash spread around her feet, dead rats, bones, the desiccated viscera of some small animal, a shiny bit of metal. She picked it up. It was Martina's Our Lady of Guadalupe medal. The chain had been broken. Then she heard the muffled, distant ringing of her phone deep inside the nest.

She dived into the hole, pushing debris away from her, swimming in it. She was unsuccessful at keeping it out of her mouth, which left her sucking for air, on the verge of vomiting, when she touched him.

He swung his arms at her in vicious swipes. No, too soft and weak for that. No strength at all behind them. These blows weren't any sort of defence. They were the sad gestures of a desperate, failing thing.

That didn't mean he wasn't dangerous. He might yet be able to hurt her, she thought, when she felt the hands around her feet dragging her out.

Delia and Martina sat on the front steps, watching as the two men loaded the deep red mahogany coffin into the back of the hearse. Lady Orlok stood nearby, murmuring cautions.

"I should have come sooner when you didn't answer your cell. I'm sorry," Martina said, brushing the filth out of Delia's hair. Delia hadn't yet had time to shower. She didn't understand how Martina could stand being next to her, much less groom her.

"You couldn't know. Your grandmother being sick, that's where you needed to be." Lady Orlok had arrived right away. As it turned out, she'd been staying in a hotel downtown, waiting for Delia's call, knowing it would come.

Martina sighed. "She is beautiful, and a strong woman. You don't suppose…"

"His condition runs in the family? The sunlight doesn't appear to bother her."

"Should we have called the police instead? This doesn't feel right."

"We didn't find any human bones, at least as far as we know. He appears to have sustained himself on the rats. I'm sorry about your medal."

"It just needs a new chain. I lost it weeks ago. I didn't want to tell you."

"Do you think you can get your cousins to come back?"

"Perhaps. Why?"

"I'm ordering several tons of gravel. I don't need a cellar, all that empty space, space I don't even own. We're going to fill it in."

BROTHER MINE

Claire Fitzpatrick

It was a quiet, drizzly night, fog rolling across the city, with rustles of domesticity around the house. The cantankerous, silver-haired laundry maid quietly folding washing; the housemaid sitting in the drawing room writing a list for tomorrow's activities; the cook preparing the kitchen for tomorrow's breakfast; the gardener preparing to leave for the evening. In the quiet of his study, Augustus Knock drew his attention to the unopened letter on his desk. A man of a rugged countenance, burly and bearded with dark eyes and a thick upper lip, Augustus had entered the parlour in dismal spirits, tired of contract signing and inheritance claims, with a bowl of hot three bean soup prepared earlier.

The parlour housed a suite of a reading chairs, a sofa upholstered with emerald-and-brown-striped brocade, and a short, upholstered piano stool. Three small tables were positioned in various corners; two were bamboo, another a polished table with three twisted legs. A warm fire burned in the grate; over the mantlepiece hung a deep plum drape with large gold daisies embroidered on it by some great aunt of whom Augustus had never met.

He placed the soup on the small drinking stand beside him, illuminated by the light of the yellow-tinted gibbous moon streaming through the window, and cut a thin slit in the envelope with his letter opener, reluctantly retrieving the scented leaf of paper. Augustus scanned the page as he made his way to his reading chair by the fire, nose wrinkling as he took in its contents, written in an unfamiliar scrawl.

September 1838

Herr Augustus Knock,

It has come to my attention your brother Heinrich is an estate agent dealing with the buying and selling of houses in Germany and abroad. I have attempted to contact him several times over the past four months, however, as of yet have received no response. I last heard he was corresponding with the aristocrat Count Orlok from the Carpathian Mountains regarding property and have sent forth inquiries to confirm.
I would be ever so grateful if you could reach out to Heinrich and inform me of his whereabouts if you are able. I have an urgent business matter to discuss with him and require his attention post haste.

Cordially yours,
Mr Arthur Ships.

Augustus stroked the fraying ends of his beard, eyes narrowed as he studied the letter. Arthur Ships? He could not recall meeting the man before, nor had his brother ever mentioned him by name. He wondered how Mr Ships had come across his place of residence. In any case, the mention of his brother gave him pause. How long since he had laid eyes on him? Three months? Or perhaps longer? While Heinrich was often away for work, it had been many months without correspondence. However, he was not one to forego business dealings, no matter how small or of little monetary worth. His attention turned to Count Orlok. His name *was* familiar to Augustus, for his brother had mentioned the recluse several times.

Frowning, he returned the letter to its envelope and looked to the window, stomach flipping. He had been meaning to visit Transylvania for some time now, though had always told himself he never encountered the right business opportunity to warrant such a trip. But he had to be honest with himself: his brother was no longer gallivanting around on a trip—he was missing, and there was every chance his brother had fallen ill or had become entangled in matters of which he required assistance. Or worse.

Augustus twirled the end of his moustache, furtively glancing over to the window, jumbled thoughts whirling around in his head. Nothing else could be done from here—he had to travel to Transylvania and fetch his brother himself.

The melancholy forest was silent, save for the gentle hoof falls of his dapple-grey steed as Augustus made his way through the inhospitable landscape. The path, a sculpture of boot- and hoofprints and the tracks of other animals along disturbed dirt and rugged stones, ventured out of the forest, weaving up the mountain. The grey-green grove of trees bent at odd angles like contorted bodies, their spindly branches jerking like puppets in the brisk wind.

He'd hired a solemn-faced guide from a nearby village, yet the man refused to leave the woods, instead pointing up to the Count's residence, ashen-faced, abandoning Augustus with a rattled horse and a swift farewell. Augustus rode towards a bridge, but the horse refused to step onto the wooden planks. It reared, threw him off into a clump of prickly, dry bushes, and galloped away. Bruised, yet not severely injured, Augustus brushed the dirt from his coat and stockings, and loosened his silk tie, setting off on foot at a steady pace towards the castle.

The journey was slow and quiet as Augustus travelled countless dusty roads, making his way across the mighty sloping terrain, the jagged rocks and pointed crags of the mountains as grey as the bestrewed masses of birch trees huddling together along the road, housing a variety of ghoulish birds. The eerie call of a barn owl and the croaks of the black-crowned night heron filled the still, hot air.

Over time, the road narrowed and almost disappeared, until finally, he scrambled up to the pinnacle, reaching the bridge leading to the Count's domain. The castle was a formidable fortress, rising steeply, its high granite walls melding with the limestone karst on which it sat, rendering it impregnable from outside forces. Great windows sat in four turrets, high enough a sling, or bow, or culverin could not reach; thick clouds hung so low as to press upon the turrets. To the west, the terrain divided into a great valley, and beyond the mountains rose giant barren peaks studded with mountain ash and thorny trees spotting the horizon.

It took another half-hour for him to reach the giant doors leading to the castle courtyard, and he paused at their size, dismayed by the termite-infested oak. Wiping beads of sweat from his brow, Augustus pulled off his travelling coat and knocked. As soon as his knuckles touched the door, they swung open of their own accord, ushering a gust of impetuous and violent wind, impelling him forwards. Gasping, he looked to the doors and stared at the thin fog enshrouding the courtyard inside, snaking around the various old stone statues of nymphs and fairies, many broken and cracked. Thunder rumbled in the distant mountains, soft at first, then hard as the crack of a whip; rain broke free from the heavens and Augustus hurried to a covered walkway leading towards an old wooden door. It swung backwards, and a thin shadow scuttled along the wall like a spider, rising atop the edges of an archway, until disappearing, replaced by a short, unpleasant-looking man. He was bald, devoid of even a wisp of hair, and dressed in a military-style coat. A rat-like overbite protruded from behind his thin lips. His elongated, ghastly fingernails, stained with a hideous yellow hue, curled towards his palms.

"Ah, Augustus, you are here."

"Yes," Augustus stuttered, expecting a servant. "And you are Count Orlok, I presume? Is my brother here?"

"Come, come inside. Your brother is quite safe."

"Safe? Has he encountered danger?" Augustus dry-swallowed as he entered the foyer, eyes darting around the large room in hopes of catching a glimpse of Heinrich.

"Oh, no, he has been a little unwell and is sleeping in his chamber. I am sure he will awake soon enough. Come, it is quite dark. I have no doubt you are eager to retire for the evening."

"If my brother is unwell, I must see him. Is he of a stable countenance? Has a doctor seen to him? Is a nurse with him?"

"Why, he is being cared for by the best doctors in all of Europe. Now, please, come inside. My home is yours. Is there anyone you need to notify of your safe arrival?"

Augustus shook his head, following the Count as he led him

through the draughty hall to a winding wooden staircase. "I have told no one of my journey."

"Very well, Augustus. Your room is on the second floor," he said, narrow, knobbly finger gesturing upstairs. "Third door on the right. There you will find writing utensils and a warm bed. I trust everything will be to your satisfaction."

The Count clasped his hands together. "Now, you must forgive me, but I have much work to do this evening, so I will excuse myself. I find I'm more attentive to my work in the night. Do you not agree?"

"Oh yes, often I feel there are not enough hours in the day."

Orlok smiled, revealing yellowed, pointed teeth. "You must remain in this wing. The castle is old and there are many hallways and many stairs, so it is easy to lose yourself in this immense labyrinth. Why, I often find myself wandering passageways and turning up in rooms I had quite forgotten about." The Count gave a short bow. "Good evening!"

Augustus waited for the Count's shadow to disappear around the corner before making his way up the narrow, steep stairs to the second floor, marvelling at the extraordinary bareness of the castle. Orlok was a *count* after all: a nobleman with wealth and connections. Where was his family crest? His rugs? Where were his bejewelled wall sconces? Why were the stairs uncarpeted? The house was as bare as an animal's cage.

Ascending the staircase did not soothe his nerves—his ears pricked up as he listened to the footsteps of Orlok retreating to his room. He imagined his brother walking up these very stairs; had Heinrich felt the same uncomfortable rising of hairs on the back of his neck? He thought perhaps to call out to the Count— perhaps he had a servant who could escort him?

The second-floor hallway was lighted, though empty; Augustus could hear no rustles of a housemaid making her way about the house. He wondered if they'd retired earlier. He followed the hallway and counted the thin wooden doors left from right, stopping at the third. He reached forward to turn the handle.

"Do you need anything before you retire?"

Augustus gasped. "Count Orlok, why, I did not hear your footsteps. I thought you were still on the first floor."

"My step is as light as my sleep. Tell me, what stops you in your tracks? Are you hungry? Thirsty? Shall I have the maid bring something to your room? How rude of me—I should have asked if you had eaten during your travels. Myself, I dine later than is custom; it is rare we should cross paths in the dining area during your stay."

"Oh, I am in need of nothing, Count Orlok. Except I would like to see my brother. I don't mean to press the issue."

"Ah, well, you see, your brother is ill, as I mentioned. Perhaps overworked. His stay has been extended by new laws and regulations, no doubt extremely complicated matters. I don't have the head for finances like he does. Anyway, you must let him rest. I doubt he would like to be roused in the middle of the night, do you? Now, return to your room, my friend. Blessed sleep awaits—how nice it sounds to close my eyes and fall into a restful slumber, bringing no fear, nor worry, but pleasant dreams."

"If I could only see my brother—"

"Goodnight."

Wild winds raged throughout the evening. The heavens broke before dawn to release a torrent of rain. A bolt of lightning shattered the darkened sky. Wrenched from his slumber, Augustus cowered under his blankets and listened to the thumping bolts, combative and catastrophic as they raged on. With his residence in the city, he'd never been subjected to such mighty roars. Rubbing his eyes, he rolled onto his side, staring at the wall. A shadow ran around the room, pressed onto the wallpaper, sliding behind the wooden writing desk and his bedhead, the only furniture in the room.

"What in the world?"

Heart thumping, Augustus searched the room for the shadow, ears prickling as the violent wind beat itself against the castle walls. A heavy scraping a rattling, emanated from his door. Augustus rose from his bed, crept to the door, turned the handle and peered outside. He gasped. Across the hall, where there had hours before been a blank stretch of wallpaper, was a golden tapestry, rippling as though roused by a breeze. Augustus stepped towards it and pulled it aside, eyes widening as he stared at a set of stone stairs descending into the dark.

Augustus stepped towards the top of the stairs, inclined his neck, and peered around the corner. While the rest of the castle was old and crumbling, the staircase was in pristine condition, boasting a luminous golden handrail. Augustus swallowed a lump in his throat as he descended, wiping the sweat from his palms on his nightshirt. How curious the stairs would be so well cared for when the rest of the great house was gloomy and drab. He imagined a servant swept and scrubbed them daily.

Biting his bottom lip, he wondered if perhaps his brother had come across the stairs, and fallen down them? Perhaps it had always been there across from his room, and he'd been too fatigued to notice it? He recalled the E.T.A. Hoffmann detective stories he had read as a child, with Doctor K, with his clairvoyant abilities, exploring hidden passages and walls, which, when leaned against, turned to reveal secret rooms. Augustus wished he had the doctor's clairvoyant abilities or at least a power granting him a sliver of confidence. He had never been as confident as Heinrich, nor as self-assured. Heinrich had been the older brother he'd looked up to, even idolised, which increased his concerns for his well-being. If anything had happened to him, he wouldn't know how to navigate the world alone. He had no wife, no close friends. Only his brother's letters of his travels abroad.

After descending the staircase, Augustus took a tentative step out into a dimly lit hallway. Three of the five wall sconces burned, though they barely illuminated the moist, moss-covered stones, cold and grimy under his bare feet. Anxiety dug its claws into his bones as he started down the hallway, twisting his stomach into knots. Though the stone ceiling was high, it felt as though the walls were closing in on him, pressing against his chest so hard he feared the air would be syphoned from his lungs. He reached the end of the hallway and looked left and right. Both directions ended in darkness. Teeth clenched, he turned left, eyes squinting as he struggled to see in the murky blackness. And then he heard it. Whispers. Muttering. Moans.

"Count Orlok—his lordship—I must return to him."

"Heinrich."

Augustus rushed forward in the darkness and dropped to his knees. Heinrich crouched in a dimly lit corner, knees drawn to his chin, arms wrapped around his legs.

Augustus could not believe the man before him was his brother. Heinrich was a strong, handsome man, known to court many ladies. Who was this ghoul before him? His face was cadaverous, eyes watery, gaze unfocused, hair thin and dry and floating around his face, lips pallid— could he truly be his brother? His breathing seemed laborious and strained, as though he had no energy left within him. His skin was covered in strange marks, purplish and bruised. And his expression, once alight and full of wonderment, was downcast as if he had just received the most terrible news. Augustus stared at him in a mixture of pity and awe at such a disturbing sight.

"Heinrich, what has happened to you? Are you ill? My concern for your safety was clearly justified!"

"Count Orlok… His Lordship… I must return to him…"

Augustus clasped his brother's shoulders, shaking him gently. "The count! Has he imprisoned you here?"

"I am…quite well. The master… Do you not hear him…calling your name? I pray you never will. For he consumes…my every waking moment…when I slumber. I must return to him…"

"Brother! This is madness! Come—I will take you home!"

"The count… He says…humans are like caterpillars…waiting for the summer to come…and in the meantime…they are grubs and larvae…ugly…easy to squash underfoot… or even eat… if you are hungry enough…"

Augustus shook his head wildly. "Brother, you are raving! You are feverish! We must leave."

"But I cannot… The count…"

Augustus clenched his fists. Had some religious mania seized his brother's wits? What was he doing here in the dark? How long had it been since he'd seen sunlight?

"What hold does the count have over you?" he exclaimed, shaking his brother's shoulders. "Tell me, brother! Are you in debt? Is he blackmailing you?"

"On his lips…fresh blood… A filthy leech, my master…yet I must obey. There was a woman… She was here… He fed… He… enters without…opening the door…"

"Fresh blood? Woman?" Augustus gasped. "What are you saying, Heinrich?"

"I went into…his room. And the box…was there. A coffin! I opened…the lid…and the count…he was renewed…his cheeks were ruby red…full…. Engorged… A mocking smile…even as he slept… He is here… even now… inside my head…"

"Please, you are making no sense, brother!"

"He opened his eyes…and they were red…like blood…and he rose…and I was paralysed… That horrid thing… My body… I could not move… Scream…run… He knows…he knows…"

"Who knows? The count? Tell me, Heinrich!"

"It is almost…akin to a savage form of love… I have many dreams, dreams which will stay with me forever… They move through me and alter the colour of my mind… Whatever blessing God once granted me is gone forevermore… I am…trapped in this abyss… I have lost…my soul!"

"What is the meaning of this?"

Augustus looked up, dropping his hands from his brother's shoulders. Orlok, followed by rats, appeared in the doorway, wearing his military-style coat, now covered in dust and dirt. His face, formerly thin and hollow, was now full. His eyes glistened in the darkness, like two bright stars in a moonless midnight sky, locked on Augustus' own.

"You have made a grievous error coming here, Herr Knock. Especially as I did not extend an invitation. How rude of you."

"What have you done to my brother? Release him at once!"

The count smirked. "Why, he is free to leave as he wishes. Do you see shackles on his ankles? His wrists?"

"You have shackled his mind! You have bewitched him! He cannot form a sentence."

"This is the manner in which he speaks. I assumed it was an impediment of speech."

"He has no such impediment! You have done something to him, I am sure of it! His addled mind and those queer marks on his neck are proof. He should never have come here. However, I wanted to give you the benefit of the doubt because of your noble status. But here is proof of my reservations!" he said, gesturing to his cowering brother.

"You know," the count said, voice icy, "people infect one another not only with disease, but also with superstition and fear. They spread dangerous ideas based on very little evidence. Your brother is weak, and we of sounder minds should not trust the weak. Cast him aside—he is but a husk with no sound substance."

Tears rolled down his cheeks as Augustus stared at his brother, pitifully inferior, cowering and feeble. He seemed smaller than the proud young man he'd known and loved.

"I will never abandon my brother! Our bond is stronger than blood!"

The count laughed, his mouth a twisted aberration of a grin and a glower. "A terrible mistake, I must say."

Before Augustus could retort, the count leapt towards him, mouth wide, yellowed teeth hungry, and Augustus held out his arms, screaming.

Augustus opened his eyes. His first instinct was to shriek. However, his mouth was so parched no voice issued from his burning lungs; instead, he gasped. His heart palpitated furiously as he struggled to comprehend his surroundings.

Am I dead? Is this Hell?

He licked his lips and felt around, quickly realising he was enclosed by satin. A coffin. He was in a coffin. Tears sprung from his eyes as he beat his fists upon the lid; sweat gathered on his upper lip and brow, and his mind whirled, unable to settle on any one thing. *Arthur Ships. The forest. The count. My brother.* How had it come to this? He uttered short, sharp breaths as he tried to focus, but the darkness and confinement brought overwhelming tiredness, and after what felt like hours, he surrendered to slumber, his sepulchral dreams a world of gloomy phantasms and fanged-toothed tyrants. When he awoke, it was to the rustle of the coffin. He was being lowered, down, down, and though he could not see through the lid, he knew he was being interred, and would never see the light of day again.

Why had the count not taken a blade to his throat? Pierced his heart? What had he done to deserve such a cruel fate? All he had wanted was to find his brother and take him home. Where was Heinrich now? They would both die here, alone. Augustus pounded his fists against the lid once more but to no avail. A poem came to mind, one his brother had read to him not too long ago. *To His Dying Brother, Master William Herrick* by the poet Robert Herrick.

"*Life of my life,*" he whispered, "*take not so soon thy flight,*
"*But stay the time till we have bade good-night.*
"*Thou hast both wind and tide with thee; thy way*
"*As soon dispatch'd is by the night as day…*"
Augustus closed his eyes.
"*Let us not then so rudely henceforth go*
Till we have wept, kiss'd, sigh'd, shook hands, or so…"

AN OLD FAMILY VOLUME

Brad Mengel

It did my heart good to see familiar sights of Wisborg again, even if they had been changed in the four years I had been away in the war. Returning to the house I had been born in, that my great grandfather Thomas Hutter had bought when he had wed his first wife, Ellen.

I turned onto the steps and before I could even think about knocking the door flew open and my father Heinrich was there.

"Come in, come in," he beckoned me. I had no sooner cleared the threshold and the old man slammed the door behind me.

Before I could ask about his odd behaviour, he was calling to rest of the household. "It's Kurt, he has returned from the war."

Suddenly, the entrance hall was crammed with people as my sister Liesel, my brother Frederick and his wife Marta, carrying young Johan, all joined my father to crush in to greet me. I caught a glimpse of my mother behind them.

There was a cacophony of sound as they all spoke to me at once. Suddenly, I was back on the front line of the Somme with English and French soldiers going over the top and charging our position.

The hands of my loved ones reaching to greet me became those of a desperate English soldier reaching for my throat as the battle left us both holding empty firearms. The Tommy soldier was here in my house trying to finish the job and kill me. Now, as then, I froze in terror as I felt my life ebb away and it faded to black.

It was with a gasp that I awoke, my hands trying to tear the ghostly remnants of the Tommy's fingers from my throat. But there was no Tommy soldier, just my dear mother sitting beside the bed. It was like I was ten again and she was ministering me through an illness.

Seeing I was awake, she left the room and in a few moments my father came in. "My son, in our joy at your return we have overwhelmed you and you fainted." I could hear the fear and concern in his voice.

He sat on the edge of the bed and patted my hand. "Take your time, rest. Your sister is cooking dinner, come down when you feel ready."

He rose and kissed me on the forehead. Just as he did when I was a boy. He tousled my hair and left the room.

I remained on the mattress for a few moments waiting for another ghostly apparition to try and haunt me. When none came, I rose slowly. I nearly tripped over my kitbag, which I kicked under the bed. I made my way to the window and looked at the empty street and derelict house across the road. There were stories about that house. My friend Rudy's father would tell of the Nosferatu that lived there around the fire on camping trips. A vile vampire with the pale skin of the dead, bald head, two sharpened rat's teeth protruding from his lips, and claws on the ends of his fingers that would tear you apart. Naturally, the Nosferatu, Count Orlok, would eat naughty boys and girls.

It was just a story to scare the children, Frederick and Marta were telling the story to my nephew before I left. No doubt I will tell it to my own children. I stared at the darkened window directly opposite mine for a few minutes as I imagined my future with Brigid, who I had been courting before the war.

I was roused from my reverie, as I caught what I thought was a pale figure moving in the derelict house. I blinked and rubbed my eyes, and I could find nothing in the Stygian darkness through the window. The scare today had made me more susceptible than usual, if I thought there was a vampire roaming around across the road.

I made my way downstairs and joined my family for dinner. The meal was more subdued than I remembered before I left. Frederick and my father would debate the latest decision of the *bürgermeister* or some other affair of the day. Now we all chewed our food in silence.

I assume that the rest of the family was as relieved as I was when the silence was broken by the shouting of the local constable. Together we rose, the scraping of the chairs on our wooden floor the only sound. We crowded around the window to watch as the officer made his way to us.

"The Spanish Flu has arrived!" he cried. "Stay at home except to buy food."

The placard strapped around his neck was hard to read in the streetlights. But he stopped out the front of the house and I finally deciphered the sign: "The hospital is closed to all but emergencies!" With that he rang his bell and moved along the street.

We all stared at each other. I had heard of the Spanish Flu and from the worried looks on my family's faces they had, too. We were stuck in the house until further notice. Everyone drifted away to their rooms.

I retreated to the library and poured myself a brandy from the bottle my father keeps, the good stuff that he doesn't think we children know about. As I sipped it, I looked through the titles on the shelves. *The Tanakh*, *The Jewel of the Seven Stars*, *Alraune*, *Gespensterbuch*, and several adventure books by Karl May. Nothing that really caught my fancy. Then I saw it.

A tatty little volume with an odd title, *Of Vampires, Terrible Ghosts, Magic and the Seven Deadly Sins*. My grandfather told me that his father Thomas Hutter had brought it with him from Transylvania in 1838.

I had seen enough of the horrors that men could inflict on each other, and thought that fairy stories to scare children might be the distraction I needed.

I took the book and the brandy to the big leather reading chair. After a small sip of the alcohol, I opened the book. The first part was titled "The Book of the Vampire".

"Out of the seed of Belial appeared the Nosferatu who lives and feeds on human Blood!" I read. "He lives in the darkest caves, tombs and coffins. These are filled with the tainted soil from the fields of the Black Death!"

I had heard of Belial, he was mentioned in the *Tanakh*—many would call him the Devil. It made sense that an evil creature like the Nosferatu would be a creature of the Devil, shunning the light. I read on about how he haunts the dreams of his victims, draining their blood. I knew how he spread disease and pestilence last time he was in Wisborg from the scary tales around the campfire and the family legend of my great-grandmother Ellen, sacrificing herself to destroy the monster, allowing him to drink her blood until the sun rose, disintegrating the creature and stopping the plague.

I flicked ahead to the next section, "The Book of Ghosts". Before the war, I may have laughed at the idea of spectres but now I'm haunted by the men I killed. They appear in my sleep and sometimes they appear when I am awake. *Shellshock*, the army doctor called it, after I woke the barracks screaming that a French soldier was trying to bayonet me.

I remembered killing the man. The call had come at dawn that the French were going over the top and the generals in charge decided that we would do the same. I climbed out the trench and ran forward. The Frenchman, barely a man, charged straight at me. I stopped and took aim, the luger bullet flew true and straight through his left eye and exploded out the back of his head. His dying synapses kept the body upright, heading for me. His rifle bayonet drove into my left thigh as he collapsed on me. His ruined face headbutted me as I heard his final breath leave his mouth.

I lost track of time pinned under his dead body, until one of my retreating countrymen found me. I next saw the French soldier staring at me with his one good eye as I lay in the hospital delirious with fever. He appeared again as I walked out of the hospital. He'd disturbed my dreams ever since.

I took a healthy sip of the brandy and continued reading.

"From deeds incomplete rise the revenants. Unable to pierce the veil to the next realm, these spirits haunt the living.

"Some spirits do not realise that they are dead and may continue as if they were still alive."

I drained the glass and refilled it before I continued.

"Many spectres are harmless and if aided in the resolution of their life's quest will pass into the next realm and haunt you no longer.

"But one must watch for the Terrible Ghosts! These are vengeful spirits who seek to do ill to the living. They may be kept at bay with a ring of salt. Or dispersed by striking them with iron."

A chill ran up my spine. I stood up and stoked the fire with the iron poker. With the flames dancing and the room beginning to heat up, I returned to the book.

"But these will only provide a temporary respite from the torments of the terrible ghosts. To stop the hauntings, one must find the Earthly remains of the person and burn them.

"Where this is not possible, one pure of heart may perform the exorcism ritual."

I was about to turn the page when I heard a noise. A scurrying and scratching in the walls. Rats or other vermin, no doubt. I was about to investigate as my mother appeared.

She would chase me off to bed as I sat up reading late at night. I went to kiss her good night as I always did, when I realised that she was not at dinner earlier, nor had she said a word when I saw her. I looked harder, there was a faint white aura surrounding her. It was then that I remembered the final letter I received from Father in the same dispatch that brought news of the Armistice. With the end of the war, I never opened the letter thinking I would see them all soon enough.

I ran to my room and pulled out the kitbag. The letter was sitting in the outside pocket. My hands trembling, I opened the envelope and confirmed what I suspected. My mother had died a month ago.

My mother was a ghost, looking over her family in death as she had in life.

Eventually, I drifted off to sleep and for the first time in a long time I slept soundly, dreaming only of a picnic with my mother.

I rose feeling refreshed and was surprised to find that it was nearly 2pm. It was a pleasant surprise as I had not slept a solid night for several months, let alone slept through the morning.

I made my way to the kitchen to find Marta just returned from the markets.

She stifled a cough as I walked in. She looked around, embarrassed, and took a sip of water.

I wished her a good day and pretended I had not noticed the cough. I made my way to my nephew, Johan, who was sitting in the corner chewing on a bread crust. He had been born just before I left for the war and the letters that found me gave glimpses of the child growing up. And now I could meet him for the first time. He let loose a whooping cough as I sat beside him.

Marta raced over and picked him up. Patting him on the back, she explained he had a touch of croup. With that she gave him a small spoonful of brandy.

"Poor little man," I said as I ruffled his hair. I could feel the heat radiating from his scalp.

The boy smiled at me before shyly burying his head in his mother's shoulder. He didn't know me, his uncle. Also, he was sick, and I remember that I only wanted my mother when I was unwell.

Just then my father came down the stairs sounding like he was going to cough up his left lung. That was three members of the household coughing. Could they be infected with the Spanish Flu?

Count Orlok's first appearance brought the plague in 1838, and I saw him again at the same time as I heard the news of the Spanish Flu arriving in Wisborg. It was clear that Count Orlok had risen from the grave on the wings of this new pestilence to threaten my family again. The rats in the walls were proof of that. I had lost so much time with my family, and was struck by the irony of surviving several battles in the war only to come home to lose my family members to the deadly plague spreading around the world.

Marta placed a plate of food before me. I formulated a plan as to how I might tackle this vampire. The idea of returning to combat twisted and turned my stomach and I could barely force down the food, but I was the logical choice. I had no wife or child like my brother, nor was I old and infirm like my father. I could not allow my angel of a mother or Marta to sacrifice themselves to this beast. I had the combat experience to tackle and destroy this monster and the plague he'd brought with him. This was my family legacy; like my great-grandmother Ellen, I must make the sacrifice to save the family.

I barely registered the talk around the table as I excused myself and returned to my room.

I knelt beside my bed and offered a prayer before pulling out the kitbag I had kicked under there the night before. I reached in and pulled out the *Nahkampfmesser*, my trusty trench knife. The blade had saved my life more than once and I was calling on it now to save my family.

The sheath clipped onto my belt, and I hid it under my jacket. There was no need to worry the family by openly carrying a weapon. I hesitated for a second and returned to the kitbag and pulled another weapon, a French nail. I'd found this in no man's land, an improvised knife made from the iron stakes that held up the barbwire. It never hurt to have a spare weapon on hand.

There was no need to search for the monster. I had seen him in his old haunt, the abandoned and derelict house directly across the road from my family home. In the last 80- odd years, the house had been bought several times, but no owner stayed long. I remembered Herr Schuler, he came from Berlin and declared that he would renovate the house. It was less than a week later that he fled the house naked. He was nearly unrecognisable as his jet-black hair had turned white overnight and his skin was covered in rat bites and scratches. The poor man had been committed to the local asylum, raving about plague rats and their master.

The town council had debated knocking the building down but the wheels of bureaucracy, that normally spun slow, had seized and frozen, leaving the derelict building to rot.

With weapons secreted on me, I made my way downstairs and into the kitchen pantry where I grabbed a lantern and a packet of matches. When I was 12 or so, I had snuck across the road on a dare and found that the outside light refused to enter its interior. I had no sooner taken three steps and I found myself in deep, inky darkness. I heard a scratching, and something brushed against my legs. I am not ashamed to say that I had turned tail and run out of the house in sheer terror. That was not going to happen again.

The town hall clock struck 3.30pm as I crossed the road. With the Spanish Flu in town nobody was on the street, and I made my way to the building unseen. The front door hung off its hinges and scraped on the floor as I pushed it open enough to admit me. Again, I made it only three steps and the light refused to follow as the darkness enveloped me. I lit the lamp expecting it to illuminate most of the room, but the light struggled to shine more than a foot in front of me.

I reached into my pocket and pulled out the French nail. With the lamp held at arm's length, I penetrated the black velvet darkness. The sounds of scratching and scraping surrounded me. I made another few steps and I felt a presence behind me. I spun, thrusting my weapon as if it might cut through the gloom. I saw a familiar pale, white face. Instead of the expected bloodless, rat-like visage of The Nosferatu, it was instead the ruined face of my French soldier, his one good eye reflecting the light of my lamp and the other oozing blood and brain matter. I slashed out instinctively with my blade and slashed across where his belly should be. The ghost screamed as the iron gutted him.

I saw another figure on my right. It was a Tommy soldier. His cold, ghostly hands grabbed my lamp hand. I felt a chill spread along my arm and the lamp slipped from my nerveless fingers. With the other hand, I began to madly slash at the darkness. I heard rather than saw the Tommy dissolve at the touch of my weapon. The darkness was punctuated with other cries and curses.

The lamp broke as it hit the ground, the spilled kerosene soaking into the wooden floor and igniting. The circle of light and flames spread, illuminating more and more of the room as the rotted timbers caught fire. Glancing around, I saw several more spectres and ghouls surrounding me; these were the ghosts of war, the terrible and vengeful ghosts that had been haunting me.

I saw a pile of wooden crates burst into flame on the other

side of the room. A plague of rats ran screaming past me as a tall, pale figure rose out of an open crate. The pallid skin, the two sharpened teeth and glowing red eyes. Nosferatu!

I turned and fled.

I carved a path through the press of ghosts bearing down on me with the rapidly spreading wildfire behind me. I felt the flames licking at my heels. A spectral slouch-hatted digger was blocking the door. I drove the blade into his throat and he faded into oblivion as I leapt through the flaming entryway.

I rolled onto the cobblestone street trying to extinguish the flames. I quickly regained my feet and pulled off my jacket. I saw another terrible ghost of a turbaned man, one of the first I had killed in battle. I punched him in his rotting face and his exposed skull made a mocking and silent laugh. I ran to the kitchen door of my house and near knocked it from its hinges as I charged through to the pantry. I grabbed the salt canister and pulled a handful of the crystals. I threw them at the turbaned figure, and he vanished.

Taking advantage of the respite, I ran to the library, grabbed the book and the iron fire poker. Then I made a protective circle of salt around my chair. I recalled what the Book of Ghosts had said but it was of little help. The ghosts haunting me had their corporeal bodies spread across the battlefields of Europe and there was no way to burn their bodies as recommended by the book. Even if I knew the exact location of the bodies, getting there would be difficult as the terrible ghosts were haunting me here and now. The book had mentioned an exorcism ritual.

I frantically flipped to the page; this ritual was my only hope. From the corner of my eye, I saw another apparition appear, I felt the hatred emanating from him like heat. When I looked, I couldn't tell what nationality this one was. He rushed me and as I raised the poker to strike him down, he stopped dead in his tracks at the line of salt. Knowing I was protected, I began to calm my breath and opened the book.

The Exorcism Ritual, it read:

"By the light of white candles six, in a protective circle of salt,
Wearing a chaplet made from white roses. Let one of pure of

heart say the following:

> "From the demon of darkness I believe you
> Terrible ghosts shall trouble me no more
> The darkness of the night is no longer home
> The song that I sing sends you to the light
> Please don't be angry, in the world to come
> After He takes us away."

This was something, but I was missing several ingredients: candles, white roses, and one pure of heart. Mrs Murchison next door grew roses and candles were easy to get. One pure of heart, that was a little harder. After what I had done in the war, I certainly did not fall into that category. These ghosts were certainly proof of that.

The ghosts seemed to have retreated for the moment. I brandished the iron poker as I stepped out of the circle. No ghosts appeared.

I now had a mission. I retreated downstairs and jumped the fence into Mrs Murchison's yard. She had kept the rose garden for over 50 years. There were numerous bushes with every colour one could imagine. Several bushes had white flowers and I quickly snapped off two dozen roses. Stealing like this did nothing towards making me pure of heart.

At that point, another ghost appeared. I hurled the poker like a javelin and it disintegrated the spectre before imbedding itself into the Murchison's cellar door.

Again, I jumped the fence and returned home. My mother always kept a supply of candles in the dining room sideboard. She never trusted the new-fangled gaslights Father had installed about ten years ago. I was relieved to find they had not been moved in my absence.

I returned to the library and the circle of salt. I sat and wove the flowers into a circle to wear as a chaplet. Just as I finished, my mother appeared. She was the best person I knew and if anyone was pure of heart, it was her.

"Mama, I need your help," I said to her, with tears flowing down my cheeks.

She smiled that sweet smile she always did. I explained that

I was being haunted and that I needed her to help remove the ghosts. I felt the temperature drop.

As she came, I noticed that I must have accidentally disturbed the salt and broken the circle. With my mother inside, I fixed the circle and lit the candles. She took the chaplet and put it on her head.

Several ghosts seeped into the room. The one-eyed Frenchman glared at me. I pulled out my French nail, but they all stayed outside of the circle. My mother cleared her throat and began to read the incantation.

A vortex appeared near the fireplace and the ghosts began to flicker and fade into a mist. I could feel the pull of the vortex as the ghosts began to disappear into it. It was almost like a weight had lifted from me as the last ghost vanished.

It was then that I realized the sun had almost set. I glanced out the window and smoke from the burning house began to waft across the road. It reminded me of something I had heard as a young child, that vampires could turn into mist or smoke.

I ran down the stairs as the smoke began to come under the door. It seeped through and began to rise and form a cloud.

The cloud solidified and began to take a very familiar shape. The red eyes glowered at me as Orlok's maw formed, with a snarl displaying his two rat fangs. He hissed at me as I leapt across the room.

I took comfort from the feel of the cold iron of the French nail in my hand. The honed point penetrated the creature's chest where the cold, dead lump of flesh it called a heart was located. The resistance was so minimal, I was unsure whether I was stabbing flesh or mist.

All uncertainty disappeared as I felt my hand press against the cold, damp black coat he wore and drive the body back. The creature screamed in agony as I pinned it to our oak door. Its face writhed and contorted into inhuman shapes as it began to disintegrate into flakes of dust and grime.

Once again Orlok had come to Wisborg, a harbinger of plague and disease to find that Ellen Hutter and her bloodline were too strong for him, ready to fight against the evil of the supernatural, ready to pay the ultimate price. I dropped to my knees, a feeling of peace coming over me, the point of the French nail buried in the door.

At that moment, the Great Death came to an end and I could feel the curse lift from the family like a carrion bird flying off to search for easier prey, vanishing in the darkness.

THE APARTMENT AT THE
END OF THE HALL

Aaron Harvie

1.

Bedford, 1982.

The billboard across the road from the Flamingo Apartments asked *Do You Know Where Your Children Are?* in big red letters, its paint old and faded and peeling. Ironically, there was a long bank of missing persons flyers posted below.

Eli Ellis got out of the car and stretched after the long drive. He was short for fifteen with a tight black afro, acne and the beginnings of a bad teenage moustache.

"Well, here we are. What do you think?" his father asked as they looked over at the dilapidated apartment complex.

Eli wanted to say was this place was a shithole and that he hated him for moving them halfway across the country away from their family and friends, all so he could take some crappy security job. But he didn't. Instead, he mustered a weak grin and said, "Yeah it's great, Dad."

"See, I told you you'd like it," his dad smiled as he unloaded the first of the suitcases. "Now make yourself useful and give me a hand bringing this stuff up to the apartment. It's Number 20 on the second floor."

Eli grabbed his backpack and carefully unloaded a blue BMX from the back of the station wagon and wheeled it inside the Flamingo. There were two things that struck him as soon as he walked into the courtyard. One was just how rundown the old building was. The U-shaped, two-storey complex looked like it was about to crumble to the ground, its pink painted stucco facade was faded and chipped, two of the units were boarded up and fire-damaged and at least half of the remaining apartments looked like they hadn't been lived in for years. Even worse, the huge swimming pool his father had boasted about looked like a green, scum-filled pond.

The second was the smell. A rank odour hung over the complex; it was kind of bitter and sweet and dark and moist all at once. It reminded Eli of the time a rat had died in the ceiling of their old place.

"Nice bike," a voice said. "I got the same one."

Eli looked around. There was a kid about his age wearing a football jersey and an infectious grin sitting on the steps nearby.

"My name's Cory."

"Eli."

"Are you moving in?"

"Yeah, me and my dad. Say, do you know what that smell is?"

"You get used to it. The caretaker says it's a broken sewer line. You want a hand with your stuff?"

Eli nodded and handed him his backpack.

"You ride much?"

"Every day back home."

"Yeah, me too. There's a pretty gnarly bowl in the park near here. You should come for a ride sometime."

Eli picked up his bike and followed Cory up the stairs. "Yeah, okay, cool."

Just then the door opened from an apartment on the opposite side of the courtyard and the most beautiful girl Eli had ever seen walked out.

"Who's that?" he asked, his wide-eyed gaze following her as she walked down the stairs.

"Oh, that's Tracy. Pretty, huh? She lives in Number 14 with her dad."

"She's beautiful," Eli agreed. He couldn't take his eyes off her. Tracy's face was perfect, with teased blonde hair, frosted eyeshadow and coral-coloured lips. She wore an old jean jacket covered with pins and badges and when she popped the collar and flicked her hair, she looked just like a movie star walking in slow motion to her own theme music.

"Get in line, man, everyone in school is in love with Tracy, including me…and I've got a girlfriend," Cory laughed. "Shame she dropped out. I hear she's working up at the Buy 'n Save as a cashier now."

Eli watched her leave. "Does she have a boyfriend?"

"Yeah, an older guy called Wayne. He's the caretaker here and a total burner, but he's pretty cool, I guess. She's totally out of his league man. In fact, she's out of all of our leagues."

They reached the door to Apartment 20 and Cory handed Eli his backpack.

"So what are you doing later?"

"I dunno. Helping my dad unpack."

"Me and my girlfriend are going to hang out at South Deering Park and watch the skaters for a bit. You can normally scrounge a beer or two if you're lucky. You wanna come?"

"Sounds cool."

"Awesome. Pick you up round seven, okay?"

For the next few hours Eli helped his dad cart boxes and suitcases up to the new apartment. When they were finished, they got hamburgers and shakes from the local diner and watched the news on TV while they ate. Most of it was the same old boring stuff, some country invaded some island, the space shuttle was launching again, blah, blah, blah…but one story caught Eli's attention. It was about the search for a missing teenager named Tommy Anderson who had disappeared three weeks ago from South Deering Park. The same park Cory had invited him to tonight. The news said that Tommy could be the latest victim of the so-called serial killer *The Stalker* who was believed to have been abducting children in Bedford for the last ten years.

Eli felt a little creeped out. He knew there was no way his father would let him go to that same park after seeing the report, especially because he was starting his new job tonight. But what his father didn't know wouldn't kill him so when there was a knock on the door a bit before seven, Eli said goodbye and ducked out, promising he'd be home by ten.

Cory and his girlfriend were waiting for him outside.

They couldn't have been more opposite. He was tall and goofy with bad hair and a permanent grin and she was dressed in black from head to toe with the sunny disposition of a nuclear winter.

"Eli, this is Jessica. Jessica, Eli."

"Charmed, I'm sure," she said unenthusiastically as she produced a silver flask from her pocket. "You want some?"

Eli looked back through the window at his father, who was sitting on the couch cracking a fresh bottle of whiskey.

"No, I'm good."

Jessica shrugged indifferently and took a swig. "More for me."

Eli followed them down the stairs to the courtyard. The smell assaulted him immediately; it was even worse than this afternoon and he curled his nose in distaste.

"My god, that reeks. How do you stand living here?"

"It's worse at night, don't ask me why." Cory noticed a little old man who was exiting the apartment on the ground floor directly below Tracy's and waved. "Hi, Mr Orlok."

The old man stopped and looked at them strangely. He was frail and stooped over and pale as a ghost. Mr Orlok wore a black suit, coat and gloves. His head was covered by a big woollen cap pulled all the way down over his brow and ears.

"Jesus, who the hell is that?" Eli asked.

"He's harmless," Cory replied. "He works nights over at the chocolate factory on Irvine Street."

"What is he, like a thousand years old?"

"You want some candy?" Mr Orlok asked in a heavy European accent, his gloved hand fishing around in his overcoat pocket.

"No thanks, Mr Orlok," Cory said.

Mr Orlok gave a close-lipped smile and shuffled on his way while Eli followed Cory and Jessica three blocks to the park.

2.

South Deering Park was the popular hangout for kids around the area.

It was nothing more than a large concrete expanse dotted with dozens of dying spindly trees, a few wooden tables and benches, and a large skate bowl in the middle. The bowl itself was lit by four towering floodlights that bathed the area in brilliant white light and cast long shadows down either end of the park.

Cory, Jessica and Eli hung out and watched the skaters till Jessica got bored and demanded to go. When Cory said he wanted to stay a while longer she whinged and complained until he relented and followed her to hang out with the group who were drinking down the far end of the park.

There were about ten kids perched on tables and benches drinking. The smell of dope was heavy in the air and loud rock music blared from a boombox. Eli noticed that Tracy was sitting there on a bench and drinking a beer, her arms draped over the legs of some guy who was sitting on the table behind her. He couldn't help but stare till she noticed and he dropped his eyes in embarrassment.

"Who's that?" asked the guy Tracy was draped over.

Cory smiled and tried to be cool. "Hey Wayne. It's me, Cory… Jessica, too."

"Who's that with you?" Wayne squinted to see in the dark; it was obvious he was very stoned.

Wayne was in his early twenties, tall, muscular and handsome with long blonde hair and the start of a beard on his cheeks. He looked at the world through round wire-rimmed glasses and wore blue jeans and a tight Judas Priest shirt with a packet of cigarettes rolled up in one sleeve.

"That's Eli. He just moved into the Flamingo today."

"Really?" Wayne sat up, suddenly interested. "You guys want a beer or something?"

"Thanks, Wayne," Cory said a little too eagerly.

Wayne passed them each a beer and lit a cigarette with a silver zippo with a *W* on it.

Eli took a drink and winced from the sour flavour. He'd only ever been drunk once before. Although he tried not to, his gaze fell on Tracy again. She ignored him or pretended not to notice.

But Wayne did.

"So new kid, where you from?"

"Ridgeway."

"How you liking our little town so far?"

"It's alright I guess."

"You guess? What's wrong with it?"

"I dunno. There's a lot of posters round town for missing kids. It's kind of creepy."

The other kids snickered at this and someone said, "Look out, he's afraid of The Stalker."

"I saw them talking about him on the news just before. They said some kid disappeared from this park three weeks ago. Tommy something, did you know him?"

The others stopped laughing and fell silent.

"Tommy lived over on Elm Street two blocks from here," Jessica said.

"I've known him since I was ten," said another.

Wayne looked less than impressed with the conversation.

"The Stalker is bullshit, alright. It's made up. Everybody knows the cops and the media are using it as a cover to hide the people that are dying from the chemical dumping in Rayburn Lake. Besides, Tommy was a fucking disease, everybody hated him. He probably ran away or some shit."

He produced a joint from his pocket, lit it and took a hit before holding it out for someone to take. "You guys wanna get high or what?"

Jessica snatched it greedily and took three deep draws before passing it on to Cory. He looked terrified. It was obvious he'd never smoked before and when he puffed on it he held the smoke in his lungs for a moment before he spat and coughed and turned red.

Wayne held the joint out to Eli.

"No thanks," he said.

Wayne didn't like that at all. "What are you, a fucking narc or something? Either take a hit or fuck off, new kid."

"Alright then." Eli reached out and took the joint, puffing several times before inhaling deeply.

The smoke was thick, hot and acrid and it burnt his lungs. All he wanted to do was cough but he held it down and casually blew out a thin plume of smoke. Eli handed the joint back to Wayne, then wandered off and sat on one of the nearby benches and sipped his beer. He felt like he was a passenger in his own mind, like he was in the back seat watching someone else operate his body.

The next few hours were a total blur. Eli tried to talk to Cory and Jessica but he kept on losing his train of thought and trailing off halfway through a sentence. At some point another kid that lived at the Flamingo joined them. His name was Ritchie. He seemed like a nice enough guy, big with shaggy red hair and kind of simple. He was telling some story about how he'd seen members from the band Kiss at the mall earlier today and that they'd asked him to come on tour with them as their new guitarist.

Eli couldn't tell if Ritchie was being serious or not but Wayne called him a fucking liar and everybody laughed him. Eli did too and once he started he couldn't stop and he laughed until tears rolled down his cheeks and his sides hurt.

Cory and Jessica left at some point. Eli was so stoned that he just sat and smiled and waved goodbye. It wasn't till Tracy came over and sat next to him that he snapped out of his haze.

"Are you okay?" she asked.

Eli nodded, not wanting to slur or say something stupid.

"First time?"

He nodded.

"Don't sweat it. My first time was the same. I laughed so hard my dad thought I was having a fit and called an ambulance."

Eli smiled and looked at her. "Really?"

"Swear to God. So, you gonna tell me why are you always staring at me?"

"I'm not."

"Every time I turn around, I catch you. You haven't taken your eyes off me since you moved in."

Eli felt the hot heat of embarrassment prickle up his spine. "I didn't mean too…"

"Well cut it out, alright? It's fucking creepy." Tracy glanced around then reached into her jacket pocket and pulled out a pill bottle with the word *Percocet* printed across the label. "Want one?"

Eli shook his head.

Tracy swallowed the pill with a swig of beer, then tossed the empty can. "So, why'd you move here?"

"You don't want to know that."

"Sure I do. I asked, didn't I?"

Eli looked at her, his eyes round and earnest and innocent.

"My dad lost his job and the bank took our house. He said living here was the best we could afford. He gambles and he drinks a lot. When my Mum was alive… I dunno, I guess he…"

Tracy gives him a reassuring smile. "I get it. My Mum died too."

"I didn't know…"

"We used to live in Plainview before we came here. My dad was pretty cool back then. Not like now. My mum, she killed herself a month after we moved into the Flamingo."

Tracy's eyes grew dark.

"There's something off with that place. Can you feel it?"

"I dunno, I just moved in today."

"It's like there's something evil in the building, I can't explain it. All I know is my life's turned to shit since we moved here." Tracy lit a cigarette. "Can I give you some advice? Get the fuck out of Bedford. I hate it here. I don't even sleep anymore, every night all I have is nightmares."

Tracy stood up. "It's getting late, I gotta go. See you round, okay?"

"Yeah alright, see you round," Eli said, a dopey grin plastered across his face.

The next few hours were a blur.

Wayne gave everyone another hit off a joint and insisted that they all shotgun beers. At some point the police arrived, the glare of their headlights causing the party to end. Wayne said he knew somewhere to go where they could keep on drinking but Eli muttered that he had to get home and wandered off back to the Flamingo.

It was almost midnight by the time he got back to the apartment.

Eli's father would have been furious if he found out he was out that late; luckily, he was working his first shift at his new job and wouldn't be home till three. As Eli plodded up the stairs, he could hear a loud argument coming from apartment 14 where Tracy lived with her dad.

Eli stopped and stood on the landing and listened in.

"…because you're a fucking slut, that's why," her father shouted. "What, you don't think I don't know about those pictures you let Jim Eidelman take of you last month? The whole town knows!"

"I was modelling, he said he could help my career!" Tracy shrieked back at him.

"How's fucking him gonna help your career? You're eighteen, he's a sixty-year-old wedding photographer Tracy… that's disgusting!"

"Disgusting?" The outrage and pain was thick in Tracy's voice. "Is it as disgusting as what you do to me, is it dad?"

"You shut your fucking mouth!" he growled at her.

Then the sound of a slap and crying.

"I swear to god, if you touch me again I'll kill you," Tracy screamed. "I'LL KILL YOU!"

Eli started down the stairs to break up the fight then froze when he heard laughing and saw two figures stumble into the courtyard. They walked over to Mr Orlok's door and knocked loudly.

After a few moments the old man opened the door and greeted his guests with a smile. It was the creepiest smile Eli had even seen, the kind of smile a serial killer flashed at a little kid while trying to lure them with candy. The figures entered the apartment and Mr Orlok closed the door behind them.

One of them was that kid Ritchie from the park.

3.

Eli and Cory sat on the stoop looking over at Richie's grandmother who was talking to the police from the front door of their apartment. Her eyes were black pits of worry. Nobody had seen Ritchie in a week.

Eli hadn't told anyone what he had seen, simply because he was terrified his father would discover he was out so late. He was mean when he was angry, and lately it didn't take all that much to set him off.

Things had been tense since they moved into the Flamingo. Eli had been plagued with nightmares and his father was barely sleeping. They seemed to argue all the time.

"Eli, get your ass down here and give me a hand with the groceries," his father snapped at him from the bottom of the stairs.

Eli knew better than to argue.

He scampered down and his father handed him two bags of groceries and pushed past him on the way up to the apartment. As Eli followed, he saw Tracy run out of her apartment in tears and slamming the door behind her. She had a fresh welt on her cheek.

"Hey Tracy, are you alright?"

"Just leave me alone," she yelled. "Everybody leave me the fuck alone."

Eli had heard fighting coming from Apartment 14 every night. It was getting worse. Tracy was right, there was something wrong with this place.

He hated living at the Flamingo.

Upstairs the TV was blaring and his father was poring over the paper while fixing himself a drink.

Eli dumped the groceries on the counter. "What's for dinner?"

"I picked up Chinese."

"Again?"

"Yeah again, you got a problem with that?" His father looked up from his paper and glared at Eli, almost challenging him to keep on complaining.

Eli shrank back and remained silent. His father took a deep, calming breath before he spoke again.

"Look, I got two hours before work. I'm tired. I just want to have a bite to eat and a drink before I have to get ready, okay?"

The news cut to another story about Ritchie. They'd stopped mentioning that Tommy kid altogether.

His father watched the report, then looked over at Eli. "You know that kid?"

The guilt Eli had been carrying around all week knotted in his stomach. Even if he was going to catch hell, he had to tell his father.

"Yeah, I met him…" Eli said, biting his lip nervously. "Dad, if I tell you something, do you promise you won't get mad?"

His father's eyes narrowed. "What'd you do now?"

"Why do you always think the worst?"

"Coz nothing good ever comes after saying 'promise you won't get mad.'"

"The night we moved in…when I went down to the park with Cory…I…"

"Out with it."

"I think I saw Ritchie go into that old guy Mr Orlok's apartment before he disappeared."

His father's eyes opened so wide the whites stood out like saucers. "You fucking what? Are you telling me you saw that kid a week ago and didn't tell anyone?"

Eli nodded and his father loomed over him.

"Why?"

"Coz I stayed out late and I was drunk and I didn't want you to find out."

Eli shrank, expecting his father to explode in rage but he just stood and stared at him incredulously.

"You stupid, selfish little shit." He looked at Eli like he didn't even know his own son. "All this time the police and that poor woman are looking for that missing boy and you don't say nothing. What the hell is wrong with you?"

His father walked over to the phone and started dialling.

Eli felt hot tears welling in his eyes.

"Who are you calling?"

"I'm calling the police, and you're going to tell them everything you know."

An hour later Eli was standing with his father and two police officers in his lounge room repeating the story about everything that happened the night Ritchie went missing. Well, almost everything. Eli left out the parts about smoking pot; he was already in enough trouble.

"So your excuse for withholding evidence from a police investigation is that you didn't want your dad to find out you were out late and drunk, is that right?" Officer Bradbury asked.

Neither of the police looked very impressed.

"Yes, ma'am."

"And how old are you, son?" Officer Harris asked.

"Fifteen."

The two officers looked at each other and shook their heads.

"Is Eli in a lot of trouble officer?" his father asked.

"Depends what happens to that boy, I guess," said Officer Bradbury, grimly staring at Eli and shutting her notebook. "Here's what we're going do. Officer Harris and I are going to go down to Apartment 11 and see if we can have a word to Mr Orlok about what your son said he saw last week. Mr Ellis, I'm going to ask that you and your son wait here in your apartment until we've concluded our interview just in case we need to speak to Eli further."

Eli's father cleared his throat uncomfortably and tried his best to smile. "Uh, look officer, I don't wanna be any trouble but I'm gonna be late for work if I don't get going soon. Any chance we could come down to the station in the morning and you could chat to the boy then?"

"I understand this is an inconvenience, Mr Ellis, but we're talking about a missing child. Time is of the essence. Now I need you to stay here with your son until we sort this out, are we clear?"

"Yeah. Thanks, Officer," Eli's father said, glaring at his son. "We're clear."

4.

It was almost dark by the time the police left Eli's apartment. Outside, the sun had all but dipped below the horizon and the fading daylight had painted the dilapidated apartment complex in muted pastel hues, its weathered facade casting long, distorted shadows across the courtyard.

Eli walked out onto the landing outside his door and watched the two officers as they made their way down the stairs and across to Mr Orlok's apartment. Inside he could hear his father on the phone trying to explain why he was going to be late for work.

Eli watched as Officer Bradbury knocked on Mr Orlok's door.

There was no answer. The officer waited, then knocked again, harder this time. There were several other residents at their windows now, watching what was going on.

Just as Officer Bradbury was about to knock for a third time, Mr Orlok's door opened a crack. It was dark inside the apartment and from where he was standing Eli couldn't see who'd answered the door. In fact, all Eli could clearly see was the backs of the two police officers as they began to talk to whoever was inside.

He needed to get closer.

Eli licked his lips nervously and glanced back over his shoulder at his father, who was arguing with his shift supervisor. He'd catch hell if he caught him leaving the apartment but he needed to know what they were saying.

"Fuck it," Eli whispered to himself, and he stole down the stairs and ducked down near a half-dead bush by the pool fence.

"...wondering if you might have a few minutes to answer some questions?" asked Officer Bradbury.

Mr Orlok stepped out of the apartment still dressed in the same outfit Eli had seen him in last week, his hat pulled low over his brow and his hands tucked deep into his pockets.

"Do you mind if my partner has a quick look around inside while we chat?" asked Officer Bradbury, trying her best not to choke from the smell.

Mr Orlok shook his head. The hunched-over old man looked bewildered and meek, like a frightened child.

"Mr Orlok, are you aware of the ongoing investigation into the disappearance of a teenager named Ritchie Brown who lived in the building?" Officer Bradbury asked while her partner Officer Harris disappeared inside the apartment.

Mr Orlok shook his head again. In the dim light his skin was the colour of porridge.

People were standing in their doorways now, watching keenly as the drama unfolded.

"Well, sir, this young man hasn't been seen for the past week and his family are very worried. We received some information today that Ritchie Brown and an as yet unknown acquaintance were seen entering your domicile around midnight last Friday."

Mr Orlok looked up over at Eli's apartment on the second floor and nodded and smiled his close-lipped smile at Officer Bradbury.

"Yes. I saw a young man and his father move into the building last week." His voice was frail and shaky.

Officer Bradbury did her best to hide her frustration. She fished out a picture of Ritchie from the breast pocket of her uniform and showed it to the old man.

"No, no, Mr Orlok, I don't think you understand," she said, speaking louder and enunciating each word carefully. "This is Ritchie Brown; he went missing last Friday. Did he come over to your apartment last week?"

Mr Orlok looked utterly confused. "Nobody has set foot in my home for ten years, Officer."

Just then there was a commotion and Ritchie's grandmother Martha Brown came bustling over in a fuss.

"Have you found my Ritchie? Do you know where my Ritchie is?"

She grabbed at Mr Orlok's shirt with tears in her eyes, her face as red as beet.

"Jesus, this is all we need." Officer Bradbury motioned to her partner inside the apartment. "Officer Harris, can you help me with this?"

Martha Brown became hysterical, falling to the ground and wailing. Eli looked around. It seemed that everyone that lived in The Flamingo was coming down to the courtyard to see what all the fuss was about.

It was time to get back home, before his father caught him.

Eli got up and made his way towards the stairs. His father was standing at the top glaring, thunderheads gathering in his eyes.

"What the fuck are you doing, boy?" Eli's father looked so angry he could spit. "Get your ass inside this instant."

Eli ran up the stairs and into the apartment. His father followed him inside and slammed the door behind him, yelling and cursing at the top of his lungs. Eli didn't say anything, he just stood and stared at his feet until his father was interrupted by a knock at the door.

It was the police again.

"Sorry to interrupt, Mr Ellis, do you have a minute?" It was obvious they'd heard him screaming at his son.

Eli's father smoothed back his hair in an effort to calm his temper and he smiled politely at the officer. "What can I do for you?"

"Well, sir, we've had a word with Mr Orlok down at Number 11 and had a look around his apartment. There doesn't seem to be any evidence that Ritchie Brown or anyone else for that matter has been in that apartment for a long time. Maybe Eli was mistaken."

Eli couldn't believe what he was hearing. He'd seen Ritchie walk into that apartment as clear as he could see Officer Bradbury standing in front of him right now.

"I'm going to leave you with my contact information, Mr Ellis. If you or your son can think of anything else, please give us a call." Officer Bradbury handed Eli's father her card and started to leave.

"So that's it?" Eli asked indignantly. "You just go down there, take a look around, ask a couple of questions and leave?"

The two officers stopped and turned to look at Eli.

"What do you mean, *is that it?*" Officer Bradbury said. "There's no one in there. That little old man isn't capable of looking after himself, let alone abducting a sixteen-year-old boy. The only thing we have to go on is the word of a minor, who was, by his own admission, heavily intoxicated at the time."

"But I'm sure I…" Eli started but his father cut him off.

"That's enough, Eli."

Officer Bradbury turned her attention to Eli's father. "Now, I don't know what this boy did or didn't see, but I do know that a fifteen-year-old shouldn't be out drinking and doing God-knows-what at twelve o'clock at night. My advice to you, Mr Ellis, is to take a stronger hand with your boy, or he could find himself in some serious trouble. Do we understand each other?"

"Perfectly," was all Eli's father said.

He closed the door and waited till he heard the police officers' steps trail down the stairs, then turned to his son. He looked at Eli like he was going to kill him.

"Dad, I can explain…"

Eli's father exploded, smacking him across the face with the back of his hand and sending Eli sprawling across the room.

"Not another fucking word," his father seethed. "We'll talk about this in the morning."

Eli's father grabbed his coat and stormed out the front door, slamming it shut so hard the wood almost cracked from the force.

Eli sat on the floor for a moment, still in shock and rubbing his cheek ruefully. He couldn't believe his father had hit him. He'd done a lot of shitty things in Eli's life, but he'd never hit him before.

Eli got to his feet, crossed to the window, and pulled open the curtains. He could see his father stalking angrily across the courtyard towards the car park. Most of everyone who lived at The Flamingo had already gone back inside their apartments, the evening's spectacle already forgotten. Everyone but Mr Orlok. He was standing in the shadows outside his front door looking up at Eli's apartment. He didn't look like some frightened little old man anymore. He looked like he was the devil and Eli felt a chill slowly creep up his spine.

5.

Eli's eye was swelling shut.

He examined it closely in the bathroom mirror, pressing tentatively at the large lump forming near the corner of his eye. He felt so mad he wanted to scream.

"Fuck him," he said to his reflection in the mirror. "I'm not gonna fucking stay here and take this shit anymore."

He was going to run away.

Back to the only place that was ever home.

Eli ran into his room, packed some clothes and wrote a note telling his father he was going back to Ridgeway.

He made it as far as South Deering Park.

The caretaker, Wayne, was sitting on one of the benches drinking beer so Eli decided to join him and get drunk.

"So why are you leaving?"

"Coz my dad's a fucking asshole and I hate this place." Eli tried to swallow the painful lump in his throat along with a mouthful of beer so he wouldn't cry in front of Wayne. "Are you going to try and stop me?"

"Nah. I met your dad and I agree, he is an asshole."

Eli tried his best not to laugh. "So where's Tracy?"

"Don't know, don't care."

"I thought she was your girlfriend."

"Man, that chick is out of her mind, you can have her. What's up with you and your dad?"

Eli told him about what he saw last Friday night and going to see Mr Orlok with the police. Then he told him about his father hitting him.

"So, you're telling me that you think Mr Orlok, that little old man from Apartment 11, he's the one that kidnapped Ritchie? Is that right?" Wayne looked very amused by what Eli was saying.

"Yeah."

Wayne chuckled and shook his head. "You were pretty wasted, man. I don't think it played out that way."

"How'd you know, you weren't there."

"Coz I know, that's how. I've worked there for five years. How long have you been there, like a week?"

"Ten days," Eli mumbled into his beer.

"Listen, dude, that old guy's harmless, I promise you." Wayne motioned to Eli to finish his beer and gave him another. "Ritchie, on the other hand, is a fucking liar, all he wants is attention. The dumb fuck is probably hiding out somewhere watching the news and loving it. I shit you not, he's gonna turn up in a week spouting some crap story how he was abducted by aliens or some shit."

Eli had to laugh at this. Wayne was probably right. He was cool, too.

"All this shit will blow over, man, I promise," Wayne said, smiling. "So are you really going to run away, little man?"

Eli shook his head.

"Good. Say, why don't you come with me? I'm going over to a friend's house. We can smoke some grass and hang out. Sound cool?"

"Yeah, okay, cool. But I got to stop by my house first. I left my dad a note telling him I was headed back to Ridgeway; if he finds it before I get back there'll be hell to pay."

Wayne looked at him strangely and smiled a huge smile.

It was off-putting.

"You left your dad a note telling him you were running away?" Wayne asked almost as if he didn't quite believe what Eli was telling him. "That's awesome."

"Yeah." Eli grinned, not knowing what was so amazing. "Why's that awesome?"

"Oh, no reason," Wayne said as he lit his cigarette with his zippo.

Wayne grabbed what was left of his six-pack and they walked back down towards the Flamingo. It took them fifteen minutes. All the way Eli pestered Wayne about where they were going next and who they were going to hang out with. Wayne never gave him a straight answer. Instead, he told him, "You'll see" and "Don't worry about it."

When they rounded the corner of Elm Street onto Lamar Drive, they both stopped in their tracks. The street outside the apartment building was choked with police cars, their red and blue flashing lights lighting up the night sky. There were people everywhere rubbernecking, all of them crowded around the entrance to the Flamingo.

As soon as Wayne saw the flashing lights he turned pale as a ghost.

"I gotta go," he said, backing away. "I'll catch up with you some other time."

Wayne ducked back down Elm Street, leaving Eli confused as to what had just happened.

"Hey, Eli," a voice called.

Eli looked over towards the crowd. It was Cory motioning to come join him.

"Where the fuck have you been?"

"At the park," Eli said, jostling to get a better look.

Two paramedics came through the front entrance of the Flamingo pushing a gurney. On top was a black plastic body bag.

"What happened?"

Cory looked at him like he was from another planet.

"Tracy killed her dad. She fucking snapped or something. Then she shot herself in the head."

"Tracy's dead?"

Eli felt the ground drop out from beneath him. He couldn't believe it; he just couldn't believe it.

It was well past eleven before the police let them back into The Flamingo. Eli trudged up the stairs to his unit and stood on the balcony looking across at Tracy's apartment. It was lit by yellow work lights that shone bright and cold like her apartment was a convenience store. There was yellow tape blocking the doors and stairs and police milled about logging evidence in plastic bags. Through the window Eli could see a spray of bright red blood on the lounge room wall.

Eli wondered if it was Tracy's.

He opened the door to his apartment and walked inside. It felt different now she was gone. Empty, maybe. Almost as if the scant happiness he'd known in this place had simply disappeared into the putrid, putty-coloured walls.

Eli found the note he'd left for his father, balled it up and threw it in the trash. Then he sneaked a sip of whiskey from the bottle his father kept in the cupboard above the sink before he lay down on his bed, not even bothering to get undressed.

But sleep didn't find him right away.

Instead, he tossed and turned for hours before he fell into a feverish slumber, his mind plagued with horrible nightmares.

Eli woke up with a start a little past two in the morning. He was shivering but it wasn't cold. The room was dark and it took him a moment to get his bearings. Something felt off. He was sure that he'd just heard a sound coming from the lounge room.

But was that a dream or real?

Eli listened intently for a moment, then decided it was nothing, relaxed and closed his eyes again.

Then the sound again.

He sat up.

He didn't imagine that. Was that the creak of a door?

Eli got up and stood next to his bed, listening for movement in the apartment.

"Dad?"

There was no answer.

Eli walked over to the light switch and turned it on. The darkness retreated and he was alone. But it didn't feel like he was alone. It felt like there was someone in the apartment. He opened the bedroom door and peered down the hall. Shadows stretched along the walls as if moving of their own accord, each one spindly and deformed like some clawed demon creeping up into his apartment to seal his doom.

"Hello?"

No answer.

For a moment he considered going back to bed and waiting till his father got home. But instead, he stepped out into the hallway.

Eli tread carefully, trying his best not to make a sound. The air felt heavy and the dim light shining from his bedroom made the hallway seem to stretch endlessly before him. He listened intently as he made his way towards the lounge room, desperately trying to ignore the panic gripping his chest like a vice and making it impossible to breath.

Was there someone here in the apartment with him?

Was it The Stalker? The killer he'd heard about on TV?

Eli swallowed hard and walked into the lounge room. It was dark and lit only by the light of the moon. Outside, The Flamingo slumbered, the apartments all dark and quiet.

He breathed a sigh of relief.

Then he noticed that the front door was wide open, the cold night air wafting in and billowing the drapes.

Ice water trickled down his spine.

He was sure he'd closed the front door when he got home.

But did he?

Maybe he didn't. Maybe he forgot and came home, dumped his bag and went to bed.

"This is stupid," he said out loud. "You're being fucking stupid."

Eli closed the front door and turned the lock, listening to the tumbler fall with a satisfying clunk. This was all about Tracy. Simple as that. It was no wonder he was creeped out; it wasn't every day you came home to a fucking murder-suicide in your building. What he needed now more than anything was some sleep.

But before that, he needed a snack.

Eli opened the fridge and squinted at the cold, bright light, waiting for his eyes to adjust. He peered at the half-filled cartons of Chinese food till he found some wontons and satisfied, he stood up and closed the refrigerator door.

Standing behind, waiting in the dark, was a monster.

It was Mr Orlok.

But he didn't look like Mr Orlok anymore.

He was tall and imposing, his head bald with ears pointed like a bat. Orlok's eyes were black pits of nothingness and his skin was pale blue and translucent.

The monster rose before Eli and the shadows seemed to form around him like a cloak. Orlok stretched out his taloned hands and hissed, baring his horrible yellow fangs.

Eli screamed like he had never screamed before and soon there was only darkness.

6.

Eli woke to the damp-sweet smell of death.

It was overwhelming.

He was in a room. It was so dark he could barely see a shape in the inky blackness around him. Disorientated and in a haze, Eli tried to get to his feet but his hands were bound and shackled to the floor. He panicked, frantically pulling at his bonds as hard as he could and shouting out desperately for help.

A voice answered from nearby in the dark.

"Eli, are you okay?"

"Who's that?"

Eli looked around in the direction of the sound. He knew that voice.

"It's me, Ritchie."

"Ritchie? What the fuck is going on man? Where are we?"

"Mr Orlok…" Ritchie began to cry hysterically. "I…I think he's The Stalker. We're gonna die Eli, we're both…"

"Calm down, Ritchie, it's alright," Eli whispered. "Tell me what happened to you."

"Wayne, uh, he invited me over to Mr Orlok's place… At first they…" Ritchie started sobbing again and it took him several moments to regain his composure. "They tricked me, with the handcuffs. Wayne got out of them easy, he…he bet me I couldn't do it…but when I put them on, I couldn't get them off. Then they… Oh, God… They killed that Tommy kid right in front of me."

There were sounds outside the room. Footsteps.

Ritchie began to cry loudly.

"Ritchie, calm down, please."

But Ritchie wouldn't listen. "Orlok…he's…he's a monster… He drank his blood…"

The footsteps were closer now.

"Ritchie!" Eli pleaded, desperately trying to keep Ritchie quiet. "You gotta help me. Where we are? How do we get out of here?"

"We're never getting out of here, Eli. We're gonna die in here."

Just then the door opened, flooding the room in a harsh white light.

Eli scrambled away from the door as far as he could, shielding his eyes from the glare. The room was bare, the walls soundproofed, and windows boarded over. There was dried blood on the floor and claw marks on the walls. Ritchie cowered in the opposite corner of the room. He was emaciated and looked like he had been tortured to the brink of death.

Orlok filled the doorway. He was a nightmare.

"Take him," Orlok commanded, pointing a long, curved talon at Ritchie.

Ritchie screamed hysterically and tore at the bonds on his wrists, trying to get away.

Wayne appeared in the doorway beside Orlok. "As you wish, Master."

Wayne rushed into the room, kicking Ritchie square in the face, then pummelling him till he went limp. He freed Ritchie then dragged him out past Orlok through an open door across the hall and slammed it shut behind him.

"Please…please don't hurt me," Eli whined.

Orlok laughed and Eli's skin turned to gooseflesh.

"You have caused me great inconvenience and for that you will know pain like no one has known before. Before night's end you will pray for death, child, but like me you will not know its sweet relief."

Eli felt warm urine soak his pants and he started screaming.

"Someone please…someone…someone please help me!"

"No one can help you." Orlok jeered. "For millennia I have walked this earth, cursed with everlasting life. In my damnation I have seen empires fall and dynasties crumble to dust, yet I have remained. Through the ages I have been known by many names; vampyre, Nosferatu, master of rats, but tonight, you will simply know me as your doom."

The fiend turned and stalked out of the room, slamming the door shut and plunging Eli back into darkness.

7.

Ritchie's muffled screams filled the darkness.

It had been more than an hour since he'd been dragged off. Eli was desperate to escape and panic overwhelmed him.

He had to get out of here before they came back for him.

He started to thrash about, wrenching against the bonds with all his might. But no matter how hard he struggled, he couldn't get free.

Then the door opened again.

Wayne was standing in the doorway splattered with blood, a maniacal grin upon his face.

"Come here, you little shit."

He overwhelmed Eli in a second and dragged him kicking and screaming into the other room. It was bare and soundproofed like the other. There was a small table in the corner and a blood-stained bucket beneath. An A-frame plywood torture board stood in the center of the room beneath a single bare bulb. Ritchie was strapped face down to one the other side, his wrists bound by thick nylon ropes affixed through holes in each corner.

He had either passed out or died from the pain.

Orlok stood watching as Wayne dragged Eli into the room

and strapped him to the other side of the board. Eli struggled to get free but it was no use. Orlok moved slowly around the room and stood behind Eli, lingering for a moment before he leaned in close and whispered in his ear.

"It was I who corrupted Tracy's simple mind, it was I who drove her to murder." Orlok cackled malevolently, the stench from his fetid mouth like that of a tomb. "And when I have finished with you, I will make sure your father suffers the same horrible fate."

Eli moaned in terror and he felt his knees buckle.

Orlok fell upon him, viciously tearing at his neck. White hot pain radiated through Eli's body and every muscle tensed as he twisted and arched away from the monster.

But nothing could stop Orlok. He sucked at his neck, gulping down the gouts of blood that spilled from his vein. A horrible trance overcame Eli and darkness danced before his eyes as the terrible rhythm of his own heartbeat thumped in his ears, strong at first, then weaker and weaker and weaker.

He felt himself slipping away.

Everything became grey and slow.

And just when Eli felt himself begin to lose consciousness, the monster stopped and released his foul grip on his neck. Eli struggled to catch his breath as the room slowly grew bright again.

Ritchie was moaning on the other side of the board.

"It is dawn. I must sleep. Have your fun with this one, but Eli must be unharmed for tomorrow," Orlok said, motioning to what was left of Ritchie.

"Yes, master," Wayne grovelled as Orlok turned and left the room.

He waited for a moment, then smiled at Eli and Ritchie.

"Now I can't hurt you, little man, you heard what the master said." Wayne stared at Eli menacingly, then made his way over to the small table in the corner of the room.

He picked up a large hunting knife and slowly unsheathed it. "But that don't mean me and Ritchie here can't have some fun."

Absolute terror and helplessness overwhelmed Eli. His heart beat like a drum and his breathing became short and shallow. He was almost paralysed with fear. Eli's mind raced. There had to be a way to get out of here. He looked around the room, desperately searching for something that could set him free. But there was nothing. There was nothing that could… Then Eli noticed the large, loose knots in the thick ropes that bound his wrists. If he could reach one of them, he might be able to free his hand with his teeth.

Ritchie began to scream hysterically, begging for mercy and thrashing about on the other side of the board.

Wayne laughed and put the knife down on the floor between his feet. "I'm just gonna get a bucket for the blood, then we're gonna have some fun, fat boy."

Wayne turned and walked back to the corner of the room to get the bucket. This was Eli's chance. He stretched up onto the tips of his toes and pulled down with his left hand with all his might, straining his neck till his front incisors snapped onto the edge of the cord. He bit down hard and yanked his head back, pulling the rope loose of the knot and allowing him to free his hand. His heart raced as he fumbled to undo the other knot.

Then both of his hands were free.

Adrenaline coursed through Eli and he quickly moved around the A-frame, bent down and grabbed the knife, just as Wayne turned back towards Ritchie.

"You ready for this?" Wayne laughed cruelly.

But his expression crumbled into fear as Eli rushed forward and attacked, swinging the knife wildly and screaming like an animal.

Caught totally by surprise, all Wayne could do was shield his face as Eli stabbed him in the neck. The knife hit bone and Wayne grunted, the color draining from his face. Eli ripped the knife from his throat and stabbed him again and again and again in a frenzy until Wayne fell to his knees, gurgling blood.

He gasped once, then started convulsing and died on the floor.

Ritchie struggled against his bonds crying uncontrollably. "Eli please…please get me out of here."

Eli stood over the corpse for a moment, his mind blank, eyes staring at the growing pool of blood radiating from Wayne's head. Ritchie called his name again and the sound snapped him back to reality.

"Are you alright?" Eli asked as he untied the ropes around Ritchie's wrists.

Ritchie tried to walk but staggered and fell to his knees.

"I got you," Eli said, putting his arm around Ritchie and helping him to his feet.

They stumbled out of the room and up the hallway. At the end was a plywood wall with a low-set, crude-looking door cut into the wood.

Eli pushed the door open cautiously, shrinking in fear as the hinges creaked loudly. He waited for a moment, listening for movement, then when he was sure someone wasn't waiting for them on the other side, he helped Ritchie make his way through. They came out into the hallway of Mr Orlok's apartment. An old wardrobe sat just in front of the doorway, leaving a narrow space for them to squeeze through. No wonder the police couldn't find anyone when they searched the place: the wardrobe would totally conceal the false wall and the door when it was pushed back up against it.

Ritchie groaned and fell to his knees; he was pale and he'd lost a lot of blood. Eli had to get help before it was too late. He helped Ritchie to his feet and urged him to keep moving, all the while expecting Orlok to suddenly appear from one of the doorways and start ripping them apart.

But he didn't. The apartment was deathly quiet and seemed empty.

Eli dragged Ritchie down the hall to the front door, his eyes wide, head darting left and right in terror.

"We're almost out of here," he whispered to Ritchie as they reached the front door and he twisted the handle.

It was deadlocked.

Eli's heart sank.

"There's gotta be a way out of here," Ritchie said as he staggered over to one of the windows and pulled aside the drapes.

The windows were boarded up.

"We're gonna die… We're gonna fucking die…" Richie began to cry again.

"We've gotta find the keys," Eli said, trying his best to not let the panic he was feeling overwhelm him. "You check the kitchen drawers. I'm gonna go check Wayne's pockets."

"I don't think I can, Eli. I feel like I'm gonna pass out."

"We're almost out of here, Ritchie, we've just got to push a little bit longer."

Ritchie nodded, but he didn't look good. He looked like he was dying.

Eli made his way back down the hall, past the wardrobe, and stood at the doorway looking at Wayne's corpse. He almost expected him to be sitting there waiting for him, but his body was right where he left it in a puddle of blood, his eyes open and staring blankly at the wall.

Eli rolled over the body and checked his pockets.

All he found was loose change and his zippo lighter. Eli grabbed the lighter and the hunting knife for good measure, then returned to the kitchen. Ritchie was slumped down next to the refrigerator on the linoleum floor.

He looked like he'd passed out.

Eli shook his shoulder. Ritchie woke suddenly, his eyes opening wide like two huge saucers.

"What the fuck? Where am I?"

Eli tried to calm him. "It's me, Eli. Did you have any luck finding the keys? Wayne didn't have them."

"Uh-uh. I could find them anywhere." Ritchie shook his head, then pointed at two crescent-shaped grooves in the lino. "What do you think those are?"

They looked like old, worn scratch marks.

As if someone had pushed the refrigerator across the linoleum, again and again and again.

"Let me see if I can move this," Eli said, grabbing one side of the fridge.

"We need to get the fuck out of here," Ritchie said as he struggled to push himself up to his feet.

Eli shook his head. "There's no way out of here, not without a key. We've got to find Orlok, get the keys from him and kill him."

Tears welled up in Ritchie's eyes.

"But he's a fucking vampire, man," he whispered.

"I know," Eli said. "But either we stop him now or he gets away and keeps on killing kids. We gotta stop him, Ritchie."

Ritchie nodded and Eli pushed the refrigerator across the floor. Beneath was a small hole that had been cut into the flooring, no wider than a man's shoulders.

A ladder was propped at the opening, leading down.

"What do we do now?"

Eli looked at the hole. It was like a pit leading to hell.

"We go down."

Ritchie shook his head. "I don't know if I can, I feel cold and dizzy."

"I'll help you, Ritchie. Let me go down first."

Eli climbed down the ladder. The room below was pitch black and the smell of death was overwhelming. When he reached the bottom of the ladder, he called for Ritchie to follow and he helped him make his way slowly down. When he finally reached the bottom, Eli retrieved Wayne's zippo from his pocket. It lit on the second try.

It must have been the furnace or some old utility room. Whatever it was, it had been sealed up and hidden for decades. In the dim, flickering light, the room looked frozen in time, wrapped in an eerie stillness. The entrance had been bricked closed long ago, the air was heavy with the musty scent of dust and the darker, sweeter odour of decay. Every surface was adorned with cobwebs and long forgotten tools lay rusted and neglected in grime-covered pegboards.

Dark shapes lined the walls.

Eli took a tentative step into the room as his eyes adjusted to the gloom.

And when he saw what was down there, he almost lost his mind.

The room was some kind of macabre tomb. Propped up against the walls were dozens upon dozens of desiccated mummies, their eyeless brown leather faces frozen in endless torment.

Eli did his best not to scream.

"Ritchie, are you okay?"

Ritchie nodded but he looked delirious.

"There's another room up ahead. Lean on me, alright? We're almost out of here."

Eli put his arm around Ritchie and propped him up as they made their way past the bodies and into the next room. The stench grew worse the further they went and the lighter's flickering glow barely kept the gloom at bay.

They reached the doorway to the second room and both stopped in horror.

Beyond, the room was piled with vile black earth. Worms and roaches twisted and squirmed amongst the diseased soil while rats, fat, slick and oily, lounged amongst the filth. Orlok lay sleeping, naked and buried to his chest in the foul dirt, his lifeless eyes open and dead to the world. He looked bloated, like a leech that had sucked too much blood, the black veins beneath his translucent blue skin pulsing like an undulating maggot.

"What do we do?" Ritchie whispered.

Eli glanced at the hunting knife tucked in his belt and briefly considered attacking Orlok as he slept; then he noticed the basement transom window up in the corner of the far wall.

It was boarded up just like the other windows.

"Sunlight kills vampires," he whispered to Ritchie. "If I can pry a board free the light will shine in and kill him."

"How you going to do that? It's nailed shut."

"Wait here a sec."

Before Ritchie could protest, Eli turned and slipped back into the other room, grabbing an old, rusted crowbar from the pegboard. When he returned, he motioned for Ritchie to be quiet and crept across the tomb to the window. He carefully slipped the crowbar under the board and breathed deep.

"Here goes nothing," he whispered.

Eli slammed the crowbar up, splintering the wood as the nail slipped out and the board fell away. A blinding beam of bright sunlight shone down into the basement crypt illuminating Orlok like a holy light from heaven. Orlok's face twisted in an ungodly rage, and he screamed like a devil, rising ominously from the earth.

Smiles cracked the faces of Eli and Ritchie as they watched the foul vampire stand before them bathed in light, expecting his skin to blister and burn and smoke at any moment.

But it didn't.

Instead, the fiend stood and laughed at them.

"Spineless worms. You dare try to destroy me while I slumber by shining a light in my eyes?" Nosferatu spat with contempt as he started towards them ominously.

"Don't you realize that is but a stupid myth, a children's tale told by simple-minded peasants so they can sleep at night? Two hundred years ago a woman in Wisberg tried the very same thing. She lured me into her home to feed on her, hoping to kill me with dawn's light. But sunlight cannot kill me. It merely weakens my powers."

Eli felt his bowels loosen as Orlok's eyes fell upon him.

"I'll tell you my secret, boy. To kill me, you must sever my head and hammer a stake through my unbeating heart. That is the only way you can defeat a vampire."

The monster's wicked laugh filled the tomb, and Eli and Ritchie fell to their knees in terror. Orlok rose and became one with the shadows as darkness engulfed them for now and evermore.

WHEN STAKES ARE HIGH, STAY SHARP

H.K. Stubbs

When Stakes Are High, Stay Sharp

Miss Ellen of The Portrait's First Lesson of Dealing with Nosferatu: Run fast and keep your eyes open.

Skin hangs white and loose on her shoulders and cheeks. Her joints ache, like her bones are rusting iron. Driven purely by fear, she runs. Her sodden shift drags through the mud and catches on branches, tearing. Despite deathly fatigue, she forces her body to dart to the next tree—supernaturally fast when she moves, inhumanly still when she stops.

She's far from the road, now, where the galloping beast's nostrils steam. His heart races in his chest, blood roaring through his veins. She hears it, it pounds in her ears as though it were her own, for she has no pulse anymore. Ellen slinks down into a creek bed on all fours, quick and smooth like a lizard. She wades, knee-deep in the bracken-thick cascades. Stumbling over rocks, she falls, claws her way over a fallen tree trunk, then runs again, splinters under her fingernails.

The horse hooves thunder faster, nearer, along the gravel road as it loops back around near the river. She glances back, eyes wide, whites shining in the dim night. The horse smells of animal, hay and manure, a stronger scent than the forest's rain and moss. The menace of the rider, the *hunter*, raises the hairs on the back of her neck. It's the whip against her shoulders, driving her on.

Where am I going? To where do I flee?

The answer rushes upon her.

Home: to Hutter, to Grace. Their family has built their lives in a cottage in the country, where Hutter endures his drunken moods that last for days, and his screaming nightmares every night. Hutter was once Ellen's husband, then, widowed, dug her grave alone and buried her deep in the forest. With a finger she rubs her gums, still seeping black blood, corroded by the garlic he stuffed in her mouth.

He married his new wife, Carol, and they had three children. Grace, his eldest daughter, is the only one awake in the cottage. Ellen has heard wisps of her thoughts and feelings since the first days the child garnered consciousness. Tonight, she smells her blood on the wind: the scrapes on her knees and elbows from days wrestling her brothers in the garden and clashing stakes with them in games of *Bite Me if You Can*, and the blood flowing between her legs with the promise of new life, as she grows into a woman.

Why am I leading this monster toward those I love? Ellen asks herself. *Why, when I'm a blood-hungry beast myself?*

Fear of the hunter woke her this night, and has driven her, madly. Terror drove her to claw up through the soil for the first time, the earth loosened by a week of rain, and illuminated by a beam of moonlight shining through the clouds, straight as the hand of a clock at midnight.

All these years she's lain in a half-sleep, connected to the living through her portrait, the same portrait Hutter took over the seas, that drew Count Orlok to her, hastened his journey here. A journey which ended in their mutual destruction.

Through the portrait's eyes she's relished Hutter and Grace's delights with them, and rued their tragedies… When little Phillip died in his sleep, just a babe in arms, Ellen's somnambulant corpse, underground, cried black tears for his loss.

Tonight, anger and hate growl in her belly, even stronger than hunger, for the man who took her life and tarnished her pure heart. Her feelings are a storm of hate, desperation and love. She hates Orlok as much as Hutter's wife hates her. The new Mrs Hutter—Carol—hides her portrait in cold, damp places. She curses: *let the devil take you, Satan's whore.*

And yet, Ellen's portrait would not burn, when Carol cast her into the fire. The flames felt real, pain scorching, as though she was burning in flesh and blood. She screamed but endured through the inferno until it dwindled, leaving only ashes and her portrait barely touched. Grace had gathered it to her bosom and said, *All will be well, Miss Ellen. Do we train tonight?*

She restored Ellen to her frame, unharmed but for smears of smoke aging her forehead and troubling her brow. She looked more like she felt, no longer the pure, innocent woman whose image Hutter had carried across the sea.

Yes. Always—we train, Miss Ellen had replied.

Tonight, the new Mrs Hutter might get her wish. The devil has come for Ellen, and she's trying to outrun him. But if she continues to flee toward Hutter, Grace, Carol and their family, the devil will take them, too.

Ellen stops, eyes wide. She mustn't take him to the family! She won't find safety with Hutter, and Grace is not ready. Grace, her little friend, her dear little listener, wielder of stakes and Holy water, garlic and fire. She mustn't lead this evil pursuer to her young hunter.

Ellen stills, a statue, tall and broad-shouldered. Her eyes, shot with black veins, narrow hatefully. Her hair is stiff and wild about her head as the wind whips it around her pale, sagging face.

She tears a thick branch from a tree, with greater strength than she's ever wielded. Teeth as sharp as razorblades, she drags her jaws along the narrow end, sharpening it to a shredded point. The hunter materialises in the distance, a blacker shadow in the darkness. His stallion's nostrils steam as he rears.

She must fight.

Ellen relishes the horse's fear in his sweat, ravenous for the salty scent. He's afraid because Ellen is a monster untamed, hungry for blood of any kind, undiscerning. She would sink her fangs through his thick skin and guzzle his blood. She hasn't yet learned to prefer the finer tincture that flows from a gentleman's delicate throat.

The hunter's eyes glow blue in the dark, and his skin glimmers. Ellen takes her makeshift spear in both hands, as the rain pours down around her, dripping from the cuffs and hem of her stained shift. The hunter kicks his steed and steers him towards her. Ellen raises her spear to fight but, as the stallion approaches, the lure of blood pumping through the horse's veins is too strong, all-consuming. His blood smells rich, hot and salty, the antidote to her deprivation.

She lunges for his neck, hands stiff as claws.

Before she can sink her fangs into his flesh, the hunter casts a dark mass towards her. It swallows her head, tangles her arms. Trapped in a thick net, Ellen stumbles. The hunter launches from his horse and hits her hard, knocking her down. Their limbs clash like marble statues, but she feels no pain, only anger and desperation.

"Let me feed!" she rasps.

The hunter rises, stands over her, binds a rope around her arms.

"You will feed, but not on my horse," he says, in a voice as deep as the thunder that shook the twilight from the world this evening past.

"What do you want of me?" she demands, as he drags her up onto his horse.

"To take you home, my abominable niece."

Miss Ellen Of The Portrait's Second Lesson of Dealing with Nosferatu: Keep your ideal weapons at hand.

For supper, Mama served pumpkin soup and thick toast with butter. Grace inhaled deeply the scent of nutmeg filling the warm cottage. By the crackling fire, Papa played cards with Grace and her little brother and sister who squabbled and giggled, but Grace heard something in the distance. She glanced at the dark window many times, pressed her face against it, breath fogging the glass cold on her lips. She turned to the portrait of Miss Ellen on the bookshelf.

When she played with her family, she lost her games of cards, one after the other.

"Your mind is elsewhere tonight," Papa said, as the twins kissed him goodnight and Mama took them off to bed. Grace sat by his side to read the Holy tome by candlelight.

"Philippians 4:8," he suggested.

Grace nodded and searched for the verse, the thin pages snapping softly as her fingers turned them. She cleared her throat and read.

Dear brothers and sisters…fix your thoughts on what is true, and honourable, and right, and pure, and lovely, and admirable. Think about things that are excellent and worthy of praise…

Grace's eyes drift away from the Bible and up the shelves to Miss Ellen's portrait. She bites her lip. "Miss Ellen is restless tonight."

Papa gasps. "Grace, what could you mean?"

"She's running. Nearer to us, for our help—"

"Grace." His eyes are wide, disturbed and afraid. "Stop this nonsense."

She moves close to him and clutches his forearm, her voice desperate. "Papa, I think she needs—"

"Enough!" His eyebrows draw down, warning that a dark mood approaches.

"Gracie, don't quarrel with Papa. It's bedtime." Mama ushers her into the hallway. With a last glance into the darkness, Grace shivers and follows her mother away to bed. Hutter is looking at his hands, appalled, as though they drip with blood. Grace's hands shake, and she shrinks away from the deeper shadows, as she walks down the hallway to her bed beside the twins.

"Are you ill tonight, my bravest?" Mama asks, feeling her forehead. "You know not to trouble Papa, lest you trigger an episode."

Grace nods and climbs into bed, rolls over to face the wall.

"Goodnight, Mama."

Beyond the wall lurks a fear that Miss Ellen flees, and Grace cannot name. It has the texture of Orlok on the night, but he is dead. Miss Ellen killed him, as he took her life.

Out in the sitting room, Grace hears the click of Papa's shotgun as he breaks the barrel over his knee and loads two shots. Hushed voices as he and Mama exchange arguments, then footfalls lead to their bedroom. There's a clunk, as he leans the gun barrel against the corner beside him. It's just inches from Grace, through the wall they share, but she cannot reach through the wall to grab it.

In the darkness of her room, Grace waits.

Miss Ellen Of The Portrait's Third Lesson of Dealing with Nosferatu: When stakes are high, stay sharp.

Grace waits until all the family sleeps, then dons her mother's oiled leather coat, packs her bag with useful things, and deliberates over taking Papa's shotgun from beside his bed. It won't stop nosferatu. It might slow them down. But the weight of it will be too much to carry on a long walk. She'll be better off with her short sword. And extra stakes.

Grace reaches high up the bookshelf and fetches Miss Ellen's portrait down. Her friend remains silent and cool, absent, in her pocket. Grace sneaks out the door, setting the lock so it will secure the door when she closes it behind her.

It's a long walk as Grace trudges east through marsh and fog. At least the drizzle has eased, as she follows the thread which joins her to Miss Ellen. The portrait—the conduit which conveys their thoughts—remains silent.

It's more than the portrait that connects us, Miss Ellen once said. *The idea of you, I implanted in your father's mind, in our happiest days of love. You are my creation, Grace, as much as you are his and Carol's.*

The sky splits open to a dawn of orange light, revealing clouds as red and raw as wounds. She walks on through the morning glow and then the midday heat, until the smell of salt, seaweed and dune grass snaps in the air. Her family will be worried, back at home, but there's nothing she can do to help them more than this.

She mounts a grass dune. The sea is a dull blue mass, in the distance, seagulls wheeling above it. On the dock a huge ship is moored, sails folded, with a familiar crest emblazoned on its hull. Dread freezes her a moment, then resolve sets in, and she marches towards the road. Her boots crunch along the firm gravel.

The afternoon is cooling when she reaches the dock. She takes a long drink from her waterskin, contemplating the great, ancient ship before her. It creaks as it rocks, testing the ropes mooring it to the jetty, as though forces within wish it to be gone, will conjure a storm to drive it over the sea.

The coat of arms on the hull is the one Miss Ellen burned onto her mind long ago, the one to be feared above all others. But he is dead! Miss Ellen killed him with the dawn light. Despite all this, the House of Orlok has returned to take Ellen away—for punishment, for revenge? Grace takes a deep breath, checks her weapons, reassuring herself that they are within reach and can be drawn efficiently.

Thousands of times she's thrust them into clods of clay, picturing fanged, man-shaped monsters slain by her blades. She leaps across the water, landing lightly on the weather-worn deck of the ship.

Miss Ellen Of The Portrait's Fourth Lesson of Dealing with Nosferatu: Strike in the day.

Across the salt-stained deck, Grace arrives at steps which lead down into the hull of the great ship. Any nosferatu on board will be asleep. Human servants might be on duty, but the only sound is creaking ropes as a light breeze tugs at the folded sails. All else is quiet, seeming deserted.

She draws her short sword from the scabbard at her back, steps down the stairs, deeper into the darkness. A scratching noise along the hall gives her pause. She squints, trying to make out what is there.

A rat squeaks as it runs close and crouches on her boot, sniffing up at her, whiskers twitching. Disgusted, she kicks it away.

She walks on. At the end of the hallway, she turns left. More steps lead deeper down. The darkness is complete, and yet her eyes adjust.

You have the eyes of a hunter.

Miss Ellen! You are here.

Her mentor does not answer, but the portrait in her pocket warms, as it does when Miss Ellen communicates with her.

More rats scurry across the hallway, and Grace turns another corner, takes the steps down deeper into the belly of the ship. Doors gape on either side. Impossible stairways spiral off, above her head, traversable only by those who crawl upside down, along ceilings.

Beneath her creeping feet, the floor begins to writhe, thick with rats squirming over each other, chittering and fighting, some of them enormous, their bodies as tall as the tops of her boots. Further on, they're even bigger, as tall as her knees. She wades through the morass, stepping over them, treading on their tails, crushing their skulls with her boots, making them scream.

A giant rat, almost as tall as she is, sits like a drunk in front of a closed door at the end of the hall. The rat wears a crown of thorny rose vines on her head, and her belly is enormous. A tiny pink rat in a yellow sac squeezes out the hole near her tail. It squirms on the floor, helpless. Two larger rats snap at it, fighting over the newborn.

"I have to pass through that door," Grace says.

"She is not the one you knew." The rat queen's voice is squeaky and tortured. "She's your enemy now. Flee while you still can. While they sleep."

"I'm going through that door," Grace says, pointing her sword at the queen's eye. "Get out of my way or I will slay you and your children."

The rat queen laughs, a bloodcurdling chitter, her children joining in with noxious giggles, surging closer, protectively, to their mother.

"Out of my way," Grace warns, slashing her sword through the pile, kicking rats out of her way, striking for the rat queen's head. Her majesty and all her subjects reveal sharp teeth and fangs. They gnash at Grace, who grabs the queen's tail and tugs her backwards. Smaller rats climb Grace's legs and bite at the flesh above her boots. She clenches her teeth against the pain and drags the rat queen down the hall. She holds the tip of her sword to her neck.

"Kill me," the rat queen warns, "and chaos descends. My plague will run wild and clash, devouring you in the madness, until a new rat queen ascends. If you spare me, you spare yourself."

What the rat queen said made sense.

"Keep out of my way," Grace says.

The rat queen waves her tiny front legs back and forth, like a conductor, directing the tide of rats, who scurry behind her.

As Grace reaches for the doorhandle to the room, her white sleeve loose around her wrist, she notes the bolt on the door. If she goes in, she might not come out alive. She closes her eyes, trying to conquer the fear burning in her veins, racing through her heart, certain that her panic would delight Nosferatu.

In her pocket, the portrait of Miss Ellen glows so hot it burns.

Do not enter this room!

"Who else will save you?"

The doorhandle is cold on her sweating palm. It creaks as it turns. She opens the door to a room where the darkness is even thicker yet, somehow, her eyes adjust. There's a coffin and a large barrel set sideways in two braces.

Does Miss Ellen lie in the coffin? Whispering words entangle in the air, words overlapping and confused as time trips backwards. Echoed conversations play again.

Let me go! Stay away! Miss Ellen cries.

Wisps of action materialise in the air. A struggle.

If I'd known you'd be so easy to catch I'd have told the servants to set sail today. But I've given them the day. On the evening wind—tonight—we set sail.

Finally, Grace understands. The younger Count Orlok is Ellen's abductor.

Let me out! Miss Ellen cried, as he shovelled dirt over her bound hands. She fought against her prison as he nailed the lid closed. With her last strains of effort, she gnawed through the ropes binding her hands. The malaise of the death-sleep rolled over her mind and body, and sucked her under.

Grace takes a tentative step closer.

You don't have to do this, she says to herself. *You could turn around, and run. The sun will set soon. You could find safety in the church, before it does.*

But she cannot. Miss Ellen never abandoned her. She taught her everything she knew about Nosferatu, in case something like him came again. She taught her that it was not enough to sacrifice herself for love. That truly winning meant escaping not only with the lives of those dear to you, but with your own life, too.

She reaches a trembling hand towards the coffin, steeling herself, seeking the strongest mettle of resolve within her, firing up her physical strength, preparing to fight.

No! whispers the portrait in her pocket, but too late, for she's touched the coffin.

Nosferatu snaps half-awake. His power's like a blast, knocking Grace backwards as the lid of his coffin slams open. The sun has not yet set, so he cannot rise, but he shivers and jerks. He will wake soon.

Good Lord, what have I done?

Grace dives for the barrel, and lays her hands on the wood. Miss Ellen is in here. This is what Orlok nailed shut.

You can't trust me, Grace! Ellen cries. *Don't let me out. Run!*

Grace glances towards the door behind her, in time to see the rat queen slamming it closed, as a tsunami of rats rolls forward to pile up behind it. The external bolt slides in, as Grace thumps against the door with her shoulder. She'll never get out that way, and there are no other doors, nor windows.

I'm no longer me, Miss Ellen warns. *He gave me his blood, soaked the soil in it, in this barrel in which I am buried, to ferment, to become a creature controlled by him alone.*

"But you remember me," Grace whispers, scrummaging in the corners for something to use to hack into the barrel. *I need your help. I'm not strong enough alone.*

Her fingers close around a sledgehammer and then a crowbar. These will do. She raises the hammer over her shoulders and smashes it down against the barrel. With each strike of the hammer, Orlok convulses nearer to waking.

Grace levers the crowbar to prise open the smashed wood. Soil falls out, and Miss Ellen's hand jerks around, grabs her wrist. She slithers out of the tiny hole—it should be impossible, but she's no longer human and her bones dislocate, break and reform.

Grace crashes through an abyss of fear as the hideous creature holds her like a vice, skin hanging from its bones. It is naked, sagging, covered in slimy dirt and blood, far from how she imagined Miss Ellen.

"I warned you," Miss Ellen growls. "Yet you reached into my

grave. You woke me before the sun has sunk and for that I will—"

Grace smashes her forehead with the crowbar, making a deep gash halfway through her skull. Miss Ellen judders and jerks, loosening her grip on Grace's arm. Free, Grace snatches the portrait from her pocket. It's glows golden, as bright as the sun.

"*This* will remind you who you are."

Grace slams the portrait into the slit she's made in Miss Ellen's brain, unsure of what will happen next, sensing this is her only hope.

As you have influenced me, I have influenced you, and it's all recorded here, in the conduit of our exchange.

Veins and neurons worm around the portrait snug in her brain. Ellen shudders and writhes. Flesh grows over the gash in her skull, remoulding like dough, as crosshairs of bone reknit. Hair sprouts from the newly formed scar as she falls to the floor, still.

Grace catches movement in the corner of her eye and turns to find Orlok looming over her, less than an arm's length away.

"Mine," he says, reaching for her, but Grace swings the crowbar towards his chest. He's too fast and snatches it out of her hand. She draws her sword, but he laughs.

"You think you'll hurt me with your little toys?"

"How about with this?" Grace grabs for her bag of minced garlic and holy water.

Before she can touch it, he's pinned her to the corner, a wrist against either wall.

"Potions and trinkets won't help you, fool," he roars, baring his fangs, leaning in, preparing to feed. Instead of the bite she expects, he tumbles away from her, folding at the waist, hauled backwards by a force too fast for her to see. His hands, still clamped around her wrists, drag her forward too. She runs, keeping her feet, breaking free of his hold.

Miss Ellen pounces away, bounds off the walls and the roof, then crouches like a monster on the floor. She dives upon him again, tackling him, tumbling with him. Grace draws a sharp stake from her leather bag, and with her sword in her other hand, races towards them as they roll. Miss Ellen crawls up his chest, wraps her arms and legs around his head, and sinks her fangs into the back of his neck. He cannot see, grabbing and punching at Miss Ellen.

Grace plunges her stake into his heart.

She draws away and watches, fascinated, as Orlok writhes and spasms. He falls still and shrinks, losing all solid form beneath his skin, which slackens and wrinkles, until his tegument dwindles and desiccates to dust. Miss Ellen's skin firms as she feeds. She grows stronger, younger, firmer. The dirt and blood fall away from her body. When he is dust, she sits back and wipes her mouth. But for the black blood dribbling down her chin, she is clean and fresh, brown-eyed with black ringlets, just like the young Miss Ellen of the portrait. The dark veins in her eyes and around her forehead are gone.

As Miss Ellen turns her gaze to her, Grace's grip tightens on her sword, with a fresh stake ready in her other hand.

"The ship's already launched," Miss Ellen says, looking upwards. Grace notices the boat shifting under her feet, rolling on the waves.

"Will you join me hunting monsters?" Miss Ellen asks, shaking out Orlok's robe. "This will have to do, for now," she says.

Outside the door, the rat queen removes the bolt, and stands back, eyeing her new master, peering inside at the remnants of Count Orlok. Her smaller children rush in and crunch the dust of her old master's bones between their jaws.

The larger rats stand either side of the hall, in a guard of honour, as Grace follows Miss Ellen through the hallway and up the steps. The crew draw back when they see the women.

"What is this?" the captain cries.

"Orlok is dead," Ellen says. "You will obey me, now, or pay the price."

She turns to Grace. "Where do we sail to first?"

Wind blowing her hair back from her face, Grace returns her sword to its sheath and looks out over the bow.

"I've always wanted to see Paris," she says.

Miss Ellen Of The Portrait's Final Lesson of Dealing with Nosferatu: There are many monsters in the world. We hunt until they, or we, are eliminated.

CELEBRATION

Jack Dann

Our little lives are kept in equipoise
By opposite attractions and desires…
—*Henry Wadsworth Longfellow*

Not knowing that her life and the lives of her "extended family" would be inextricably changed and shortened that very night, Eva Lutz Wagner, née Eva Fae Nosferatu, parked her prototype white Mercedes SSK Roadster in front of the Central Park South entrance of the Plaza Hotel and signaled to the uniformed doorman to look after it.

I shan't be a minute, she thought; and the doorman—mazed and not realizing that she had casually possessed him—left his post to open the door for her and stand guard beside the car as she walked into the hotel.

Eva walked through the sumptuous U-shaped lobby, her gold high heels clicking like little hammers on the mosaic floor. She took the elevator to the nineteenth story, which belonged to her father, and sighed impatiently as the liveried elevator boy fumbled to unlock the door to the private landing. The entrance hall was old fashioned but immaculate and led to a bronze *Porta del Paradiso* door framed by two iconic paintings by Giorgio de Chirico: "The Disquieting Muses" and the 1917 "Great Metaphysical Interior."

The great door opened into what could have been a ballroom; and Eva said, seemingly to the empty air, "Well, *mein vater*, I see that you have not lost your infatuation with irony and displacement."

Casimir Vsevolod Nosferatu, now known as Alvar Wagner,

was seated behind a partners' desk. He stopped writing and looked up at her. The exquisite beauty of his daughter's face was evident, even under the protective makeup that seemed to be sculpted rather than applied. She was an Amazon dressed in a tight-fitting white satin evening dress and an open sable cocoon coat. She wore a cloche hat with a Cartier brooch over her shingled black hair, gold-threaded scarves, and differing lengths of perfect pearls; and she emanated physicality and strength. In contrast, Nosferatu was a shade, just another still shadow in this darkened room.

In a thin and whispery voice, he said, "And I see that you have lost your respect for privacy"…*and respect for the poisonous influence of sunlight,* he thought.

"I was just saving you the trouble of getting up," Eva said, surveying the room. The faded silk and velvet damask curtains that covered the windows allowed just enough light to turn the room into a chessboard of shadowy shapes: cushioned sofas, overfilled breakfront bookcases, lacquered cabinets and secretaires, tallboys, Chippendale desks and chairs, and what her father liked to call his "concatenation of art." She was relieved that the wan darkness dampened the expensive abominations her father had acquired since she had been here last. She hoped he had gotten over his infatuation with that young upstart who called himself Dali, as if the 'i' in his name was to be translated into a succession of e's.

"Modern heterotopians do not shrink from the light," she said as she sat down in a chair near her father. She smiled triumphantly and turned on a lamp.

Unfazed, her father continued to write.

"I see your eyesight has not diminished."

Nosferatu smiled weakly, sadly. "You mean my eternity has become only a bit clouded."

"You have allowed yourself to become a fugacious old man," she said angrily; and he had: his skin was blotched, his strong face seemed to have melted into wrinkles below which hung a dewlap. He had given up immortality for human transience. Purposely.

He laughed. "Yes, that I am, daughter. Human frailty can be

ugly when viewed from…a different perspective." He put down his fountain pen; and without moving his lips, he thought (said), *"Now get on with it. Tell me what you want."*

Eva felt the force of his dismissal…and the surprising potency of his phrenic, paralyzing power. Without moving a muscle, she slapped him hard in retaliation. He nodded as a blush appeared on his right cheek. "It's not just what *I* want," she said. "It's what the rest of your family wants. Remember them? Your family?" *Enough*, she thought. Guarded, impenetrable thoughts. She would make quick work of this. *"With or without your agreement, you* will *attend the conclave."*

Unperturbed, Nosferatu said, "Yes, darling, I do remember everything. Now sit back down and let me make you a drink, and then you can tell me everything at leisure."

She felt a palpable pressure on her shoulders, pressure she could have easily withstood; but she acquiesced and lowered herself back into the cushioned yet uncomfortable chair. He poured her a brandy, handed it to her, then sat down on a sofa across the room.

"I did receive an invitation to the conclave," he said.

"You did not respond."

"Because I wasn't sure if I would attend," he lied. "It's not exactly my sort of thing anymore."

"It is exactly your sort of thing, which is why you are going and why I am taking you."

Nosferatu nodded, transmitting what Eva could only imagine as…*love*. Such a distant and alien notion.

"Your friends—your family—have vindicated you," Eva said, guarding herself from him.

"I have no wish to be vindicated, nor do I wish to witness whatever reprisal the conclave has planned."

"*Herr* Dieckmann and Grau named their film after *you*, Father! Presumptuous poseurs. And they filmed it in Lübeck…at the *Salzspeicher,* where we used to conduct business."

"We did well with the Hanseatic League," Nosferatu said, a hint of nostalgia in his voice. "There was good business in salt. But that was three centuries ago, child. I can barely remember, much less entertain a blood grudge against this unknown so-called film company.

"They used your name!"

Nosferatu shrugged.

Eva tried to penetrate his thoughts, his emotions, his reactions; but he was…empty. How much of his potency had he really lost since he renounced hunting? Since he *elected* to become prey with its burden of human mortal emotions? Without allowing a stray thought to pass unguarded—yet adhering to a plan borne out of something that was the cold equivalent of love, affection, familial duty—she leaped out of her chair, leaped upon him like an animal, as if he were indeed the prey he had sought so diligently to become; and she sunk her needle-sharp secondary incisors into the hollow between his neck and shoulder; and she tasted blood, blood that still retained the acridity of her kind, but was also so lusciously and overwhelmingly sweet that she felt its deliciously caustic heat in her groin.

Then, dazed and disconcerted, she pulled away from him.

And vomited on his crimson eighteenth-century Aubusson carpet.

Nosferatu held his daughter as she slept, having pulled her back onto the couch. Sated, she snored. Her head rested on his lap; and had her eyes been open, she would have been looking right up into his. She was stone cold, yet intensely alive, as only the undead could be. She could feel hunger, but not grief nor remorse; Nosferatu remembered the freedom that presented, the exhilaration that was the normal state of being, an exanimate joy. He felt a deep, burning ache where she had bitten him; and at that moment he wished to be what he had been: cold and hungry in the best possible sense; but his race, his family—including his daughter, for whom right now at this moment he could feel human affection—had to be exterminated. He could but regret becoming human, a process that had taken him a human lifetime; yet he was still a sanguinarian. He still needed a ration of blood. Only now he drank from a bottle rather than an artery. That was his pledge to humanity.

The phone rang, jolting him out of his reverie and awakening Eva, who pulled away from him as if she was profoundly repulsed. Dizzy and weakened, Nosferatu walked over to the telephone cabinet and lifted the receiver from the switch hook.

"Yes…"

"Doctor Wagner, this is Chimes at the desk. I'm sorry to disturb you, but we've been looking after your visitor's automobile; and the doorman has asked me whether you would like it garaged or—"

"No," Nosferatu said, "please take two ten dollar bills out of my private safe: ten for you and ten for the doorman, who I'm sure can be persuaded to look after it until we come downstairs." Ten dollars was almost a week's salary for the doorman, and certainly a nice tip for Chimes.

"Yes, sir, of course. Consider it taken care of."

When Nosferatu hung up the phone, Eva was sitting erect on the couch as if she was preparing to stand and escort her father out of the suite. Her gaze was intense. She smiled and said, "You've made the right decision, Father."

"I'm sure you think so. Now please relax while I change clothes. Would you like another drink?"

But Eva had closed him off and was seemingly impenetrable.

"I shan't be more than a few moments," Nosferatu said as he left the room, his steely thought-voice invading her privacy like a stone smashing crystal.

He stood naked in front of the mirror of his ebonized dressing table He looked hard at himself, seeing as if with double vision what he had been and the skeletal, ugly quasi-human chimera he had chosen to become; and then feeling an intense mixture of sadness and guilt, he opened a drawer and removed a wooden box that contained a brass hypodermic syringe and a glass vial. He inserted the needle into the rubber top of the vial, drew back the hypodermic's plunger, and then injected the prepared pathogen into his cephalic vein. When he was finished, he carefully placed the instruments back into the satin-lined box and then dressed: black swallow-tailed jacket, trousers with shiny silk stripes on the sides, wingtip collared shirt, diamond cufflinks, ivory vest, matching bow tie, and black leather pumps with white shoe covers. Donning a velvet-collared coat, he twisted an ostentatious crimson silk scarf around his neck and left his private rooms to poison his daughter with his very presence.

"Now I am death.

"Now I will kill what was once my kind and kin.

"And myself…"

It was dusk as they left the hotel, and there was a chill in the damp air.

Eva sat silently behind the wheel, the dark tinted windows rolled tight to the roof, the leather seats radiating the autumnal damp. It was rush hour in the city, but Eva navigated little-used lanes and shortcuts and when she reached the 125th Street ferry dock, she cut through a block-long line of waiting cars and drove onto the automobile deck without hindrance or complaint. The ferry crossed the Hudson River to Edgewater, New Jersey, and then Eva drove the next few miles in first gear; the Palisades rose like serrated walls from the moonlit river. She tried to penetrate her father's thoughts, but couldn't; he was as opaque and as silent as the sheer cliffs below them.

"I suppose I should apologize to you before we arrive at the castle," she said when the road became more easily navigable. "It won't be long now. I just wish that cousin Wolfgang had chosen a less gaudy abode."

Nosferatu shut down his persistent, nagging thoughts of his pharmaceutical plant near Andermatt in Switzerland, such a pretty town, such a profitable business; and his secret lab would certainly benefit humanity, for it was there that his team had developed his selective airborn pathogen, a pathogen that was itself immune to any counteractant…purposely so. The deadly fire that had destroyed everyone and everything in the small lab was regrettable—especially as he had developed a fondness for the staff—but necessary.

He looked over at his daughter, who was driving with relaxed concentration: he could not (yet) allow his daughter to see that she and everyone attending his so-called celebration would have only hours to live. He would explain when the time was ripe. "I should probably apologize for being such dull company, but I am trying not to retaliate for your incestuous assault," he said, isolating himself further, protecting himself from her and his abhorrence of what he was about to do.

"It was certainly *not* pleasurable," Eva said. "But…it was necessary and won't need to ever happen again."

Nosferatu chuckled. "Do you really believe that you've cured me by intermingling our vital fluids?"

"Cure you? *Nein, Vater,* perhaps redirect you would be a better way to put it."

"Ah," he said, but he thought, *If our lives were not now measured in hours rather than centuries, I would tell you that I read you while you slept and dreamed of penetration.* He closed his eyes. *You dreamed you were a child being sucked and penetrated…by me. Dein vater. At least I was not responsible for that.*

After traveling mile after mile of winding roads, Eva said, "There's the castle," indicating a halo of gauzy light that illuminated the hills ahead in shifting pink, lavender, and yellow, along with sudden shots of white light. She turned on the windshield wipers to clear the moisture from the glass and drove over the next hill to a bylane that was one of the private entrance roads to the property. They could hear the echoic sounds of distant music and the soft roar of laughter as they passed through the first gate; and the rowdydow became louder and louder as they passed through the second gate, which closed behind them like a clam on a coral reef.

Damp and chilly though it was, there were crowds drifting on the well-lit terraced lawns and manicured gardens. There were guests wearing beaded headbands and sequined fringed dresses that reflected the moonlight and lamplight like mirrors. There were women dancing in casual cardigan and sweater daywear, and women dancing the Charleston in drop-waisted, hooped *robe de style* frocks that would not have looked out of place at an eighteenth century cotillion ball. There were men in lounge suits, in Oxford bags and plus-fours, in formal Savile Row black tie and tails and in sportswear; and one young man was naked except for a narrow brimmed trilby hat and Oxford shoes. They were all drinking, frolicking, laughing, shivering, shouting, arguing, and dancing to Paul Whiteman's "Hot Lips," conducted by the maestro himself. A bluestone promenade flanked by grotesque topiaries led to the central colonnaded gallery of the enormous white terracotta clad mansion. The house was bathed in even brighter light than the gardens, an uninviting, excoriating light that blotted out the moon with its unnatural intensity.

Eva stopped the car and paid no attention to the liveried servants who opened the doors for them, bowed, and then drove the roadster to a concealed parking lot. She and her father strolled through the crowds of partygoers, past buffet tables covered with crystal decanters of wine and whiskey and porcelain platters of hors-d'oeuvres, spiced hams, game roasts, sliced turkey, and salads glowing as green as the grass and promenade topiaries.

A well-dressed drunk wearing a dented top hat reached out to Eva, trying to grab her by the arm, but fell dead before her. She stepped over the corpse as if it was just a spot of vomit. Nosferatu shook his head, troubled by his daughter's casual act of senseless murder. The orchestra began playing the "Black Bottom," and the partygoers danced and gyrated, shuffling back and forth and waving their arms to the syncopated rhythms. "There are obviously more prey out here than our own sanguinarians," Nosferatu said.

"Food for thought," his daughter replied, her smile unnoticed.

As they approached the house, they saw a portly, smooth-faced man waving to them from a portico above the stone steps of the entryway.

"Welcome Cousin Casimir, and, of course, his ever-lovely perfection Eva."

He did not have to shout, nor articulate words that could be heard by anyone other than Nosferatu and Eva. *"We—and I speak of all of us, for the family—are so pleased and proud that you could attend.*

We could not help but notice that you have become a bit—shall we say reticent—to mingle with those whom you give—and take—succor."

Eva heard her father think *"blowhard"* as he embraced and kissed the owner of the great house. She smiled as she embraced her cousin Wolfgang, nee Count von Wangenheim of Wisborg. He allowed his hand to drop to her buttock, giving it a quick caress before saying, "I think you will find the company inside more agreeable than that of the *kine* grazing in the gardens." Then he led them through the central *corps de logis* with its Corinthian pilasters and arch headed windows, past a grand ballroom lit by a hundred chandeliers and crowded with revellers of the same ilk as those outside. When Eva scowled at the guests, Wolfgang smiled and said, "Patience, *Cousine* Eva," and gestured to a recessed doorway. He unlocked the door; and as soon as he locked it closed, the noise outside and behind them became nothing more than a faint susurration. They continued on past a billiards room, salons, and a dining room with coffered ceilings until they came to a stair hall overwhelmed by a curved, crimson-carpeted grand staircase. Genteel voices and soft laughter could be heard above.

"Here we are," Wolfgang said, and suddenly, as if by telesthesian command, the voices and laughter ceased…until Nosferatu and Eva climbed the stairs.

Into a ballroom that occupied the entire floor. Chandeliers bathed the tapestries, Renaissance paintings, murals, sculptures, the white tablecloths, bloody plates and decanters—and, of course, the immortals, impeccably dressed and groomed sanguinarians—in buttery light. It certainly was a family welcome, everyone surging around father and daughter, calling, applauding, and raising glasses to them—but really to Nosferatu, the most favored one, the eldest, their purported leader, the prodigal father returned to the cold bosom of his deathless community. And Nosferatu received all their praise and accolades with his usual detached attention; and then with smiles, kisses, whispers, caresses, and all the secret expressions of mutual consanguinity, all lies and deception on his part; but he would act his part until the hour when he could reveal himself to Eva. Although it would make no difference, he felt he owed her that.

He looked around at his family, these confident demigods who were more like kine than the humans they fed upon, who lived to feed and feed and feed forever. He was not surprised that he had almost no feelings for them. He had experienced human affection and warmth, but such sympathies could not be extended to the cold and the ambulant dead. He was, however, surprised at the depth of affection he felt for Eva. Although it bordered on sexuality, it was not quite the same. But he could not dwell on his confusion, for Wolfgang and company insisted on presenting him with "gifts."

Wolfgang reiterated what Eva had said in his apartments and continued on with the usual tribal homiletics of secrecy, retribution, and the dangers of exposure as he prodded Nosferatu, along with Eva, through a series of rooms that led to the servants' quarters and kitchens. "I think this is the gift station," he said, opening a door that led into a large vapor compression cold room. Fruit and vegetables, cheeses, and all manner of delicacies were arrayed on the floor-to-ceiling shelving. Slabs of beef, mutton, and game dangled from hooks, as did the desiccated corpses of the producers, directors, and the entire cast of *Nosferatu the Vampire*. Everyone connected with the film, including the hapless screenwriter Henrik Galeen, production workers, grips, investors, distributors, financiers, painters, and camera assistants claimed the majority of the refrigerated space, which was substantial. And Nosferatu conflated his memory of the crystal chandeliers hanging like stalactites in the ballroom downstairs with these mummified corpses clustered before him.

Wolfgang stood beside Eva and Nosferatu while the rest of the family maintained a respectful distance, forming up according to rank, wealth, and power, filling the kitchens. Those with a superior vantage ignored the family members jostling for position behind them.

Speaking loudly, as if he was standing on a dais, Wolfgang said, "Your good name has now been cleansed, dear cousins." He gestured to the corpses. "It is as if that abomination of a film had never been created. It has been erased; every cell, every copy has been erased." He paused for effect, and then said to Nosferatu, "Welcome home, dear cousin."

At his signal, the family applauded.

Nosferatu pulled on his cuff and surreptitiously glanced at his diamond Cartier watch, which Louis Cartier had made to his specifications.

He had, so to speak, several hours left to kill.

Eva stayed close to her father throughout the night. She didn't excuse herself to go downstairs or outside to feed on the guests, but kept trying to penetrate her father's thoughts, deftly prodding, looking for weakness, any attenuation through which she might push; and Nosferatu experienced a novel sadness and poignancy as they drifted from room to room and party to party, conversing with old friends, making small talk with those who had been relegated to the edges of their sanguineous society.

By 4:00am, as the revelers were quieted and the family having reached an agreeable torpor, Nosferatu opened up to his daughter. It was finally time to reveal himself, which he did without saying a word. They would both be dead within the hour; the rest of the family would find graduated demises, according to the time they came into contact with Nosferatu, his daughter, and the others infected throughout this quietly apocalyptic night.

And Eva, now able to access her father's thoughts...now able to experience his intentions, justifications, memories, and emotions, emotions which were as alien to her as the surprising strength of his affection, his love for her. She felt his humanness, not yet fully actualized, felt his fear; and she stepped over to a window overlooking the balustraded roofline and the remains of the feeding frenzies in the gardens below. She surveyed those who were satiated and those who were fed upon, the unconscious, the drugged, the inebriated, the exhausted, the awakened, and the dead. Then she turned to her father, her thoughts now as transparent as his, and asked, "Shall we find a private alcove in the gardens?"

Nosferatu nodded and took her by the hand.

"I had expected more of a reaction when I revealed what I have done."

"Did you then?" she said.

"It would only be natural—"

She laughed. "And so you consider us to be natural?"

"I consider it to be natural to balk upon the discovery that you have been murdered," Nosferatu said.

"Ah, but I have not *yet* been murdered, have I?"

When Nosferatu did not respond, she said, "You overwhelmed me. I experienced you rather than understood you. Now it is all part of me. Which is what you wanted. And, as you have made clear over the years, I have never been endowed with an abundance of emotion, except for what you have just foisted upon me…your traitorous embrace of humanity."

"So once again, I have underestimated you."

"Indeed, *Vater*, once again…"

Then they left the mansion, stepped down broad perron stairs onto the lawn and then through the private east garden where they found a wrought iron table and chairs situated near a series of fountains, some that shot rainbow spires of water into the air, others that created pools resembling boiling springs. They sat down together, and Nosferatu began to recite a poem:

> *From a golden faucet pours a wave*
> *Its clarity purer than a soul…*

which Eva completed:

> *A turquoise and silver wave that creates*
> *rainbows in this basin,*
> *rainbows from this faucet of gold.*

Nosferatu smiled at his daughter. "So you are familiar with the poet Azraqi."

Eva laughed softly. "No, I just took the lines from you."

Nosferatu looked at his watch again and said, "Sadly, I don't believe we shall see the golden dawn. *My apologies, daughter. I wish I could have spared you.*"

"*That was never your intention.*"

Nosferatu closed his eyes and waited, but Eva interrupted him.

"*You look younger, Vater.*"

"Tricks of the artificial light."

"No, I think not."

Nosferatu straightened. "So you think your little love bite earlier has transformed me?" He chuckled. "If so, I fear the change will be short lived," and with that he who had become death put his arm around his cool-skinned daughter and waited…

and waited as the sun rose and burned off the dank moisture of the night.

BEING THERE!—IN SEARCH OF NOSFERATU FILM LOCATIONS

Julia Kruk

Universally acknowledged as one of the most influential master-pieces of silent cinema, F. W. Murnau's 1922 expressionist classic, *Nosferatu*, still haunts viewers today, still exerts an uncanny power. It was ground-breaking in so many ways, not least because it was not studio-bound, being shot almost entirely on location… If, like me, you are a horror movie buff and love this film, then it's hugely exciting to anticipate being there—visiting the actual filming locations of one of your favourite movies. And for *Nosferatu*, all the information is well documented, allowing us to put together an itinerary to visit those iconic locations in Germany and Slovakia where it was principally filmed.

To put all this in context: I did not do this alone. Members of the Dracula Society (of which I am currently Chair and Treasurer) love to travel. One of the Society's founding objectives back in 1973 was to visit Dracula's homeland, Transylvania, at a time when tourism to Romania barely existed. Since then, we've travelled to Egypt (mummies), Prague (the Golem) and Paris (*The Phantom of the Opera*) in search of authentic locations. But our reverence for *Nosferatu* has taken us to Slovakia no less than three times (2001, 2011 and 2022), and to Germany twice (2012 and 2019).

Let us return, then, to Murnau's masterpiece *Nosferatu*, and we'll begin with Thomas Hutter and his wife Ellen, at their home in the fictional German town of Wisborg, which we visited in 2019. This is, in fact, Wismar, a gorgeous Hanseatic port city on the Baltic coast. The opening shot of Murnau's film is taken from the tower of the Marienkirche (St. Mary's Church), looking down at the market square with the Wasserkunst (an elaborate wrought-iron fountain) clearly visible on the left. Sadly, the hexagonal spire that we see in the foreground of the shot no longer exists, the rest of the church having been destroyed in a bombing raid in April 1945. The Markt with its fountain appears now much as it did in 1921 when Murnau was filming there.

The first and most obvious location we identified was the Wassertor, the harbour gate of Wisborg, through which Graf Orlok carries his coffin into the city in that wonderful blue-tinted scene. You don't see the top, crenelated gabled part above the gate in the actual film, but it's an impressive structure. And of course, who can forget that ominous shot in the film where Orlok's death ship, the *Empusa*, slowly glides into harbour from the right of the frame, presaging the disaster to come?

It's was pleasing to see that Wismar is aware of its *Nosferatu* film connections, with helpful plaques set in the ground at important locations around the city to remind tourists of the fact. There was one by the Wassertor, and another in the courtyard of the Heiligen-Geist-Kirche (the hospital Church of the Holy Spirit), the other main location here used in the film. This courtyard is where ship-owner Harding lived, and where Ellen stayed to be looked after by his wife Ruth, when Hutter departed on horseback on his fateful journey to Transylvania. The courtyard looked pretty much as it does in the film, although on our visit there was some building work going on, with an area cordoned off by red and white tape.

While the exterior shots of ship-owner Harding's house in Wisborg *were* actually filmed in Wismar, we had to travel to Lübeck, another German city on the Baltic coast, to seek out four other important filming locations. The first was Count Orlok's new residence, which was virtually impossible to miss: you just pass through the western city gate (the Holstentor), stroll along the Upper Trave River, and there they are— six tall, historic salt storehouses (Salzspeicher), two of which are gabled and are instantly recognisable from their rows of small black windows. Comparing the window configuration with a screen grab from the film, we were even able to pinpoint the actual window Graf Orlok stares out from.

With the aid of google maps and more screen grabs, we went in search of the other locations. Hutter's house was easily identifiable in a small square near the churchyard of St. Aegidien, just a short way off a street called Depenau, which we recognised from the scene in which coffin bearers carrying plague victims make their slow procession. Many of these streets were used in the scenes where the townspeople are on the hunt for Knock. The final Lübeck location we tracked down was from an early scene in which Hutter encounters Professor Bulwer: this was the medieval Fuchting's Courtyard off Glockengassen Strasse, looking just as calm and peaceful as it did in 1921.

That was most of the Germany film locations ticked off, but what about Transylvania? Murnau didn't actually take his film crew to "the land beyond the forest". He went to Slovakia instead. Hutter's journey through the mountains and valleys was filmed in the High Tatras and the Vratna Valley in northern Slovakia. And his destination, Count Orlok's castle, is Oravsky Hrad—the magnificent Orava Castle—perched high on a rock overlooking the Orava River. Probably still my favourite of all the castles I've ever visited, Orava never fails to impress. (Mark Gatiss obviously thought so too, as he went there to film it as the location for Dracula's castle in his BBC TV adaptation of Stoker's novel in 2020).

Our first visit to Orava was in 2001, when the experience felt arguably the most authentic. Our guide had to phone the keyholder to come and let us into the castle, so there were no tourists, just us. Everywhere we looked brought back a scene from the movie: the approach to that great arched door where Orlok welcomes Hutter to his home, the inner courtyard and the circular tower with its dark, pointed roof, and the small domed structure by a balustrade where Hutter writes his letters to Ellen. There were no restrictions in 2001. In 2011, this area was roped off, but our guide did manage to gain us admission. Not so in 2022—a padlocked gate barred all access. But that is how progress works: Orava castle now attracts hordes of tourists, with timed admission for its two-hour tour, and souvenir stalls, cafes and restaurants have mushroomed up all around. But on the plus side, Murnau's landmark movie is now publicised everywhere: a large banner at the castle entrance referenced *Nosferatu*'s centenary in 2022, there's an exhibition devoted to it in the citadel on the highest level, and on our visit, even a display of Count Orlok artwork—all by school children!

Still in Slovakia, some sixty-odd kilometres from Orava, is one other location in the film that we finally managed to tick off our list, on our 2022 trip. You know the one? The shot of Orlok's ruined castle at the very end of the film. This has long been established as the ruins of Starý Hrad ("Old Castle"), which towers high above the Vah River. Probably, most people would content themselves with just viewing the ruins from the road below, just as you see them in that final shot. But not our little group—we just had to climb the steep path up through the forest to clamber over the actual castle. But just as we emerged at the summit, everything got strangely surreal… There before us was a unit of Wehrmacht soldiers, encamped around the castle ruins. Had we suddenly passed through a time warp? Or been transported into a real-life version of *The Keep*? Alas, no—just a group of WW2 re-enactors preparing to recreate a major battle the next day. (We encountered several groups of partisans on the way back down). An experience at a *Nosferatu* castle evoking another, very different, vampire movie… Not particularly relevant to my reminiscences of visiting the 1922 *Nosferatu* sites perhaps, but—all part of the adventure.

And finally, we come to a couple of locations that are appropriate to mention here—particularly at the end of these recollections. Back in Germany, to the south-west of Berlin, are two cemeteries. The Wilmersdorfer Waldfriedhof, in the Berlin suburb of Stahnsdorf, is a large forest cemetery, and with the help of a German speaking fellow-Dracula Society member, we managed to locate the grave of Max Schreck. Neglected for many years, a new granite slab was erected in 2011, bearing the simple words "Max Schreck, Schauspieler" (Actor), with the dates of his birth and death. F. W. Murnau's grave, by contrast, has a much more imposing resting place, as you might expect, and this can be easily located in the nearby, quite separate, cemetery of Sudwestkirchhof.

Murnau died in a car accident in California in 1931, but in classic Dracula style his body was shipped to Berlin for interment. There he lay undisturbed until July 2015 when his grave was broken into and his skull stolen. Wax candle residue found at the scene suggests some sort of occult ceremony may have taken place and the whereabouts of his skull is unknown to this day.

At both graves, Dracula Society members raised a toast to the memory of two men who helped create one of the most powerful and influential horror films of all time.

Plates:

Although now tourist attractions, various sites in F. W. Murnau's silent masterpiece *Nosferatu: A Symphony of Horror* have been preserved and remain largely unchanged:

1. Courtyard inside Orava Castle—In the original movie, Hutter walks towards the camera in this scene.

2. Wismar ("Wisborg" in the film—the harbour gate through which Orlok is seen carrying his coffins.

3. Lübeck—the restored Salzpeicher (salt storehouses) used by Murnau as Orlok's "new" residence.

4. Inside Orava castle—the heavy double doors leading down to Orlok's crypt.

1. Courtyard inside Orava Castle - Hutter walks towards the camera in a similar shot

2.   Wismar ('Wisborg' in the film) - the harbour gate through which Orlok is
seen carrying his coffins

3. Lübeck - the restored Salzpeicher (salt storehouses) used by
Murnau as Orlok's "new" residence

4. Inside Orava castle - the heavy double doors leading down to Orlok's crypt

Contributor Biographies

LEVERETT BUTTS (story contributor) is the award-winning author of the *Guns of the Waste Land* series, a four-volume retelling of the King Arthur legends as an American Western. His short fiction (written both by himself and with Dacre Stoker, great-grandnephew of Bram Stoker) has appeared in in various publications and anthologies such as *Weird Tales* magazine, the *Kolchak 50th Anniversary Deluxe Special*, *Classic Monsters Unleashed*, *Dracula Unfanged*, and *Shakespeare Unleashed*. He teaches American literature at the University of North Georgia, and lives in Carrollton, Georgia, with his wife, son, dog, and cat.

GREG CHAPMAN (cover designer) is an illustrator and graphic designer based in Queensland, Australia, specialising in the horror field. Trained as a graphic designer and visual artist, Greg has provided artwork for various magazines, comics, graphic novels and promotional designs for the Horror Writers Association and the Australasian Horror Writers Association. He also specialises in book cover design and has created cover art for many authors and publishers, including IFWG Publishing. Greg is also a Bram Stoker Award, Australian Shadows Award and Aurealis Award-nominated author. You can find out more about his writing at www.darkscrybe.com.

SAL CIANO (story contributor) is an author and editor based in South Florida. When not working or spending time with his friends, family and dogs, Sal spends time appreciating and delighting in the strange parade of the completely absurd, absolutely weird, heartbreakingly ephemeral, and breathtakingly bizarre experiences that comprise living life in South Florida.

JACK DANN (story contributor) has written or edited over eighty books, including the international bestseller *The Memory Cathedral: a Secret History of Leonardo da Vinci*, *The Rebel: an Imagined Life of James Dean*, *The Silent*, *Bad Medicine*, and *The Man Who Melted*. His work has been compared to Jorge Luis Borges, Roald Dahl, Lewis Carroll, Ray Bradbury, J. G. Ballard, Mark Twain, and Philip K. Dick. *Library Journal* called Dann "…a true poet who can create pictures with a few perfect words," and *Best Sellers* said that "Jack Dann is a mind-warlock whose magicks will confound, disorient, shock, and delight."

He is a recipient of the Nebula Award, the World Fantasy Award (twice), the Australian Aurealis Award (three times), the Chronos Award, the Darrell Award for Best Mid-South Novel, the Ditmar Award (five times), the Peter McNamara Achievement Award and the Peter McNamara Convenors' Award for Excellence, the Shirley Jackson Award, and the *Premios Gilgames de Narrativa Fantastica* award. He has also been honored by the Mark Twain Society (Esteemed Knight).

His latest novel is *Shadows in the Stone: a Book of Transformations* (IFWG). *New York Times* bestselling author Kim Stanley Robinson called it "such a complete world that Italian history no longer seems comprehensible without his cosmic battle of spiritual entities behind and within every historical actor and event." His most recent books include *The Writer's Guide to Alternate History* (Bloomsbury) and the collections *Masters of Science Fiction: Jack Dann* (Centipede Press) and *Islands of Time* (Cemetery Dance).

Dr. Dann is also an Adjunct Senior Research Fellow in the School of Communication and Arts at the University of Queensland. He lives in Australia on a farm overlooking the sea.

CLAIRE FITZPATRICK (story contributor) is an editor and award-winning author of speculative fiction and non-fiction. She is the 2020 recipient of the Rocky Wood Memorial scholarship fund for her non-fiction anthology *A Vindication of Monsters—Essays on Mary Wollstonecraft and Mary Shelley* (IFWG Publishing International 2023) and the winner of the 2017 Rocky Wood Award for Non-Fiction and Criticism for *The Body Horror Book* (2016). Her article 'How Mary Shelley Continues to Influence Modern Science Fiction'

(*Aurealis* 145) was nominated for the 2022 William Atheling Jr. Award for Criticism or Review. Her fiction collection *Metamorphosis* was hailed as "a wickedly gruesome collection", "graphic and disturbing", "engaging and darkly beautiful", and "simply heroic". Claire is the current president of the Australasian Horror Writers Association and runs a women-in-horror blog. She lives in Brisbane with a menagerie of animals and her two eldritch offspring. Visit her at www.clairefitzpatrick.com.au.

CHANTAL HANDLEY (cover artist) was born in England and graduated from Griffith University in Brisbane, Australia in 1998 with a BA in Character Animation. Chantal now has over 20 years' experience in animation and graphic design and has a studio in Queensland. Her art is inspired by the films she loves, mostly horror movies from the '70s and '80s, but she adores anything "Halloween". Her artwork is handmade using soft pastels on paper. Her work can be seen in *Fangoria* magazine, the *Printed in Blood* art books, *The Little Shoppe of Horrors* magazine created by Richard Klemensen, Kensington Gore Publications and *The Creators Unite* magazine. Chantal was inspired by the work of Mike Hill to create her cover piece for *Nosferatu Unbound*.

AARON HARVIE (story contributor) is a former rock band manager, cook and TV show host. He is owner of the retro horror brand *Blood, Brains & Aliens*, author of the novel *The End of Everything We Know* and was a AHWA Shadow Awards finalist in 2022 for the anthology comic book *Frankie's Drive-In Ozploitation Marathon.* Aaron is also the writer, director & producer of the chart-topping sci-fi/horror podcast *Baron Sordor's Theatre of the Doomed.*

NANCY HOLDER (story contributor) is a *New York Times* best-selling author of approximately a hundred book-length projects and hundreds of short stories, essays, and articles. She received the Faust Grand Master Lifetime Achievement Award from the International Association of Media Tie-In Writers in 2020. In 2020, she won the Bram Stoker Award for Graphic Novel for *Mary Shelley Presents Tales of the Supernatural,* and she received her seventh Bram Stoker, the Lifetime Achievement Award, from the Horror Writers Association in 2022.

ALAN PHILIPSON (story contributor) has written more than 130 novels and other projects under his own and house names. He has been a professional editor and book doctor for three decades, working on fiction, nonfiction, and memoir.

Although Nancy Holder and Alan have collaborated informally for many years, they formed a writing partnership in 2015, producing comic books, graphic novels, and short fiction for a variety of publishers. Nancy and Alan both live in the Pacific Northwest. Go to: www.nancyholder.com, and facebook.com/holder.nancy/ for news of both.

Their story in this Nosferatu collection is a prose prequel to their second noir comic and graphic novel series *They Call Me Midnight* for IPI Comics, which features art by John K. Snyder III. "In the Lands of Thieves and Phantoms" details the supernatural "birth" of their character Mezzanotte, a vampire-who-is-not-a-vampire, plagued with all the memories—and bloodlust—of his progenitor, Count Dracula, and yet he has never tasted blood. Rejecting his vile heritage, but accepting the burden of its guilt, he has become a monster all his own.

STEVE KILBEY (poetry contributor) is Australian rock music royalty. He has written, performed and produced over 22 solo albums, 30 with rock legends *The Church*, and frequently collaborates with notable artists worldwide. However, he is a prolific artist in many media; his creative oeuvre spans three books, 750 songs, pages of poetry and hundreds of paintings. Genre material is one of his talents, as seen by horror-oriented prose-poetry that appeared in *Cthulhu Deep Down Under Vol 3*, and the dark historical-fantasy, *Vale of Tears*, co-written with Nicole Madunic and illustrated by Keith Donald, that is underway for IPI Comics."

LESLIE S. KLINGER (introduction contributor) is is the editor of the highly-acclaimed *New Annotated Dracula*, *New Annotated Frankenstein*, and the two-volume *New Annotated H. P. Lovecraft* as well as the anthologies *In the Shadow of Dracula* and *In the Shadow of Edgar Allen Poe*, featuring 19th century supernatural fiction. Together with Lisa Morton, he's also edited the anthologies *Ghost Stories Weird Women*, *Weird Women* II, and *Haunted Tales*, all with extensive selections of Victorian horror. He co-edited (with Eric Guignard) the HWA's eight-volume *Haunted Library of Horror Classics* and an edition of *Phantasmagoriana*. His latest book is *New Annotated Strange Case of Dr. Jekyll and Mr. Hyde*.

JIM KRUEGER (story contributor) is one of the top-rated writers currently working in American comics. Significant successes include the prestigious *Earth-X* Trilogy from Marvel Comics, and *Justice* (a *New York Times* Bestseller, and winner of an Eisner Award) from DC Comics, with colleagues Alex Ross and Doug Braithwaite. In addition, he has had notable projects with *Avengers*, *X-Men*, *Star Wars*, *The Matrix Comics*, *Micronauts*, and *Batman*. With Ross again, and others, he did *Avengers/Invaders*, and *Project Superpowers* for Dynamite Entertainment. He has been a creative director at Marvel Comics, and is also a freelance comic book writer/property creator whose original works include *The Foot Soldiers*, *Alphabet Supes*, *The Clock Maker*, *The High Cost of Happily Ever After* and *The Last Straw Man*.

JULIA KRUK (essay contributor) is Chair of the Dracula Society, probably the oldest and longest-running Society devoted to Bram Stoker's novel—and its myriad incarnations—anywhere in the world. Her love of supernatural fiction (and cinema) led her to join the Society way back in 1977, taking over as Chair in 1998. Julia's teenage years were spent devouring Pan Books of Horror Stories, classic Gothic fiction, and spending evenings watching double bills of obscure US and European horror films at the local fleapit cinema. Pioneering works on horror cinema, such as Carlos Claren's *An Illustrated History of the Horror Film* and David Pirie's *A Heritage of Horror* were a huge influence, while at the same time studying the Gothic novel at university.

Joining the Dracula Society meant that she finally found herself amongst kindred spirits—with those who love Gothic and vampire fiction in general, as well as those whose main passion is for horror movies. Over the past twenty-five years Julia has sought to combine both the Society's cinematic and literary interests: *Frankenstein* trips to Geneva (the Villa Diodati, where Mary Shelley's novel was born) and to Germany, as well as repeated trips to Romania (from Vlad the Impaler's birthplace in Sighisoara to the location of Dracula's fictional castle in the Borgo Pass).

When she is not planning where to travel, Julia also reviews books and plays for the Dracula Society's magazine, and has co-edited two anthologies of vampire and *Dracula-* related short stories. She also attends as many fantasy, horror and ghost story festivals and conventions as she can fit in, and visits her local cinema every week. She lives in London with her partner and two cats, in a house that's far too small for their vast joint collection of genre DVDs, Blu-rays and books.

KIRSTYN MCDERMOTT (story contributor) has been working in the darker alleyways of speculative fiction for much of her career. She is the author of two award-winning novels, *Madigan Mine* and *Perfections*, along with numerous pieces of short fiction and poetry. Her most recent works are *Hard Places*, a collection of short fiction, and *Never Afters*, a novella series of retold fairy tales. She produces and co-hosts a literary discussion podcast, *The Writer and the Critic*, and holds a PhD in creative writing. Kirstyn lives in Ballarat, Australia, with fellow writer Jason Nahrung and two distinctly non-literary felines. www.kirstynmcdermott.com.

BRAD MENGEL (story contributor) is a lifelong reader and pulp fan so it was only natural that he would turn to writing. His non-fiction book, *Serial Vigilantes of Paperback Fiction*, was the first major work on the paperback heroes of the '70s and '80s, such as The Executioner and The Destroyer. He is also the author of *The Unofficial Guide to The Scorpion and The Mummy Universe*, exploring the world of the Brendan Fraser Mummy movies. His fiction work includes new adventures of Sherlock Holmes, Domino Lady and Senorita Scorpion. He is the author of the novel *Australis Incognito*, a new pulp novel set in Australia with a team of multi-generational heroes. For IFWG he has contributed to *Sherlock Holmes and Doctor Was Not* and *Dracula Unfanged*.

JASON NAHRUNG (story contributor) grew up on a Queensland cattle property and now lives in Ballarat with his wife, the writer Kirstyn McDermott. The author of four vampire novels and more than 20 short stories, his fiction is mostly anchored in the speculative genres and typically is darkly themed. This interest has expanded into the realm of climate fiction, which led him to complete a PhD in creative writing from The University of Queensland. Having developed a liking for editing during 30 years of work as a newspaper journalist, he also offers freelance editing and manuscript appraisal services. Find him online at www.jasonnahrung.com.

DILLON NAYLOR (internal art contributor) is an award-winning Ballarat-based artist and writer who has been a central part of the Australian comic book scene with long-running characters including "Da 'n' Dill," "Batrisha the Vampire Girl" and "Rock 'n' Roll Fairies" since the early 1980s. He is currently collecting his previous work into hardcover books and developing new projects using his distinctive brush and ink style.

STEVEN PAULSEN (editor) is an award-winning speculative fiction writer and editor. His bestselling spooky children's book, *The Stray Cat*, illustrated by the acclaimed artist Shaun Tan, has seen publication in several English and foreign language editions. His horror, science fiction and dark fantasy short stories have appeared in books and magazines around the world. The best of his weird tales can be found in his short story collection, *Shadows on the Wall*, which won the Australian Shadows Award for Best Collected Work. His new YA Historical Fantasy novel, *Dream Weaver*, set in 15th century Ottoman Turkey, was released by IFWG Publishing in 2023. Find him online at: www.stevenpaulsen.com.

PETER RAWLIK (story contributor) is a long-time collector of Lovecraftian fiction, and in 1985 stole a car to go see the film *Reanimator*. He successfully defended himself by explaining that his father had regularly read him *The Rats in the Wall* as a bedtime story. His first professional sale was in 1997 but he didn't begin to write seriously until 2010. Since then, he has authored more than fifty short stories and the Cthulhu Mythos novels *Reanimators*, *The Weird Company*, *Reanimatrix*, and *The Eldritch Equations*. In 2014 his short story *Revenge of the Reanimator* was nominated for a New Pulp Award. In 2015 he co-edited *Legacy of the Reanimator* for Chaosium. Somewhere along the line he became known as "the Reanimator guy," but he fervently denies being obsessed with the character. He lives in southern Florida where he works on Everglades issues and in his spare time tries to go fishing.

CHRISTOPHER SEQUEIRA (editor) is an award-winning fiction editor and anthologist (and also a writer himself), specialising in comic-book and prose material in the mystery, horror, science fiction and fantasy genres. Previous anthologies for IFWG Publishing International include *Cthulhu Deep Down Under* (Vols 1 to 3); *Cthulhu Land of the Long White Cloud; Caped Fear: Superhuman Horror Stories; Sherlock Holmes and Doctor Was Not; Dracula Unfanged*, and the forthcoming comic book chapter-novel anthology *Superhumanity Vol 1: The SuperAustralians*.

DEBORAH SHELDON (story contributor) is an award-winning author and editor from Melbourne, Australia. She writes short stories, novellas and novels across the darker spectrum of horror, crime and noir. Her award-nominated titles include the novels *Cretaceous Canyon, Body Farm Z, Contrition* and *Devil Dragon*; the novella *Thylacines*; and the collections *Figments and Fragments: Dark Stories* and *Liminal Spaces: Horror Stories*. Her most recent work is the novella *Redhead Town*.

Deb's collection *Perfect Little Stitches and Other Stories* won the Australian Shadows Best Collected Work Award, was shortlisted for an Aurealis Award, and longlisted for a Bram Stoker. Her short fiction has been widely published, shortlisted for numerous Australian Shadows and Aurealis Awards, translated, and included in various "best of" anthologies.

She has won the Australian Shadows Best Edited Work Award twice: for *Midnight Echo 14* and for the anthology she conceived and edited, *Spawn: Weird Horror Tales About Pregnancy, Birth and Babies*. As a senior editor at IFWG Publishing, Deb specialises in horror anthologies.

Other credits include TV scripts such as *Neighbours, Australia's Most Wanted* and *State Coroner*; magazine feature articles; non-fiction books (Reed Books, Random House); stage plays; poetry; and award-winning medical writing. Visit Deb at http://deborahsheldon. wordpress.com.

JIM SHEPARD (story contributor) has written eight novels, including most recently *Phase Six* and *The Book of Aron*, which won the Sophie Brody Medal for Jewish Literature, the PEN/New England Award for Fiction and the Clark Fiction Prize, and five story collections, including *Like You'd Understand, Anyway*, a finalist for the National Book Award and Story Prize winner. Seven of his stories have been chosen for the *Best American Short Stories*, two for the *PEN/O. Henry Prize Stories*, and two for Pushcart Prizes. He's also won a Guggenheim Foundation Award, the Library of Congress/Massachusetts Book Award for Fiction and the ALEX Award from the American Library Association. He teaches at Williams College.

DACRE STOKER (essay contributor) is the great-grandnephew of Bram Stoker and the international best-selling co-author of *Dracula the Un-Dead* (2009), and *Dracul* (2018). Dacre is also the co-editor of *The Lost Journal of Bram Stoker: The Dublin Years* (2012). Dacre is a native of Montreal, Canada. He taught Physical Education and Sciences for twenty-two years, in both Canada and the U.S. He has participated in the sport of Modern Pentathlon as an athlete and a coach at the international and Olympic levels for Canada for 12 years. Dacre has consulted and appeared in recent film documentaries about vampires in literature and popular culture: *The Real Vampire Files* (2010 History Channel), *The Tillinghast Nightmare*, (2014 Historical Haunts), *Secrets of the Dead* (2015 PBS), *Mysteries at the Museum*, (2017 Travel Channel) *Legend Hunter* (2019 Travel Channel) and *American Vampires* (2022 Fox Nation).
He currently hosts tours to Dublin Ireland, Whitby England, and Cruden Bay Scotland, to visit places where Bram Stoker lived, was educated, worked, researched, and wrote *Dracula*. He also leads groups to Transylvania to explore both the life and times of the historic Vlad Dracula III and also the locations where Bram Stoker set his famous novel.

H. K. STUBBS (story contributor) is an Australian writer, journalist and creative producer who loves following stories and paths for the discoveries along the way and the surprise at the end of the journey. Stubbs's stories and essays have been published in *Apex Magazine, Nightmare Fuel Magazine, Kaleidotrope, Midnight Echo,* and books published by CSFG, Black Beacon Books and IFWG Publishing (*Killer Creatures Down Under, Spawn, Spawn II,* and *A Vindication of Monsters*). Her non-fiction appears in *We Are Gold*

Coast, Nevertheless and Binna Burra's *Art Nature Science*. She won the Aussiecon 4 short story competition with "The Perforation." Her story "Uncontainable" was shortlisted for an Australian Shadows Award, and she won a Ditmar Award for Best New Talent. When not writing or caring for her kids she's happiest rock climbing and exploring the mountains of South East Queensland. Follow her adventures and climbs on Instagram @helenstubbs, Twitter/X @ superleni, and her blog https://helenstubbs.wordpress.com.

STEVE RASNIC TEM (story contributor) is a past winner of the Bram Stoker, World Fantasy, and British Fantasy Awards. His novel *Ubo* (Solaris Books), a finalist for the Bram Stoker Award, is a dark science fictional tale about violence and its origins, featuring such historical viewpoint characters as Jack the Ripper, Stalin, and Heinrich Himmler. He has published over 500 short stories in his 45+ year career. Some of his best are collected in *Thanatrauma* and *Figures Unseen* from Valancourt Books, and in *The Night Doctor & Other Tales* from Macabre Ink. You can visit his home on the web at www.stevetem.com.

www.ingramcontent.com/pod-product-compliance
Lightning Source LLC
Chambersburg PA
CBHW051256210726

48287CB00002B/535